SAVE
ONE THING

SAVAGE ACADEMY

J. Wolf

Author's Note

Dear Reader Friend,

Although Save One Thing isn't a dark book, it does touch on subjects that may be sensitive to some readers, such as:

-past mentions of sexual assault

-drug use and addiction

-mild violence

Please treat yourself kindly when choosing whether or not to read this book.

Xoxo,

Julia

Prologue
Luciana

Age 13

IT TOOK A LOT of pleading, but my sister finally agreed to let me spend the entire weekend with her at Savage U. She lived in this cool house with two other girls, and her boyfriend lived in the house right next door.

How sick was that?

They were definitely going to get married. Theo and Helen were like *the* couple. She was beautiful and badass, and he completely adored her. Theo was nice to me too, but because I was Helen's little sister, he kind of had to be.

I was hanging out on campus with Helen and her friends and wondered if all the college kids could tell I was only in middle school. I'd be in eighth grade soon, which was practically high school—okay, yeah, they'd probably clocked me as a kid a mile away.

Whatever.

We were getting ready to watch a drumline show. One of Helen's friends, Julien, had brought his little brother too. Helen shoved us together, telling us to talk to each other since we were the same age. I didn't really like talking to most guys, but I tried to be friendly for my sister's sake. I didn't want her to think I was uncool and not let me stay with her again.

The kid—Beckett—was a total beanpole. He had to be almost six feet tall, with long, lanky limbs. His clothes were preppy. No one in my school wore khaki shorts or deck shoes. I guessed it worked for him, but to me, he looked like he came from an entirely different world. My Vans had a hole in the toe, and my Dickies, which I'd cut into shorts, had once belonged to a man named Charlie—that's what was written in Sharpie inside the waistband anyway.

Beckett was staring at me, barely blinking his crazy blue eyes, making me feel like a bug under a magnifying glass.

"What grade are you in?" I asked him.

"Almost in eighth," he grunted.

I smiled. "Same."

He scowled in response.

"Um..." I racked my brain for something else to ask him. "Do you play any sports?"

"Soccer."

Based on the handful of words I'd heard him say, his voice was surprisingly deep. I almost told him he looked more like a basketball player but refrained, figuring he heard that a lot.

"I mainly skateboard, but recently got recruited to play field hockey. It's weird, playing a sport in a skirt, but it's kind of fun."

He didn't say anything, but I guessed I hadn't asked a question. Fortunately, the drum show started, letting me off the hook. I really hoped Helen didn't expect me to entertain this kid when we went back to her house for the cookout. I could already tell he was *not* my number one fan.

· · · · ● · ● · · · ·

The only time I had ever counted myself lucky was when my dad died and I got to move in with my mom in Savage River. Not that living with my mom was the good part—it was the worst part. But now, I was in the same town as Helen.

I seemed to have used all my luck up in one big swoop.

Instead of hanging with Helen's cool college friends while they drank and played badminton, I was stuck sitting on the deck with freaking grump-face Beckett.

Couldn't everyone see this kid hated me? Honestly, the feeling was beginning to be mutual. I kept asking him questions just so I wasn't stuck in awkward silence, buried under the weight of his glare.

"When's your birthday?"

His eyes narrowed. "September."

I wiggled my brows. "I'm older than you. Mine's in June."

"Did you get held back or something?"

My stomach curdled. I'd been trying to be nice to this guy all afternoon, but he ranked up with the top ten rudest human beings I'd ever met—and that was saying something since my dad had been a drug dealer and my mom was a...how had Helen told me to say it? Oh yeah, an indiscriminate lover.

"No. My dad forgot I was supposed to start kindergarten when I turned five, so I didn't go until I was six. That's the beginning of my villain origin story."

I paused for a laugh. I would have even accepted a scoff. The kid gave me neither, glaring at me with his freaky eyes.

"I've never seen eyes as clear blue as yours," I blurted.

He shrugged. "They're better than plain brown, I guess."

I flinched. Wow. My eyes were dark brown, almost black, with the tiniest bit of gold swirling through them. I'd always wished they'd had a little more pizzazz, but this was the first time someone else had insulted the color.

Leave it to this guy.

I pushed back from the patio table. "I'm going to go inside and grab a drink."

Escaping into the kitchen through the sliding glass door, I went straight to the fridge and grabbed the soda Helen had bought especially for me. I cracked it open and took a long swig while I checked my phone. My friend Giselle was begging me for updates. She was a romantic, so when I'd sent her a picture I'd sneakily snapped of Beckett earlier, she'd immediately 'shipped us.

Me: *He's cute, but no personality. He called my eyes plain.*

Giselle: *Oh, gross. Okay, we're over him.*

Me: *I would like to remind you I was never into him!*

Giselle: *Yeah, right. You wouldn't have sent me a pic if you didn't think he was cute.*

Me: *I just knew you'd think he was cute, that's all!*

The door slid open, and Beckett stepped into the kitchen. He stopped and looked at me for an incredibly long moment before heading to the fridge. When he came out with one of my sodas, I almost told him he couldn't have it, but since I was currently ignoring him, I bit my tongue.

He leaned against the counter across from me, sweeping his gaze from my feet to the top of my head.

"Where are you going to high school?" he asked.

"Savage River High." I jerked my chin at him. "You?"

Please don't say SRH. Please don't say SRH. Please don't say SRH.

"Savage Academy." He grimaced slightly. "It's where my dad went."

Yesss.

"That's nice."

"Why do you say that?"

I lifted a shoulder. "I guess I'm just being polite."

"Hmmm." He drank my soda and glanced around the kitchen. "It's a shame you have to go to public school. The field hockey team is really good at Savage Academy."

He said all this while eyeing the house scornfully.

"I think Savage Academy is above my price range," I answered.

His judgy gaze landed on me again. One brow lifted, and he nodded. "Probably."

I had to laugh. "Oh my god, what's your deal? Why are you being so rude to me? Do I stink or something?"

Beckett put his soda down on the counter and leaned forward, bringing his nose a few inches from my hair. Then he took a deep whiff.

"You smell like you've been outside all day." Blue eyes flicked to mine. They narrowed on me, then he straightened, putting space between us again.

He's basically just confirmed I stunk...which, no. I *had* spent the day outdoors, but I knew for a fact my deodorant was still doing its job. This kid was just a stuck-up jerk.

"Good. I hope I'm so smelly you stay far, far away from me," I volleyed back.

He flinched and stuffed his oversized hands in his pockets. "You have an attitude."

"Not really. Only when provoked. I've been nice to you all day, you know."

"Do people like you?"

I rolled my eyes. I loved my sister, but man, oh man, she was asking way too much if she expected me to spend another minute with Beckett.

I folded my arms over my chest. "I've never done a survey or anything, but yeah, I have friends."

"A boyfriend?"

"That's none of your business."

He chuffed. "You don't."

"How would you know?"

He rocked back on his heels. "I bet you've never been kissed."

Well, I hadn't, but he didn't need to know that. Besides, it was my choice. Boys my age were stupid—case in point, this dude—and the thought of pressing my lips to some unhygienic, sweaty guy gave me the heebie-jeebies.

"What's it to you?" I challenged.

He rocked forward, tipping his chin. "If you want to get it over with, I'll kiss you."

My mouth fell open. "Are you kidding me?"

His shoulders bunched around his red-tipped ears. "No. I don't normally make jokes."

"I've figured that out." I sipped my soda to give myself something to do. "I'm not kissing you."

"You should."

"I'm not interested."

"That's a mistake," he warned.

"I really doubt it. I don't think I'll ever think about you again once this day is over."

I inwardly cringed at myself. That might have been a little harsh. Not that Beckett showed it. Aside from the cocky wing of his eyebrow, he remained stoic.

"Disagree. My brother is friends with your sister. We'll see each other again."

Deflating, I sighed. "Fine. Whatever. If we *do* see each other again, can you do me a favor and not talk about us kissing? That's never going to happen."

Something changed in him. His mouth spread into a slow smile, transforming his whole face. For a second, my stomach fluttered, forgetting he was a jerk and I wasn't interested in boys.

But only for a second. Then he spoke.

"Don't worry. When we kiss, it will be because you asked for it." He crossed one ankle over the other, casual as could be. "I'll be waiting."

My head exploded, and I groaned. "You, Beckett Savage, had better get used to waiting. My lips touching yours will never, ever happen. Dream on!"

I stomped upstairs to Helen's bedroom and locked the door.

Beckett could go make out with a bag of razors for all I cared. I would never kiss that egotistical a-hole.

And that was final.

CHAPTER ONE

Luciana

MY LOADED DUFFEL BAG went flying across the room. I let go of the trash bag filled with shoes I'd been carrying and spun around, raising an eyebrow at my sister.

"That could have taken my head off."

Helen laughed. "Oh, please. Your head is way too hard to be knocked off by a tiny little bag."

I poked the fifty-pound duffel. "Tiny? My entire wardrobe is in here."

She nodded at the garment bag laid neatly beside it. "*That's* got your wardrobe. The duffel has your poor, neglected weekend clothes."

Moving to the bed, I picked up the garment bag and unzipped it, taking out the blazers and pleated skirts. Since ironing wasn't my thing, these needed to be hung in my closet immediately, or I'd be wearing a wrinkled uniform on the first day of class.

"My weekend clothes don't have feelings, so don't feel too sorry for them." I bounced by Helen, pausing to tickle Madelina's downy soft cheek. She was asleep, of course, since that was what two-month-old babies did and she *always* zonked out the moment Helen strapped her to her chest.

I still couldn't quite get over my sister being a mom.

As soon as I unzipped my bag, Helen was reaching around me and tugging out one of my beloved pairs of Dickies. She wrinkled her nose at them like she always did. What kind of skater didn't like Dickies? My sister, that's who.

"Aren't you ready to outgrow these?" She flapped my Charlie cutoffs in front of her. "You're a senior now. These are from middle school, kid."

I snagged them from her and held them to my chest protectively. "And? These things would survive a nuclear blast. I'll be wearing them at my funeral when I'm ninety-two."

She covered Madelina's ears. "Don't you dare talk about dying so young. You'll scar the baby."

Rolling my eyes, I laughed. "You're not helping me unpack, you know. I thought that was the whole reason you were hanging around."

"Wrong. I'm here to try to talk you out of this whole living-on-campus idea. It's not too late to pack up your crusty Dickies and come back home with us."

"I'm not even going to list the reasons I'm living on campus this year since we've already talked about it two dozen times."

Helen pursed her red lips and batted her lashes. "I'm Luciana, and I love field hockey so much I can't live with my beloved sister anymore. I'm a traitor to the Ortega name."

I would have shoved her smart ass if my baby niece hadn't been attached to her. The decision to board at Savage Academy hadn't come easily. Since I'd started attending my sophomore year, I'd been commuting from home a half hour each way. At the end of my junior year, my field hockey coach informed me my scholarship had been increased to include room and board. Coach Thompkins had pressed me hard to accept it.

Helen had bucked against the idea, and Theo too. And, okay, maybe I'd doubted it as well. But once Madelina was born, my decision was made. They deserved their time as a family without me third-wheeling.

"Shut up. You know I'll be visiting every weekend."

She sighed and swayed a little, patting Madelina's bottom. "If you don't, I'll show up here and embarrass your sassy little ass."

My bedroom door swung open, and Theo, Helen's husband, trudged in, carrying my bedding and a box of books and other odds and ends.

Dropping the box at his feet, he threw the bedding next to my duffel, then swung around, his hands on his hips.

"There are boys living at the other end of this floor. Did anyone tell me that?" He raised an eyebrow at me, then Helen.

"Luciana doesn't like boys, so it didn't occur to me that it mattered," Helen answered.

I tipped my head at my sister. "What she said. And I definitely told you this is the athlete's dorm. I never said it was all female athletes."

My not liking boys wasn't exactly factual. I had been attracted to one or two over the years, but finding a boyfriend was not on my radar. Getting through high school and landing a field hockey scholarship for college was my focus. Too many girls got sidetracked by the drama that inevitably came with high school relationships—*especially* at Savage Academy, where we were essentially together twenty-four seven.

Theo's blue eyes narrowed. "That was absolutely a purposeful omission."

I used to think Theo only cared about me because I came as part of Helen's package, but those thoughts had been erased a long time ago. He was more of a father figure than my own shitty dad had been. His protective streak was wide, but instead of being smothering, it blanketed me in warmth.

Helen picked up Theo's arm and draped it around her shoulders. "Don't be mad at us."

He immediately softened, pulling her closer. His other hand went to Madelina, rubbing her back through the wrap holding her against Helen's chest.

"I'm not mad." He looked from her to me, making sure we understood where he was coming from. "And I trust Luc. It's the boys I don't trust."

I picked up my field hockey stick and hefted it over my shoulder like a baseball bat. "If they even look at me funny, I'll set them straight."

He couldn't hold back his grin. "Just like your sister."

"Hells is way tougher than me. How many guys had you beaten up by my age?"

She started counting on her fingers but gave up. "Too many. Be glad you haven't had to take a swing at anyone, dude."

My sister was a legit badass. She'd grown up hard because she'd had to be. If she'd been afraid to swing a bat at the men who'd seen her as a slab of meat, she wouldn't have survived.

She became my permanent guardian as soon as she graduated college, but she'd been protecting me from all the evils in the world a lot longer.

She kept me soft, and sometimes I wondered if that was a good thing.

"Actually, I saw Julien's brother moving in down the hall." Theo glanced toward the door, rubbing the back of his neck. "I'm going to ask him to look out for you."

The idea of Beckett Savage looking out for me was laughable. But since I didn't want to get into it, I just groaned and acted put upon by Theo's protectiveness, though it really made me feel safe and cared for.

"I've got my entire team looking out for me, Theo. You don't need to recruit random boys to do the job."

Helen held her fist out for a bump. "Damn straight."

Theo raised his hands in defeat. "All right, all right. You can't blame me for being protective of my girl."

I was Theo's girl. Not quite a daughter, but more than a sister. When he and Helen got married, we both took his last name. What we were to each other didn't really have a name other than family.

The two of them helped me unpack and set up my bed, even though I told them I could do it myself. Then Madelina made herself known, so Helen unwrapped her and fed her before handing her over to me.

"Tell her you're leaving her," Hells ordered. "You break it to her. I don't have the heart to."

Madelina blinked up at me, gurgling milk bubbles. God, this baby was the cutest. She'd probably be bigger the next time I saw her. If she forgot me, my heart would break.

Before the guilt could set in my suitemate, Delilah stuck her head in my door.

"Hello, everyone."

"Hey, girlie." I waved her into my room. Her twin sister, Evelyn, followed. They both met Helen and Theo last year when they'd transferred to SA, so introductions weren't needed.

Delilah cooed over Madelina while Evelyn swept her gaze over the room, studiously avoiding the people standing in it.

"If you ever need a babysitter, please call me," Delilah offered Helen.

Evelyn stopped her sweep to stare at Delilah. "You have no experience, though."

Delilah was unfazed by Ev's quiet but blunt critique. "Quite true, but I imagine I could figure it out."

Theo chuckled. "They let us take her home from the hospital with a 'good luck, now get out.' The secret is we make things up as we go." He raised an eyebrow at Hells. "Isn't that right, baby?"

Hells nodded. "The most important rule is not to drop them."

I sputtered a laugh and held the baby a little tighter. "I hope no one had to tell you that."

She scrunched up her face at me. "Hey, kid, remember who's the nurse in the family?"

My shoulder shook from giggling. "I also hope they didn't have to teach you not to drop babies in nursing school."

She broke free from Theo and came at me. "Give me my baby back."

Before she could take Madelina from me, Theo swooped in and tucked her against his chest. "I'll hold her. You say goodbye to each other."

Even though I'd thought I was ready to spend my senior year living at Savage Academy, panic suddenly struck me in the gut. This was really happening. I wouldn't see Helen, Theo, and Madelina every day. I'd be sleeping under a different roof, having dinner on my own, watching Netflix without them.

Helen snagged me around the neck and pulled me into a fierce, almost painful hug.

"I know I'm being a bitch because I'm going to miss you like whoa, but I'm so damn proud of you, dude. I can't even put into words how proud you make me."

"If you make me cry, I'll step on your toes," I warned.

Her arms banded around me even tighter. "Nah, I'm done with the sentimental stuff. Just be good and maybe have a little fun—just not Helen-level fun."

She let me pull away from her, both of us laughing, ignoring our wet eyes. "I don't think I would have any idea how to have Helen-level fun."

"It's illegal, so that's a good thing." Theo leaned down and kissed my forehead then ruffled the top of my head. "Be good, kid."

"She will," Helen answered for me. "That's one thing we don't have to worry about."

CHAPTER TWO

Luciana

A WHILE LATER, DELILAH sauntered back into my room, perching on the end of my bed. I was making a valiant attempt to arrange aesthetic squares on the wall behind my headboard, but I was about to give up since I couldn't form a straight line to save my life.

"Did you see the text? There's a party on the quad tonight."

"Really?" I blew an errant strand of hair out of my eye. "Who's throwing it, and how are they getting away with it on school grounds?"

"It's school sanctioned, so don't expect a *discoteca* in Ibiza."

I snorted a laugh. "I don't think you have to worry about that. *Some* of us have never been farther than Mexico. Not the fun parts either."

Delilah groaned. "Oh my, I'm an incredibly out-of-touch twat, aren't I? Sometimes I forget that."

"At least you're self-aware, unlike the majority of the people who go to SA."

Savage Academy's student body was composed of the offspring of some of the wealthiest people in the world. They weren't the one percent, they were the point-five percent. I'd gone into culture shock when I'd transferred in from Savage River High my sophomore year. We all wore uniforms to level the playing field between the haves and have-nots, but some people simply screamed money no matter what they wore. It was the offhanded mentions of wintering in the Mediterranean, casual connections to presidents and royalty, designer shoes and bags that probably cost more than all my, Helen's and Theo's shoes combined.

Delilah and Evelyn had been attending boarding schools since they were six. They were Greek, but they had what they'd informed me were *international* accents due to going to school in several different countries. I'd been teaching her California slang. Hearing her say "dude" in her accent still killed me.

When they'd landed at SA last year, and Delilah took on the job of manager for the field hockey team, we'd slid into an effortless, tight friendship. My bond with Evelyn had taken longer, but that was Ev. You had to really know her to love her, and she wasn't easy to know.

"That isn't saying much, is it?" Delilah got on her knees beside me, shoving me gently to the side while tsking. Without saying a word, she started taking down the squares I'd taped to the wall.

I wasn't offended. I'd been hoping she'd take pity on me and pick up the reins of this job.

"Are we going to the party?" I asked.

"Did someone say party?"

Delilah and I swiveled around at the sound of Bella's voice. She was the fourth roommate in our suite and my teammate.

Delilah waved off her excitement. "It's on the quad."

"Oh." Deflated, Bella trudged to my bed and flopped down on the end. "It can't be a party if teachers are there. That goes against the very definition of the word."

I raised an eyebrow. "Does it? I'm not sure Merriam-Webster would agree."

Delilah let out a tinkling laugh. "Or teachers. At our last school in Spain, our literature professor routinely came to class straight from the bar."

"He told you that?"

She smiled at me like I was an adorable little lamb. "No, precious, he showed up smelling like a distillery. I suppose he could have been getting pissed at home, but I liked to think he had company whilst destroying his liver."

"Ehhh…" Bella made a buzzing sound and swatted Delilah's butt. "You said 'whilst.' Minus ten points."

Delilah glanced from Bella to me. "'Whilst' is a useful word. You won't pry it out of my cold, dead hands."

Bella and I were both on a mission to cure Delilah of her internationalisms. She'd finally succumbed to saying cookies instead of biscuits, but we hadn't gotten her to stop referring to french fries as chips.

The flip side was Bella's Texas twang was rubbing off on all of us. Now, Delilah sounded like a Southern Euro Californian. I'd even caught Evelyn saying "y'all" at the end of last semester.

Bella lifted her head from my bed. "That sounded very American, D. Nice job."

Delilah grunted in response. "I'm still not sure why I should want to sound American."

"I thought the goal was neutral," I reminded them. "So you can be a woman of mystery. No one will be able to place where you're from."

"Always keep them guessin'," Bella added.

I turned around to poke her bicep. "But you, bluebonnet trollop, will never be able to hide your identity."

Bella pumped her fist. "I have never once aspired to be a woman of mystery. My book is wide open."

Evelyn appeared in the doorway. "I thought that was your legs," she said dryly.

Evelyn deadpanned her way through life. Her joking cues were subtle, but I'd slowly learned them. Like now, she rose up on her toes and tilted her chin down, the corner of her lips barely curving.

Bella shot up from the bed, attempting to be offended for half a second, then flopped back down. "Yeah, I can't even be mad about that."

I threw a pillow at her. "Shut up. Don't talk about yourself that way."

She tossed the pillow back at me. "Didn't you just call me a trollop?"

"Lovingly," I told her.

Evelyn sat beside Bella. "Having two lovers doesn't make you a slut. And even if you were a slut, I would still love you."

"Thanks, Ev." I could see Bella's hands twitching. She was a hugger, and holding back from hugging Evelyn was probably making her crazy, but she knew better. Hugging Ev without warning would have been a bridge way, *way* too far.

"No one answered me before. Are we going to the quad party?" I asked.

Bella shrugged. "I'm in if y'all are. Maybe it'll bore me enough I'll go to bed early tonight since my hard-ass team captain is making us run at six in the freakin' morning."

I gave up on the pretense of helping Delilah hang my pictures and spun around to face my mutinous teammate, my eyes narrowed.

"Your team captain just mentally added a hundred jumping jacks to your warm-up."

The groan that Bella released from her compact body was so deep and resounding it sounded like it had come from a man three times her size.

"You're supposed to be nice, Luc."

I had to laugh. "Oh, please. You've played two seasons with me. You know I'm not nice on the field."

"To the other teams!" Bella shouted, making Ev cringe. "You should be nice to your teammates."

Ev glanced in Bella's direction. "I'm in the pool every morning by six. I've never complained."

"Well, I'm way lazier than you and require a lot more beauty sleep. You roll out of bed looking like a Greek Snow White while I look like Merida's haggard blonde cousin."

Bella tugged on her white-blonde corkscrews for emphasis. Of course she was exaggerating, but I'd slept over with her a few times last year, and the girl did have insane morning hair.

"Psh—*anyway*..." I held my hand up, blocking her out. "What does one wear to a quad party?"

"I certainly know what you're *not* wearing." Delilah lowered her chin, giving me a pointed look.

I threw out my arms. "Are you seriously about to gang up on me with *Helen*? There's nothing wrong with my crusty Dickies."

"They're crusty, Luc. That's what's wrong with them."

I nudged Bella's side with my foot. "Traitor. For that, you're doing two hundred jumping jacks."

Bella caught my foot in one hand, the other poised like a claw, ready to tickle my insanely sensitive arch. "You can't punish me for telling the truth."

I tried to jerk my foot free. "If you tickle me, it'll be three hundred."

"I like your style," Evelyn said.

"Thank you, Ev." I wrangled my foot away from Bella and tucked both underneath my butt. "As always, your opinion is the one I treasure most."

She nodded. "You look like a small child wearing their big brother's clothes. It's very endearing."

Delilah's lips pinched together while her shoulders shook with silent laughter. Bella didn't even attempt to hide her reaction to Ev's burn. And from the way Ev's mouth curved, it was very evident she'd meant it as one.

No one was on my side.

"Fine! I give up. You guys can dress me tonight."

I trusted them. Sort of.

CHAPTER THREE

Beckett

A RHYTHMIC KNOCK SOUNDED on my door. Without waiting for me to answer, Rhys opened it and strolled into my room, his hands tucked in his pockets, his head swiveling back and forth, checking everything out. This was my first year with a single. It barely had space for a single bed, desk, and wall shelving, but after three years of bunking with three other guys, I would have slept in a closet to get some privacy and alone time.

Rhys focused on me, giving me a wry look. "Wow, this room is smaller than my asshole."

I sat up in my bed, my eyebrow winging. "Is there something you'd like to tell me about your summer activities, Astor?"

He took a seat at the minuscule desk tucked against the wall. I guessed he was here for the long haul.

"Is this where I detail my liaison with a French whore who taught me the joys of pegging? I think I'll keep that to myself, thanks. I prefer to maintain an air of mystery."

I rubbed my forehead, torn between laughing and yelling at him to get the hell out of my room. Fortunately, for the sake of our friendship, I didn't have to make a decision. Rhys got to the point of his intrusion.

"Let's go. We're hitting a house party in Malibu to celebrate the start of the school year."

I dropped my hand from my face and blinked at him. "I have to be up at death o'clock for practice. I'm not partying tonight."

"It'll be low key. Safe. We'll have you tucked into your beddy-bye, all on your own, before midnight. You'll get your beauty sleep, gorgeous."

Rhys Astor was nothing if not persistent. He bit into an idea and didn't let go until he'd consumed it. There was no fucking way he'd leave my room without me alongside him.

I blew out a long breath. "Who's going?"

He lifted a shoulder. "Charles and Felix. The usual suspects. No one unwanted will be there."

I thought it over. "Felix isn't staying on campus to guard Isla?"

"I've convinced him to drop his baby sister's reins for the evening."

I stood up, twisting my torso left and right, waking myself up. "Finally. The kid is going to give himself an aneurysm from the stress."

I'd been going to school and playing soccer with Felix Santos since we were freshmen. Isla, his younger sister by a year, had been living at home and attending an all-girls school up until this year when her father was transferred to France, choosing to attend SA with her big brother instead of moving overseas. Felix had basically gone from Bruce Banner to the Hulk ever since.

"Which is why we need tonight," Rhys said. "Now, put on your finest duds and get moving. It's nearly departure time."

I scoffed. "Duds? Really? I'm ashamed to know you."

"You aren't."

"Fine. I'm not. But can you stop talking like someone's pappy?"

Rhys chuffed at that. "Pappy? Why, I never. If anything, I speak like a grandpapa."

I pointed to the door. "Leave. Immediately. Before I change my mind."

"All right, all right." He pulled out his pocket watch. "You have fifteen minutes. If you're not at the elevators by then, I'll tell everyone you spooned me at my tenth birthday sleepover."

"Out."

He walked by me, clapping me on the shoulder. "Make sure to dress pretty. I need my wingman looking fine tonight."

I knocked his hand off me. "You have far too much confidence for a man with red pubes."

A maniacal laugh burst out of him. "Always thinking about my pubes, Savage. That's something to discuss with your therapist at your next session." He waggled his eyebrows. "She had no complaints about my pubes, by the way."

I slammed the door on his hastily retreating back. Rhys had been convincing me to do things I didn't want to since Halloween in fourth grade when he went as Frodo Baggins from *Lord of the Rings*, and I, of course, was his faithful buddy, Samwise. Fucking Rhys Astor.

· · · · ● · ● · · ·

My friends were already by the elevators when I showed up. Rhys tapped his pocket watch, giving me a threatening look.

Really. A threatening look from a guy with a pocket watch.

"I'm on time. Not even a minute late," I said.

"You cut it dangerously close." He slipped his watch back in his pocket, the little chain that attached it to his belt loop swaying.

"Give the kid a break, Astor." Felix held his fist out, and I bumped it. "He's our DD, after all."

Blinking, I swiveled my head back and forth between the two of them. "I did not agree to that."

Charles slapped my back. "You don't drink. Why wouldn't you be the DD?"

I gave him a quick once-over. I hadn't seen him over the summer, and it appeared he'd doubled his muscle mass in that time. If he wasn't juicing, I'd have been *really* surprised.

"Don't assume I want to drive a carful of drunk idiots around the hills of Malibu."

Rhys pressed a hand to his chest. "Are *we* the idiots? That isn't nice, Beck."

"I have never once claimed to be nice."

The elevator arrived at the same time the door to the girls' side of the hall opened. Four girls poured out, arms linked, chattering and carefree, dressed up like they were going out to be seen.

We stepped into the elevator, and Felix hit the "open" button, waving them in with us.

"Lobby?" he asked as they huddled together on the opposite side of the car.

The one with white hair answered him. "Yep. Thanks for holding the door for us."

He winked at her. "No problem."

Charles leaned his shoulders against the wall opposite the girls. "Where are you beauties headed all dressed up?"

One of the Kastanos twins—the one who smiled more often, Delilah—turned her head, sweeping her gaze over him, and made the barest smirk but didn't reply.

"We're going to the same place you are," Luciana Ortega-Whitlock informed him.

Rhys chuckled. "Oh, I highly doubt that."

Her black brows angled down. "Aren't you headed to the quad?"

Rhys laughed even harder. "Now, why would we do that?"

"What's happening on the quad?" I asked.

Luciana glanced at me over her shoulder, which was bare except for the dental floss crisscrossing her tan back, somehow securing her shirt to the front of her body. "Some back-to-school party. I was told it happens every year."

I shrugged, eyeing her exposed skin. She never wore scraps of material like that. It was either a school uniform or sports gear. "I wouldn't know."

"Sorry, ladies," Felix slipped in. "School-sponsored events are the land of the geek and the home of the lame."

Delilah Kastanos held up her phone. On the screen was the younger Santos sibling, duck facing for the camera. "Is that why Isla's meeting us there?"

Felix's shoulders expanded. "My sister is going to the party?"

"It barely counts as a party," the blonde, Bella, said.

"It's not like it's a *discoteca* in Ibiza." Luciana giggled at herself and leaned into her friend, who petted her thick, dark ponytail.

Felix's jaw clenched. I saw where this was going, and I couldn't dig any disappointment from my bones.

He spun to face Rhys. "We're going to the quad."

Rhys rolled his eyes and groaned. "My god, cut the cord. I went to one of these back-to-school shindigs my freshman year. They make you wear nametags, Santos." He smoothed his hand down his well-fitted waistcoat. "I'm not sticking cheap adhesive to this. It's bespoke, man. My tailor would shun me if he knew."

Before I could tell him to stop speaking, Delilah did it for me.

"You are a caricature. Did you know that? I'm fairly certain you're the reason people want to eat the rich."

Rhys tapped away on his phone, unperturbed by her spot-on insult, but Charles pushed off from the wall, crossing his arms over his bulging chest, his mouth pulled down as he raked his gaze along her body.

"It looks like you got a good start on the eating."

My molars clenched. Why would he insult a girl in a small, confined space surrounded by her protective friends? He was asking to have his shrunken testicles walloped.

Luciana stepped in front of her friend, leveling us all with a sharp gaze before stopping on Charles.

"Are you five? Are we really insulting bodies? If that's the case, should I point out your tits are bigger than mine, and mine aren't exactly little?" She popped her hip, her fists balled there.

Bella swooped in beside her, equally pissed and unafraid of Charles despite the red climbing his cheeks and the tendons in his neck standing out like railroad tracks. "The nineties called, they want their insults back, *Charles*."

Three things happened at once.

1. Charles lost what little control he had and lunged forward.

2. The doors slid apart.

3. I threw myself in front of Charles to stop him from doing something he couldn't take back.

The four of them hustled off. Once they were safely out of his reach, Bella spun around and held up both middle fingers, sticking her tongue out. Luc laughed and hooked her arm around Bella's neck, dragging her away. The Kastanos twins were glued to each other, hurrying off into the night.

Felix helped me hold Charles back until the girls were gone. Then we shoved him out of the elevator while Rhys strolled out, whistling.

"That was wholly unnecessary, Bloomberg," Rhys drawled.

Charles shoved us off and smoothed his ruffled clothing. "Fuck off. I was defending *you*."

"Like I said, wholly unnecessary. You could pull out all my fingernails one by one, and I couldn't even hedge a guess on what was said about me. I stopped listening as soon as the yammering began." Rhys took out his pocket watch, checked the time, and sighed.

"Overreaction," Felix muttered.

"They had a point, you know." I tipped my chin at Charles. "Fat jokes went out in elementary school."

Charles shrugged. "It wasn't a joke. Just pointing out facts. Girl shouldn't throw stones when she lives in a glass house."

"Whether it's true or not, picking a fight in an enclosed space with all her girls around her was fucking stupid, Chuck." If he were on the soccer team, I'd have him out on the track, running laps until he realized what an idiot he was being. "Besides, do you even understand what 'eat the rich' means?"

The corner of Rhys's mouth quirked. "'When the people shall have nothing more to eat, they will eat the rich.' I missed the quoting of Jean-Jacques Rousseau while I was daydreaming about all the Spanish pussy I sank into over the summer? Tragic."

I elbowed his side. "I thought your summer whore was French."

Rhys pressed his palm to his chest. "Do you honestly believe I discriminate?"

Felix released a pained groan. "Come on. We have to get to the quad. Did you see what Isla's wearing? Not a chance I'm leaving her alone to the wolves."

He stalked off, leaving the rest of us with the choice to follow. I exchanged glances with Charles and Rhys.

Charles rolled his shoulders. "I'm good either way. If we stay, I can get an early look at all the new game on campus."

Rhys rolled his eyes. "I have a feeling I'm being outvoted, so *fine*, I'll go to your little *rah-rah-rah* school spirit event, but I won't be happy about it."

Charles hurried to catch up with Felix, leaving Rhys and me trailing behind.

"He's out of hand," I muttered.

Rhys chuckled, watching our massive friend stalk down the lit path ahead of us. "He's been out of hand since birth. Testosterone and ego have only made it more pronounced."

"He's on something."

That made Rhys laugh even harder. "No shit, Captain Obvious. Your girl had a point. His tits *are* bigger than hers. Nature had nothing to do with that." He flicked his hand. "Nothing we can say will change Charles Bloomberg. I'm not about to waste my breath trying."

"He was going after those girls."

"Hmmm." He slid his hands into his pockets. "I guess we'll never know if he was going for a scare or a kill." He shrugged like it didn't matter either way. "I'm more pissed I'm being forced into staying on campus. I have a beauty waiting for me in Malibu, all primed for the plucking. You owe me one."

I narrowed my eyes at him. "I do? I think it's Felix."

"Meh. I could live without Felix."

If it were anyone else, I would have laughed. Rhys wasn't kidding, though. He could live without friends and family. An island of a man. He claimed I was the one person he'd be able to tolerate if the apocalypse wiped everyone else out, while I was pretty certain he'd shove an apple in my mouth and have me rotating on a spit roast at the first sign of a food shortage.

Until the day he ate me like a supermarket rotisserie chicken, we were as tight as two guys raised in the deep end of toxic masculinity could get.

"*I* can't live without my goalie." I gave Rhys a shove in an attempt to snap him out of his lackadaisical pace. "We need to get ourselves to the quad before Felix spots an uninformed underclassman looking at Isla a little too long and rips his head off. If Felix gets suspended, our season will be over before it begins."

Rhys winked. "Sure, sure. Balls. Sports. All things I care about deeply. Let's make like the wind to save our mutual friend Felix before he makes an unwise decision and busts some freshmen heads."

· · · · •· • · · ·

As much trouble as he gave me, as soon as we hit the quad, where a surprising amount of SA's population was milling about, Rhys vanished, saying something about a pussy appointment he couldn't possibly miss.

I found Charles and Felix perched on a stone wall, watching the event that really couldn't be called a party.

"What's the news?" I asked as I took a seat beside them.

Felix's jaw rippled. "She's here, but she's hanging out with the girls from the field hockey team. As long as she's with them, she'll be fine."

Charles grunted. "She'll be in class all day without your supervision. She'll be fine then too. Can we stop talking about baby sisters and discuss the little blonde beside her? Who is that?"

Felix shook his head. "Pretty sure she's a sophomore."

Charles raised a brow. "So?"

Felix smacked his arm. "So? You'll be eighteen soon. She's fifteen, at best. That's a charge waiting to happen. No sniffing around underclassmen."

While they argued the propriety of seniors dating the younger girls, my attention narrowed on the small group near the refreshment table. Luciana and her friends were filling up their cups with school-appropriate drinks. There was no chance that rule follower would have ever snuck a splash or two of vodka into her lemonade, even though it would have made this sorry excuse for a party more enjoyable.

Then again, after finding myself in a situation I never wanted to repeat, I hadn't had a drink since the beginning of my junior year. Luc was probably the smart one for avoiding alcohol altogether.

No friendship had blossomed between us since that day we met at Savage U when we were kids. But after attending the same school with her since we were sophomores, I knew a lot more about Luciana Ortega-Whitlock than I had back then.

She made friends easily and often.

She'd never had a boyfriend and had responded to anyone who asked that she wouldn't consider dating until college.

She was serious when she needed to be but laughed more often than most people I'd encountered.

The only people who had anything bad to say about her were those who were jealous. There was plenty of that. When you were given everything your entire life, it was difficult reconciling a girl who wasn't given much yet still had a lot more than you.

And Luc had plenty. Good friends. She did well in class. Her talent at field hockey was unmatched.

The most irritating thing Luciana did: she kissed *everyone*.

Their cheeks, their forehead, their hands. To greet them, to comfort them, as a goodbye, congratulations, just because. Her lips were always connecting with someone else's skin.

A tall, lanky guy approached the table. Freddie Spencer, one of her many, many fans. Luciana lit up and launched herself at him. He picked her up, her feet dangling off the ground. She held his face in her hands and kissed both his cheeks twice.

Were four kisses necessary?

He pecked her on the lips before setting her down, keeping her firmly molded to his side. They looked like a couple, but having known Freddie for years, I was well aware he wasn't interested in what was under Luciana's skirt.

Charles's massive shoulder bumped mine. "Who are you checking out?"

He could be a dog with a bone. If he thought I had an inkling of interest in any girl, even if it was curiosity or for science, he wouldn't drop the matter until I admitted it or he fucked the girl himself. Since I'd never admit anything remotely personal to him, he'd fucked plenty of girls he had assumed I was interested in.

Like no one had ever accused me of being nice, absolutely *no one* had ever claimed Charles was a good friend.

"Freddie Spencer." I jerked my chin in his direction. "He got taller over the summer."

Charles rubbed his chin. "I could give a fuck about Freddie Spencer." He stood, stretching his arms over his head. "I'm going to make a lap and see what I can see."

If it weren't for Felix needing supervision, I would have escorted myself back to my bedroom. It would be an early morning on the track before the boys showed up for practice. Six a.m. was going to arrive before I knew it.

A kid walked past Isla's group, and Felix's fingers gripped the edge of the wall. When the kid kept going without even glancing at Isla, he still didn't relax.

I would have told him to save his focus for the field, but my breath would have been wasted. Felix was always going to be scarily overprotective. Nothing I could have said would have changed that.

I folded my arms across my chest and settled in, scanning the crowd for a moment before my gaze was drawn back to Luciana.

Just in time to watch her smack her lips on yet another person.

I shook my head, releasing a heavy exhale. She gave her kisses out like candy on Halloween.

Since the very first time I watched her do it, it had made my stomach curdle.

What else did she give away?

Did she even value what she was giving?

Girls at SA were either free loving and unashamed or tight lipped and closed legged. There'd never been rumors about Luciana. She'd never dated anyone at SA either. But the girls around here, who could be catty when they were threatened, hadn't labeled her a prude either.

She was just Luc, doing her own thing without a fucking care, and liked by most anyway.

Smiling, always.

Kissing everyone.

There was something there, though, under her surface. Where the light didn't reach. Those murky, unexplored waters churned, unseen.

My fingers twitched, wanting to dig.

To find her darkness.

Expose it to the light.

And see if it matched my own.

This year. This year, I'd find out.

CHAPTER FOUR

Luciana

MY FEET HIT THE track in a steady rhythm. *Thwack, thwack, thwack.*

I'd been athletic from birth. Helen had gotten me on a skateboard as soon as I could stand. Had told me I'd been a natural. Of course, she was my sister, so she had to say that. She'd had a kid and *still* kicked my ass at the skate park, but I held my own.

It wasn't until middle school that I participated in a team sport. The money just hadn't been there before that, much less the guidance from either of my parents.

My mother still thought I played hockey on ice.

But my middle school gym teacher saw something in me and recruited me onto my school's field hockey team. The rest was history.

And a lot of work. *A lot.*

My summers weren't for lounging. I trained, ran, lifted weights, went to camp, and studied videos of games. I was the captain this year, so everything was ramped up a notch.

Savage Academy didn't play around when it came to athletics. They bred champions. Not winning wasn't really an option around here. For some, that might have been stressful, but for me, it lit a fire under my ass. Our field hockey team was the current state champion, and I intended to get there again this year.

So, I was out before my girls, getting my run in. I'd run with them too, but that was more to encourage them and push the stragglers. This time, on my own, was when I pushed myself.

I wasn't alone on the track this morning. Beckett Savage was half a lap away, his long legs carrying him at an enviable pace. He'd arrived a few minutes after me and had kept the track between us at all times.

I didn't mind sharing the track with him. To tell the truth, even though SA was a closed campus, being out here alone at sunrise probably wasn't the smartest decision. Helen may have tried to keep me wrapped in fleece so the monsters of the world didn't get to me, but I'd had my eyes wide open. I knew what went bump in the night weren't little fairytale creatures. Reality was a lot scarier.

Having Beckett within screaming distance made me feel like I could really lose myself in my workout, which I did. Music pumping, singing along with the lyrics pouring into my ears, I got caught up and hadn't noticed Beckett disappearing until there was a gentle tug on the end of my ponytail.

Gasping, I whipped my head to the side, shocked to find him jogging beside me.

"You scared me!" I yelled.

His mouth moved, but I had no idea what he was saying. He pointed to his ear, then mine, and I remembered I was wearing my earbuds. I yanked one out.

"You scared me," I repeated.

He held his hands up. "Didn't mean to. You slowed down so much, I caught up to you."

I shot him a glare. "I didn't slow down. My pace has been steady my entire run."

"Then how did I catch up?"

"You..." My nose crinkled. "Your legs are twice the length of mine. Of course you'd catch up. It's science."

He chuffed. "Science, huh?"

"Yeah. I'm pretty sure Newton wrote a paper on it."

That made him let out a breathy, deep chuckle. "I'll have to look it up. It sounds riveting."

"You won't find it easily. It's one of his lesser-known works. Very rare."

"Damn. I guess you're going to have to tell me all about it sometime." He tugged my ponytail again and took off, leaving me in the dust.

What was that?

Was Beckett...bantering with me?

He couldn't have been. Beckett scowled and skulked and glared. He didn't make jokes. If he said anything, it was to be an asshole—not to make me laugh.

He'd hated me since the day we met, and nothing had changed over time. I would never understand his instant loathing for me, but during the intermittent years between when we met and when I started at SA, he'd held strong to it.

So strong, he'd tried to get me kicked off the field hockey team when I'd transferred here my sophomore year—which would have meant leaving SA entirely since I was here on scholarship.

Of course, he'd been born wealthy and would be buried beneath stacks of money when he died. Me losing a scholarship had probably seemed like a fun prank to his twisted self. He had no stakes. His life would end up rosy no matter what he did.

The school we both attended bore his family's name, after all. You couldn't walk down the street anywhere around here without seeing "Savage" emblazoned on a building or a road sign.

What must that have been like to have his last name splashed high and low? For people to think he owned the town and all its contents, including the people?

Probably a head trip.

No wonder Beckett was such a jerk.

Fortunately, he had been easy to avoid. Other than noticing his perpetual judgment face from time to time, he wasn't really on my radar.

It might be different this year, living on the same floor in the dorm.

Beckett Savage didn't worry me, though. I had more important things to think about.

Like tearing apart every team we came up against limb from limb.

· · · · ● · ● · · ·

There were a lot of things I loved about SA. The uniforms weren't one of them. I felt like a kid playing dress-up in the pleated skirt that hit my knees, white button-down, and blazer. It wasn't that the clothes didn't fit me, it was that they didn't *fit* me.

Delilah looked adorable as hell in her uniform. Then again, she walked around with an air of sophistication that belied her age. Not to mention, she had boobs, hips, and a butt. She filled out every crevice of her starched and pressed clothes with her Greek-goddess curves.

And it wasn't that I didn't like my body. It worked well for me and did its job. But if I was going to drown in clothing, I'd rather have been comfy in my skater gear.

Delilah slapped my hand. "Stop fidgeting with your collar. You're going to make me nervous too."

I dropped my hands, tucking them under my thighs. "I'm not nervous. It's just hard for me to go back to wearing this stuff after a summer of being in shorts and a tank top."

The first day of class always made me antsy but not *nervous*. We'd gotten to English literature early, so we were waiting to see who else would be in this period with us. Unfortunately, Ev and Bella weren't, but a few of the girls from the team were.

She plucked at one of the buttons on her jacket. "Do you really believe I love wearing this? I don't. I just accepted my fate a long time ago."

I perked up in my seat. "Let me see the picture of you and Ev in your straw hats."

Her dark eyes narrowed. "No. Absolutely not. My trauma is not for your entertainment."

I batted my eyes. "But you were so cute."

Delilah had made the mistake of showing me a picture of her uniform in kindergarten. She had looked like she'd stepped out of the pages of *Madeline*, with her little blue swing jacket and yellow straw hat. Since then, I'd asked her to show it to me whenever I needed cheering up.

Sighing, she pulled out her phone, tapped the screen, then handed it to me. I immediately cooed at tiny Ev and Del, holding hands and staring at the camera with stony, serious little faces.

"Aw, I die. I just want to scoop the two of you up and squeeze you."

As I sighed at their sweetness, a shadow fell over me, then a hand plopped on my desk and Rhys Astor bent down to check out the screen.

"Is your biological clock already ticking away, Ortega?" His teasing words ruffled the hair that had fallen loose from my ponytail around my ears. "Looking at small children makes your womb lonely?"

Rhys wasn't the worst SA had to offer, but he was far from the best. My mother believed in all kinds of superstitions, including the one about redheads having no souls. She'd told me more than once that every freckle on a ginger represented a soul they'd stolen.

I'd always rolled my eyes, but then I met Rhys Astor and wondered if he was the reason the myth came to be. I could easily picture him crouching over some innocent, sleeping person, and sucking their soul out of their body, licking his chops at the delicious, soul-y flavor.

I jerked away from him, pressing the phone against my chest. Unless I wanted to fall out of my chair, I couldn't go too far. "For a guy whose junk is right at my elbow height, you're being awfully unpleasant."

"Wow. First day of school and you're already thinking of my junk." He tucked the wisps of hair behind my ear. "That's really sweet, doll, but you're not my type."

"Because I have a brain?"

He chuckled and straightened, smoothing a hand over his tie. "Exactly. Why fill up your head with gray matter when you could fill it up with—"

He was shoved out of my face before he could complete his disgusting sentence. Beckett scowled at him, and Rhys laughed, his shoes squeaking on the wood floor.

"Sit down," Beckett gritted out to his friend.

"I was only making conversation," Rhys countered, amusement lacing his words.

"And now it's over." Beckett's hands went to his hips. He didn't crack even a hint of a smile, despite Rhys dancing down the aisle, away from us, cackling as he went.

I tipped my face up to look at Beckett. He was watching Rhys, then suddenly, he was watching me, his intense, searching gaze sweeping over me like he was checking for injuries, which was strange. Rhys had been teasing me in a tolerable, if not annoying, way since the day I'd started here, and Beckett had never had a problem with it.

Maybe he was mad at his friend over something else. That was probably it.

"Did you have a good practice?" I asked.

He flinched like my question had been a physical blow. I was only asking to be polite—a habit I couldn't seem to rid myself of.

"Better than yours," he muttered, shoving his hands in his trouser pockets.

I cocked my head, straining to look at him so high above me. "What does that mean?"

"You don't look ready."

"I think you should stick to soccer. I'm pretty sure you don't know a thing about field hockey."

I would never admit he was right. Our practice had been a shit show. New girls weren't picking up on our plays. The team wasn't meshing well yet. And to make things worse, two players had gotten in a fight over a freaking *boy*.

Of course, the soccer team practiced in the field adjacent to ours, so Beckett had been a witness to all this.

He rocked back on his heels. "I never said I was an expert, but I know what I saw." He shrugged, a slice of black hair falling across his forehead. "You should practice with the new players more. They need it if you expect to maintain the level the team played at last year."

I had to bite down on my bottom lip to stop myself from cussing this arrogant asshole out. He played *soccer*. What did he know about my sport?

"Excuse me," Delilah interjected, and Beckett slowly turned his head in her direction. She took her job as team manager seriously and Beckett had raised her hackles, which was a hard thing to do. "As far as I know, you weren't asked for your opinion. If we ever need unsolicited advice in the future, you can be sure we'll come to you now that we know you love giving it."

Clutching Del's phone, I crossed my arms over my chest and nodded. "Exactly."

Beckett leveled me with another hard, intense stare. "If you don't want to win, that's your business, I guess." He held my gaze for another long, drawn-out moment before his lips parted and he exhaled. It seemed like he might have had something to say, but our teacher arrived before he could. As he sauntered past, he ran his hand over my ponytail, then he gave it a gentle tug, sending strange ripples through my stomach.

Delilah and I exchanged wide eyes. "What was that about?"

I handed her her phone and swallowed down the disconcerted feeling Beckett had left behind. "I have no idea."

Beckett was the captain of the soccer team. How had he found the time to watch our practice at all, let alone so closely he knew where our troubles were stemming from?

Class was called to order, and we were told to push our desks against the wall, grab a pillow, and sit down on the floor. There was some moaning and groaning, but we all did as we were told.

Somehow, during the shuffle, I ended up beside Beckett. I tucked my legs under my skirt while his were stretched out in front of him, crossed at the ankle. He raised a brow at me, and I turned to Delilah on my other side.

"Remind me to wear trousers to class from now on," she murmured, smoothing her skirt over her thighs.

"We're not going to spend the semester on the floor, are we?" I whispered.

"I don't know. I've heard Dr. Burns is unpredictable. We should be prepared for anything. Rain gear and snorkels might even be necessary."

I snorted a laugh. "I can't swim, so that might be trouble."

Growing up poor would do that to a girl. It was my secret shame since I lived within a few miles of the coast. Delilah was one of the few who knew that about me.

Her pinkie snagged mine. "Oh, precious. This year, I'm teaching you, and I won't hear any arguments."

"So you say. I'm pretty sure I'll sink like a stone."

"Not with..." she trailed off, distracted by the guy who'd walked into class. A new student since I didn't recognize him, and he was definitely recognizable.

"Who's that?" I whispered.

This new student paused to speak to Dr. Burns, towering over her. When he bent his neck, tattoos peeked out from beneath his unbuttoned collar, his tie slung loosely down his chest.

"I have no idea," Delilah whispered hoarsely.

Dr. Burns gestured toward the cushions. The only one free happened to be beside Delilah, who was frozen, her pinkie still curled tightly around mine.

"Oh god," she hissed.

Delilah never lost her cool. Even when assholes like Charles Bloomberg insulted her, she kept her head high, letting it roll off her back, but when the tattooed, lanky boy started in our direction, I felt her vibrating beside me.

He dropped his bag on the floor, then lowered himself to the cushion. Much like Beckett, he stretched his legs out in front of him, then turned his head toward us and tipped his chin.

"What's up?"

He had a deep, thick timbre to his voice, the kind of sound only tall men made, like Kylo Ren or Beckett Savage. Unlike Beckett, this new kid had an accent softening the edges of his words.

"Hey." I gave a little wave. "I'm Luc."

"Ivan." He glanced at Delilah. "And you?"

"Delilah," she squeezed out. "I'm Delilah."

Beckett leaned into me, his shoulder against mine, and stretched his long arm out. "Beckett Savage."

Ivan's sharp brow furrowed as he stared down at Beckett's offered hand, his lip curling like it was covered in dog crap instead of a polite gesture.

I recognized what this was: a pissing contest I was right in the middle of.

Great.

I should have brought my rain gear after all.

CHAPTER FIVE

Beckett

"WHO THE HELL IS that kid?" Rhys didn't bother lowering his voice. That would've implied he gave a shit who heard him, and he very clearly did not.

"No idea."

The new kid sat down beside Luc's friend, making himself right at home, giving Luc all his attention. Covered in tats, eschewing the dress code, stupid name, and worse accent, we hadn't exchanged a word and I could tell I wasn't going to get along with this guy.

I leaned into Luc's side and introduced myself to him anyway. "Beckett Savage."

"Ivan Sokolov." This kid slapped my hand like we were bros. "Is that your name on the big sign out front?"

"Family name, yeah."

He cocked his chin. "Must be proud."

"It is what it is," I answered as if he was commenting in good faith, though his sneer and superior expression were evidence to the contrary. "Do you play a sport?"

"I swim," he replied curtly.

"Oh!" Luc brightened. "Delilah's sister, Evelyn, is on the swim team. Are you going to try out?"

He nodded, sweeping his gaze over Delilah, then Luc, his nostrils flaring. "I plan to."

"You definitely should. SA has sent more than a dozen swimmers to the Olympics." She flicked her hand. "Well, I don't know if that's your goal. What I mean is they're excellent."

"That is not my goal," he answered, his mouth curving into something like a smile. Not the sneer he had sent my way. If he was attempting to flirt with her, he'd be out of luck. For two years, this girl had sent every interested guy packing with a friendly pat on the back. He'd get the same treatment, even with his tattoos and accent.

I pressed into Luc's shoulder. "Luciana is captain of the field hockey team. She's taking them to state."

Even if she wasn't interested in him, Ivan needed to understand he was the newcomer. He didn't know her, and he never would—not the way I did.

She turned her head, bringing her nose so close to mine they almost touched. I hadn't been near her like this since we first met. Hadn't touched her, even in passing.

Her skin was smooth gold. A swipe of mascara on her lashes, something rosy on her high cheekbones, gloss on her heart-shaped lips, the rest bare and natural.

And she still smelled like sunshine after all these years.

Her lips quirked. "I thought we were a mess. Now we're going to state?"

I smirked at her exasperation. "I have confidence you'll fix what's not quite working yet."

"That means the world to me," she quipped without an ounce of sincerity.

"You're welcome."

Her swirling brown eyes narrowed. "Tomorrow, I'm going to watch your soccer practice."

"Bring on the critique. Though, from what I saw today, your team needs all your focus."

Her forehead crinkled. "Just when I thought you were being nice."

"Nice is useless."

"That's extremely pessimistic."

"How do you win games, Luciana? By being nice?"

She opened her rosy lips to deny my point then clamped them closed and glared at me.

I grinned. "See?"

"You can't hold my behavior on the field against me. That's not real life."

"On the contrary. I don't hold it against you. Your ability to go from girl next door to absolute beast is an admirable quality."

She sucked in a breath. "Did you just call me a beast?"

I tilted my head, trying to get a read on her. I couldn't tell if she was offended or complimented.

"You know how you play," I said slowly. I hadn't kept track of the other players, but I was almost certain Luciana had earned more yellow cards than anyone on her team.

"I'm surprised *you* know how I play, considering you wanted me off the team in the first place."

"Is that what you think?"

Her mouth pursed. "It's what I know."

She didn't quite have her story straight. When she was ready to listen, I'd explain the truth. Since this was the longest, most civil conversation we'd had with each other, now wasn't the time. Her little pink cheeks were going to be awfully red when she fully understood my past actions.

"I'm not sure you know all that much, Ortega."

Dr. Burns stepped into the middle of the circle, pulling Luc's attention away from me. I craned my head to catch Ivan's eye. He raised a brow. I jerked my chin. The message had been sent and received. He needed to look for friends elsewhere. Luciana wasn't going to be one of them.

Dr. Burns passed a beach ball between her hands and informed us we were going to play a getting-to-know-you game. There were groans all around the room. We were seniors now. We knew each other well enough. If I wanted to know any of these people more, I'd speak to them. If I hadn't...well, there was a reason for that.

If this middling, unoriginal, unwanted game was a sign of how this class was going to be, this semester was going to be painful.

Dr. Burns tossed Ivan the ball first. He stared at it like he had my hand, so Dr. Burns reminded him of the rules. "Answer the question your thumb landed on then throw it to someone else. Go on."

He looked her straight in the eye and said, "No." Then he rolled the ball left, hitting my legs.

Dr. Burns stood there, stunned. The kid had turned her down flat without any hesitation. I admired that, but I was never going to like him.

Even though I wanted to follow in Ivan's footsteps, I couldn't. My sister-in-law, Sera—my brother Julien's wife—worked at SA, assisting the band director. If she got wind of my being insubordinate, she'd give me one of those looks. Not angry. She wasn't the angry kind. No, Sera would go for the jugular and tell me how disappointed she was in me.

With a heavy exhale, I picked up the ball and read the question beside my thumb. "What insect could you live without?" I glanced at Rhys, then Luc, and mouthed, *"What the fuck?"* "Excuse me, what is the purpose of my answering this question?"

Dr. Burns gave me a condescending smile. "It gives us insight into how you think, which is a more interesting way of getting to know one another than asking for your favorite color. Don't you think?"

"No, I don't think."

I was poised to throw the ball across the room, but Luc elbowed me. "Come on, Savage. Are you afraid to let us see inside your thoughts about bugs?"

"What's your answer?"

She breathed out a laugh. "It's not my turn. It's yours."

"Fine." I shoved my fingers through my hair. "Fuck. I don't know. Cockroaches are out."

From across the circle, Bianca DeSoto scoffed and tossed her raven hair behind her shoulder. "Nice job destroying the entire ecosystem, Beckett."

Dr. Burns shook her finger at Bianca. "There are no wrong answers in this game, and we will not judge what each other has to say."

I tossed the ball away from me, annoyed at myself for even participating. Bianca raised a brow and shifted her legs so her skirt rode up her thighs. This move of hers was so practiced, I'd seen it a thousand times, and I'd never once been impressed. In fact, Bianca turned my stomach every time I saw her.

I swiveled to my right, finding Luc watching me.

As soon as our eyes met, she leaned away and lowered her gaze to her lap, refusing to look up even as I bumped against her.

"Luc," I gritted out.

She shook her head. "Shush. I'm trying to listen."

"No you're not."

Her eyes flicked to mine. Pink flushed her cheeks. "Why are you talking to me so much today? Is this because of Theo?"

"What?"

I had no idea what she was talking about. Theo was a friend of my brother's, but I didn't know what that had to do with anything. It was on the tip of my tongue to ask her to clarify when Bianca sent the ball sailing toward Luc's head. Reaching out, I swatted it out of the air before it could make impact and dropped it onto her legs.

"Your turn," I whispered.

She frowned at the ball, reading the question. "You're stranded on a desert island. Are you alone or with your worst enemy?"

She had the audacity to look at me and bite her bottom lip. "I'd like to be with my worst enemy. I'd let him build me a shelter and teach me all the survival skills he knows, and when he got too annoying, I'd eat him."

Laughter broke out. Rhys howled over little Luciana being bloodthirsty as fuck. Even Dr. Burns giggled, which would have been disconcerting if I'd given myself a second to process it.

"Naturally," Bianca called over the din. "It makes sense a girl like you would suck dry all the resources around her without contributing anything."

"What does that mean?" Luciana asked, her shoulders tense. "A girl like me?"

I leaned forward, pulling my legs in, wanting the same answer. Bianca had always been a bitch, but this was the first time I'd seen her direct any of her ire toward Luciana.

Laughter died off. Bianca shifted her legs again, unruffled at the sudden attention. "On scholarship, obviously. You're here for free because our parents pay. I bet you look down on all of us while you're taking from us. We all know how the poor view the wealthy."

Luciana shook her head. "That isn't true."

Bianca dragged a long strand of hair forward and smoothed it between her fingers, simpering her pouty lips. "Sure it is."

She winked at me, and my hands flexed on my knees—hands that were tied because of my family and role here at school. If I said what I wanted to, told that bitch to go fuck herself, that she was an unoriginal, boring heap of nothing in a skin sack, word would get back to my coach. My sister-in-law and brother. And worse, my father. God, if I had to listen to my father lecturing me about tarnishing the family name one more time, I'd walk off the edge of the earth.

There were other ways to deal with Bianca, though.

"That's enough, Ms. DeSoto," Dr. Burns scolded. "If you'd like to discuss scholarships, I recommend making an appointment with the headmaster. Otherwise, it's irrelevant to this classroom."

Ivan reached over and plucked the ball from Luciana's hand. "I got a question," he announced.

Dr. Burns sputtered, having lost control of the classroom. "Mr. Sokolov, as long as it's from the ball, I—"

He squeezed the ball in his overgrown hands. "Does being a dumb cunt come from growing up with money, or is it an attribute you're born with?"

Bianca gasped, her hands flying to her chest. So tenderhearted and offended. "Dr. Burns! You can't allow him to speak that way."

So fucking hypocritical.

Dr. Burns, the poor dear, was seconds away from imploding. Red-faced, her maw flapped like a hooked fish and her hands clenched at her waist.

Ignoring Bianca's outrage and Dr. Burns' feeble attempt at regaining control of the class, Ivan went on to answer as if the question was actually written on the ball. "In my experience, you have to work at being that level of dumb cunt."

Rhys patted my shoulder as the class erupted in chaos. "You know, I think I like the new guy."

Funny, I had just been thinking his valiant show of white knighting had put him right at the top of my shit list.

Chapter Six

Luciana

THE PONYTAIL TUG DIDN'T startle me this time.

All week, Beckett Savage had been out on the track at the same time as me. I sort of suspected this was part of Theo's request for him to watch out for me. What didn't make sense was how he continued to interact with me, both on the track and in class.

"Slowing down." I read his lips, his voice drowned out by my music.

"Shut up," I shouted.

Grinning, he kept pace with me, which must have been painful on his giraffe legs. Also strange. Other than when he'd tried to get me kicked out of SA, Beckett Savage had lived on the periphery of my time here, yet this week, he'd been shoving himself directly into my line of sight.

Our schedules aligned—and not just on the track. We had almost every class together, we ate in the dining hall at the same time, and we'd ended up riding the same elevator in the dorm more often than not.

All of this was probably part of some nefarious plot that ended with me in a ditch somewhere. I'd never heard rumors of Beckett putting girls in ditches, but it didn't seem outside the realm of possibilities.

I tugged one of my earbuds out. "If I'm slow, why are you running beside me?"

"Isn't it obvious? I'm trying to push you to go faster."

I narrowed my eyes, glancing from the track to him. "Why would that work?"

"Because you want to keep up with me."

I huffed. "Says who?"

He nodded toward my feet. "Says you, chugging like a little determined choo-choo train."

Groaning at his condescension, I shoved my earbud back in. "Shut up, Savage."

That made him laugh but not run away from me. I really had to work on becoming more threatening off the field.

He stayed beside me for the rest of my run. By the time we slowed to a walk to cool down, some of his team was starting to show up, as was mine. Beckett turned around, walking backward. Reaching out, he plucked my earbuds from my ears and stuffed them in his pocket.

My mouth fell open. "Are you kidding?"

"Don't worry, little light. I'm not going to keep them."

"Then why take them in the first place? To be rude?"

He chuckled. "If you say so. Don't you think it's rude to listen to music when you're running with someone in the first place?"

What was up with him? Why was he teasing me like we were buddies?

"You're confusing." I braced my hands on my hips. "And no, it's not rude because I wasn't running *with* you. You chose to run next to me uninvited."

He clutched his chest. "Wow. Way to drive the dagger deep. I can see this past week meant nothing to you."

"I'm glad you see things clearly. Maybe next week, I can go back to running in peace."

He scoffed, and I worried what that could've meant.

"Luuuc!"

I spun around, grinning as Bella waved both arms over her head from the other side of the track. Cupping my hands around my mouth, I yelled her name.

"Don't you live together?" Beckett asked when I spun back.

"Yes, why?"

He threaded his fingers together behind his neck as he fell into step beside me again. "You're incredibly excited to see someone you spend most moments of the day with. It doesn't make sense."

"To you."

"Right." He peered down at me. "It doesn't make sense to me, which is why I'm pointing out the oddity."

"You don't ever get excited to see...I don't know, Charles?"

He dropped his arms, letting them slap his sides. "No. I've never felt anything when Charles appears."

"Isn't he your friend?"

"I wouldn't call Charles my friend. He's just there and has always been there. If he wasn't there, I wouldn't think about him."

I crinkled my nose. "He's awful, you know. If you don't care about him, why hang out with him? People judge you by the company you keep."

"What's so awful about him?" Beckett sounded genuinely interested, like he'd never thought about it.

While Beckett didn't have a reputation for leaving girls in ditches, Charles Bloomberg did. Well, not the ditches part, but everyone around SA knew what he was about—and it wasn't sticking around, even if he made promises to.

It wasn't just his "come and done" behavior that made me avoid him like the plague, though. There was something intrinsically about him that gave me the ick. Plus, he was just a jackass. He let his mouth run when he would have been better off shutting it.

Out of the group Beckett hung around with, Charles was the worst. He was an eighties high school movie villain. If he had changed his name to Blaine and flipped his collar, he would have fit in seamlessly.

The fact that Beckett didn't see it said a lot about him.

"You were there in the elevator when he made fun of Delilah."

"Ah." He nodded as if I'd jogged his memory. "In defense of Rhys."

"Who didn't need defending. I'm not sure he was on the same plane as the rest of us. If he was, he didn't seem at all broken up about what she said." I shook my head at him. "I can't believe *you* would defend Charles making fun of Delilah's looks. But I suppose that's why you keep him around. You don't have a problem with that behavior."

"It's a low form of banter, I'll give you that."

I could not believe my ears. "Banter? Insulting a girl's body is not banter! You and I were bantering but—"

"Wait, we're not now?"

"No." My fingers curved into a fist. "I'm yelling at you."

"You yell very gently." He scratched the side of his sweaty head. "It's not unpleasant."

Frustration ripped through me. I hadn't thought of Beckett often since we first met, having filed him away with Charles, Rhys, and the rest of the rich, stuck-up, egotistical douche lords of his ilk, but for a second, I'd considered maybe he was different. I'd clearly been wrong. Beckett might not have made fat jokes, but he'd stood by while they were being made, and that was just as bad.

I stuck my hand out. "Can you give me my earbuds back? I have to go to practice, and so do you."

He made no move to comply. "I thought we were talking."

I shook my hand. "Right, well, that's done. Earbuds, please."

I felt his gaze on the side of my face for a long time but stared straight ahead. Finally, he sighed, and from the corner of my eye, I watched him stick his hand in his pocket.

"You're coming to our game tonight," he stated.

"Am I?"

God, I just wanted to get away from him. His impassive expression annoyed me. More than that, the fact that I'd questioned my own judgment about him was really grating on me.

"You are. It's required when you live on campus."

I huffed, out of patience. I already knew that and had been planning to go, but now that he'd all but ordered it, I wanted to tell him to suck it.

Since he'd most likely spot me in the stands, I bit back the response.

"Then I suppose I'm coming to your game."

He dropped my earbuds into my palm, and I yanked my hand away, not wasting any time before cutting across the field to put distance between us and join my teammates for practice.

Bella and Delilah intercepted me as soon as my feet left the grass and hit the track.

"Was he bothering you?" Delilah asked.

"He was being a typical SA guy." I just wanted to close the subject. I'd had enough of Beckett Savage for the day.

Bella crossed her arms over her chest, her lips curling. "I don't know. I got here a while ago and y'all looked awfully buddy-buddy. I didn't know you two were friendly like that."

"We aren't." I sighed, giving in. "He's been running at the same time as me all week and he's been strangely chatty."

"Chatty?" Delilah raised a brow. "What do you and Lord Savage have to talk about?"

I snorted at the title. "He tells me when I'm slowing down."

That made Bella gasp. "I didn't get a close look at him. How black is his eye from when you punched him?"

"No violence." I held up my hands. "I think he's doing it to push me, which is effective. I don't know, I think Theo asked him to watch out for me, so I'm pretty sure that's what's going on."

Bella shimmied her shoulders. "Are you sure he's not into you?"

"No." That was definite. I didn't even have to think about it.

"I don't know, precious." Delilah's gaze flitted over my shoulder—probably to Beckett—then back to me. "I noticed he touched you a lot on the first day of English lit. And his face almost turned purple when Bianca said those hideous things to you."

Ugh, I'd blocked Bianca's snobby opinions out of my memories.

"Speaking of Bianca, did you hear?" Bella glanced around at us, her eyes alight.

"No, tell me," I demanded.

"She's suspended indefinitely. I heard an anonymous call was made that she was keeping drugs in her room." Bella sounded delighted by this.

My mouth fell open. "What did they find?"

She shrugged. "Probably uppers, knowing how manic she is half the time."

"That's too bad," Delilah said with absolutely no sincerity. "I'm surprised Beckett didn't have her thrown out, given this is *his* school and—"

"This isn't Beckett's school. It has his, like, great-great-great-grandfather's name."

"Which is his name," Delilah argued.

"I don't know why we're still talking about Beckett Savage." I tilted my head to the side. "Can we talk about how you were barely able to breathe when Ivan sat down beside you?"

She didn't try to deny it. That was the thing about Delilah—she was who she was. Before Ivan Sokolov entered the room, I had never seen my friend unsure or shy. Ivan had *flustered* her in a big way.

Which was how I knew she had it bad for him.

"Did you see him?" Her blinks were long and pointed. "He's beautiful. It would have been criminal to keep my cool in front of him."

Bella grinned. "I'm betting Luc didn't have that problem."

"Because Luc doesn't see boys as an option," Delilah explained.

I raised my hand. "Maybe Luc just doesn't let pretty skin suits fluster her."

My friends exchanged a long glance then laughed at me. Delilah shook her finger. "See? You have shut your brain off to boys for so long you only see them as skin."

"Are you gonna be able to turn that switch back on in college?" Bella asked.

I shrugged. "I'm not too worried about it. If I end up a spinster, I'll just move in with one of you and be the eccentric aunt to your children."

"Nope," Bella proclaimed. "You're too hot. I don't need my future husband to have any eye candy besides me."

I glanced at Delilah, who shook her head. "My children, if I choose to have them, will already have eccentric Aunt Ev. Sorry, presh. You might have to live on your own—*or* stop thinking of boys as 'pretty skin suits.'"

I laughed. "Whatever. I can't even think that far in the future." I stretched my arms over my head, then raised my voice so the rest of my team could hear me. "Who's ready to run?"

I could always count on Bella to yell the loudest and most enthusiastically, and this morning was no exception.

Chapter Seven

Luciana

Every year, Savage River High and Savage Academy faced off in a pride match that didn't count as part of the regular season. The coaches touted it as community outreach, but everyone knew what it really was.

SA wanted to show the locals they were superior in every way.

SRH wanted to show the richies' money didn't buy talent.

My competitive heart sang, but I was torn on who to root for. Since I'd gone to SRH my freshman year, I had friends on the team and in the school. But I was an academy girl now. I couldn't exactly cheer against my schoolmates.

So, I took a seat in the middle of the stands.

Neutral territory.

Bella and Delilah were chatting with some of the girls from the team at the bottom of the bleachers, and Ev was back in our dorm. This was so not her scene.

Both teams were out on the field, running drills and warming up. My eye kept inadvertently following Beckett as he dribbled the ball with smooth ease. I'd been to soccer games before but had never paid special attention to him. Now, I wondered how I hadn't. His control of both his body and the ball was impressive.

My breath caught in my throat when he suddenly stopped, his foot on top of the ball, his head swiveling my way. He found me after one second of searching, and even from a distance, I could tell he was smirking.

As if he knew I'd been watching him specifically.

I mean, he was right, but he didn't need to know that.

"Luci-loo!"

Ripping my gaze away from the field, I hopped up and opened my arms for Giselle, my friend from when I went to public school in Savage River. She threw herself at me, knocking me to my butt. Fortunately, I fell back into my seat and not on the ground.

"Holy enthusiasm, girl. You took me out." I kissed her dimpled cheek twice and shoved her onto the bleacher beside me.

"Sorry about that. You know me." She ruffled my hair and grinned. "You look hot."

"You do too, baby girl."

That made her beam, showing off the gap between her front teeth. Giselle was like a puppy, bouncing and happy all the time. She got into trouble like one too.

She tucked her arm in mine and gestured to the guys hovering two steps down from us. "Come here, boys. Say hi to Luci." Two was a low number for her. She was usually surrounded by a cavalcade of them.

Giselle still went to Savage River High. She was here to cheer for her team since she was a major soccer fanatic and followed them everywhere.

I recognized one of the boys with her from my year at SRH.

"Hey, Cris," I greeted.

He reached out and bumped my fist, giving me a chin jerk.

Giselle bumped my shoulder. "This is Adrian. He just moved to Savage River."

Adrian held out his hand. After a beat of hesitation, I slipped my palm against his, and we shook. He let me go immediately, not creeping by trying to hold on to me for too long. That was nice. His face was nice too.

More than nice.

Adrian was really good-looking, which, as my girls liked to point out, wasn't something I often noticed. He wasn't too tall but wasn't short either. He was lean and rangy, with a mess of dark curls on his head, thick brows with a slash running through one, and another scar over his upper lip. He was wearing cutoff Dickies, a vintage Smashing Pumpkins shirt, and beat-up Vans on his feet.

"Do you skate?" I asked.

His head jerked like I'd startled him with my abrupt question. "Uh...yeah. I do."

Giselle plopped down beside me and threw her arm around my shoulders. "My girl skates too."

Adrian's brow went up, and he took me in again, this time scanning me from head to toe. We were required to wear our academy gear at home games. My khaki shorts and Savage Academy polo didn't exactly scream "skater girl."

I held up three fingers. "Scout's honor."

Adrian laughed, nodding toward my legs. "I was checking out your knees. I believe you."

Straightening my legs in front of me, I rubbed the scars on my knees. "I spent a lot of time skating on broken sidewalks when I was little. I've face-planted more times than I can count."

He cocked his head. "Your face looks like it made it through without a scratch."

Just as I was about to show him the scar under my chin, a ball came sailing straight at me, knocking my words away. I threw up my arms to shield my face, but the ball whizzed over my head, landing right behind me.

"Oh shit." Cris yanked Adrian down a second too late. If the ball had been aimed at him, it would have hit him already.

Shooting to my feet, I peered at the field. Beckett stood on the sidelines, his hands on his hips, staring at me, and I just knew he'd done that on purpose.

I grabbed the ball and stormed down the steps. Beckett met me at the rail, standing a few feet below me, and held up his hand.

Looking down at him, I palmed the ball. "Oh, you want this?"

"Give it to me, Ortega."

"If you wanted it, you shouldn't have kicked it at my head."

His jaw tensed. "If I had been kicking it at your head, you would have felt it."

"Where were you aiming then? The moon?"

"I was aiming exactly where it landed." Without warning, he grabbed the railing and lifted himself so we were on the same level. "You know, fraternizing with the enemy is frowned upon. Not a good look for an SA athlete."

I moved the ball behind my back. "How do you even know who I'm talking to? Shouldn't you be paying attention to what's going on on the field?"

"Sit on the SA side of the bleachers, Ortega."

I scrunched up my face at him. He was taking Theo's request a little too far.

"I'm sitting in the middle because I have friends on both sides." I shook my head. "Not that I have to justify myself to you."

"People are watching."

My eyes flared. "I really hope you're not one of them when the game starts."

"I won't have to if I know you're sitting in the right spot."

"Is that why you kicked a ball at my head? Because of where I was sitting?"

He reached around me, laid his hand over mine holding the ball, then he dipped his head, bringing us eye to eye. His normally crystal-blue eyes had gone dark, and his mouth was drawn into a tense, straight line.

"I told you I wasn't aiming at your head." He swallowed hard, his throat working. "I would *never* do that."

My mouth had gone dry, and my voice cracked like I'd been wandering the desert for months. "You fooled me."

Pulling me into the railing, bringing our chests together, he inched the ball from my grasp, rolling it up my back until he had it in his palm, then tossed it over his shoulder, but didn't seem to be in a hurry to leave.

"Isn't your team waiting for you?" All I could force out was a whisper, and I had no idea why.

"They are. I'll go back to them when I'm sure you're going to do the right thing." His eyes flicked to the stands behind me before coming back to mine. "Who are your friends?"

"Why?"

"I told you, I'm making sure you're doing the right thing."

"Because of Theo."

The muscles around his mouth twitched, but he didn't bother answering me.

I huffed, deciding to take the path of least resistance. "Giselle is a good friend from SRH. I went to school with one of the guys, and the other one just moved to town. Is that good enough?"

"Did she bring them here for you?"

"What?" I barked a laugh. "No. Of course not."

"Because you don't date."

Not a question. A statement of fact.

"How do you know?"

He lifted a shoulder. "I know."

"Then why would you ask if Giselle brought guys for me?"

"Maybe she doesn't know."

"She knows."

His lips flattened as he stared at me for a drawn-out moment. I was so stupefied by his behavior. That I had the option to walk away didn't even enter my mind until his coach hollered his name.

Beckett tapped the railing. "Remember whose side you're on, little light." And with that soft yet somewhat ominous warning, he hopped down and jogged back to his team, leaving me more confused than ever.

· · · ● · ● · · · ·

The Savage boys played soccer like they were battling for their lives. The field was a bloodbath. Since this wasn't part of the official season, the refs seemed to be letting elbow jabs and pushing slide without issuing warnings.

The teams were pretty evenly matched, so the score was low. At halftime, SRH was ahead 2–1.

Giselle slapped my arm. "I never knew you could scream so loud."

I pressed a hand to my throat. "I'm hoarse."

On my other side, Bella burst out laughing. "Of course you are, girl. You haven't shut up since kickoff."

"Sorry," I rasped sheepishly.

"Don't apologize." Delilah stood up, stretching her arms over her head. "I quite enjoyed watching you go savage."

"I'm only feeding off the boys' energy," I protested. "They're the ones drawing blood out there."

Adrian and Cris were on Giselle's other side. After coming back from my confrontation with Beckett, I made sure to scoot a little farther into academy territory. Not because Beckett had told me to but because of the optics. How would it look for a team captain to be cheering for the opponent?

I also wanted to put some distance between Adrian and me. Boys were off the table for me, so I tried my best not to lead them on. Not that my ego was so big I thought a dude like Adrian had fallen in love with me at first sight or anything.

But it was better to be safe than sorry.

Bella hooked her arm through mine. "Let's go for a walk. You need water."

I grabbed Giselle and Delilah, and the four of us made our way down the bleachers. When we reached the bottom, I glanced up to find Beckett straddling the bench on the sidelines, watching us as he wiped his face with a towel.

He'd been vicious out there. From the stands, I had seen him exchanging words with a couple of the SRH players before kickoff. If that had been the catalyst for how dirty both teams were playing, I didn't know, but I was curious.

Giselle nudged me. "I'm gonna go talk to my boy Johnny." She pointed to one of the players Beckett had clashed the hardest with. "I'll meet you back at the bleachers."

She ran off toward the field, and Johnny started toward her, along with a couple other guys from the team. Boys had always flocked to Giselle, so I wasn't surprised.

Delilah, Bella, and I got in line at the refreshment stand. "What are the chances no one walks away from this game without a serious injury?" Bella asked.

I rolled my eyes. "Right? What are those boys doing? They have a whole season to play, but they're acting like it's the last game of their lives."

Delilah pursed her lips. "Who would like to place bets on how many laps their coach will make them run after this showing?"

Bella snickered. "Coach Watts is a hard-ass. Did you see him yelling from the sidelines?"

"Someone must have stolen someone else's girlfriend." It was a guess, but I couldn't think of another reason for the bloodshed on the field. "Boys get crazy when their egos are bruised."

A throat cleared behind us. I glanced over my shoulder. Rhys and Charles were in line too. Charles had his normal, pissy expression, while Rhys's head was cocked toward us, obviously listening in.

"What?" Bella put her hands on her hips. "Did your mummy not give you enough attention, so you need some from us?"

Rhys chuckled, clearly not intimidated by Bella's five-foot-nothing ball of challenge in a cherubic form. "If that's an offer of special attention from you, I'll gladly accept. I prefer some privacy, but if it needs to be here and now, I can make an exception."

"Gross," Delilah muttered, keeping her back turned on them both.

Bella stomped her foot, her cheeks flaming. She had to know he was antagonizing her, but her fiery temper always got the best of her. "If you take your spindly, inflamed from too many STIs, sorry excuse for a dick out, I'll rip that sucker off."

"Well, now, that was a vivid picture you just painted." He slapped Charles on the arm. "Wasn't it?"

Charles crossed his arms over his barrel chest. "Little girls should learn to keep their mouths shut unless they're asked to open them."

He swept his eyes over our trio. "Speaking of, where's the quiet one?"

That got Delilah's attention. She glared at him over her shoulder. "That will never be any of your business."

Charles swiped his hand over his mouth, muttering, "Ugly twin," under his breath. Delilah swiveled back around, her spine rigid and tense.

"That's enough." I hooked arms with Bella and grabbed D's hand. "I'm not that thirsty. Let's skip the water and go back to our seats."

They both agreed with nods of their heads. My throat was dry, but I'd deal if it meant not having to listen to Charles and Rhys for another minute.

As we brushed by them, Rhys said my name. I paused, raising a brow. "Yes?"

"You were curious why the game's been so violent," he stated.

"I lost my curiosity," I answered, though it wasn't really true. I just wanted to get away from him.

"I don't think you did." Rhys tucked his hands in his trousers, cool as a maniacal cucumber. "The guy you're sitting with—the one with the bad haircut? His cousin's on the team."

"And?" Bad haircut? He must've been talking about Adrian since Cris's hair was buzzed.

"And think about it." He reached out and tapped my forehead. "You were talking to Beck before the game. Now you're sitting with the enemy. You've given them ammunition, and they've been busy shooting it at Beck."

I shook my head, almost laughing at how ludicrous his lie was. "That's not true." Beckett was looking out for me upon Theo's request, but there was no way he'd give a damn if his opponents trash-talked me on the field.

He tilted his head, leveling me with a long look. "Isn't it?"

Absolutely no way.

CHAPTER EIGHT
Beckett

I DROVE THROUGH THE parking lot on my way to an obligatory appearance at my family home and pressed on the brakes behind Luciana's car.

She kicked the back tire and groaned, her hands balling into fists at her sides.

I rolled down the window. "Need help?"

Her fingers raked through her hair. "No. Unless you can change a flat."

"Sorry. Not in my skill set." I could, but I wasn't going to. Not today.

"I figured."

"Where are you headed?"

Bending down, she swiped her bag from the ground and swiveled around to face me. For once, she was out of anything that was Savage Academy–issued, wearing cutoffs with an oversized T-shirt tucked in the front and Pumas on her feet. It wasn't particularly sexy, but I got stuck eyeing her tan, muscular thighs, trailing down to her defined calves.

"Going home for the weekend. I guess it'll have to wait until next week."

Tearing my eyes off her legs, I nodded toward my passenger door. "Get in. I'll drive you."

Her mouth fell open. "What? No, I couldn't—"

"It's on my way, Ortega. You're not putting me out."

She worried her bottom lip with her teeth then started to approach, only to pull up short. "Are you sure? I'll need a ride back too. Hells has to go to work in the morning, and I can't ask Theo since he has the baby, and—"

"I'm sure." I leaned over and opened the door. "Come on. We don't need to have a long discussion about it, that will only end in us back where we started. I'll drive you and bring you back."

Those with cars were allowed to leave campus on the weekends. If I left, I normally stayed with Julien and Sera, but on occasion, my mother and father requested I show my face in their home. This was one of those occasions.

"If you're sure..." she trailed off, glancing to the side. Like an invisible force pushed her, she tipped forward and grabbed my car door, tossing her bag in first. "Thank you, Beckett. I hate to admit it, but I was about to cry."

"The flat tire upset you that much?"

"No. Well, I was frustrated about the tire." She buckled herself in then tucked her hair behind her ear. It was rare she wore it down. I bet it would be scraped back in a ponytail by this afternoon. "I hadn't realized how homesick I was until it looked like I wouldn't be able to go."

My hands tightened on the wheel as I drove off campus. "You have my number, don't you? If something like that happens again and I'm around, I'll get you there."

Her breath caught. "That's...thank you. I'm hoping this is a one-off, though. What are the chances of my tire randomly going flat again?"

"You never know."

"I guess. Thank you for driving me anyway."

I felt her stare on the side of my face. At the first red light I hit, I turned. She didn't bother pretending she hadn't been looking at me. "What?"

"I was checking you over for injuries."

I laughed once. "Were you? For what reason?"

"I was at the game last night, you know."

"Oh, I know. I haven't forgotten that."

Her infuriating naivete nearly drove me out of my mind. How did she not get that her loyalty lay with Savage Academy now? She may have started at Savage River, but that was her past. Her sitting with her old friend and those idiots hadn't been acceptable. Girls looked to Luciana as an example. They followed her lead. If she crossed the line, so would they.

Not that I gave a damn about those lemmings.

"I expected you to have a black eye, at the very least," she quipped.

I chuffed and leaned toward the door so I could pull up the side of my shirt. She gasped at the bruises mottling my ribs.

"Should have seen the other guy," I intoned.

"How did that happen?" She twisted in her seat, her lashes fluttering like hyper butterflies as she blinked. "Who did that?"

"Like you said, you were there. It wasn't a clean game."

"I saw you exchanging words with the other team."

"That happened, yeah."

"Rhys said the conflict had to do with me sitting near Adrian."

My eyes sliced sideways. Rhys had a big mouth when it suited him. This was him stirring the pot, gleefully waiting to see what would boil over. Too bad for him, he didn't get to watch the results of his machinations.

"Adrian?"

"Yeah. One of the guys who came with my friend Giselle."

My fingers drummed on the steering wheel. "Ah."

"Ah? That's all you're going to say?"

I glanced at her again. My chest was tight with the same fury that had burned through me last night. We talked trash on the field. It was part of the game—especially when *Johnny* was on the field. If kids at SA were entitled, he was in a league of his own. I'd played against him before, but last night was the first time he'd drawn a reaction out of me.

When Luciana's name was brought up with *implications* she belonged to SRH, like they had some kind of claim to her, I'd had enough.

"Do you really want me to repeat the filthy shit some of those guys had to say about you?"

Savage Academy had welcomed them into our *home* like we did every year, and this time, they'd lived up to their scummy reputation. How a girl like Luciana had survived there even a year was beyond me.

She did *not* belong to them.

"I—" Her hand went to her chest, her mouth, then fell back to her lap. "Why would they be talking about me? I barely know any of those guys."

"The captain—Johnny—he knew you. Knew the guys you were sitting with too. Your buddy, Adrian, is his cousin."

"I literally just met Adrian last night. I don't see how much fodder I could have given Johnny."

I shrugged. "He had a lot to say about you and what his cousin would be doing with you later. I warned you it mattered where you sat. I *told* you."

She shifted to face forward again and crossed her arms over her chest. "Rhys said they were going after you specifically because they saw you talking to me before the game."

Rhys had a really fucking big mouth. I'd be talking to him when I got back to campus.

"That might be true."

"Then you only have yourself to blame."

"Hardly." When her head turned, I shot her a hard look. "I don't mind defending you, Ortega, but do me and my ribs a favor and listen to me next time."

She went silent for a while, the low hum of the road and quiet music from the radio filling the silence. The drive to Helen and Theo's place took a half hour. It wasn't really on the way to my dad's house, but since I wasn't in a hurry to get there, I didn't mind.

I had turned into her sister's neighborhood when she spoke again. "Why don't you mind defending me?"

That wasn't a question I'd been expecting. I had to be careful with how I answered.

"Do you see me as the kind of person who would let anyone run their mouth?"

"I—I guess not."

"I'm not, Luc. My patience is miles long when something is important to me. That little scuzzy cunt *Johnny* is not important to me in the least. There was no way I would let the things he had to say stand."

I pulled into the driveway and put the car in park. When I faced Luc, she was already looking at me, a line between her brows.

"You really won't tell me what he said?"

"I told you. Filth. That's all you need to know."

Her mouth flattened, and she shook her head. "I won't apologize for hanging out with Giselle. I did nothing wrong."

I huffed. "I'm not surprised you think that."

Her hand darted forward, landing on my forearm. "Thank you, Beckett. I appreciate you defending my honor, even though I wish you hadn't gotten hurt in the process."

I froze. This was the first time Luciana had ever touched me. Some might question how I could be certain of that. Luc and I had been around each other off and on for years, after all.

But I knew.

I was sure.

Some things weren't forgettable.

I swallowed, my words coming out more bitter than intended. "Your thanks aren't necessary or needed."

She withdrew her hand. "Well...okay then. I won't thank you for driving me home either."

I lowered my chin. "Text me when you're ready to go back."

After agreeing, she swiftly exited the car and jogged down the long driveway, disappearing inside without a glance back.

···•••·•···

Since my parents had ordered me home, one would think they'd be there to greet me when I arrived.

If one had indeed thought that, they didn't know Gretchen and Josh Savage.

I threw a load of laundry I'd brought with me into the wash. SA had a laundry service, but I didn't trust them for anything other than dry cleaning my jackets. One pair of pink underwear had been enough to write them off for good.

My mother didn't appear until I'd already washed and dried one load and was in the middle of another. The *click-clack* of her heels on the hardwood floors was like nails on a chalkboard. The floors had been repaired and replaced more than once due to her heel habit, but she was a hurricane that couldn't be stopped.

"Beckett"—she stopped at the laundry room doorway, her arms crossed over her chest—"you don't need to do that, honey. There's a service—"

I slammed the dryer door, cutting her off. "I know about the service, but I prefer to do my own when I have the chance." I got a good look at her face and winced. "Let me guess, you're coming from Dr. Abadir's office."

She rolled her shoulders back, bringing her hand to her face but not touching it. "Am I bruising already?"

"No, but your lips look like a pair of balloons about to pop. I'll never understand why you do that to yourself."

She waved me off. "You know they always look crazy the first few days after I get filler. They'll settle." Then she opened her arms. "Come hug me before you insult me again."

I went to her, wrapping my arms around her small, overexercised body. She was fragile in ways that made it impossible for her to be a good mother.

Losing her looks terrified her so brutally she developed an addiction to plastic surgery. The irony was she'd become a caricature of her former self. Puffy in some places, skeletal in others.

She was a poorly stitched-together doll, one strong breeze or gentle jostle away from going to pieces.

I'd never been able to go to her with scrapes or bumps when I was little or lean on her with any of my emotional turmoil when I got older. She'd fallen apart the few times I'd attempted to do either.

She tried, though, and she *did* love me in her own selfishly encapsulated manner, so I humored her. I hugged her gently and kept most of my thoughts to myself. Wrecking my mother was the last thing on my agenda.

She patted me on the back before straightening her arms and looking me over. "Handsome as ever, my guy. Soon, I'll have to tell people you're my brother. I can't possibly be old enough to have a son as old as you."

"If you do that, I'll call you Gretchen."

Her lips attempted to pucker. "You know I hate that."

I chuckled. "I do know that."

"Fine." She let out a long sigh. "I suppose I'll keep claiming you."

"Thanks, Mother."

She rolled her eyes but couldn't hold back her giggle. "Don't make me laugh, honey. My face needs a few days before I move it that much."

"And yet, you continue injecting yourself with botulism..."

She didn't laugh at that.

·······

My father arrived in time for dinner with no explanation for where he'd been all day. That was Josh Savage. He answered to no one. I guessed it came with the territory of living in a town named after your family.

If you let it. I had no intention of becoming my father.

The three of us sat together awkwardly like cyborgs attempting to portray a real family. It wasn't going so well. Our house was grandiose, and our dining room fit right along with the theme, our chairs spread too far apart to create any sort of intimacy.

These days, I preferred it that way.

My mother was pushing her dinner around her plate, a trick she'd used for years to appear like she was eating. "We have to discuss your list for your birthday."

"What list?" I asked.

My father heaved a sigh. "We talked about this, Gretch. Beckett doesn't like big parties."

She let her fork drop with a flair of drama, bouncing off her plate. "Honestly, Josh? Beckett only turns eighteen once, then he'll be off to college. Do you think he'll allow me to throw him big parties then? This is my last chance. I wish you wouldn't give me a hard time."

Dad wiped his mouth with sharp precision. "Since it's clear you haven't even asked our son if he *wants* a party, much less for his input before this very moment, I think we know who this party is really for."

"Aren't I his mother? I've raised him into adulthood. I think I deserve a little celebration too."

He chuffed, then continued to eat, exiting the conversation.

Leaving me to deal with her.

"I don't really want anything big," I started. "Or formal."

Her shoulders slumped. Gretchen Savage was all about big and formal—precisely why I'd put in that stipulation. "Okay, honey. We can do it a little more low key. I'll need your list ASAP since it's only three weeks away."

I had to laugh. "Are you trying to convince me you haven't invited anyone to an event that's only three weeks away?"

Her cheeks pinkened through her makeup. "Of course I've already invited my guests. I assumed your friends don't need as much notice..."

My father cleared his throat. "Christ, Gretchen. I wouldn't put it past you to put your own name on the birthday cake."

Her lips formed an *O* that looked a lot like a pool float. "Why would you say something like that to me? I'm proud of my baby. That isn't a crime."

Her chin quivered, but my dad was unmoved. He jabbed his knife in the air. "I'm proud of him too. Do you see me throwing myself a party?"

She sniffed, then, in fine Gretchen Savage form, pushed back from the table and ran out, sobbing just loud enough for both of us to hear her.

Though it panged my chest, I remained in my seat. I'd long since stopped chasing my mother during one of her emotional breakdowns. It didn't help either of us. I knew that, but it would always bother me to see her that way.

Dad shifted, heaving a sigh. "You can tell her no."

"I'm not going to."

The skin around his eyes pinched. "Your mother doesn't know you came home at the beginning of the week."

My movements stilled. "But you do." No doubt he personally monitored the security cameras all over the property. How else could he leave the house if he wasn't in control while not there?

"I do. You didn't stay long."

I shrugged. "I had to pick something up. It wasn't a social visit."

He rubbed his chin as he eyed me. The curiosity in his gaze faded as his demeanor hardened. "I heard about your game last night."

Ah, this was what he *really* wanted to talk about.

"Did you hear we won?"

"I heard you behaved like a thug out on the field. Coach Watts called me this morning while your team was running laps. He told me while the others were culpable, you were the main instigator."

I worked my jaw back and forth, grinding my molars to stop myself from saying something my father would find disrespectful.

"The other team—"

He held up a hand. "The other team is not responsible for your behavior. There's no one to blame but yourself, Beckett. You're lucky Coach Watts didn't suspend you. If it had been in season, you can be sure he would have."

I could have argued, told him nothing like this *would* have happened in season since last night's events were squarely due to the pieces of shit sharing the field with us, but why waste my energy? If he wanted to blame me, he would. Besides, having to explain why hearing *Johnny* run his mouth about Luc had set me off didn't interest me in the slightest.

"Message received. It won't happen again."

He looked at me for a long time, probably ensuring I wasn't being a smart-ass. But I wasn't known for that around this house. I toed the line because that kept my dad out of my face. If he wanted me to promise to be a good little soldier and salute him, I would. In less than twenty-four hours, I'd be back at Savage Academy, and we'd both go back to forgetting the other existed.

CHAPTER NINE

Luciana

BECKETT: *WHAT TIME DO you want me to pick you up?*

I'd convinced myself Beckett would have forgotten about me. Out of sight, out of mind, and all that. To my surprise, I woke up to a text from him.

Me: *Is two okay? I have to run a couple errands.*

Beckett: *Two's fine. Doing anything exciting, Ortega?*

Me: *Just family stuff. You?*

Beckett: *I'm at Julien and Sera's new house.*

Me: *Nice. Well, as long as you're sure two is fine, can you pick me up at the entrance of Chance Park? My errands are in that area.*

Beckett: *Don't tell me you're going skating.*

Me: *If I was, do you honestly think I'd tell my narc to pick me up near the scene of the crime? Be for real, Savage.*

Beckett: *Not happy with your sass...or being called a narc.*

Me: *You know what you are.*

Beckett: *Yeah, I do.*

Me: *As much fun as this has been, I hear my baby niece making cute noises, so I'm going to go snuggle her. See you at two.*

Beckett: *Send me a pic.*

Me: *Really? Of the baby?*

Beckett: *You holding the baby, yeah. Send it.*

Me: *You're being strange. I'm going to go.*

Beckett: *Don't forget the pic, little light.*

· · · · · · ● · · · ·

Tossing my phone aside, I scrubbed my face. I had a few things to do today, but I was procrastinating. The longer I stayed in bed, the less time was left for the unpleasant things I didn't want to do but would anyway.

When I finally trudged out to the kitchen, Helen had already left for work, and Theo was hanging out at the massive island, sipping coffee. Madelina was in her bouncy seat, perched on top of the island.

"Morning, kid."

I waved at Theo and stopped to stroke Madelina's cheek on my way to the fridge. "I'm grumpy."

"Impossible. You don't get grumpy."

"It won't last, don't worry."

I poured myself a glass of orange juice and let out a long breath.

Sometimes, there were moments like this where it hit me hard how beautiful our house was. We'd only lived in it for a couple years, and I hadn't really gotten used to it yet. The kitchen alone was bigger than my mom's trailer—the trailer Helen had lived in her whole life. I'd been lucky to only spend a few years there before Hells got me out. Of course, where I lived with my dad before he died hadn't exactly been paradise.

Helen and I both tended to forget we weren't poor any-more—contrary to what Bianca DeSoto thought. Helen and Theo had great jobs, sure, but they wouldn't have been able to afford this house on a nurse and mechanic salary. She'd been left a substantial sum of money—I'd never known the exact amount, but it was in the millions—by a dying woman she'd taken care of in her final year, and it had changed all our lives in ways we were still coming to understand.

I plopped down across from him with a glass of orange juice. He cocked his head, studying me.

"Something in particular getting you down?"

I shook my head then nodded. "Mom visits are never fun."

His mouth went flat. "You don't have to do that. Helen and I can take care of it."

"You guys do enough, and you have Madelina now." I picked up my glass but didn't drink from it. "I want to see her. Is that terrible?"

Theo shifted in his chair and leaned forward, catching my gaze. "There's nothing terrible about wanting to see your mom, Luc. Despite her flaws and fuckups, she's still your mom and you're you."

"I'm me?"

"Yeah." He gave me a soft grin. "Still as sweet as you were when I first met you back when you were a scrappy little twelve-year-old trying to hook me up with your big sister. You'll always see the best in people, and that's not a trait a lot of people have. Never change that, kid."

My skin had gone hot, and I took a big gulp of my juice. I didn't really know what else to do. What did I say to that?

He knocked his knuckles on the table. "Sorry to embarrass you."

I put my glass down, swiping my mouth with the back of my hand. It was time for a change of subject. "Speaking of embarrassing, can you ask Beckett to back off? He's taking his protection job a little too seriously."

Theo stopped mid motion, his coffee cup hanging in the air. "I'm not sure what you mean. I never actually spoke to Beckett when we dropped you off."

"You didn't?"

"No." He frowned at me, his expression growing stern. "Is he bothering you? I can talk to Jules—"

"No, no." I held up a hand. "Please don't. Beckett's fine. I just thought him hanging around all of a sudden was because of you. Since it's not, I'm sure he'll get tired of whatever he's doing soon enough."

At least, I hoped he would.

· · · · ● · ● · · ·

"Mom?"

I pushed open the crooked, ripped screen door and stepped into the stale air of my mother's trailer. Bottles and other detritus I wouldn't be looking too closely at covered the barely standing coffee table. My mom was in the kitchen, scowling hard at something in a frying pan.

"Hey, Mom."

Her shoulders jumped. "Luc? Is it that time?" Her glassy eyes raked over me, and she gave her head a violent shake. Her long, dark hair was unwashed. It lay around her collarbone in strings. "Are you early?"

Putting grocery bags on the counter, I reached around her to flip off the burner. "I'm on time." My nose wrinkled at the charred contents of the pan. "Looks like you lost track of time."

She huffed. "I thought I'd make breakfast for you." Disappointment made her voice wobbly.

"That's okay. I already ate. Thanks for thinking of me anyway."

One hand went to her forehead, the other braced on the counter. "That's right. Why would you eat here when you can be in Helen's fancy new house, living the high life?"

"It's not like that." Even though my mother's kitchen was one step up from disgusting, I'd spent a few years living here after my dad died. I wasn't a snob and had never once thought of myself as above anyone. But Mom had been a victim her whole life. She didn't know how to be anything else, even with her own daughters.

Waving me off, my mom grabbed a crushed pack of cigs with shaking hands and stuck one in her mouth. She didn't light it. For once, she seemed to remember I wouldn't be sticking around if she smoked with me in the house.

We unloaded the groceries together, and I went through her cabinets and fridge, tossing out anything moldy or expired. She didn't eat much, preferring to ingest her calories in liquid form, so food tended to go bad often.

"I got you those chocolate chip pancakes you like," I said.

"Thanks, lovey. You're too good to me."

I pressed my lips together, watching as she splashed vodka into her coffee. She used to hide her habit when I was little, but those days were long gone.

"I want you to eat."

She nodded, gulping her coffee. "I do, but without you girls here, sometimes I forget."

"Do you want me to text you a reminder? Or I could set up an alarm on your phone."

She waved her bony hand. "Don't worry about it. I can't find the thing. Haven't seen it in ages."

"You lost your phone?" The phone I'd convinced Helen and Theo to buy her over the summer after she'd *misplaced* the last one.

She shrugged.

"Did you sell it?"

She shrugged again, refusing to look at me. Irritation crawled up my spine. Despite *everything*, her neglect, mistreatment, outright abuse, Helen bought her groceries every single week. When I was able to, I brought them to her, cleaned her house, made sure she was okay.

We didn't ask for anything from her. Not even a thank-you.

And *this* was the only kind of thanks our mother willingly gave us: a slap in the face for our kindness and care.

I was the one who made excuses for her. Maybe because I hadn't lived with her for most of my childhood—I still had some patience left, unlike Helen. Or maybe because I'd been shielded from the worst of the worst about her. Helen would never tell me just how bad it had gotten.

"*Mom*," I rasped. "How could you?"

Her shoulders bunched with tension. "It's not like Helen can't afford it. Livin' in that big house, working at the hospital, sending you to private school."

"I have a scholarship."

I wanted to yell at her to take Helen's name out of her mouth. My sister deserved every ounce of good she had, and my mother begrudged her for it.

"Yeah, but she could foot that bill if you asked, just like she could give me money to get me by if she wanted to. What am I supposed to do for cash, lovey?"

"Get a freaking job!" I snapped, for once not holding my temper. Trash-talking my sister was my line in the sand, and she was well aware of that.

Mom's lip trembled, the cigarette stuck between her lips quivering. "I can't work. You know I'm sick. Just standing here exhausts me. How could I go to work in this condition?"

"Mom—"

She held up her hand. "In fact, I'm going to take a nap now. You should go." Just like that, she shambled off, disappearing into her bedroom on the other side of the trailer. Of course, she'd taken her mug and the vodka with her.

Mad at myself for letting her get to me, I stomped out of the trailer, letting the rickety screen door slam behind me. I'd planned on being there another hour, but there was no way I'd stick around to clean her kitchen after the things she'd said.

My feet carried me over cracked and crumbling pavement, out of the trailer park, onto the sidewalk. I'd never longed for my skateboard more than I did now. I would have given almost anything to whip down the road, wind on my face, my hair flying. Instead, I was stuck walking.

By the time I made it to Chance Park, I still had time to kill, so I had sat on a bench near the skate ramps and watched the skaters. My wrist twinged, reminding me why I wasn't out there with them. It didn't make it easier, though. Skating had been part of my identity my whole life, and it had been stripped from me.

My coach would kick me off the team if she caught me on a skateboard. Sometimes, I wondered if giving up the one thing I loved most was worth the sacrifice.

I always came to the conclusion it was. This was my last year at SA, my last season on the field hockey team. If I kept my eyes on the prize—college—it was easier not to think about what I'd had to let go of.

Before I stood up to leave, I spotted Adrian doing tricks on a low rail. For being as tall as he was, his balance was impressive.

Until it wasn't.

He fell on his ass and sprung up laughing, fist-bumping another guy. Remembering that feeling where the falls were funny as hell and didn't hurt until later, I grinned. That was when Adrian's eyes swung in my direction, spotting me too.

After a beat, he raised a hand. Embarrassment at being caught flooded through me, but I managed to wave back. When he took a step in my direction, I spun and raced for the park's entrance.

My timing was perfect. Beckett pulled into the parking lot at the same time, and I threw myself into his car, out of breath.

He watched as I buckled myself in, attempting to calm my fluttering heart.

"You okay?"

"Yeah. Sorry. I thought I was going to be late meeting you, so I ran."

"What were you doing in the park?"

"Watching the skaters."

His hand shot out, tugging the end of my ponytail. "Not skating?"

I jerked my head away from him, too bitter to play along. "No, Beckett. I wasn't skating. Can we go? I have homework to do before tomorrow."

For once, he listened. His arm stretched behind me, resting on the back of my seat as he backed out of his spot. My breath caught, and I sat stock-still until we were on the road and his hand returned to the wheel.

Only then did I release a long, tension-filled breath.

He glanced at me. "You didn't send me a picture."

It took me a second to understand what he was talking about. "I thought you were kidding."

"I wasn't."

"I didn't know you were such a fan of babies."

His thumbs tapped a lazy beat against the leather steering wheel. "I'm not."

I almost asked why he'd wanted a picture of Madelina and me if that was the case but stopped myself when the implication hit me. He'd wanted a picture of me.

But why?

"Next time," he muttered.

"You'll have to wait a while. With my games and schoolwork, it might be a few weeks before I go home again."

"I'm good at waiting." We stopped at a red light, and Beckett turned his head, giving me a long once-over. "Good visit?"

"For the most part."

"You don't seem like you're happy."

"I'm okay. Family stuff, you know."

He raised his chin. "Oh, I know. Believe me."

"I take it your visit wasn't so good?"

His sigh was tired and ragged. "Parents requested me home, but they were barely around. They still managed to get pissed that I spent the night at my brother's instead of their place. Oh, and my mom's throwing me a birthday party I don't want."

I blinked at the admission. I'd expected him to give me a short answer and end the conversation. Instead, he'd given me a glimpse into his imperfect life.

I didn't know how to handle sincere Beckett, so I teased him.

"Oh, that's right. You're turning eighteen soon. I forgot how young you are."

The surprised laugh that burst out of him told me I'd made the right choice. "Kids these days, ruining everything."

That made me giggle and shake a fist in front of my face. "Youths!"

The corner of his eye crinkled. "You may be older, but are you wiser?"

"I like to think so." I shifted in my seat, tucking my foot under my opposite leg so I could angle myself toward him. "Why don't you want a party?"

He shook his head. "The party's not for me. It's a show. And even if it weren't, I don't care to be the center of attention like that. A few friends, some good food, the beach, and I'm set. Caterers, open bars, and tuxedos aren't exactly in my wheelhouse."

"No? I bet you own your own tuxedo."

His brow lowered. "Of course I do. I can't imagine putting rented clothing on my body. Do you really think they clean those?" He shuddered, and I laughed.

"Most guys I know wear a tux once or twice in their lives."

"We know different kinds of guys."

"No kidding."

"It's not like I enjoy wearing them. But it's part of life."

My hands spread on my knees. "Not my life."

"Maybe. Maybe not. You're in a different stratum of society than you were. Who knows where you'll go after college."

"It won't be wherever the tuxedo set is. I know that."

"Never say never, Ortega."

"Never," I whispered.

The profile of his wide smile halted my breath. I could probably count on my hands the number of times I'd seen Beckett Savage smile a genuine smile in my presence. I'd chalked it up to not being his thing. Some people weren't smilers.

His face transformed, even from the side, and I wished I was looking at him head-on. The corner of his eye lifted, the edges of his chiseled cheekbones and jaw softened, and his teeth gleamed. Seeing him like that, smiling with abandon, prodded a place deep in my chest. Maybe Beckett *was* a smiler, but he was out of practice.

I was beginning to wonder a lot of things about him.

• • • • • • • • • •

Easy conversation filled the rest of the ride. Beckett parked, and I climbed out of the car, slinging my bag over my shoulder. He popped his trunk, taking an oversized duffel out.

I raised a brow. "You forgot to bury the body?"

He took my bag from me, carrying it along with his. "Everything I do is with purpose, Ortega." I tried to take my bag, but he looked at me like I'd spat in his face. "Not gonna happen."

I shoved my hands in my pockets. "Fine. I didn't want to carry it anyway."

He chuckled and bumped me with his arm. I glanced up at him, finding him peering down at me, the slightest grin curving his lips.

"Come on, little light. You have homework."

I trudged with him to our dorm, holding the door open for him despite his glower. I guessed, along with their tuxedos, men from Beckett's world maintained old-fashioned views. Not that I minded him carrying my bag, but I didn't deserve a dirty look for holding the door open.

We were the only two in the elevator, and Beckett chose to stand right beside me.

"So, what's in the duffel, if not a dead body?"

"Laundry."

I narrowed my eyes at him. "You took your laundry home for your mom to do?"

"Cute assumption." He smirked. "I don't think Gretchen even knows where the laundry room is, much less how to run the washer."

"That means you did your own laundry?"

He bowed his head. "That's what it means."

"Hmmm."

Stepping out of the elevator on our floor, Beckett nodded in the direction of my suite, then followed me to my door. Only then did he slide the strap of my bag back onto my shoulder.

"Thanks. And thank you for the ride. You saved me."

"Any time, Luciana. All you have to do is ask." He gave my ponytail one last tug, sliding his fist down the length of it. "See you."

Beckett Savage sauntered away from me, and something wholly unfamiliar swooped low in my belly.

Whoa.

What was *that*?

CHAPTER TEN

Luciana

I ARRIVED AT THE dining hall for dinner before everyone else. My stomach rumbled as I went through the line, begging me to grab the fried chicken and mashed potatoes.

I patted my abdomen. "When it's off-season, I promise."

Someone behind me laughed lowly. Twisting around, I found Ivan smirking and nearly shuddered. Ivan's smirk looked like it had come directly from a Medieval painting of the devil. All that was missing were the pointed teeth.

"Yes?"

He cocked his head, curiosity and amusement dancing behind his eyes. "Were you speaking to your stomach?"

"Mmhmm. And it was a private conversation."

"Excuse me for listening in." The timbre of his voice was so deep it sounded like it was coming from somewhere under the crust of the earth, not his throat.

Since his first day, Ivan had been quiet in class, keeping to himself, ignoring the curious stares aimed at him. He was the definition of unbothered, and I admired that.

Even though there was something about him that scared me.

"You're forgiven."

We moved forward in the line. Ivan grabbed the fried chicken while I was responsible and took the grilled. When he scooped mashed potatoes onto his tray, I nearly wept, and my stomach waged a riot when I settled for roasted veggies.

"Why not eat what you want?" he asked.

"It's the beginning of my season. I'm trying to treat my body right so it doesn't get mad when I go hard on it during my games." I slid a glance at him as we walked toward the tables. "As a swimmer, I'm surprised you eat like that."

"I'll fit in my Speedo. Don't worry."

He said this so deadpan I nearly dropped my tray and snorted a laugh. "Thank you for that. I was definitely thinking of your poor Speedo." I nodded toward an empty table. "Want to sit with us?"

"Us?"

"My roommates and me. They should be here soon."

He hesitated and scanned the dining room as though he were checking for a better offer. Finally, he looked at me, giving me a sharp nod.

"All right."

We sat at a circular table big enough for ten people. As I took my first bite, a burst of rowdy laughter rose above the din of conversation. I looked up from my boring food in time to see what appeared to be half the soccer team strolling by. Another burst of laughter sounded, and one guy jumped on an unwitting guy's back, shifting the group so Beckett Savage was no longer hidden behind his teammates.

As if sensing me, he turned his head, still grinning, then his lips slowly slipped into a flat, annoyed expression. I gave a little wave, which he did not return.

Okay. I had no idea what that was about. Since he gave me a ride last weekend, we'd picked back up on our new habit of running together. I kept my earbuds in most of the time, so conversation had been minimal, but sharing the track with him hadn't been *unpleasant.*

"That your boyfriend?" Ivan asked.

"No." I shook my head. "I don't date."

"Does he know?"

"That I don't date?" Ivan lowered his chin. "Yeah, he knows. Everyone around here does."

"Hmmm." He went back to shoveling his chicken and potatoes in his mouth with a surprising amount of gusto.

"Why do you ask?"

Someone palmed the top of my head. "Ask what?" Freddie Spencer plopped down in the seat next to me. "What did dear Ivan ask you?"

"Freddie!" I leaned in to kiss his cheeks. When we first met, he'd informed me he was a two-cheek kisser. "I haven't seen you in ages."

An exaggeration, to be sure. I hadn't seen him since dinner two nights ago, but it had *felt* like ages.

"I know, I know. Mock Trial is consuming all my time, even my sleep. I've woken up yelling, 'Objection!' It's absurd. I'd quit if it didn't look so fucking good on my college apps." Freddie pointed back and forth between Ivan and me. "You never said what Ivan asked you."

I wasn't about to repeat Ivan's ridiculous question, but Ivan had no such qualms.

"I asked her if the Savage kid knows she doesn't date."

Freddie canted his head. "Oh, really? And what brought on that discussion?"

"He seemed displeased to see Luciana having dinner with me," Ivan answered.

I rolled my eyes. "Ivan's clearly delirious. That did not happen."

Freddie rubbed his hands together, his eyebrows bouncing. "Tell me more."

"There's nothing to tell," I protested. "I was barely aware of his existence before this year."

Ivan hissed between his teeth. "Very cruel."

Freddie cackled. "Our dear girl is like that. She doesn't give a single boy besides me—and now you, I suppose—the time of day. That makes them want her more, of course."

"Ah." Ivan nodded. "A challenge. I understand."

"I'm not a challenge." I wagged my fork at them both. "If I were, I'd be winnable, which I am not."

Freddie patted my head. "I know that. Ivan obviously knows that too. It's the rest of the boys at SA who don't believe or understand it."

"You say that like I have dozens of boys banging down my door. That isn't the case."

Freddie slung his arm around my shoulders. "Maybe not. But I have to put up with the 'boys will be boys' locker room talk, and you, my dear, are often a topic of discussion."

I wrinkled my nose. "Gross. I don't want that mental image in my head."

Delilah, Evelyn, and Bella arrived then. Delilah slid into the chair beside Ivan, possibly without realizing who she was sitting beside until it was too late. When she looked at him, she immediately flinched and turned beet red.

Evelyn took the seat beside her, and Bella sat next to Freddie.

Freddie twined one of Bella's curls around his finger. "Hello, my angel."

"My love." She leaned over, kissing his cheeks. "What were y'all talkin' about?"

"That the boys here see Luc as a challenge," Freddie said.

"Oh, sure." Bella's nod was vigorous enough to bounce her ringlets. "That's a fact."

I groaned, nearly face-planting into my chicken. "Stop it and change the subject. Tell Ivan about the time you made out with Freddie."

Bella bit into a roasted carrot. "Which time?"

Ivan's fork paused midair. "There have been many times?" His brow lowered. "I thought—"

Freddie winked at him. "If you thought I was gay, how dare you." He pursed his lips, crossing his arms over his chest. Ivan stared him down until he broke. "Kidding, love. I am decidedly homosexual, but these things happen."

"Do they?" Ivan intoned.

Delilah nodded. "Freddie and I have also..."

Ivan turned to her. "You too?" Then he raised a brow at me. "You?"

My eyes darted around, then I held up two fingers an inch apart. "A little bit." Making out with Freddie was almost a rite of passage in our friend group. The kid could kiss, too.

A deep, resonant guffaw burst out of him, and he slapped the table. "I did not expect that."

Evelyn's hands flew to her ears for a moment before she forced herself to drop them. The only reason I took note of this was that Ivan did as well.

"Am I too loud?" he asked at a much lower volume.

Ev shook her head. "No, it's me. My problem. Not you."

Ivan peered around Delilah to better see Ev. "I'll keep it down. Don't worry."

"It's fine," she murmured.

Ev wasn't shy in general, but she really didn't like when her quirks were the center of attention. Luckily, Ivan seemed to pick up on this and shifted his focus back to Freddie, asking him to point out all the girls he'd made out with in the room.

Freddie's arm swung around wildly before landing back on our table, winking at Ivan. "I stick with my main beauties."

Bella slapped his arm. "Oh, please. Everyone knows you made out with Ms. Rose." She leaned toward Ivan, cupping her mouth to whisper conspiratorially. "Ms. Rose teaches freshman English."

Freddie booped her nose. "He only asked who I'd kissed in this room."

"He's got you there," I quipped.

Bella and Freddie went on to share more gossip about the teachers at SA. Since I'd heard it all before, I tuned them out, allowing my eyes to wander the dining hall. I couldn't lie to myself. They went searching for Beckett and found him. He was with his boys, a crowd of girls that ran in their circle filling in the rest of the seats. Beckett was shoveling his dinner into his mouth, not paying the girls any attention, nodding as Rhys spoke in his ear.

A ribbon of tension unfurled in my stomach, and I didn't understand it. Who Becket spoke to or dated had never been in my line of sight. He'd simply never been on my radar. But something had changed, and I didn't know what. Whatever it was, I couldn't stop myself from noticing him now.

His eyes flicked up, homing in on mine, and he licked his lips before wiping his mouth with his napkin, never looking away from me. Even from across the room, I felt the intensity of his gaze gliding over my skin like cashmere, warm and rich.

I sucked in a breath. Heat suffused my skin in a completely unfamiliar way.

I had no idea how long the moment stretched. It wasn't until Ivan's shoulder pressed against mine that I remembered where I was and who was around me.

"Are you sure he knows?" Ivan murmured.

Ripping my gaze from Beckett, I turned to Ivan. "Knows what?"

His lips curled. "That you don't date." I snarled a little, making him pull back and hold up his hands. "Okay. I understand. I won't ask again."

"Thank you. If you do, I'll cut holes in your Speedos."

That made his smile grow more devious. "If you want to see my dick, you can just ask."

If he'd been anyone else, I would have been annoyed, but I already had a read on Ivan. Despite his tattoos, scary demeanor, and blunt way of speaking, he liked to play.

"Not right now, dear. I left my microscope back at the lab."

He patted his chest like he was wounded, and I couldn't hold back a giggle. My gaze flitted back to Beckett, but his chair was empty.

Scanning the hall up and down, I couldn't find him.

Beckett was gone.

My stomach sank like a stone.

This had better not become a problem. I really didn't want to feel anything for Beckett Savage, much less *this*. I was a logical, levelheaded girl. If I ignored whatever this weirdness was, it would go away.

Definitely.

Any time now.

· · · · • · • · · · ·

After an unplanned but great visit home on Sunday—Hells had bribed me with a picture of Madelina along with a text that my niece missed her favorite aunt, and I'd been toast—and a crappy one with my mother, I ended up at Chance Park again. This time, Adrian spotted me right away and skated over.

"I *thought* that was you hanging around here a couple weeks ago."

I grinned at him. "It was me, creeping on the skaters. How are you?"

"Good." He glanced around the ground. "Did you bring your board?"

I held out my empty hands. "I'm only watching."

That made his brow crinkle. "Do you want to borrow mine or something?"

I did. God, how I did. But I couldn't. I'd signed a contract stating I *wouldn't*. And even though I could probably get away with it and not be caught, I would know. My word was something I didn't go back on once I'd given it.

"Not today. But you should go ahead and get your skate on. I'm going to hang here for a while."

He cocked his head, then glanced back at the ramps. There were a lot of skaters out today. Listening to the wheels rolling over concrete, shit talking, the groans when someone didn't land a trick, the cries of victory when they did, filled me with a deep sense of longing. If only skating could land me a scholarship to college...

But it couldn't. Field hockey was my ticket, and staying in one piece so I could play had to be my priority.

"Actually—" Adrian cleared his throat, drawing my attention to him, "—I was thinking I might go grab a milkshake at the T. You hungry?"

My lips parted in surprise. I'd been expecting him to skate off into the sunset, not ask me to join him for a milkshake.

At my hesitation, he shook his head. "Never mind. It was—"

"No, wait." I jumped up from the bench. "I *am* hungry."

I said no to a lot to reach my goals. After the crappy couple hours with my mom, I didn't want to say no to this.

"Yeah?" His happy grin made me nervous, but I really needed to get away from this place, or I might've cried. "Rad. Let's get out of here."

The T was a mainstay of Savage River. I had no idea how long it had been here, but it gave '50s diner vibes, with metal siding and a cute laminate counter with swiveling seats. However old it was, it was adorable and made me feel instantly at home.

Adrian and I chose a booth by a window for easier conversation. He ordered a strawberry milkshake while I went wild with a plate of cheese fries. Not my normal diet, but I was a little sad—desperate times and all that.

Adrian was easy to talk to. We stuck to skating and school, but there was a lot of ground to cover with those topics. I also dropped very clear hints this wasn't a date. We were to be friends—and only friends.

After we finished our food, Adrian ran to the bathroom, and I texted Beckett.

Me: *Can you pick me up outside the T instead of the park?*

When I'd gone to my car this morning, the strangest thing had happened. My tire had been flat again. Even stranger, Beckett had arrived right in time to give me a ride.

He'd mentioned I most likely had a slow leak from a small puncture. Since I only drove once a week at most, it made sense it would go flat again.

It was plausible enough to be believable, so I hadn't pressed. Besides, it would have been insane for Beckett to have been purposely letting the air out of my tire. Even forming the thought sounded ludicrous.

Yeah, I'd keep that suspicion to myself.

Beckett: *No problem. You didn't send me a picture.*

Me: *I'm still considering it.*

Beckett: *What's to consider?*

Me: *If I want you to have a picture of me.*

Beckett: *What could I possibly do with a picture of you, Luciana?*

Me: *I don't even want to consider the possibilities. I don't know why you would want one anyway.*

Beckett: *To put with your contact info.*

Me: *Oh, right. That makes sense. You can take one when I see you.*

Beckett: *You don't want to get your best angle in a selfie?*

Me: *Lol, no. I don't really care what my pic on your phone looks like.*

Adrian slid back into the booth, so I tucked my phone away.

"Can I ask you a question?"

I nodded. "Sure. Go for it."

"Why don't you skate? You were looking at the ramps the way a starving man looks at a thick, juicy steak."

Laughing, I pressed my hand to my forehead. "Oh god, do I really look that desperate?"

He cocked his head, grinning at me. "Want me to lie?"

"No, no, please don't. I'm aware I'd been practically drooling." I sucked in a breath, drawing up my shoulders. I hadn't had to talk about this in a while. Everyone knew. "It's a sad story."

He rolled his hand. "Go on."

"I got a scholarship to go to Savage Academy my freshman year for field hockey, then the weekend before school started, I went skating, took a bad fall, and broke my wrist."

He cringed. "Aw, fuck. No!"

"Yep. Playing field hockey with a broken wrist is pretty much impossible—and that meant losing my scholarship and going to SRH."

"Damn. I'm sorry. That sucks. I mean, SRH is fine, but you were all set to join the big leagues."

"Yeah. It was pretty damn heartbreaking." Losing the scholarship and my field hockey season had been a hard pill to swallow. The fact that it had been due to something I'd done to myself had made it that much more bitter.

"But you obviously got another shot."

"I don't even know how, but yeah, I did." My nose crinkled. "I didn't learn my lesson, though. My stubborn little skater self kept going to the park with my sister. It was our thing, and I didn't want to give it up."

"Don't blame you."

"Well, other people definitely did." A seed of anger burst in my belly at the memory of what Beckett Savage tried to do to me. "This guy from school—I don't know why he hates me, but he does. He saw me at the park and took pictures and a video of me skating."

"What?" Adrian fell back against his seat in shock. "What the fuck? What'd he do with them?"

"Totally narced. He sent them to my coach and the headmaster. I was called in to a meeting with them, my guardians, and the head of the athletic department. They were *this* close to yanking my scholarship."

"Jesus," he uttered. "That's fucked up."

"Yeah. It was an awful, terrifying situation. My sister went hard for me, convincing them she'd keep me off the skateboard if they let me stay. In the end, I had to sign a contract stating I won't skate until I graduate."

His head jerked like he'd been hit. "Even in the off-season?"

"I can't skate at all. If I break my wrist again, it might do permanent damage, you know? I get it. I really do. But I miss it like breathing. I've been a skater practically my entire life."

"It's part of your identity," he supplied in understanding.

"You get it."

"I do, for sure." He clicked his tongue. "Damn, I'm sorry."

"Me too. But I *know* it's worth it. That's the only reason I agreed to the contract."

"I'd probably do the same in your shoes." His mouth pressed together in a pained line. "Glad I'm not though, to be honest."

That made me laugh. "No kidding."

"You ever get back at the guy who snitched on you?"

"I'm not really one for revenge. I've just avoided him all these years."

Until now.

Speaking of Beckett, my phone vibrated. I checked the screen, finding a text from him telling me he was out front.

"My ride's here, so—"

"Yeah." Adrian's smile was soft but tinged with regret. "You're cool, Luc. Too bad about the whole friend zone thing."

I snorted a laugh as I slid out of the booth. "Come on, I never used those words."

He held up his hands. "I know what zone I'm in. I don't have to be told. And listen, I can always use more friends, so I'm not even mad."

Adrian was a legit good guy. Chill to the core and nice on top of it. And still, I didn't feel even a twinge of desire for him. Not like—

Nope. Not thinking about *him* that way. Not when he was right out front.

Not ever.

CHAPTER ELEVEN

Beckett

I TAPPED ON THE steering wheel, waiting for Luciana.

She didn't hold me up long. A minute later, she pushed out of the old diner, a bright smile on her face. I sat up straight, keeping a keen eye on her. I'd just seen her this morning, but it felt like longer. In that short time, she'd already changed. Hair was now swept up in a ponytail when it'd been down before. Her skin was a shade more golden like she'd spent the day in the sun. She was lighter too, like visiting her family had eased her load.

Studying her as closely as I had was how I'd momentarily missed that she wasn't alone. I didn't notice until she turned around to speak to the guy behind her. He had a skateboard tucked under his arm, stupid shaggy hair, and was wearing some kind of ratty old band tee. Her type.

I recognized him as the guy she'd been sitting with at the game. Johnny's asshole cousin. What the hell was she doing with him?

I rolled down the passenger window, intent on putting an end to whatever was going on.

"Luciana."

Glancing at me over her shoulder, she held up a finger, telling me to *wait*.

The asshole pulled her into a hug, which she reciprocated. My stomach clenched as I watched them. This wasn't supposed to be happening. She didn't date. So why did it look like I was picking her up at the end of one like her schmuck of a dad?

I fought the urge to slam my hand down on the horn.

I gave her a ride as a favor, not to watch her make out with some random dick who very clearly wasn't good enough for her. Who walked around in a Nickelback shirt unironically?

This guy, apparently.

Go back to Canada with that shit, you goon.

"Luciana. Time to go." It came out harsher than intended, barking her name, my patience fried.

She glanced at me again, this time frowning, then turned back to the big doofus. Up she went on her toes, her hand curving around the back of his neck, her lips pressed against his cheek.

She kissed him.

My hand went to the gearshift. Because fuck this. I was not this girl's chauffeur, and she didn't get to disrespect me like this.

Before I could put the car in drive—or truly decide if I was going to—Luciana opened the door and slipped inside.

"Hey, thanks for picking me up here. Sorry I made you wait."

She was breathless, like that guy had made her heart beat faster.

Taking a deep breath, I drove away from the curb in silence. If I spoke now, it wouldn't be polite. Luciana must have sensed my mood, staying quiet too. The air between us was thick, fraught with tension. I didn't want to be angry at her, but I couldn't find my way out of it.

Unable to take another second without saying something, I broke the peace. "You were on a date."

"What?" she squeaked in surprise.

I slid my eyes sideways. She shifted in her seat to face me, tucking her legs underneath her.

"A date. You had me pick you up from a date."

In my periphery, she shook her head. "No, it wasn't a date. I don't do that, and, god, if I did, I wouldn't expect you to pick me up from one."

"You kissed him."

She threw out a hand, sighing heavily. "I kiss everyone. It's how I greet people and say goodbye."

"Not everyone," I muttered, my molars grinding together.

"Well, not *strangers*."

"Is it even special to you, Luciana? Does it mean anything?"

"What? Does what mean anything?"

I exhaled heavily through my nose, grasping at my elusive patience. Finally, I answered her. "Kissing. You give them away like scattering confetti. Doesn't that make them meaningless?"

She studied me without replying. Possibly considering how she would. I waited because I wanted to know what she would say if I gave her the space to think.

At the next stoplight, I turned to her. Her fist was raised to her mouth, her cheeks flushed, and when she found me looking, she sniffled.

"Did I hurt your feelings?" I was somewhat incredulous this could be a possibility. It certainly hadn't been my intention. Hurting Luciana was the last thing I'd wanted.

"That was mean, Beckett. How could it not have hurt my feelings?"

Her fist opened, the tips of her fingers pressing against her lips.

"It was asked out of genuine curiosity." I chuffed, giving my head a slow shake. "I'm sorry I hurt you. I can see that I did. I was thrown off by seeing you with that guy. You know Johnny's his cousin, don't you—the one who said some really hideous things about you at the game?"

"I remember." She lowered her fingers to her chin, revealing her chewed-on lips. "I know what Johnny's like, and I really don't think Adrian's anything like him."

"Adrian," I muttered, pressing hard on the gas when the light changed.

"I was having a really bad morning, so I went to watch the skaters. Adrian was there and offered to grab some food with me at the T. I accepted because I thought it would cheer me up."

"Did it?"

"It did...until a few minutes ago when you cut me to the quick."

My fingers flexed on the wheel. Leave it to Luciana to give me the blunt truth. "I'm sorry."

"I get that. And thank you for apologizing. It was a good apology, so ten points for you."

I almost laughed. "It's that easy for you to forgive?"

"I don't know if it's a character flaw, but I have a tendency to give people a lot of chances."

"It's a flaw," I stated unequivocally. "Fortunately, you don't have many."

"Wow, for someone who was *just* forgiven, you're being awfully opinionated. And fine, it's a flaw. I guess you're lucky I have it since it worked to your benefit this time. Although, your apology was top tier. I hate when people say, 'I'm sorry *if* I hurt you.' Like, yeah, dude, I'm sitting here sobbing because of you. I'd say whether you hurt me is not in doubt."

"Who's made you sob? Give me a name."

She snorted a laugh. "Nothing serious. You can't go back and beat up Danny Eisen for snapping my training bra in fifth grade and then saying I didn't even need one since I had no boobs."

My jaw tightened. "Danny Eisen, you say?"

"Shut up, Beckett. That's a made-up name. Don't go stalking some poor, innocent guy."

"But someone did that to you?" I shot a glare at her, and her lips pressed together, holding back her amusement.

"I'm not telling you."

"Don't laugh. This pisses me off."

"I can see that. Thank you for being angry in my honor. I'm over it since I *do* have boobs now."

I didn't know how to respond to that without coming off sounding like a perv, so I let it lie. She huffed, though, like she was offended I hadn't agreed with her about her boobs. Still, I bit my tongue.

Eventually, she sighed. "It wasn't a date, Beckett. I made that clear to him, and he was cool with being my friend. I kissed him on the cheek to thank him for brightening my day."

"Yeah? A diner trip did that?"

"Good company and a plate of cheesy fries."

I glanced at her. "You ate cheesy fries? You never eat garbage like that during the season."

"Why do you even know that?"

I shrugged. "I have a knack for noticing patterns. You always eat chicken and veggies during your season."

"You realize it's sort of weird that you know what I eat when we've never shared a meal, right?"

"Possibly. Like I said, I notice things." My thumbs tapped on the wheel, and my stomach churned. "We could, you know."

"What?"

"Share a meal."

"Could we? I don't know. You and I seem to get along in short spurts, but your friends...plus my friends. No. Sorry, Beckett, but I don't think it would work."

"Your friends are fine." For the most part. Truly, I could take them or leave them.

"Well, your friends aren't. Sorry."

"Ha."

Her head whipped my way. "What was that?"

"Nothing. It's just you made a big deal about my apology being top tier, and frankly, yours was bottom rung."

"Because I didn't mean it."

"Then why offer it?"

She folded her arms across her chest. "I take it back."

"You really have to work on your apologies, Luc. I can give you pointers."

"Wow, Beckett. That's the last time I compliment you."

I huffed a laugh. "I doubt that."

"Don't be cocky. It's really not an attractive personality trait."

"I'm the furthest thing from cocky around you."

"*Okay*, sure."

Luciana really had no idea who I was. But she would.

"Can you tell me why you had a really bad morning? I thought you got along with your sister and her husband."

"Oh, I do. That part was great." She twisted some of the strings on her cutoffs. "My mom is a mess. Some people say their moms are messes and it's because they wear pajamas all day or tell embarrassing stories when they're tipsy on wine. That's not my mother."

"Okay."

"Please don't repeat anything of this, Beckett."

I would've been insulted she'd felt the need to extract that promise from me, but like I'd said, she didn't know me yet.

"Of course, Luc."

Pulling in a long breath, she yanked a string off her shorts and began to wrap it around one of her fingers as she spoke.

"Helen helps our mother with food and pays her utilities, but other than that, she has nothing to do with her. I can't seem to cut myself off from her that completely, so when I'm home, I take her the groceries and help her around her house. It's fine, you know? She's a mess, but I expect that of her. Except...today's visit was a surprise."

My spine went rigid as I raced through my memories of Luciana on the sidewalk. I hadn't seen any injuries on her, but my focus had been fractured by the dipshit who'd been staring at her with hearts in his beady eyes.

"Not a good surprise?"

"Not for me." She sighed, and it was filled with years of disappointment and melancholy. This was the darkness I'd known was somewhere deep inside her. She'd built walls around it, made of her never-ending good moods and fortified by her ceaseless friendliness with barbed wire bright smiles keeping even the most curious on the other side.

"Some guy I'd never seen before was in her living room, all set up to shoot poison into my mom's veins. I was so shocked at *everything* about the scene, I fell back on my manners and actually said 'excuse me,' as if I'd done something wrong by interrupting them."

"Luc..."

"I know, I know. I snapped out of it pretty quickly, though. My mom started screaming for the guy to get out, trying to play it off like he was an intruder, which is just...I don't know what goes through her mind. But he left, wearing freaking church clothes, probably going back to his wife and kids. The entire thing was gross and made me feel dirty just witnessing it."

Stopping, she pressed her hands into her thighs. The string was wrapped tight around her index finger, turning the tip deep red.

"You're cutting off the circulation," I grumbled.

"Oh." She held her hand in front of her face. "I guess I am."

She unraveled the string and went on. "I went in, and Mom was trying to hide the stack of money on the coffee table and the needles. I guess it was heroin. I don't know. Can you inject other drugs?"

"I don't know, Luc."

"Yeah, me either. You'd think I would, being the child of two addicts. I guess I probably should know what she's taking, in case I ever need to tell an EMT or—"

Her voice broke, and she clamped down on her lip with her teeth. She wasn't crying, but her fingers were digging into her knee, holding it all back.

"Helen probably knows. You should ask her."

"If I do, I'll have to tell her what I saw today. She won't let me go back."

"You've never seen that before?"

She shook her head. "Helen got her to promise not to do any of that in front of me when I came to live with her. Even now, Mom wants me to keep visiting. She's cranky with me, but I know she looks forward to it. And I—I don't know if I look forward to it, but I *need* it. Even if it hurts." The way she swiped at her cheeks looked like it hurt. "Anyway, I don't even know why I'm telling you all this. You probably just got a lot more than you bargained for, huh? I bet you're wishing you'd kept on driving this morning instead of offering me a ride again."

"I'm not wishing that." I turned into Savage Academy, driving through the gates, a long, smooth road in front of me. "You're probably tired of repeating the same story."

"What do you mean?"

"You told the guy in the diner and then me. I was thinking—"

"No. I didn't tell him. We just talked about skating and school, stuff like that." She let out a shaky exhale. "I can't believe I just unloaded like that on you."

"I told you I don't mind. Feel better?"

"To be honest, yeah, I kind of do."

"Better than cheesy fries?"

She slapped my bicep with the back of her hand. "Be for real, Beckett. There's nothing better than cheesy fries. Not even you can argue."

Luciana jumped out of the car as soon as I pulled into my parking spot, then waited for me at the front of the car. We started off toward our dorm, neither of us in a hurry.

"By the way, I've always kissed hello and goodbye. I don't know if it's cultural or just something my family does. We're kissers. Anyone who's around us is subject to being kissed." She smoothed a hand over her ponytail. "But I don't think that makes it meaningless. There are different types of kisses. Greeting kisses, friendly kisses, thank-you kisses, I'm-sorry kisses, sorrowful kisses, romantic kisses, passionate kisses."

"I see. And Diner Kid was a thank-you kiss?"

She waved her hand. "A mix between friendly and a thank-you."

"Okay." I tucked my hands in my pockets. "And have you ever had a passionate kiss?"

Her elbow met my forearm. "I almost said that's too personal, but then I remembered I just told you intimate details about my addict mother, so I guess we're getting personal."

"Yeah?" I waited for her reply on tenterhooks.

"Yeah." She rubbed her lips together. "I haven't experienced a passionate kiss yet, and I'm in no rush for it."

"Romantic?"

Her shoulder lifted. "That's stretching it. Sloppy making out isn't really the epitome of romance." She raised a brow at me, and I had to work to keep my expression neutral. "What about you? Have you experienced romance? Passion?"

Mimicking her, I shrugged. "That's personal, Ortega."

A laugh burst out of her. "I see how it is, Savage. You get me to spill the beans, and when it's your turn, you shut it down. Next time, I'm digging your secrets out first."

She ducked under my arm when I held the door open for her, getting to the elevator first to press the button. It came quickly, and we climbed on.

I tugged the end of her ponytail, then let go when what I really wanted to do was wrap it around my fist. It would have looked nice that way.

Luciana flashed me a grin, her earlier darkness hidden behind her beaming lights. It might've still been there, but something that felt a lot like pride brimmed inside me from the knowledge I'd been there to help it recede.

The doors slid open. Luciana stepped out and spun around. I stopped in front of her, waiting to hear what she had to say.

She crooked her finger. "Come here."

Brow pinched, I dipped down, bringing myself to her level. She stepped closer and leaned in, tipping her face to the side. Time slowed. Her nose grazed my cheek, then her cheek brushed mine. An exhale heated my skin. I sucked in a breath, her sunshine scent traveling to my foggy head, making it even foggier.

An eternity passed by the time her lips connected with the hinge of my jaw.

A touch.

One press of her soft lips to my hard jaw.

And then a whisper next to my ear.

"That was a thank-you kiss, Beckett."

She backed up, her deep-brown eyes fluttering to mine. They were vulnerable. I held her secrets now, and we both knew it.

I caught her by the nape, tugging her into me again. Not allowing myself to overthink it, I bent and touched my lips to the spot above the arch of her right eyebrow.

"Friendly kiss, Luciana."

Dropping my hold on her, I backed away toward my end of the hall. She was probing the spot I'd kissed, and I had to stop myself from doing the same to my jaw.

A big part of me was reluctant to end this. Something had shifted during the span of that drive, sending my curiosity into overdrive. I wanted to dive into it, discover exactly what had changed, but I'd wasted an entire day driving around when I should have been writing a paper.

So, with a final nod, I turned around and headed to my room.

Chapter Twelve

Luciana

"OH MY GOD, I'M so stupid."

I kicked the door to my suite shut and leaned against it, groaning. Two sets of wide, alarmed eyes were on me.

"What's all this about, precious?"

Delilah and Bella were spread out on the plush area rug in the center of our small, shared living space, books and computers surrounding them. I'd obviously interrupted a study session with my drama.

Evelyn popped her head out of her room. "You aren't stupid, Luciana. Far from it."

"Thanks, Ev." I ground the heel of my hand into my forehead. "I might not be stupid, but I'm sure acting like I am."

Bella and Delilah both sat up. Evelyn inched her way out of her room, worrying her bottom lip with her thumb.

"Right now?" Ev asked. "Or do you mean in general?"

"Neither. I mean Beckett Savage is making me act like an idiot."

Her mouth popped open. "Oh. That doesn't sound so good."

"What's goin' on?" Bella asked. "I thought you were goin' home today. What's Beckett got to do with it?"

I flung myself down on the tiny love seat, my legs hanging over the end of it. "He gave me a ride, and on the way home, I unloaded some of my mom trauma on him."

Bella scooted over to me on her knees and touched my forehead with the back of her hand. "You're not feverish. Make it make sense."

I swatted her away. "He's a shockingly good listener. He didn't judge, he was just...*there*."

"Okay." Bella glanced behind her at Delilah then turned her attention back to me. "Nothing about what you just said makes you stupid, so I'm gatherin' there's something else."

I squeezed my eyes closed. I couldn't look at her—or any of them—when I admitted this part. "When we got off the elevator, something came over me, and I kissed him."

Bella gasped. Delilah made some kind of choking sound. Tentative fingers stroked the escaped strands of hair off my forehead.

I peeked, finding Evelyn standing over me with a crumpled expression. "Was the kiss very terrible?"

I shook my head. "It was only his cheek." I pressed a finger to the same spot on my face. "Well, his jaw. But—"

"What?" Delilah pressed. "You can tell us anything, you know."

I knew that, but if I said it out loud, it would be real, and that terrified me. I'd never once said this kind of thing out loud.

"If it wasn't terrible, did you like it?" Leave it to Ev to cut right to the chase.

Covering my face with both hands, I nodded. "I did. My stomach felt like I'd downed a gallon of tea, all sloshy and warm."

"Oh," Ev whispered. "That sounds really lovely, actually."

I grabbed the tips of her fingers, which were still stroking my hair, and she allowed it.

"It was," I whispered.

"What did Beckett do?" Delilah's voice was closer now. And even though I wasn't ready to look at them, it was a comfort to have all three crowding around me.

"I started to back away and said goodbye, but he caught me by the nape—"

Twin gasps from Delilah and Bella. Ev's fingers wiggled in my hold.

"And then?" Bella sounded breathless.

I swallowed hard. "He pulled me closer and kissed my temple."

"Oh, girl," Bella cooed. "This is...I don't even know what to say."

"I think this is a crush, guys." I had to push the words out, and they felt strange on my tongue.

"Yes, precious. I'm pretty certain that's what this is," Delilah agreed.

Bella sighed.

"Are you sad, Luciana?" Evelyn wiggled her fingers again, and this time, I let go, my hands falling from my face.

"I'm—I don't know. Confused is probably the best way to describe it. How can Beckett Savage be my first crush? Why is it *him*?" I pressed on my swooping belly. "I don't like it at all."

"He's hot as shit, that's why," Bella quipped.

Delilah nodded. "He is. And he's always watching you."

"No, he's not." I didn't know why I was trying to deny it. It was a fact that Beckett had been everywhere I was lately. But that could have been a coincidence. "Maybe this isn't a real crush. It could just be my mind tricking me because he's always around."

"Freddie's always around. Are you crushin' on him?" Bella cocked a brow.

I snorted a laugh. "Shut up, you. Beckett's probably planning my demise since his first attempt didn't work."

Bella rolled her eyes. She didn't believe me, but then again, I didn't believe myself either.

"Well, do you want to—" Delilah paused, giving me a very pointed look. "Do you want to make this into something?"

"No. You know my stance." As emphatic as I made myself sound, I didn't quite feel it on the inside.

"Then enjoy the sweet, beautiful pain, precious." Delilah took my hands and pulled me upright.

"Pain doesn't really sound enjoyable."

"It isn't." Evelyn circled around the love seat to perch on the arm of it. "I don't think pain is the right word. Or perhaps it's not specific enough."

"An ache," Bella supplied. "Like a deep, deep bruise you can't stop yourself from pressing on."

"But it's exciting too. Seeing him, thinking of him, hearing his name and your heart beating faster. Everything feels more vibrant. Waking up is easier because you have something to look forward to." Delilah sighed. "That's the sweet."

"Since you don't want anything to come of it, you won't get caught up wondering if he's into you too," Bella added.

"I truly despise that part," Ev said.

Delilah faltered for a moment. "As do I."

"The worst," Bella agreed. "Luc is a lucky bitch not having to worry about it."

Swiveling my head, I looked at all my friends. "You guys don't think I'm stupid? I mean, it's Beckett. He tried to get me expelled. He's the last person I should be having warm fuzzies about."

Delilah waved that fact away. "You aren't dating him or *marrying* him. Inappropriate crushes are a rite of passage."

"A really, really confusing one," I lamented.

Since there was no possibility of denying these feelings, the most I could hope was for them to fade as quickly as they'd appeared.

· · • • • • • • • · ·

Delilah had been right about one thing. I woke up on Monday filled with anticipation. My stomach had been so swirly from the moment I'd opened my eyes I skipped my early run.

And maybe I was avoiding alone time with Beckett.

Because as good as those last few seconds we'd spent together yesterday were, they weren't worth throwing away my convictions. Especially not for Beckett, who didn't have my best interest at heart.

I just had to ride this out while taking my girls' advice and enjoying the ache.

Maybe I spent a little extra time getting ready for class after morning practice, taking extra care blowing out my hair and swiping on my cherry gloss. Nothing over the top, but it felt *necessary*.

I was running late because of this. Delilah had ditched me to grab our seats in English. That was what she'd said, at least. What she hadn't said was that she'd wanted to make sure she could sit beside Ivan too.

Who was I to judge? I was making myself pretty to see the boy who'd once tried to derail my life.

My shoes squeaked on the floor as I rushed down the hall. Dr. Burns was frazzled most of the time, but she really didn't appreciate tardiness. The last thing I wanted was to be called out in front of the class, especially when I was already embarrassed over the extra effort I'd made getting ready this morning.

Spotting Beckett propped against the wall outside the classroom, I nearly stumbled over my feet and ducked into an alcove to pull myself together. My heart tumbled around inside its cage. Pressing one hand over the fluttering beat, I peeked out, checking if he was still there.

At first, I only saw him. Tall and lean, he was gazing down, his dark brow furrowed. I followed his line of sight. Bianca DeSoto was standing close, her palm on his chest.

"Come on, Beckett." Bianca used a sexy baby voice, poking her plump bottom lip out.

"What are you doing here? I thought you got kicked out."

She flicked her hand. "My father took care of that." Like a parking ticket instead of controlled substances, if the rumor mills were true. I should have been used to how far the influence of my schoolmates' parents stretched by now but still found myself surprised.

Beckett paused. Inhaled. His head canted. "Did he?" Each word was carefully enunciated like he was forming them from blown glass.

"Mmhmm. I told him they weren't my pills. Naturally, he believed me, so he made the whole thing go away." Another flick, her troubles vanishing as easily as her fingers flung about particles of oxygen.

"Good for you." More blown glass, this time brittle.

"Aw, don't act like you weren't sad I was gone." She poked the third button on his shirt with a sharp, red fingernail. "Admit you missed the eye candy."

"Eye candy. Hmmm." He tipped his head down, whispering something to her I was glad I couldn't hear since it had Bianca pressing her front to his.

I flattened my back to the wall of the alcove. I might've had to listen, but I definitely didn't have to watch. My stomach had gone from butterflies to rabid bats. The swirls were raging rapids, and I had to keep swallowing so I didn't gag.

"Oh, Beckett, that isn't what you were saying when my lips were wrapped around your dick."

"True, but I wasn't saying much, now was I, Bianca?"

I was so disgusted I couldn't help the loud, wet cough that escaped.

"What was that?" Beckett gritted out.

Squeezing my eyes closed, I held my breath, waiting to be caught.

"Who knows? Probably a freshman regurgitating her breakfast. So gauche. No one wants to hear that."

A muttered, "Shut up," then slow, measured footsteps neared.

"Mr. Savage? Ms. DeSoto? Are you joining us today?" I had never been so relieved to hear Dr. Burns's voice.

The footsteps faded off in the other direction, joined by the clack of Bianca's heels and then a click of the door closing. I chanced another peek, finding the hallway empty.

I waited several minutes, hating every second that ticked by, making me later and later. And of course, I blamed Beckett. This was his fault. If he'd never begun this strange campaign that had brought him to my attention, I wouldn't have been feeling this way—nauseous and stupid and, god, unaccountably let down.

Of course Beckett had hooked up with Bianca DeSoto.

They went perfectly together.

Rich, beautiful, mean, entitled.

I'd forgotten that for a little while. I wouldn't anymore.

"Luciana?"

My head jerked up. Sera—no, Mrs. Umbra at school—was standing in the hall just outside the alcove, concern etched on her face.

"Um...hi."

She took a step closer. "Are you okay?"

"Yeah, I'm fine." My nose scrunched. "Cramps. I just needed a minute to let the medicine work before I went into English. Dr. Burns makes us sit on the floor—"

She held up a hand. "Oh, I get it. Believe me. Sitting on the floor when you feel like your insides are being scooped out with a dull spoon is no fun."

I laughed. "That was a vivid description."

She fluffed her red curls, grinning. "I try my best to keep it real. *And* I made you laugh, so I'd say my work here is done. Don't tell the other teachers. They're already a little jealous of me."

My brows popped. "Are they?"

"Have you *seen* my husband?" She winked, making me laugh again.

"I have, and I get it."

Sera and her husband, Julien, had gone to college with Hells and Theo. Their friendship had carried on after graduation, which meant I'd seen them often over the last few years. Sometimes it was hard for me to go from my sister's friend Sera to Mrs. Umbra when I ran into her at school, but she was part time, so it didn't happen a lot.

"Are you ready to go to class?" she asked.

I sucked in a breath and straightened. "I think so."

She beckoned me to come with her. "I'll walk you in and make an excuse."

"Would you? Thank you so much."

"Of course. Besides, Beckett's in there, and I never pass up a chance to say hi to him—loudly and enthusiastically." Sera pushed open the door, going in ahead of me. "Sorry to interrupt, Dr. Burns. I needed to borrow Luc for a minute and made her late."

Dr. Burns wrung her hands together, seemingly flustered by the interruption, but motioned for me to come in. Sera patted my arm as I passed, whispering for me to feel better.

I kept my head down once I found Delilah, taking my spot on the empty cushion next to her as quickly as I could. Awareness prickled down my arms. Beckett was on my other side, but he wouldn't be receiving any more of my attention.

"Hi, Beckett," Sera called. "I hope you remembered to eat breakfast this morning."

He grunted. "Yeah, I did."

"Good going, champ. Well, have a great day of learning, everyone."

Sera disappeared out of the room, and Dr. Burns got back to her lesson.

As subtly as possible, I scooted closer to Delilah. "Did I miss anything?"

She shook her head and whispered into my ear. "Not much. We're going to read *Pride and Prejudice.*"

I nodded. I'd read it twice and had watched the movies countless times, so I was looking forward to this unit.

I gave Dr. Burns my full attention, even though I was never unaware Beckett was beside me. As class went on, I shifted closer and closer to Delilah until we were shoulder to shoulder and there was nowhere left for me to go. She gave me a searching look, but I just shook my head. I'd tell her later, and most assuredly, she'd be as grossed out as I was.

· · • • • ♦ • • · ·

It was after math when Beckett caught up to me. Mr. Caraway had kept me after to talk about one of my answers on a quiz, and when I'd rushed out of the classroom, Beckett was there.

"You didn't run this morning," he grumbled, falling into step beside me.

"I overslept." My pace was hurried, my gaze focused on the ground in front of me.

"That's unlike you. Are you sick?"

"You don't know me well enough to say it's unlike me."

"I think I do."

"Obviously not."

I really couldn't smooth my thoughts out. I recognized I was angry at Beckett but had no real right to be. He wasn't responsible for my crush, and over the last few weeks, he'd been nothing but friendly and generous with me. Well, not *nothing but*. He was still Beckett, after all, and that meant surly and grumpy too.

But that wasn't the point.

The point was, so what if he had messed around with Bianca in the past or was planning to mess around with her in the near future. That wasn't my business.

That was rational, but the thoughts in my head were wrinkled, like a paper that had once been balled up. Logic couldn't seep into the creases.

He reached for my ponytail, but it wasn't there. My hair was down because I was stupid and had wanted to look prettier today. I started to dodge him, but Beckett smoothed his hand down the back of my hair and then my arm to my elbow.

"You're in a bad mood," he stated.

"Oversleeping does that to me."

"Is that it?" He didn't sound at all convinced.

"Yes."

"What were you doing with Sera this morning? How'd you help her?"

I used Bianca's method of flicking my troubles away. "It was me who was late. She just said that to help me out."

He made a low sound, a rumble in his chest. "She's cool like that."

"You're lucky to have her for a sister-in-law." What was I doing? He was pulling me into a conversation I definitely didn't want to be having. When he was around, it was like I couldn't help talking to him. It was too natural.

"I am, for certain." He touched my hair again. "It's down."

"Yeah." I picked up a strand from my shoulder. "I'll probably put it up soon."

He dipped his head, squinting at me. "Your mouth looks different."

"Gloss."

"Hmmm. Did I do something between bringing you home yesterday and English this morning?"

I shrugged, avoiding having to lie by not saying anything.

"Do I smell like shit, Luciana?"

I practically squeaked out a yelp at his blunt question. "What? No. Not that I've noticed, anyway."

He sniffed. "I think you'd notice."

"Probably."

He put his arm in my path, forcing me to stop. Taking my shoulders, he turned me to face him. We were two doorways from psychology. I'd almost made it.

Beckett dragged his hands down my arms then let me go. "If I don't smell, then why were you scooting away from me in English?"

"I wasn't scooting away from you, I was moving closer to Delilah."

"Hmmm."

I didn't like the sound of his hum. It said more than words. Like he didn't believe me. He probably didn't, but that was too bad for him.

"We're going to be late for class."

"Maybe."

He wasn't holding me, but I was pretty sure he'd stop me if I attempted to dart by him.

"Beckett, I don't know what you want me to say. My actions don't have anything to do with you. You don't—" I cut myself off from being too harsh.

"Don't what, Ortega? Give it to me. Tell it to me straight."

I turned my head, huffing. "There's nothing to say."

He exhaled through his nose. "Are you—Luc, are you embarrassed about the things you told me yesterday? Is that why you're avoiding me?"

The careful way he formulated his question and the quiet intimacy with which he asked almost undid me. But Bianca's voice was stuck in my head, and the image of the two of them—nope, not going there.

Not going anywhere with Beckett.

"I'm not avoiding you, Savage." I flicked my eyes to his. "I don't know what you want me to say. Tell me, and I'll say it."

His cool gaze stayed locked on mine as though he were trying to peer inside my jumbled thoughts to drag out the truth. I stared back, pushing away my disappointment and frustration to remain as blank as I could.

Beckett sighed. "Go to class."

"Aren't you coming?"

His lids lowered to half-mast. "Don't worry about me, Ortega. I'll do what needs to be done."

His glass words were heavy with lead and meaning. They settled between us, and I took a step back. When he didn't stop me, I took another. He watched me warily but never moved.

Finally, I put one foot in front of the other, wondering if this was the fastest a crush had ever crashed and burned.

Chapter Thirteen
Luciana

THE STANDS FOR OUR first home game of the season were nowhere near as packed as they'd been for football or soccer. But I didn't thrive off cheers from fans. My buzz came from the game itself.

Today's game was the kind I loved to play. We were ahead the whole time, but the other team didn't stop fighting until the final whistle blew. They'd pushed us to level up, and my girls had risen to the call.

At the end of the game, I dropped my stick and tipped my face up to the sun. Sweat and dirt coated my face and limbs. Satisfaction and pride rushed through my system.

He'd watched the whole thing. The soccer team had come out to support us, as they always did for our first home game of the season, but it was Beckett's eyes I felt on me while I played. And strangely, that had spurred me on. I'd gone harder, digging into my reserves, wanting to show him I was just as skilled at my sport as he was at his.

At the sound of my name, I opened my eyes. Bella charged toward me, throwing her arms around me. The rest of the team followed suit, all of us woven together into a cheering, yelling, sweaty ball of victory.

"You guys did that," I yelled.

Bella raised her arm to point at me over her head. "You did that, Ortega!"

I threw my head back, laughing, adrenaline and happiness buzzing beneath my skin. There was nothing better than this feeling.

This was why I played hard—not to show off for a boy. My team, this victory, the giddiness that our blood, sweat, and tears were worth the sacrifice—they were my reason.

Bella and I walked to the locker room, her arm slung around my shoulders. The captain from Brookside Prep, Jenny, stopped us.

"Good game, ladies."

"Thanks, girl," Bella answered. "You too."

Jenny waved her off. "I wanted to extend an invite to the bonfire we're hitting tonight. Some kids from Brookside and Marshall will be there. Maybe Savage River too. It should be low-key good times."

Bella turned to me. Even if she wanted to go—and knowing her, she did—she'd follow my lead on this. It was on the tip of my tongue to turn Jenny down. She'd invited us before, and I'd declined automatically.

This time, I hesitated. I didn't really want to spend another Saturday night in my room, and hanging out in the common area of my dorm was out of the question since Beckett seemed to appear whenever I did and I had been strategically avoiding him all week.

I couldn't quite come up with a good reason to say no—not after playing my last first game of high school.

So, I told her yes.

And *really* hoped I wasn't going to regret this decision.

· · • • • · • • • ·

Beckett, Rhys, and Felix were hanging around the locker room entrance when we poured out after a postgame rundown with our coach. Felix grabbed Isla, pulling her into a hug and congratulating her on a good game. He might've been crazy overprotective, but he never failed to be there for her.

"Nice playing out there," Beckett said to all of us, but his focus was on me.

"Thanks," I murmured, keenly aware of my sweat-soaked tank and how damp my ponytail was.

"It's an interesting game," Rhys drawled.

Bella stepped up to him, her arms crossed, her little chin tilted in a stubborn pose. "What was so interesting about it?"

His gaze dropped to hers. "The skirts."

I huffed at his remark. "Why am I not surprised that's all you found interesting?"

Then I accidentally made eye contact with Beckett. He'd already been looking at me, and his head cocked when I looked back. My body froze, except for the flip-flops in my stomach. Some kind of twisted amalgamation of butterflies and bats haunted that part of me, fluttering and clawing in equal measure. I couldn't remember a time feeling this helpless over my own emotions, and I hated it.

"Do I look like the kind of man who enjoys watching girls whack a small ball around a field for an hour or more without some further enticement?" Rhys straightened the collar of his crisp, white polo.

"You *sound* like a guy who begs to have his balls ground into dust by a whip-yieldin', spiked-heels-wearin' dominatrix while thanking her for the privilege of havin' his manhood destroyed." Bella linked her arm with mine and shot Rhys a smug grin. The girl thrived on arguing and was never one to back down.

He held up a finger. "One, we don't abide by kink shaming."

"Who's kinky?" Felix slid over to the guys after letting go of his sister, who came to stand with us.

"Bella is," Rhys went on, ignoring Bella's sputtering protests. "Two, you should really consider taking a gender studies course since you equate testes with manhood."

Bella's mouth fell open then closed on repeat. Isla turned toward her, her lips pinched.

"He has a point," she conceded.

While the rest of them argued, Beckett stepped into my space, dipping his head down to speak to me.

"Are you going home this weekend?"

I shook my head. "No. Not this weekend."

"You sure? I can drive you."

I laughed softly. "I can drive myself. After all, what are the chances of my tire being flat a third time?"

"Slow leak," he murmured.

"I've checked it every day this week. It's doing okay. It would be weird if it were suddenly flat today."

"Stranger things have happened."

"Sure. But if it's flat again, I might start to get suspicious."

The tips of his fingers brushed my bare shoulder. Goose bumps sprouted in his path, and my lungs constricted at the featherlight contact.

"Of what, exactly?" he asked.

"That someone is purposely removing the air from my tire." I gave him a pointed stare.

He stared right back, the clearness of his eyes almost unsettling. "Who would do something like that?"

I licked my lips, suddenly parched. "I have an idea."

Bella groaned, interrupting whatever was happening between Beckett and me. "Oh my god, can we go? I need to shower like whoa."

"Yeah, let's go." The sweat on my skin was starting to dry, which I hated more than most things. But not more than the way Beckett had begun to affect me.

Beckett tugged Rhys away from us by the back of his shirt. "Shut up," he grunted.

Rhy ducked out of his grip and checked his collar again. "Mind the attire, Savage. You dragged me out here for this, you can't be surprised I have an opinion."

Leaving them to sort out their bickering, Bella, Delilah, Isla, and I started to head for the dorm. Felix tagged along, going over some of the plays Isla made with her.

"Why does Rhys exist?" Bella gnashed her teeth together, her cheeks flushed with anger.

"To teach you patience," I supplied. "It's really the only reason I can think of."

Delilah snorted. "I'm not certain he's real. Can you imagine him outside of SA? Going shopping at Target? Filling up a car with gas?"

I giggled. "Actually, no, I can't."

Isla waved her hand in front of her. "Once when I was visiting Felix, I saw Rhys sleeping."

"Was he in a casket?" Bella asked.

"Or charging in a closet?" Delilah added.

Isla's eyes rounded. "Even more eerie. He was asleep in his bed, his mouth was open, and I'm pretty sure I saw drool."

All of us snickered at Rhys being caught doing something so *human*. It seemed utterly impossible. Well, all of us except Felix. He wasn't amused Isla had been anywhere near Rhys and a bed without his knowledge or permission.

The kid really needed to cut the cord.

As we were walking into the dorm, I caught Isla's wrist. "Hey, we were invited to a bonfire tonight with some kids from Brookside—"

Felix slung his arm around her shoulder. "No. She's not going."

Isla rolled her eyes. "Thanks for asking, or at least attempting to ask. If I went, my brother would probably toss every guy who looked at me into the bonfire."

Felix nodded. "Damn right. If you don't want to be responsible for that, stay in your room like a good girl."

Bella started fighting with him about his overprotectiveness, and I tuned them out, having heard it a thousand times before. My mind was on tonight, a thrill riding through my veins at the possibilities of what could happen.

Just about anything.

CHAPTER FOURTEEN

Luciana

I WAS A GOOD girl.

Helen always told me that. She'd been bad most of her life, so she'd know.

But I was also curious. I had never been to a bonfire. Or even a house party. I'd been invited once or twice, but staying in with my friends and trying out a new makeup palette or watching a movie had always been more enticing.

My natural aversion to breaking the rules was helped along by my desire to never become anything like my addict mother. Plus, while Helen had sugarcoated a *lot* of her high school and early college years, she'd told me in soft, easily digestible terms drinking and getting high had led to her being in situations that had irrevocably changed her.

So, when Jenny offered me a beer from a huge cooler when we arrived at the beach, I didn't hesitate to turn her down. Bella and Delilah accepted, and I didn't judge them. They didn't share my baggage.

The three of us wandered around the raging bonfire, which was taller and emitting more warmth than I'd expected. Outside of its perimeter, it was almost pitch dark, with only a sliver of the moon for light.

The telltale scent of weed mixed with the smoke of the fire. On a quick glance, I spied several burning cherries. Judging by the smell, and since I rarely saw anyone smoking cigarettes around here, I came to the conclusion weed was plentiful tonight.

That worried me a little, but not more than the coolers filled with alcohol. We'd be in trouble if we were caught with either.

That was the good girl in me trying to take control of my thoughts. Nothing was going to happen. Kids did things like this all the time.

I took a deep breath to calm my nerves. And maybe, if I inhaled deeply enough, I'd get a little contact high and *really* chill out.

"Did you ever do anything like this at your last school?" I asked Delilah.

She chuffed. "No, precious. We walked out the front door of school to go clubbing."

"Gah, you're so sophisticated." Bella chugged from her beer can and swiped her mouth with the back of her hand. "Where was that again? I can't keep track of all your schools."

"Spain. We didn't stay there long. They didn't treat Evie right." Delilah took a more delicate drink from her can.

"Are we all losing our bonfire cherry tonight?" I threw my arms around their shoulders. "There isn't anyone else I would have wanted to share this experience with."

Bella's giggle ended in a soft burp. "Oh my god, excuse me. You can't take me anywhere. Now, let's go see if there are any cute public school boys for me to flirt with. I'm out of practice."

Since Bella was a tiny Texas tornado, Delilah and I let her sweep us along, stopping to look at boys then dismissing them as not cute enough to stay. She did this to a few groups before one of them said my name.

"Luciana? That's you, right?"

I squinted, peering up at the dude with dark, buzzed hair and a cocky smirk. "Hey, Johnny. What's up?"

He shook his head and slowly wiped his mouth as he looked me over. "Never thought I'd see little Luciana Ortega at one of these things." Then he addressed the three other guys he was with. Guys I vaguely recognized from Savage River High. "This girl is so squeaky clean I bet she's never had a single drop of alcohol."

"Not true." I laughed, but I was uncomfortable.

"Oh yeah?" He raised his chin. "What, have you had Communion wine?"

I folded my arms over my chest, and Bella copied my stance, putting herself halfway in front of me.

"Why does what Luciana drinks matter to you?" she snapped at him.

His eyes slid lazily to her. "Ooh, we got a feisty one. Lookin' like a little cherub, though." Then his attention went back to me. "You never answered the question."

"It's not your business." I tugged on the back of Bella's shirt. "We're gonna go."

One of the other guys moved closer to Delilah. "Nah, why don't you hang out. Johnny'll be good. He's just playin'." It was Cris, the guy who'd come with Giselle to the soccer game a couple weeks ago. "I've seen you before. What's your name?"

Delilah sipped her beer, and even in the firelight, I could tell she was unimpressed by all of them. "Why do you want to know?"

He dipped his head to get in her face. "I need to know what name I'm going to be writing in my diary tonight."

Okay, that was sort of cute. Too bad he was hanging around Johnny. That negated all his charm.

I hooked my arm through hers. "Her name's Not-A-Chance."

Cris rocked back on his heels. "Original. Is that French?"

Delilah released a breathy laugh, which she quickly swallowed down. "No, Greek."

"Hmmm...Greek. My favorite. I could bathe in tzatziki." He held his hand out. "I'm Cristiano."

Before Delilah could react, Bella slapped her palm to his like she was high-fiving him.

"Get outa here with that." She made a shooing motion with her fingers. "No one's fallin' for it. Be gone."

"Thanks for the invitation, boys," Delilah said in her smooth, Euro accent. "I see someone we really must speak to, though, so it'll be a rain check for us."

Cris staggered back. "You're breaking my heart. That accent. Those curves. Come on, mama, stay a while. Tell me your real name."

Bella waved at someone who definitely wasn't there. "I see our friend. We have to jet."

The boys didn't physically stop us, but they groaned and called out rude things about our asses—specifically Delilah's. Hers was worth yelling about, but no one wanted to hear it from creeps who didn't know how to take a freaking hint.

We kept trudging through the sand until we got to the cooler on the other side of the fire. My girls grabbed another drink, then we took a seat in some camp chairs.

Bella tipped her can toward Delilah. "You know, the one who was flirting with you wasn't really half bad."

"He was fine." Delilah remained unimpressed.

"Better than Johnny." I rolled my eyes. "Thank everything above I don't have to go to school with him anymore. I feel sorry for Giselle."

But knowing Giselle, she could hold her own against Johnny and his buddies. She didn't let boys intimidate her or give her a hard time.

Bella tucked herself into a ball in her chair, her legs underneath her jacket. "Okay, so if Cris is just *fine*, then who's more than fine?"

I pressed my lips together. "I think we all know who Delilah thinks is more than fine."

Bella smacked her knee. "Someone better enlighten me, or I'm going to throw a fit."

Delilah flicked her manicured fingers. "If you must know, it's Ivan. I think he's hot, and he makes me feel extremely stupid inside."

"Still? I would have thought you'd be over him by now." Bella was probably surprised because of Delilah's tendency to get the ick about boys as often as other people changed their socks.

"It's a crush," Delilah shot back. "I don't really know anything about him. It's possible he's completely intolerable."

We'd been in school with Ivan for a few weeks now, and he definitely wasn't intolerable, but it was true he remained an enigma. That was most likely part of the appeal. We knew *way* too much about the other guys we went to school with.

"Probably. When you look like he does, you don't have to have a winning personality," I said, and they both agreed.

"Like Beckett," Bella supplied.

I let my head fall back. "Let's not bring him up, okay? He's over."

"I'm still in disbelief he let Bianca touch him," Delilah said.

"I'm not. She's awful, but she's hot." I rubbed my arms to stop shivering.

"That's all that matters to those boys," Bella said.

"Stupid idiot boys," Delilah agreed.

Jenny stumbled over to us with a few of her teammates and some guys from Brookside Prep. They were all pretty hammered and passing around a weed vape. We declined the vape, but Bella and Delilah had another drink.

Needing to stretch my legs and walk off the sour mood that had come over me at the mention of Beckett, I got up from my chair to go hunting for the cooler with water in it. Delilah offered to come with me, but I told her to stay.

It took me a while, weaving through a lot of drunk, friendly people, to find a cooler. I bent down and opened the top, but there were only cans inside. I would have settled for a soda, but it was beer or hard seltzer—nothing I wanted.

I wandered some more, farther away from the crowd and finally came across another cooler. When I opened this one, I found one lonely bottle of water. Grabbing it, I held it up like a prize.

"Yes! I win."

A low chuckle came from way too close behind me, then something that felt like fingertips brushed my hips. I spun around to find Johnny standing there, the firelight casting shadows that made his grin look wicked.

He clicked his tongue on his teeth. "See, I knew it. Good girl's drinking water. They teach you to be like that at your fancy school?"

"I thought drinking water was common knowledge." I glanced behind me. "I need to get back to my friends."

He snatched my wrist before I could blink. His hold was firm, but it didn't hurt. Still, he shouldn't have been touching me.

"Don't go yet. I wanna catch up with you, Luciana. What've you been doin' all these years? I never see you with your girl, Giselle."

"It's hard to get together these days." Not that it was any of his business.

"Oh yeah? I heard you were hanging out with my cousin. You into Adrian?"

"I barely know him."

"That's not what he said."

"I'm not responsible for what he said." I shook my wrist, but he didn't take the hint, so I went for the direct approach. "Let go of me, Johnny."

He tugged me closer, sending me stumbling into him. I bounced off his chest with an *oomph*. That gave him the opportunity to grab my hip with his other hand, keeping me flush with him.

Shocked by my sudden change of location, it took me a moment to react. When I did, he was already inching his hand down my butt.

"Get off me." I slapped his chest and squirmed.

"We're just talking, Luci. No need to get all dramatic, baby. I'll let you go in a minute."

"I want to go back to my friends." I went firm this time, and I got loud. No more freezing. "I'm two seconds away from screaming if you don't let me go right now."

He laughed in my face, moving his hand off my backside to the center of my back, flattening my chest to his. Then he let go of my wrist to stroke my cheek.

"There's no need for any of that. I'm a friendly guy, and sometimes I get carried away."

"You're not friendly, you're rapey. Get your hands off me, Johnny." I yelled that time, but between the waves, the crackling fire, and the music someone had turned up to blasting, I was wasting my breath.

Fear I'd never once felt closed in on me like a blanket weighted with shrapnel. It held me in place, digging into me to take me over. My mind raced as quickly as my pulse. Why had I come here? Even more importantly, why had I wandered off on my own? I wasn't naive, but man, was I acting like it. Johnny could drown me in the ocean, and no one would notice until my body washed ashore. We were a world apart from the rest of the crowd. There were no rules here, only Johnny's will.

Out of nowhere, a hand came down on my shoulder from behind. I jumped, but Johnny still had a tight grip on me, so I barely moved.

"You're going to remove your hands from Luciana."

Beckett?

There was no time to process whose voice it was as a cacophony of panicked shouts rose above it. At first, I couldn't focus enough to make out what they were yelling. Then, one word became clear.

"Cops!"

The three of us heard it at the same time. Beckett's fingers curled into my shoulder, the dull pain a focal point for my scattered mind. Johnny shot me a vicious glare as if whatever was happening was my fault.

Time stood still, at least for us. The world whirled around us. People streaked by like shooting stars against the midnight sky. Cans were tossed, vapes abandoned, and the fire danced. Blue and red lights reflected in the distance, the beams of flashlights bouncing around the beach.

Johnny was the first to wake up to what was happening. He gritted out a "Fuck you, bitches," before he shoved me to the ground with the force of a freight train.

Sand flew into my face, stinging my eyes. My hands took the brunt of the impact, and my wrist twinged enough to take my breath away. Johnny kicked more sand at me when he ran. Frantic to see, I swiped at my eyes, but my hands were covered in sand too, making it worse.

"Stop, stop." Firm fingers wrapped around my wrists. "Stop, Luc. I'll help you, but we have to run. Cops are coming."

I shook my head. "I didn't do anything wrong. I wasn't even drinking."

"They're not going to see it that way." He tugged me to my feet then swept me right off them into his arms. "Hold on to my neck, I'm going to run."

I hesitated, but he didn't. He took off, carrying me through the sand. With my eyes squeezed shut, I held on to him with all my might, trusting him not to drop me and get me to safety. His heart thrashed against my cheek, but his panic soothed me, like he'd taken mine and added it to his.

My eyes were sealed closed, so I had no idea where he was taking me. I could only hope it was somewhere safe. I had to trust him, whether I wanted to or not.

CHAPTER FIFTEEN
Beckett

MY ONLY FOCUS WAS getting Luciana to safety. Then I would think about what I'd just witnessed happening to her. If I tried to wrap my head around it now, or what could have happened had I not come tonight, I'd fall to my knees and tear apart the world.

This beach was in a cove with a craggy outcropping of rocks framing it on both ends. I ran with Luciana in my arms into the rocks, finding a small spot that fit the two of us. We weren't the only ones who'd had this idea. A few other kids were ducking behind rocks. Once they were down low, the black night ate them up so completely they disappeared from my sight, even though I knew they were there.

That eased the tension flowing through my veins slightly. If they were that well-hidden, so were we. And now that we were relatively safe, I could concentrate on clearing the sand off Luc's face.

Sitting cross-legged, I held her in my lap. She was huddled against me, panting for breath. Leaning away from her, I yanked my shirt over my head.

"What are you doing?" she whispered.

"Sit still. I'm helping you."

"Okay."

Cupping the back of her head, I used my shirt to wipe her face. I could only see the outline of her features. Going slow so I didn't hurt or poke her, I stroked the soft, worn cotton against her skin, periodically shaking off the sand I'd removed.

"I could do that myself." But her protest was weak. She didn't even reach for the shirt.

"I've got it. It's easier for me to do it."

Her shoulder and arm hit my chest. Skin to skin. Her body was vibrating. "Are you using your shirt?"

"Mmhmm. That's all I have. Let me work, Ortega."

"All right. My eyes still feel really gritty. I don't want to open them."

"If you could open them, you wouldn't see much. It's really dark."

"Where are we?"

"Hiding."

Her fingers clamped down on my arm. "I'm scared, Beckett. I need you to talk to me, otherwise I think I might scream. I really, really don't want to scream."

"Please don't scream. That will defeat the entire purpose of staying hidden." I moved to her eyes, using the corner of my tee to wipe her lashes and delicate lids. "We're behind the outcropping of rocks at the end of the beach. I tucked us into a shallow cave. There are other people here, so we're not alone, even though I can't see them."

"Do we have to stay here a long time?"

I blew on her face, hoping some of the sand would fly away. She shivered, though it wasn't cold tonight. "I don't know. I've never been in this situation before."

"You've never been to a party that's gotten busted?"

"I haven't. I'm not a big party person." Only when Rhys annoyed me into agreeing to go with him, which was rarer than he liked.

"I don't think I am either."

She'd never sounded so small. Her voice wobbled, and if I could have seen her, I bet her chin would have been too.

I stroked the back of her hair while wiping her other eye. "Nothing bad's going to happen to you, Luciana. I've got you, and we're safe where we are. We just have to wait out the cops, okay?"

"Do you think it'll be a long time?"

She'd just asked me that, but I answered her again anyway. This time, I lied to her. "I don't think so. We'll be on our way soon."

Her fingers dug into my arm. "Don't leave me. Please?"

"I promise you I won't."

Her shuddering breath was hot against my chest. My heart thumped a frantic beat for an entirely different reason than the danger we were in.

I finished wiping her eyes as best as I could with what I had. "Do you want to try to open your eyes now? You won't see much, but it might make you less afraid."

"Okay." She moved against me, still holding on tight to my arm. "I think—I think you got most of the sand." Then her hand slid up to my shoulder, following the path to my neck, ending at my jaw.

I leaned down, putting my face closer to hers. "Can you see me?"

"Barely," she whispered. "Enough to make me feel like I'm not alone."

"You aren't."

She went quiet for a minute, keeping her hand on my face. Her fingers spread wide, curling into the light scruff on my jaw. Digging my fingers into her hair, we were locked together, anchored to one another in what felt like an infinite black abyss.

"This is so strange, isn't it? I feel like I'm floating in space."

I exhaled a low laugh. Her thoughts were echoing mine. "Have you ever seen a sensory deprivation tank?"

Her snort was soft and breathy. "No, I haven't. Well, not in person. Think this is what it's like?" Her fingers traced the line of my jaw, from my chin back to the corner. The same place her lips had been a week ago.

"My mother has one. One of her therapists told her it would help her face her childhood trauma. I tried it once, and it freaked me out. Guess I didn't want to face *my* childhood trauma."

A shiver ran through her, and my arms tightened around her, drawing her closer. "I don't think I would like that, especially after this."

"This isn't so bad. It was being alone with nothing but my thoughts that made me panic."

"Oh, I—crap, Beckett."

"What?"

"I was with Delilah and Bella. What if they were caught? They were drinking. I don't even have my phone. They have to be worried about me too."

Letting go of her with one arm, I reached into my pocket and tugged out my phone. I took her hand from my face and placed the phone in it. "Send them a message. Tell them you're with me."

She turned the screen on, cupping it against her so the light wouldn't give us away. "You have to enter your passcode."

"It's zero six one three."

She tapped the code in, and her thumb swiped to my messages then went still. "Beckett."

I knew what was coming. "Yeah, Luciana?"

"You—" She struggled for what to say. I nudged her hand.

"Send your friends a message."

"Um. Okay." She tapped out a short message, saying she was with me, using my phone, and asking if they were safe. A reply came in within a few seconds, telling her they were with some girl named Jenny and they were fine.

Clutching my phone between us, she leaned into me. "Did you know your passcode is my birthday?"

"Yeah."

"Oh. But why?"

"I think you know." She had to, right? The fact that I'd made my passcode her birthday wasn't exactly subtle. To me, none of my attention this year had been.

"But..." If I could've seen her, would her brow have been puckered as she mulled over our every interaction? Was she rubbing her lips together like she did when she was deep in thought? "You hate me, Beckett."

"I don't." Fuck, I shouldn't have been doing this here, where I couldn't get a read on her. But there was no taking it back now that it was out there.

"How can you say that? You tried to get me expelled from school."

"No. I was *saving* you, Luc."

"What does that mean?" she pleaded lowly. "How can you believe that's what you were doing? My sister had to basically tap dance to get them to let me stay. I thought I was going to lose everything for good that time."

"I'm sorry you were afraid, but maybe you needed to have that fear."

She pushed against me, trying to create some distance between our bodies. I let her have a few inches, but no more. Since we were having this out now, I wasn't going to part from her until she understood my motives.

"That sounds insane, Beckett. If you'd been worried about me, couldn't you have just told me to be careful or something?"

I scoffed at her argument. There was no way she truly believed a conversation between the two of us would have convinced her.

"I saw you at the park that day, and I honestly didn't believe what I was seeing. After what happened freshman year, the way you hurt yourself and lost your scholarship for the year, you were still taking chances. What if you'd fallen again? You could have fucked up your wrist permanently."

"But, Beckett—"

"No, Luc, you can be mad at me all you want, but I decided to go to your coach because I didn't want you screwing yourself. You're talented as hell, but one wrong fall and it would have been gone. All that hard work, done."

"It was my decision to make."

I could almost hear her molars grinding. She was angry at me. Not hearing me. But I was telling the truth about my motivations.

"Maybe. But as an athlete, I found it personally offensive to watch you play it fast and loose with your body's wellness. You already knew what the consequences were, and you flipped them the fuck off like they didn't matter to you."

"I—" Her hands moved toward her face, and for the thousandth time in the last five minutes, I wished like hell I could see her. "I don't know how to wrap my head around this."

"I was helping you, Luc."

"I get that you think that."

Frustration swelled in my muscles to the point it was difficult to remain still.

"How do I make you understand something that makes complete sense to me?"

"I don't know. I've been under the impression you haven't wanted me to be at SA the entire time, but now—"

"It's the opposite."

She sighed so heavily I felt it on my skin. "This is a mind trip. All of tonight is. We're sitting in the pitch-black—"

"In space."

"In space. Or our sensory deprivation tank for two. Whatever. We're hiding from the freaking cops, and now you're telling me something I knew to be true for the last two years is actually all wrong? And the thing with my birthday as your passcode...I—"

I slid my hand from the back of her head to her chin, holding the stubborn little pad of it between my fingers. Before I could say anything else, there was movement nearby. Rocks tumbled, followed by several voices, then multiple flashlights.

Luciana immediately dove into my chest, tucking her head in the crook of my neck. If the circumstances were different, I would have taken the time to memorize what it felt like to have her in this position.

But I'd promised to keep her safe, and I would. I went on alert, listening to the voices, which didn't sound like cops.

Finally, I picked up on where they were coming from. Not the beach but the surrounding rocks. Then I made out what some of them were saying.

"The cops are gone," I told Luciana. "Everyone's clearing out."

She clung to me tighter. "How can they be sure?"

"Do you want to wait?"

"Um. What do you think?"

"I think we should go. I want to get you home."

· · · · · · ● · · · ·

The ride back to SA was quiet. Luciana had curled into a ball in the passenger seat, her face tucked into her hands. She'd been shivering when we got in the car, so I'd grabbed my hoodie off the back seat for her. She'd zipped it up and pulled her knees underneath.

"You okay?" I asked.

"I'm good. Really tired, though."

"Adrenaline crash. We're almost back, then you can pass out in your bed."

"Thank you."

"Anything."

She didn't understand exactly what I meant by that yet, but she would.

CHAPTER SIXTEEN
Beckett

MY ROUTINE HADN'T CHANGED, even though Luciana's had. I got to the track early every morning, getting in my miles before my team showed up for conditioning. It was a habit I'd taken from Luc, and it was a good one.

I was only half surprised to find her on the track Monday morning after a week's absence. She didn't slow for me to catch up, and I gave her space for a lap or two. Then I picked up my pace to meet up with hers.

Like a magnet, my hand went right to her ponytail and tugged. "You decided not to be lazy this morning?"

"If you're going to insist on running next to me, can you try to not be an ass?"

"I make no promises."

She huffed. "Of course not."

After a minute, I tugged her ponytail again. "I didn't see you yesterday."

"I didn't really leave my room. The whole thing Saturday night took a lot out of me, I guess."

I believed that, but I was pretty sure she was also avoiding me, as she had a tendency to do. But I had plans and pressing her wasn't part of them. Luciana was skittish. If I went after her too hard, she'd bolt.

This was the long game I was playing.

"How did you know where I was?" she asked.

"Felix. He mentioned you'd invited Isla to a bonfire."

"And you showed up."

"Bad things are known to happen at bonfires."

"You came to protect me."

I didn't feel the need to confirm that. We both knew why I'd shown up that night.

"Are you okay?" I asked after a minute or two.

"I'm fine, but I feel pretty stupid for nearly getting arrested the first time I broke the rules. I guess I'm a good girl for life."

"Nothing wrong with that."

Her brow winged. "Says the boy rules don't apply to."

"Why do you think that? Have I given you the impression I'm out pillaging every weekend?"

"I don't know, Beckett. I don't have a clear impression of you, but I do know what money can erase. If you had gotten in trouble, it wouldn't have lasted for long."

I grunted, insulted, even though she wasn't wrong.

"You're right that you don't know me well."

"I know."

"You should, though. You'd like me."

She laughed, too surprised to hold it back. "Are you ever not blunt?"

"Never." I tugged her ponytail again, keeping it in my grip instead of letting go. "Are you coming to my party this weekend?"

"I'm thinking about it."

"I want you to."

"I don't know if I'm fancy enough to enter the Savage estate."

"You're not. I don't think I am either. Anyway, my mother's party is in the house. Mine is by the pool."

"And never the twain shall meet?" she quipped.

I chuckled. "Dr. Burns would be fucking thrilled you casually quoted Kipling."

"I'll be sure to mention it if I need extra credit."

I slid my fist down to the end of her ponytail. "Come."

"I'll think about it."

"Don't let me down on my birthday."

"Saturday isn't your real birthday."

I almost stopped running. "You know when my birthday is?"

Her lips rolled over her teeth, and she shook her head. "No. Um...I just know for...reasons. Forget it."

"Reasons that have nothing to do with being obsessed with me?"

She snorted. "Yes, very different reasons."

"I won't try to pry it out of you if you agree to come to my party."

She made me wait, sighing long and heavily. "Fine. But you better not get me arrested."

I held up my hands. "That was all you, bad girl."

That earned me a smile. "Shut up, Savage."

"Anything, Ortega."

· · · ● ● · ● · · ·

Rhys let himself into my room, eyeing everything inside of it with disdain. "How can you stand to live in this shit can?"

"Aw, it's *my* shit can. Nobody talks about my baby that way except me."

Since I was sitting at my desk, he parked himself on my bed, his back against the headboard, his feet stretched out in front of him. Fortunately for him, he'd kicked off his shoes first, or his face would have met the ground when I threw him off my bed.

"What's happening with you, Beck? You keep disappearing on me lately."

I shrugged. Out of anyone, Rhys was the person I shared the most with. He might've been an asshole, but he was a loyal one.

"A shrug? That's all I get? Where did you wander off to this weekend? I know you didn't go home since I wasn't treated to a rundown of Gretchen's latest procedures and how big of a douche Josh is."

I shot him a sharp look. "I'll be sure to keep my repetitive complaints to myself."

"You misunderstand me, you overly sensitive twat. You complaining about your parents is like a comfort meal to me. Knowing Josh and Gretchen are up to their same old antics means the world is still on its axis, even if it feels like it's falling apart."

My eyes narrowed. "I don't know how to take that."

He heaved a sigh. "You know feelings disgust me, Beck. But if you insist on me putting aside my toxic masculinity to stroke your fragile little heart, I will because I'm a great friend. My ear is always open to you, all right?"

I cringed. "Put your toxic masculinity back on. Sensitive you is alarming."

He rolled his eyes. "I tried to tell you this, but you insisted."

"I made a mistake."

Relaxing back into my pillows, he put his hands behind his head. "So, tell me where you were if not with Gretch and Joshy."

Rhys wouldn't leave if I didn't give him a real answer. He'd take up residence in my shit can of a room until he died from starvation. Since I had no desire to share a room with his rotting carcass, I gave him something to chew on.

"I went to a bonfire."

His brow furrowed for less than a second before he jackknifed upright and clapped his hands.

"You fucking followed her, didn't you? I knew it! I *knew* it. The second Felix mentioned that bonfire, I saw your mind working." He was smug, running a hand through his hair. "You're not going to leave me hanging now, Beck. Tell me the rest of it."

"I got there right before the cops showed up. There was weed and booze everywhere. It could've gone bad for her."

"If not for her white knight."

"She doesn't see me that way, but she trusted me to keep her safe. We had to hide out for a while before we could leave, and we talked. She thought I hated her all this time."

He cackled. "Why would she ever think that?"

"Because, according to her, I tried to get her expelled."

He cackled even harder. "You poor fucker. No wonder she hasn't looked at you a single time since she started going to school here. Did you get her to listen to you?"

"I don't know how much got through. I was careful with how much I said."

That made him shake his head at me. Rhys didn't agree with how I was handling Luciana. He never had. But he'd always been a bull in a china shop, charging in and fucking shit up when he wanted something. He didn't have the patience I did.

"I will never understand you, Savage."

"You don't have to. I know what I'm doing and that's all that really matters to me."

"There are girls who would fall on their knees for you at the snap of your fingers. You know that, don't you?"

"I do know that." My nostrils flared. "But why in the hell would I want that? They'd do the same for half the seniors here. There would be no meaning behind it."

"The meaning would be having your dick sucked in a consensual act." He noticed my flinch, but since he *did* know me well, he didn't acknowledge it. "Fuck. Forget that. All I'm saying is, things could be a lot easier. You don't have to choose the most difficult path, though I know you love a challenge."

"Easy paths are boring."

He waggled his pale brows. "But fun. Especially when they bring a friend."

"Fuck off, Rhys. Be supportive or get out."

He swung his legs over the side of the bed and steepled his fingers. "I support *you*. That doesn't mean I'll blindly follow you around, jerking your dick, telling you what a good boy you are. I'm not a 'yes' man. I'm going to ask questions and make sure you're not setting yourself up to fail."

"That's your version of support?"

"It is. Take it or leave it."

"And if I left it?"

"I'd haunt your dreams until you came back for me. I'm your herpes. Never getting rid of me."

"You should write greeting cards."

"This is why we're friends. I offer you advice on your paltry love life, you pay me back by setting me on my future career path. It's symbiotic." He got up and patted my shoulder. "In all seriousness, I do care. I want you to be sure the challenge of Luciana is worth the reality of her."

"I appreciate your concern."

"But it's going in one ear and out the other?"

My jaw was set tight. "I know what I'm doing."

His sigh was heavy. "I really hope that's true."

CHAPTER SEVENTEEN

Luciana

BEFORE ARRIVING AT SAVAGE Manor, as I had started referring to it in my head, I had an idea of what it would be like. Massive, sprawling, intimidating. It was all those things, but the reality of the enormous wealth Beckett came from was a bucket of cold water on my head.

Sobering.

Especially in contrast to the places I'd lived in most of my life.

What must it have been like to have *this*?

I was no architect, but I knew the square footage of Helen and Theo's new house, so I could guess how big this one was.

"Holy shit," Bella breathed in my ear. "This is bigger than my house by double."

She came from Texas, so that was saying something.

Delilah didn't say a word. I had a feeling this ostentatious display of wealth was something she was used to.

Our limo came to a stop, and my stomach lurched. We were running late because Bella had insisted on squeezing her D-cup boobs into one of my dresses. Since my boobs were half the size of hers, Delilah and I had to shove and smash and tape to make the dress fit. The result was hot, though, so the effort had been worth it.

The door beside me was opened by a white-haired gentleman in a tuxedo. He held his hand out, helping each of us out of the car, and directed us to the path on the side of the house.

Candles and twinkling fairy lights illuminated the way. Bursts of flowers in SA's colors—white and burgundy—sprayed out of hip-height vases every few feet.

"I still can't believe Beckett sent us a limo," Bella whispered.

"I'm sure it was his mother." When you had money like this, you could hire cars to drive all your son's school friends to his party. "I'm glad I didn't have to drive my car here, though. The pavement would have ejected my tires as soon as they'd tried to roll down the driveway."

Delilah giggled. "Do you know how many people would invest in that product if it were real?"

I smoothed a hand over my stomach. "I don't want to think about it."

Music and voices filtered through the air. Nerves bit at my insides. Something told me the crowd wasn't going to be comprised of my favorite people. Almost none of the field hockey team had been invited. I supposed I was lucky to have Delilah and Bella with me. Then again, I never would have come on my own.

I still wasn't sure why I'd agreed to come at all.

We rounded the house, and the path opened to a sprawling stone patio flanked by a glittering pool with votives floating on the surface.

"I thought there would be a lot more people here," Bella remarked as we looked around.

"Me too," I agreed.

Waiters carrying trays with canapés wove through the small, well-dressed crowd. If I had to estimate, I would have said there were fifty people here. The soccer team comprised a good number, but there were the usual suspects as well, like Bianca DeSoto and her friends.

Beckett's crowd—not mine.

The fact that many of them were gathered around a bar that appeared to be serving real alcohol separated us even further. In this case, it wasn't about wealth. It was how this world treated their children. I may have been eighteen, but Theo and Helen would have laughed in my face if I'd suggested having alcohol at one of my parties. I was a kid. Their responsibility. If I wanted to drink, I'd have to sneak it like every other kid my age.

In my world, at least.

I spotted Beckett leaning an elbow on the corner of the bar, nodding at something Rhys said. Charles was nearby, hulking over them as usual, while Felix threw back a shot.

"Shall we find a drink?" Delilah asked.

"Hell yeah." Bella shimmied her shoulders a little. "I can barely breathe, so I'm gonna need a drop or two of alcohol to loosen my lungs."

I puffed out a breath. I really didn't want to go to the bar, but I couldn't exactly deny my girls. This was a party, after all—one I'd dragged them to. "When in Rome, I suppose."

As if called upon by fate, a waiter passed with a tray full of champagne. The three of us grabbed glasses, and I was relieved not to have to stand in line at the bar and fake my way through ordering.

We trailed along the patio together, pausing at the game area. There was a Ping-Pong table and foosball. I wondered if Beckett played. I couldn't picture him being carefree enough to enjoy something like that.

I spun one of the handles on the foosball table. "Want to play?"

Bella stepped up to the other side. "Our teams are uneven. We need Ev here to make it fair."

Evelyn would have rather munched on rocks than show up at an event like this. Tonight, she was blissfully spending time in her favorite study cube in the library.

Delilah frowned at the game. "I don't think Ev or I would be proper teammates. I've never played."

"Then you should be on Bella's team since you barely count as a player," I quipped.

Delilah arched a brow. "That sounds like a challenge, and I'm competitive enough to take it."

But before we could get started, a shadow fell across the table. I jerked my attention to Beckett, who was backlit by the fairy lights strung from posts across the patio and yard.

His eyes were on me. "Hello." Then he nodded to Bella and Delilah. "Thank you for coming. I was beginning to think you weren't showing."

Bella raised her hand. "It's my fault. I was havin' wardrobe issues."

He gave her a sweeping once-over. "You look nice."

"Thank you." She visibly perked up, her spine straightening. "This is Luciana's dress. None of mine were workin'."

"That must be why I like it," he intoned, flicking his gaze back to me. "I don't think I've ever seen you in a dress. It's surprising you own more than one."

My hand fluttered to my chest, which was more bare than I was used to due to my dress's sweetheart neckline. Since I spent a lot of time running around in a tiny field hockey skirt, I had no problem with the short hemline, but being this exposed all over was new for me.

"I do." I grinned sheepishly. "Two, to be exact."

The corners of his lips tipped as he raked his eyes over me. I'd worn my hair down, done in soft curls by Delilah, red gloss on my mouth to match the hue of my dress, and heels on my feet added height to my short frame.

"You're lovely." He said it so low I knew it was just for me, even though there was no way Bella and Delilah hadn't heard.

"Thank you, Beckett. You look really nice too."

At school, he was always in his uniform, so wearing a collared shirt and slacks wasn't a new look for him, but this version was entirely different.

He wore navy cigarette pants that fit the line of his muscular legs like they'd been made for him—and maybe they had. On top, his light-blue button-down was open at the collar, the sleeves rolled up to his elbows, but his vest, which matched his trousers, was buttoned to midtorso.

He looked more than nice. This was slick, hot, sexy. Older than his age. Mature and serious, yet still casual enough, he didn't look like a kid playing dress-up.

I received another quirk of his lips. Almost a smile, but not quite.

"Thank you, Ortega." He nodded toward the table. "Do you need a teammate?"

Delilah patted Bella. "I'm so sorry."

Beckett turned to them. "Why are you sorry?"

She brought her champagne to her mouth. "Poor Bells is stuck with me, who's never played, and Luc gets you, who has certainly played often."

Beckett slapped one of the handles, sending it spinning. "I used to, but if it makes you feel any better, it's been a long time. I'm rusty."

His arm brushed mine, and warmth emanated from the contact. I sucked in a breath and glanced up at him, unsurprised to find his gaze already on me.

"I haven't played in years either," I admitted.

The corners of his clear eyes crinkled. "Somehow, I really doubt you'll be bad at this game."

Bella made a sort of strangled sound that shredded the strangely intense moment. I looked away from Beckett in time to see Delilah's elbow connecting with Bella's bicep.

My friends knew all that had happened at the bonfire—except his passcode. I'd wanted to keep that clutched close to my heart, only for me—and they were seeing in real time that maybe my feelings hadn't crashed and burned as hard as I'd thought they had. All three of us were getting front-row seats to what it looked like when Beckett Savage stopped disguising his own feelings.

It was heady and intimidating. I had no idea what was to come, nor did I really know how far his infatuation with me went, but it was impossible not to want to linger in the center of his attention.

I grinned at my girls. "Let's play."

· · · ◆ · ◆ · · · ·

Three games later, Delilah had been replaced by Charles—he'd insisted—who took foosball as seriously as football. And he was an outright monster on the football field.

Sweat beaded my forehead, and during a time-out, Beckett had produced a hair tie from his pocket for me to pull my hair back in a ponytail.

I slapped the handle hard, sending the ball straight past Bella and Charles's goalie.

"Oh, come on!" Charles yelled, his fury intense despite having absolutely zero stakes in the game. "That's bullshit."

"You're the goalie, doofus," Bella argued. "It was your job to stop it."

He glared at her. "Switch sides. See if you can do better."

Beckett chuckled, his hand gripping my nape. "Having fun yet?"

I laughed past the goose bumps fanning out from where he was touching me. "I absolutely am. Although, I should apologize to Delilah. She spent an hour on my hair, and I think I sweated all the curls out."

He slid his palm under my ponytail. "I like how hard you play."

"I'm just lucky you had a ponytail holder."

"Not luck, little light. I've been carrying it since I was thirteen. I'm going to want it back when the night's over."

I swallowed. He'd called me 'little light,' and it wasn't the first time. I'd noticed then, but this time, it really sank in.

"That's a long time to carry a ponytail holder."

I wanted more information, but he just gave me one of his enigmatic, almost smiles and turned back to the game.

A crowd had gathered. More than a crowd. Most of the party had migrated to surround the table. They'd chosen sides. Charles and Bella were understandably the underdogs. Most of the cheers were for Beckett and me by association.

Charles cursed and spit, hitting the handles so hard I thought they were going to snap off. Bella and I kept exchanging glances across the table. I felt bad she'd been teamed up with him, but this was our final game. The poor girl could get away from him in a couple minutes.

Charles glared at Beckett. "Don't think I'm going to let you win just because it's your party."

Beckett cocked his head. "Do you think I want you to go easy? Give it all you've got. That way, I can gloat when we win."

Rhys groaned from the sectional nearby. "Oh god, do you have to be so dramatic? You're playing an actual children's game."

"Shut up, Astor," Charles growled. "Let's play."

We went after each other hard. Bella and I trash-talked—good-naturedly—while Charles devolved into a snarling, sweaty beast. Beckett was all silent concentration, slapping back against every one of Charles's and Bella's moves.

He was a freaking boss at foosball. If this was him out of practice, he'd probably be a world champion if he devoted time to honing his skill.

And why did that make me like him more?

Helen once told me how attractive she found it when Theo did *things* like fixing broken appliances or putting together furniture with ease. His competence made her want to jump on him—those weren't her words, but I'd read between the lines.

I understood what she meant now.

Beckett slammed down on a handle, shooting the ball like a rocket straight past all the other team's players into the small goal.

"Fuck yeah," he gritted out, then turned to me. My eyes rounded.

"We did it!" I exclaimed.

"Hell yes we did."

Victory bubbled under my skin, and I leaped at him. He caught me easily, spinning me in a tight circle. My arms clasped around his neck, and I threw my head back, laughing.

"We did it!" I yelled.

Charles was losing his mind, spouting expletives in the background of our celebration. His fury brought me down to earth. We weren't alone. My dress was riding high up the back of my thighs, and if Beckett didn't put me down, my ass was going to be on display for a good portion of my classmates.

I patted his chest. "Hey, can you put me down?"

His arms tightened around my waist. "Not yet." Our chests were flush, so close together, I couldn't tell if the throbbing beat of a heart was mine or his.

He made me nervous. I had never been in this position with anyone else, much less where everyone could see us. Though I noticed for the first time Beckett had moved us off the patio into the grass.

I kicked my dangling feet. "My dress, it's slipping, and—"

He didn't wait for me to finish before turning me away from where everyone was hanging out. Slowly, carefully, he slid his hand down my back. His eyes were locked on mine as he continued past the curve of my waist, lightly grazing my butt. My breath caught, but he didn't linger there, moving on to where the hemline of my dress was rucked up just below it. The tips of his fingers teased my exposed skin, then his chest rumbled.

"Sorry, Ortega," he grunted, gently setting me on my feet. His fingers hooked the bottom of my dress, tugging it back to where it was supposed to be. "Better?"

"Yes. Thank you." I backed up a step and smoothed my hands over my dress. "Sorry for jumping on you. It's a habit from—"

"You shouldn't be sorry for that. You have to know I liked it."

I did know that. While he held me, I felt how much he liked it pressed against my belly. I might have been naive and inexperienced, but I knew I'd made him hard.

"Beckett!" Rhys's voice cracked between us. I jumped back, even though we hadn't been touching, and Beckett scowled.

"What?" he yelled back without turning away from me.

"Your dear sweet mother would like your presence on the patio. It's time for the birthday boy to blow out his candles."

I laughed at Beckett's disgruntled expression. "Cake," I said. "You can't be mad about cake."

"It isn't the cake I'm mad about." With a sigh, he held out his hand. "Come on. Your heels have to be sinking in the grass. Let me help you."

I slipped my hand in his, and he pulled me to his side. Though my heels were sinking slightly, it felt like an excuse, especially when he wove his fingers between mine.

It lasted maybe thirty seconds, and I hadn't wrapped my head around how I felt about it before we were separated again. Beckett going toward his beautiful mother beside his elaborate cake, me huddling with Delilah and Bella, softly singing "Happy Birthday" with the rest of the guests.

"You were holdin' hands," Bella whispered.

I sighed. "I know."

"What do you think that means?"

"I have no idea."

CHAPTER EIGHTEEN
Luciana

BELLA, DELILAH, AND I ate cake, sipped champagne, and dangled our feet in the pool. I reminded Delilah she still owed me swim lessons, and she promised to teach me when the season ended.

We were having a good time because we always had a good time together, no matter where we were.

When I snuck peeks at Beckett, I couldn't really get a read on what kind of time he was having. He was never alone, that was for sure. His boys were around when they weren't flirting with anyone in a dress. Bianca approached him once, lingering for a moment before she propped herself up nearby.

I wondered if he'd let her wrap her lips around his dick tonight. She was dead sexy, without a doubt, and her sights were definitely aimed at him. Beckett was his usual aloof self, but that probably only made him more attractive to her.

A sour taste in my mouth made me queasy at the thought of them together. I hoped I was long gone if a hookup between them happened. I had no desire to witness that for many reasons.

Bella patted my arm. "Let's have one more glass of champagne and dance."

"I'm already tipsy," I protested. "I don't want to be hammered."

Delilah stroked my ponytail. "Oh, precious. Three glasses of champagne spread out over an evening won't get you hammered, I promise."

"You're patronizing me."

She winked in a way only Delilah could, appearing cool and un-bothered instead of cheesy. "A little, but only because I love you."

They tugged me toward a waiter, and we plucked flutes of cham-pagne from her tray. There wasn't really a dance floor, but there *was* music, so we made our own, drinking and moving to the beat.

While we'd been dipping our feet in the pool, the vibe had changed around the sectional on the patio. Random people were kissing each other, and it took me a minute to understand they were playing Spin the Bottle, except with an app on someone's phone.

Seeing Charles shove his tongue down the throat of a junior girl made me gag.

"That is disgusting." My fingers pressed against my lips as I swal-lowed and darted my gaze away. I landed on Beckett, who was watching me and laughing.

I shook my head and rolled my eyes, then I mouthed, "Disgust-ing."

He bowed his head, his whole face lit up by his wide grin. I couldn't remember a time I'd seen him that free with his happiness. He should've practiced more. It looked delicious on him.

Bella took my hand, spinning me in a dizzying circle. The cham-pagne had definitely gone to my head, thinking of Beckett as deli-cious. That so wasn't like me.

Laughter bubbled out of me as we danced. Delilah curved her arm around my shoulders, and Bella stayed latched on to my hand. We swayed and sang along to the music, ignoring the game playing out only a few feet away.

Except I couldn't stop myself from sneaking peeks at Beckett, and every time I did, he was watching me, his lips curved with pleasure. He seemed relaxed, arms thrown over the back of the cushions. I hadn't seen him take a sip of alcohol tonight, but I'd probably missed it. No way he'd become that laid-back naturally. Not Beckett.

"This isn't as terrible as I expected it to be," Delilah said.

Bella held up her half-full glass. "That's because we make our own good time wherever we go. It's us."

Wisps of my hair that had escaped my ponytail tickled my cheeks and nose. I brushed them aside, but a slight breeze set them loose again.

"We had fun earlier though, right?" My brows rose. "With Beckett?"

Bella squeezed my hand. "*You* had fun with Beckett."

"I—" I couldn't speak. My gaze had flitted back to him just as Bianca crawled over him and planted her mouth on his.

Time stood still. My heart stopped beating. Music was replaced by static roaring in my ears.

And then Beckett erupted.

Shooting to his feet, he practically threw Bianca off him with a roar. She landed sprawled on her back on top of a pile of plush cushions on the ground.

The next moment, Beckett was standing over her, his hands clenching into fists. *Open, close, open, close.* Rhys was at his back. Charles was nearby. But I didn't think he noticed them. His focus was on Bianca, who was trying to sit up and scoot away at the same time.

"Fucking cunt." Beckett spat on the ground in front of her, maybe on her. It was hard to tell, except that she flinched. Each time she moved, he followed her, looming and glaring, his nostrils flaring like a raging bull.

"You're done here. Pack your bags. You won't be staying long." His tone was flat, and if he weren't locked and loaded, I would have believed he didn't give a damn. But he was close to exploding. All he needed was a little spark.

"Come on. Back up." Rhys squeezed his shoulder, putting pressure on it.

"Who invited this cunt to my party?" Beckett's head whipped around, swinging his pointed finger at his guests. "I find out who brought her here, they're done too. Pack up, motherfucker."

"*Beckett.* Ease up," Rhys pleaded. "Not now."

Beckett shrugged him off. "No, I want to know why this bitch thought she could come here. She knows what she did. And not only did she come here, after every-fucking-thing, she dared to put her mouth on me." He threw his arms up, and his voice cracked with rage.

I had no idea how I knew it, but I was certain he needed me right now. Without thinking about my actions, I kicked off my shoes and took off at a run straight for Beckett.

Jumping over the back of the sectional, I landed on a cushion and climbed to my feet. I was behind him, afraid to touch him or sneak up on him and spook him.

"Beckett."

He whirled around, ready to fight. His jaw was tight, but his fists were even tighter. My heart was a hummingbird trapped in my chest. When he found me standing on the couch a foot behind him, he closed the distance in a second, his arms banding around me. Lifting me off my feet, he strode off the patio, holding me against his chest, passing everyone without uttering a single word.

Beyond the pool was a small guesthouse. Beckett punched in a code and let us in, then he kicked the door shut with so much force something cracked.

His chest heaved, his exhales hot on the side of my neck. On instinct, I smoothed my hands down the sides of his neck, sliding to his nape and back again.

"You can put me down. I'm not going anywhere," I whispered.

He grunted, holding me tighter.

"Want to talk about it?" I tried.

"Not really."

"You don't want to tell me why you're so mad? It was a game, right? Everyone was playing."

His chest vibrated against mine. "I wasn't playing."

I didn't understand his reaction. He'd hooked up with Bianca before. Why was he so furious she'd kissed him tonight? It didn't make sense.

But just because I didn't understand didn't mean I couldn't comfort him when he was so clearly upset. Slowly, as I rubbed his shoulders and made soft shushing noises like Helen did with Madelina,

Beckett eased me to the ground. Once I was on my feet, I kept my hands on his shoulders, showing him I wasn't going anywhere.

He peered down at me, and I was surprised to see a deep sadness had overtaken his rage. It absolutely pummeled me.

"Oh, Beckett. Tell me why you're so upset. *Please*."

His hands traveled over my arms, dragging up my shoulders to the back of my head. Sliding the ponytail holder out, he let my hair spill around my shoulders. He slipped the band back in his pocket and cupped my cheeks. "She is the last person I wanted to kiss tonight."

I licked my parched lips, racking my mind for the right thing to say. "Well, did you kiss her?"

His head canted to the side. "You saw what happened."

"I saw her put her mouth on yours, but did you *kiss* her?"

His lips parted, and the divot between his brows deepened. "I—" He shook his head. "No. I pushed her off me as fast as I could."

"Then you didn't kiss her, Beckett." My fingers delved into the back of his hair, scratching lightly at his scalp. He shuddered, his eyes closing. We stood like that for a while, him holding my face while I soothed him. A question beat at my mind, and finally, I had to ask. "Who's the first person you wanted to kiss tonight?"

His eyes opened and locked on mine. "I think you know, Luciana."

Yeah, I did.

"Do you want to kiss me?"

His head dipped. "I do."

When he didn't move, I realized he was waiting for my invitation. And even though it wasn't smart, went against all my convictions for myself, I desperately wanted to be kissed by Beckett Savage. "Will you please kiss me, Beckett?"

His lids fell to half-mast, and the fingers on my cheeks flexed. "Yes," he rasped.

The first touch of his lips to mine was soft, barely more than a graze, but it made me whimper and grasp his shirt in my fist so I wouldn't fall. He pressed his lips to mine again, so warm and sweet my toes curled against the tile floor.

"Beckett," I sighed into his mouth. "More."

I parted my lips, then he parted his, slotting us together. His movements were slow and searching, so unlike what I expected. His gentle, careful kisses were making me ache all over. Even the backs of my eyes burned. If he kept this up, he'd be tasting my tears.

I would never have thought Beckett Savage could kiss this way. Before his mouth had touched mine, I hadn't known this level of tenderness could be directed at me.

The sweep of his tongue across my lips made my knees weak. Beckett's hand slid from my face down to the center of my back, holding me close. I wrapped my arms around him, drawing myself even closer.

My tongue met his, drawing him into my mouth. His groan traveled down my throat, spread through my overstuffed lungs, and settled in my core. Awareness of the heat pooling there tingled in the back of my mind, but my main focus was on this kiss.

Was it one kiss or a thousand? Even when our lips parted, Beckett's remained on me, kissing around my lips, my chin, the divot under my nose, then the tip. He only let seconds pass before he covered my mouth with his again, giving my tongue soft, sliding licks until I mewled like a little kitten.

My sounds seemed to spur Beckett on. Chest rumbling, he dug his fingers into my hair, tipping my face back even farther. His tongue slipped deeper into my mouth, lapping at the back of my teeth, tasting me everywhere. He was meticulous, so unlike the sloppy, rushed kisses that had come before him. I barely remembered those anymore. After this night, Beckett's mouth would be the shining star in my mind.

We parted, both of us breathless. His forehead rolled against mine. He stroked through my hair and ran the tips of his fingers up and down my spine.

"I knew it," he murmured.

"That it would be good?"

His soft laugh was a hot breath across my swollen lips. "I hoped like hell it would be good. That was better than anything I could have imagined, though."

I tipped my head back, still foggy from having the daylights kissed out of me. He peered down at me, the corners of his mouth curved into a smirk. Something about his expression made me feel strange.

"You look pleased with yourself." I unraveled my arms to brace my hands over his heart, which was much calmer than mine.

"I am, Luciana." His head fell back, and he released a long, victorious sigh at the ceiling. "I knew this would happen."

"What?"

"I knew you'd ask for me to kiss you if I stayed persistent." He grinned at me, his hands dropping away to drag over his face. "I didn't think it would happen this soon, but I'm not mad about it."

I was thrown back to the dining hall when my friends informed me the boys at Savage Academy viewed me as a challenge. A sickening feeling crashed into me.

He rocked back on his heels, so very pleased with himself. "I told you you'd ask. I think I should be rewarded for being right." He held a hand out to me, and it was only then I realized I'd taken a few steps back. "Come here, little light. This time, I'll ask you."

My back hit the door, knocking a breath out of me. "You—you stayed persistent?"

"Don't you remember? When we met, I told you you'd ask me to kiss you one day. And I was right."

God, this was worse than I thought.

"Was I a challenge?" I hated how wobbly I sounded, but he'd affected me, and I couldn't hide it.

Some of his mirth dropped away, and he spoke to me like a skittish baby animal. "Come on. I like you, but you have to admit, you're not easy to know." He raised a brow, his smile coming back. "But I got in there, didn't I?"

The burning in the back of my eyes came back in full force. Only this time, the tears that threatened were due to the realization of how big of a fool I was. I'd never been this angry at myself. I let myself have feelings for this boy, feelings that went in contradiction to my convictions and goals, and look where it had gotten me.

"I can't believe you." I fumbled for the door behind me. "You're as bad as the rest of them. Just—leave me alone."

I flung the door open, retreating into the night. Beckett looked stunned, his eyes wide, the rest of him frozen.

Seeing him surprised I would want to leave after he'd ruined the most perfect, beautiful moment of my life only made me angrier.

"You should go find Bianca," I hissed. "The two of you are a perfect match."

Then I ran. Beckett cried out my name, and if I hadn't already hardened myself toward him, I would have said he'd cried it in anguish. But that was just another ploy to get me back there. He hadn't yet achieved the ultimate prize by fucking me.

He'd just fucked me over.

Delilah and Bella were waiting for me. They didn't ask questions. One look at me, and they were surrounding me, hustling me to the limo.

Only when we were inside with the doors locked, driving away from Savage Manor, did I let the tears fall. My friends gave me the time and space to be sad, and I was so grateful for it. I didn't have the strength to recount what had happened in those lost minutes inside the guesthouse.

When we arrived at the dorm, I headed to my room. Delilah followed me, stopping me with a soft touch on my shoulder.

"I'll let you process, precious, but I need to know one thing. Did he hurt you?"

I nodded, pressing against my sternum.

"My heart. He hurt my heart."

Chapter Nineteen

Beckett

Age 13

JULIEN'S FRIEND HELEN SOUNDED like she was underwater. She told me her sister's name was Luciana. Luc for short. She was my age. We should talk.

I would have talked, but the only thing I seemed capable of doing was staring. My brain was misfiring, and I couldn't really compute what I was seeing.

The girl in front of me was scruffy. Poorly dressed. Almost certainly wearing used men's trousers she'd cut off at the knees. Her head barely came up to my chest, and her orange Adidas T-shirt hung off her like a curtain.

She was, without a doubt, the most beautiful girl I had ever seen.

Her face was golden perfection. She smiled at me, and all of her lit up. She even bounced on her toes when she said hello. One of her front teeth was slightly crooked, but it didn't take anything away from her perfection.

Her dark-brown hair was pulled back into a ponytail on top of her head, revealing ears that were softly pointed at the tips. My friend Rhys would have wet his pants over that feature. He'd been obsessed with *Lord of the Rings* since fourth grade, though he was starting to pretend like it had been a phase.

The idea of Rhys seeing this girl made my hands ball into fists.

Luciana stood beside me, facing the drummers preparing to play. She tipped her face up to me, and the sun caught on her eyes. I'd thought they were black at first, but in the light, they almost looked like marbles. Shades of brown swirled around burnt amber.

"What grade are you in?" she asked.

Oh crap. Did she see me staring?

"Almost in eighth." That was all I could force out. Girls didn't make me nervous, but that was because I had never cared how they saw me.

She smiled again, and it punched me in the gut with its force. "Same."

Why am I reacting like this? She's going to think I'm an idiot.

Her slanted black eyebrows pinched. "Do you play any sports?"

This was my chance. Something I was good at. Maybe I could get her to come to one of my games.

"Soccer."

Holy crap, what was wrong with me? My thoughts weren't reaching my mouth.

"I mainly skateboard, but recently got recruited to play field hockey. It's weird, playing a sport in a skirt, but it's kind of fun."

Instantly, my brain was taken over by the image of Luciana running down a field in a little plaid skirt. Then it slipped to her on a skateboard, the breeze picking up her hair as she flew around a skate park.

When I finally forced myself back to reality, the drums had started, and I'd completely lost her attention.

· · · • • · • • · · ·

It was rare for things I *really* wanted to go my way. Sure, I was given anything I asked for, but there were things I knew not to ask for, my parents' time and attention being the biggest. I never would have asked for Luciana to hang out with me back at her sister's house, but she was.

While my brother and his friends hung around each other, Luc and I were on the deck.

I couldn't stop looking at her. Her cheeks were rosy from the day in the sun, and a few wisps of hair had escaped her ponytail.

She turned her head, finding me staring, and sighed.

"When's your birthday?" she asked.

"September." *When's yours?* The question wouldn't come out, no matter how hard I tried to force it.

She made a cute little face. "I'm older than you. Mine's in June."

She was almost fourteen. I was used to being the oldest in my class since my birthday was right after the cutoff date.

"Did you get held back or something?"

Curiosity had overridden my broken tongue, but the words that finally came out weren't what I meant to say. From her sour expression, she wasn't much of a fan of me.

"No. My dad forgot I was supposed to start kindergarten when I turned five, so I didn't go until I was six. That's the beginning of my villain origin story."

I was too stuck in my head to really hear her. She rolled her eyes, so I guessed I'd missed an important social cue. This was a disaster.

"I've never seen eyes as blue as yours," she remarked.

I shrugged off her comment. They were my dad's eyes, and since he was a POS, I hated being complimented on them. Besides, Luciana's eyes were far more interesting.

"They're better than plain brown, I guess." Like my mom's. Gretchen tried to make up for her mud-brown eyes and tepid looks with heavy makeup and plastic surgery.

Your eyes contain a galaxy, Luciana.

Luciana excused herself to grab a drink inside. I tried to play it cool, but a minute later, I followed her. My cool had gone out the window the second I met her.

She was drinking a Sprite. For the most part, I avoided soda, but I grabbed a Sprite from the fridge and cracked it open. I had the urge to fill my mouth with the flavor on her tongue.

I propped myself against the counter opposite her. Her hair was down now, spilling heavily over her shoulders. I could barely breathe.

She'd been texting when I'd walked in but put her phone down on the counter beside her discarded ponytail holder and sipped her soda.

"Where are you going to high school?" I asked.

The chances were low she'd be attending Savage Academy, but I held my breath waiting for her answer.

"Savage River High. You?"

Dammit.

"Savage Academy." I grimaced, waiting for her judgment. It was a rich kid's school and had a reputation for educating the coddled children of the wealthy. "It's where my dad went."

"That's nice." She didn't sound like she meant it.

"Why do you say that?"

"I guess I'm just being polite." That made more sense. Through all my bumbling, Luciana had been unfailingly polite.

"It's a shame you have to go to public school. The field hockey team is really good at Savage Academy."

What if she got a scholarship? Then I would see her every day. I could show her how popular I was. When she saw the way other kids treated me, how they all wanted to know me and say they were my friend, she'd like me better.

"I think Savage Academy is above my price range," she quipped.

I nodded. It was out of most people's price range. "Probably."

She laughed, but it was dry and kind of caustic. "Oh my god, what's your deal? Why are you being so rude to me? Do I stink or something?"

I was completely taken aback. Nothing had come out right, but I'd been hoping she'd get that I was nervous. Guess not.

I put my soda down on the counter and leaned forward, breathing in her hair and warm skin.

"You smell like you've been outside all day."

Like sunshine and fresh air. Pure and delicious. I had to stop myself from smelling her again.

"Good. I hope I'm so smelly, you stay far, far away from me," she retorted.

I winced at how harsh she sounded. I hadn't expected that from her. "You have an attitude."

"Not really. Only when provoked. I've been nice to you all day, you know."

Yeah, she had. I'd never met anyone as nice and friendly as Luciana. She must've had friends coming out of her ears. There was no way she wasn't the most popular girl in her school.

"Do people like you?"

She folded her arms over her chest. "I've never done a survey or anything, but yeah, I have friends."

A thought occurred to me, and panic swarmed my chest and gut. "A boyfriend?"

She raised her chin. "That's none of your business."

Relief made me sigh. "You don't."

"How would you know?"

If she had one, she would have said. Maybe she didn't want a boyfriend. Maybe she wasn't allowed to have one yet. That was probably it. I bet she came from a strict household.

"I bet you've never been kissed."

I hadn't had my first kiss yet. Girls were interested, but I wasn't, at least until now. I was very interested in everything about Luciana.

"What's it to you?" She sounded defensive, so I guessed I was still getting this all wrong. I wondered if she felt like she was behind. Had all her friends already had their first kiss? A lot of mine had. That was why Rhys hid his *Lord of the Rings* fanaticism. Girls didn't go for guys who liked to LARP as elves on the weekend.

"If you want to get it over with, I'll kiss you," I offered.

Her mouth gaped. "Are you kidding me?"

Stupid. She seemed absolutely horrified at the idea of kissing me.

"No. I don't normally make jokes."

"I've figured that out. I'm not kissing you."

"You should."

We can learn together. I'll be nice. I won't take anything you don't offer or brag about it to my friends.

"I'm not interested."

"That's a mistake."

Guys our age would be dicks. They would tell all their friends they kissed Luciana, and there was no way they'd recognize how special she was.

"I really doubt it. I don't think I'll ever think about you again once this day is over."

Not if I can help it.

"Disagree. My brother is friends with your sister. We'll see each other again."

She sighed. "Fine. Whatever. If we *do* see each other again, can you do me a favor and not talk about us kissing? That's never going to happen."

It dawned on me that I'd been going about this all wrong. I'd been letting my nerves get the better of me. When I played soccer, I still got nervous before the ref blew the whistle, but I never let it show. Channeling that manufactured confidence, I grinned at her.

"Don't worry. When we kiss, it will be because you asked for it." I crossed one ankle over the other, aiming for casual. "I'll be waiting."

She groaned. "You, Beckett Savage, had better get used to waiting. My lips touching yours will never, ever happen. Dream on!"

After that declaration, she stormed upstairs.

I picked up her discarded Sprite and raised it to my mouth, putting my lips exactly where hers had been, making myself a promise.

I'm not kissing anyone until I kiss Luciana. No matter how long it takes, she'll be worth the wait.

Determination settling in my bones, I tucked her ponytail holder in my pocket and walked outside to find my brother.

CHAPTER TWENTY

Luciana

HISTORY WAS BORING AS hell. I mean, I did want to learn about Mesopotamia, but did my textbook have to be so unforgivably dry? I'd almost nodded off in my room, so I moved outside to the courtyard behind my dorm to wake myself up. As it turned out, having lain on a blanket in the grass was just as conducive to napping as my bed.

I was nodding off again when a shadow fell over me, blocking out the sun.

Shaking off my sleepiness, I looked up, finding Rhys Astor looming over me.

His expression and features were indecipherable with the light at his back, but I'd recognize the swirls of his hair anywhere.

"Hey. What's up?" I didn't want to assume his standing over me had anything to do with what had happened at Beckett's party last night, but since he hadn't sought me out in the past, I was pretty certain it did. My stomach was immediately in knots.

"Can I join you?" He nodded to my blanket and held up a book.

"Um. Okay." I sat up, tucking my legs to the side to give him plenty of room.

He stretched out on my blanket, taking all the space I'd given him and then some, and cracked open his book as if what was happening right now was perfectly normal.

"E.E. Cummings?" I asked.

He held up his book of poetry. "I respect a man who eschews the rules of grammar. Capitalizing letters is so fucking pedestrian."

I snorted. "Have you even read any of his poems or only looked at his name on the spine?"

He shot me a glare. "I'm incredibly insulted you'd ask me that." He swiveled the book around to glance at the spine. "But now I'm curious. Why do you ask?"

I tapped his hardback. "Because it's a myth, Rhys. His publisher printed his name in lowercase for the aesthetic. The man himself signed his name the proper way."

His brows drew together in a hard line. "That, I do not believe."

I shrugged. "You could Google it or look at the freaking book. He played with lower and uppercase, but he used both very deliberately. Did you pay attention in eleventh-grade poetry at all?"

His eyes rolled. "I got an *A*. That's all that matters."

"If you say so. I personally wouldn't feel great about walking around spouting incorrect facts, but that's me. I have a feeling you don't care what you say."

His harrumph was pointed. "You're one to talk."

"Am I? What does that mean?"

"The things you said to Beckett last night were wholly incorrect. You're going to feel like a fucking idiot when you understand the truth about him."

It was my turn to roll my eyes. "I understand just fine."

He jerked upright, looking me square in the eye. "If you did, you wouldn't have run out on him. You would have paid attention to how he's always—fucking *always*—treated you, even if I don't think you deserve it."

"I don't know what you're talking about." I folded my arms over my chest. "And since you apparently heard Beckett's version of events, your facts are skewed heavily in his favor."

Rhys clucked his tongue like he was ashamed of me. "He didn't tell me *everything*. He could barely string a few words together. Even if he'd said nothing, it would only have taken one look at his face when he finally dragged himself from the guesthouse to make it obvious you'd destroyed him."

The gravity of Rhys's admonishment pushed me down, but I had to scoff. Just like his supposed facts about E.E. Cummings were made up of half-truths, so too was his opinion of what went down between Beckett and me.

"I'm not going to tell you all he said to me, but your boy made it pretty clear I was only a challenge to him."

Rhys's eyes bulged so much they almost burst out of his head. "Oh my Jesus, fuck. Have you ever met yourself? Of course you're a challenge. *Only* a challenge, though? That's laughable."

In fact, he threw his head back to cackle like a madman. Passersby stopped to stare, but when they saw it was Rhys making the same sounds as a gaggle of dying chickens, they quickly moved on.

"Stop it," I hissed.

His freckled face was flushed when he focused on me again. "He pines."

"What does that mean?"

He took a moment to brush his hand over his waves and down his face, sobering somewhat. "Beckett has been pathetically, pitifully pining over you for years. I have never seen him show even a hint of interest toward anyone else."

"That isn't true."

He raised a brow. "The only reason I'm telling you this is because I refuse to allow you to make him miserable any longer. Before, you didn't have all the information, so you had an excuse. Now, you know."

I shook my head, trying to absorb what he was saying, but I couldn't seem to really grasp it.

"He hasn't been pining over me. I know for a fact he was with Bianca."

Rhys's normal bored, slightly unhinged expression darkened in an instant. "You know nothing, Luciana. If you think even for a second about throwing Bianca DeSoto in Beckett's face as evidence of his disloyalty to his fucked-up obsession with you, I'll tell you right now to forget this conversation. Walk away and never look back at Beckett Savage."

"He shoved himself into *my* face this year."

Why was I defending myself? It wasn't Rhys's business. I owed him nothing. But he was getting under my skin. Somewhere in the back of my mind, I was beginning to doubt my own version of events.

I couldn't help but picture how violently upset Beckett had been when Bianca had crawled all over him. He hadn't faked that. Although I knew what I'd heard between them in the hallway, it was possible context was key in this case. I didn't have it, and without it, I might have misunderstood.

A horrifying thought scratched at the back of my mind, but I shoved it away for now. I couldn't go there. Not when I had such little information. I'd only torture myself if I considered Bianca had—

No. Not right now.

"Did he force himself on you?" Rhys raised an eyebrow at my flinch. But damn, his choice of words was uncanny, considering where my thoughts were. "Did you like the attention?"

My teeth clamped together so I could swallow down the bitter taste on my tongue. "I don't know."

"He's not who you seem to think he is, Luciana. Maybe you should stop judging him by the house he grew up in. Look at his character. Pay attention." He slammed his book closed. "I'm not convinced you're good enough for him, and *not* because you're here on scholarship. I may be an elitist, but not that kind."

"Good to know," I intoned. My emotions were too scattered to have any patience with Rhys. "Why don't you get off my blanket?"

"Because I'm not done listing the reasons you're not good enough for Beckett. They begin with you shoving him into the box you've placed the vast majority of us in, rich assholes. I deserve that, sure, but Beckett doesn't."

I wanted his accusations to slide off my back, but they were sticking. Mostly because he wasn't wrong. Beckett had been kind of a jerk to me half a decade ago, and I'd written him off with the rest of the assholes since then.

It didn't help that I'd been under the impression he hated me so much he'd tried to ruin my shot at going to school here. But if I'd stopped to ask *why* back then instead of slamming the lid shut on him, things could have been different.

Rhys climbed to his feet, his book tucked under his arm. The flat look he gave me made my stomach cramp and roil. Rhys Astor, who didn't seem to bother caring about very much other than himself, and apparently Beckett, was making his disdain for me clear as day in his expression and stance.

And that panged hard in my chest.

"The list of reasons ends with you purposely shutting your eyes to the best kid I know, who is absolutely gone for you." He shook his head. "I don't know why, but he is."

He left me there feeling like I'd been run over again and again by a Mack truck. Absolutely flattened and ruined.

Was this how Beckett felt when I'd left him?

Or was Rhys off his rocker, spouting madness?

Even if he was right and Beckett had been carrying feelings for me for a long time, I had no clue what to do with that. I'd only opened my eyes to him. A crush I could've accepted. Soft, stolen kisses were welcome. But that wasn't what Rhys was talking about.

He'd implied something far bigger.

And that I wasn't ready for.

A conversation had to happen, though. That was obvious. Even if I confirmed everything that had gone down last night, at least I'd be able to smooth out my ruffled thoughts.

Snapping my history book shut, I released a heavy breath. There was no time like the present. Ignoring the dread weighing down my bones, I folded my blanket up and marched back to the dorm.

The entire elevator ride, I rehearsed what I would say, but as soon as I knocked on Beckett's door, my mind went blank. And when he swung his door open, my mouth went desert dry.

His glare shot straight through my heart. "What?" Soft but hard at the same time. So different from the way he normally spoke to me.

I licked my lips, but it was no use. My tongue was a dried-out husk. "I have a question."

He leaned his shoulder against his doorframe, his arms folding over his chest. Clearly, he had no intention of inviting me into his room, so I guessed we were doing this here.

"Ask it."

I cleared my raspy throat. "Am I only a challenge to you?"

His nostrils flared as he sucked in a sharp breath. "No."

It was only one word, but the meaning behind it was so powerful I had to brace myself so I wouldn't stumble backward.

I grasped the outside of the doorframe, my fingers centimeters from his shoulder. "Do you have real feelings for me?"

He blinked at me, long and slow. "Yes."

Another blow, but at least I'd been holding on this time.

"Did I—" I licked my lips. "Did I get it all wrong last night?"

His lids lowered, and it was then I noticed the purplish circles beneath his eyes. Another pang in my chest. I'd only slept last night because my heartache had taken it all out of me. It didn't appear Beckett had slept at all.

He dipped his head, bringing us eye to eye. Our noses nearly grazed, but he was careful not to touch any part of me.

"So fucking wrong, Ortega."

Ortega, not little light, or even Luc. I didn't like how that felt. Not one bit.

"I'm sorry," I whispered, swallowing hard.

His head cocked, but he stayed close. "Okay."

"I don't know what any of this means."

He stepped back and to the side. "Come on. Get in here."

I only hesitated for a moment before accepting his invitation. His room was immaculately clean except for the open notebook on his bed and the stack of textbooks on the floor. It was also so small there was no extra space with the two of us standing in front of each other.

He nodded. "You can sit at my desk if you want."

There was still something different about his voice. He'd dropped most of the hardness, and he was definitely exhausted, but there was something else.

He sat down on the edge of his bed, one hand cupping the other between his knees. One by one, he cracked his knuckles, then smoothed his palms over his joggers.

That was when I recognized the difference in him. Beckett was nervous.

"You're the last person I expected to come knocking on my door," he said.

I was nervous too. This was a first for me. Boys didn't really make me nervous since I never cared what they thought of me. That wasn't the case with Beckett, which struck me hard.

I care what Beckett Savage thinks of me.

"Rhys found me," I told him. "We talked about poetry, making assumptions, and you."

He huffed a dry laugh. "You never know what will come out of that kid's mouth." He narrowed his eyes. "What'd he say about me? Things he shouldn't have?"

"He has your back. Let's just say that."

Beckett tensed. "Not yours? Did he say inappropriate shit to you?"

"No. Well, not any more than I would expect from Rhys. His loyalty to you is pretty fierce, though."

He nodded once. "He's unshakable in that way. Then again, I have pictures of him cosplaying as a hobbit."

"Something tells me he wouldn't even care if you leaked them."

He lifted a shoulder. "I don't know. Rhys cares about a lot more than you think."

"I'm glad you have a friend like that." I scooted to the edge of my chair, and my knees grazed him, but I didn't pull back.

Beckett did.

"What are you doing here, Luciana?"

"Rhys made it clear I misunderstood what happened last night. I really want to understand."

"Why?"

I rubbed my lips together, hating the feeling of being on the outside of a closed door that had previously been open to me. It had been open to me for so long I'd never noticed.

"Because when we were close, it was—" It was beautiful, perfect, almost magic, but I couldn't say that. That was too much. "I really liked being close to you."

"I liked it too."

My heart skittered around in my chest like a lunatic. It was all I could do not to press on my chest and beg it to behave. Now wasn't really the time to swoon over Beckett. We were far from settled.

"But your reaction after, I don't understand it. I'd like you to explain it."

He nodded, his head dropping as he raked his fingers through his uncombed hair. "You don't remember much about when we met, do you?"

My skin inexplicably prickled. "You were kind of a dick to me. But you were a kid, so I can't hold that against you. Well...maybe I have been, but I won't anymore. It's not fair."

"Thank you for that." He tapped his steepled fingertips together. "I was tongue tied all day. Nothing I meant to say would come out of my mouth. I came across as a dick because I was stumbling over my own thoughts."

Brooding, gorgeous, popular Beckett stumbling over his thoughts due to *me* seemed impossible.

"You said my eyes were plain."

Again, he huffed. "No, I said blue was better than plain brown, and I was referring to my mom's eyes, which she's always called mud brown. She overcompensates for what she finds lacking in appearance by piling on so much makeup I don't even know what the real her looks like. In my head, I was thinking your eyes contain galaxies, the way the gold and brown swirled with black."

My mouth parted in shock. No one had *ever* said anything like that to me. "Really?"

"Yeah. Really." He took a deep breath, his chest expanding. "You make me stupid, Luciana. If I've said rude things to you, I promise you the truth is the opposite."

"Maybe I should learn to read your mind."

His clear blue eyes locked on mine. Fathomless seas to swirling galaxies. "No, you shouldn't. I'd scare you off in a heartbeat."

"What are you thinking now?" I pressed.

"I'm thinking you don't remember the promise I made to you in your sister's kitchen."

I racked my brain, but I was coming up blank. "Tell me, please."

"When we kiss, it will be because you asked for it. I'll be waiting."

If I had known back then how pivotal those barbed words we'd exchanged would be, I would have committed them to memory. I wished I could take a shovel and dig through my mind to bring them back to the surface.

"That's what you said?"

He hadn't let go of my gaze. "That's what I said, and I followed through. I waited for you to ask. I was so fucking happy you asked. So happy I got stupid after. I said the wrong thing."

"Yeah," I breathed out. "I didn't like that part."

"You liked the rest of it?"

"Of course I did. That's why it sucked to feel like it had meant nothing."

Everything about him became more intense. His hands curled into tight fists. The line of his shoulders bunched. His jaw ticced as he stared at me in a way that made me feel like he could see straight through me.

"It meant everything. I waited for that, Luciana. All this time, I waited because I knew nothing would compare."

"What do you mean?" This was more than waiting me out, but surely he couldn't have been saying what I thought he was. That was unimaginable.

"I *waited* for you to be ready, Luciana. What I mean is there has been no one else. Last night was the first and only time I have ever kissed anyone. I was saving that for you."

"Beckett…" I almost wanted to deny what he'd just admitted. To yell that he was lying, that it couldn't be true. It sounded too far-fetched and fairy tale–ish.

This beautiful boy spotting me at age thirteen and never kissing another girl while he waited for me to finally see him? The idea made me dizzy and warm all over, but I had trouble believing that someone—that *Beckett Savage*—would do that for me.

But when I looked into his eyes, his vulnerability was laid bare. I couldn't picture Beckett claiming I was his first kiss if it wasn't true. As romantic as it was—and god, I hadn't really wrapped my head around how incredibly, profoundly romantic it truly was—it just wasn't *cool*. Guys at SA plowed through girls like it was a Midwest winter. And girls hopped dicks just as readily. That was how things were done here.

I believed him, but I didn't know how to feel about it.

"I know it wasn't your first, and I don't give a shit about any of the others that came before me."

He sounded like he gave a shit. So much his molars were grinding into dust.

"Beckett—"

A tumultuous storm flashed in his eyes. "Stop saying my name like that, Ortega."

"Don't call me Ortega and let me speak," I snapped back.

He held his hand out. "All right, Luciana. Speak."

I sighed in frustration. "Did you like kissing me?"

"Yes."

"I liked kissing you too. Do you want to kiss me again?"

"Yes."

"I want to kiss you again too. Are you ever going to bring up the fact that I didn't save my first kiss for you again?"

The corners of his mouth pinched. "No."

"Thank you. What do you want from me?"

"Everything."

My heart was a ghost. Exploded, dead, the pieces buried. Beckett Savage terrified me, but the longer we spent in a state of brutal honesty, the more I wanted to be with him.

But I didn't do boyfriends, and Beckett would be way more than a boyfriend. Being with him would be all-consuming. *Everything.*

"I don't know if I can give you everything. Can I think about it?"

More molar grinding. They *were* dust by now. "Of course."

I wanted to hug him, to touch his jaw and rub away the tension. To press my lips to his and recapture those perfect moments. I didn't know if he'd welcome it when we were in limbo and I wasn't saying what he wanted me to, but I was out of my chair and in front of him before I could stop myself.

My fingers grazed his jaw. "I'm going to go, but I was wondering if maybe I could kiss you first?"

His sigh was hot against my hand. "Come here." He tugged me closer until my knees hit the bed and I spilled into his lap. His arms looped around my waist, and my hands went to his face.

Dipping down, his nose touched mine. I tipped my face to the side and slotted my lips with his. His mouth was warm and lush and just as gently probing as I remembered. As we kissed, slow and soft, never moving beyond lips meeting lips, he held me closer.

I'd been kissed a few times, but I'd never been *kissed.* There should have been a different word for what we were doing.

We pulled apart, staying forehead to forehead. "I don't know what to call this, but I know it's my first time," I whispered.

I felt his smile, as small as it was. "I'm glad you saved one thing for me."

"Beckett..."

"Don't say my name that way, Ortega."

I laughed, the intensity of the moment dissipating. "I don't know why, but I *do* like you."

"I know exactly why I like you."

"One day, maybe you'll tell me." I touched my lips to his, kissing his smile. "You're a really good kisser, you know."

"Luciana." He growled my name like he was exasperated with me but tangled his fingers in my hair and pressed a hard, biting kiss to my lips in the next breath. "Weren't you leaving?"

"Yes." I kissed him one more time. "I'm going now. Mesopotamia waits for no man."

"Don't be cute when I'm trying to let you leave without giving me the answer I need from you."

He gave me a light shove to get me moving. I was more reluctant to hop up from his lap than I would have expected, but I did it. It wasn't fair for either of us for me to linger. Especially now, when I understood Beckett's feelings for me ran deep.

It wasn't until after we'd said goodbye and I was walking back to my room with Beckett's gaze on my back that I remembered the whispered conversation I'd overheard between him and Bianca.

Some of the magic of being Beckett's first kiss blew away like fairy dust at that stark dose of reality.

Beckett had saved his first kiss for me, but was that all he'd saved?

CHAPTER TWENTY-ONE
Beckett

AFTER SPENDING YEARS IN this maddening stasis, one more day should have been easy. Being with Luciana hadn't even been part of my plan until after graduation. My time line was months ahead of schedule.

And yet, every fucking part of the day was torture. Seconds dragged on like hours. Minutes were days. Hours were centuries.

I was old and grizzled by the time school let out.

The fact was, tomorrow could be more of the same. Giving Luciana space was a necessary evil, but I was resentful that it was.

If things had gone according to my plans, she wouldn't have needed to take time to consider being with me. I would have had the whole school year to become such an integral part of her life she would have accepted becoming mine as easily as breathing.

But my plans were based on nothing but logic and reason. They didn't account for Luciana's own feelings developing, and they sure as hell didn't include Bianca putting her filthy, disease-ridden mouth on mine.

I'd been planning to get Luciana to the point where she'd ask for me to kiss her, but Jesus Christ, never in my wildest dreams had I fathomed it would happen a month into the school year.

Not that I would take any of it back. Even though I'd fucked it all up after, it had been worth it to have her.

I reminded myself of that as I headed out for soccer practice. Patience was my finest virtue. I could wait for Luciana to come around to me. If her visit to my room yesterday had meant anything—and I thought it'd meant a lot—I wouldn't be waiting long.

A pair of waving arms caught my eye as I jogged across the grass. Stopping, I fully turned toward my sister-in-law, Sera, who was assisting the marching band practice.

She tapped her watch and pointed to me.

I gave her a thumbs-up.

She made a heart sign with her fingers.

I had to stop myself from flipping her off. That was our vibe, and Sera would have found it hysterical, but I figured it was best not to give the finger to a faculty member, even if she was essentially my relative.

I waved to her instead and continued making my way to practice. I'd see her tonight, which she'd been attempting to remind me of with her random hand signals.

The next hour was another test of my self-control. As always, the field hockey team was practicing on the field adjacent to ours. I only allowed myself to look three times. The first, Luciana was running passing drills. The second, they were scrimmaging and Luc was charging down the field. The final time was during their cooldown.

Stretching. They were stretching.

My resolve was stretching too. Paper thin by now.

Their practice ended before ours, and the girls cut through our field on the way to their locker room. I made sure to be in their path. When Luciana walked by, I waited to see what she would do.

She was talking animatedly with Bella and Isla, but her gaze snapped to mine like she knew I was watching. Her grin widened, that front tooth of hers still ever so slightly crooked. She remained the most beautiful girl I'd ever seen, and her imperfect smile never failed to fuck me over. Now that it was directed at me, I was rocked to my core.

"Eyes on the game, Savage."

"Get off my field, Ortega."

She laughed, continuing on her way with her girls. I took one step in her direction before a ball slammed into my shoulder. Lurching around, I spotted Felix waving at me unapologetically.

"Just because it's your birthday doesn't mean you get to take it easy, man," Felix called. "Practice isn't over. Stop looking at the girls and move your lazy ass."

The girls were gone, so I moved my lazy ass, throwing all my frustration, anger, and pent-up desire into practice. This wasn't the first time. I had a feeling it wouldn't be the last.

· · · • • · • · · ·

The parking lot was pretty deserted as I strode across it. I should have been in my car ten minutes ago, but I got held up, so now I was going to have to book it to Jules and Sera's house.

I pulled up short when I approached my parking spot. My car was tilting to one side. I bent down, checking the front tire. It was completely fucking flat.

Great. The perfect cherry on top of this endless day. This had been the one thing I'd been looking forward to, and now I was stuck. Rideshares took forever to arrive around here if they even accepted our ride requests, which they often didn't.

Rising to my feet, I braced my hands on top of my head and bit back a groan. I'd have to cancel. I had no other choice.

A silver car rolled to a stop behind mine. "Flat tire?"

My eyes flicked up from my phone. Luciana was behind the wheel, her arm resting on her open window.

"Yeah."

"Do you need a ride?"

Her timing seemed too perfect for this to be a coincidence, but she wouldn't have done this. She hadn't even known I was heading to my brother's house.

I walked over to her car, bending down so I could get a good look at her. She didn't appear guilty. No, she seemed amused by my predicament.

"Depends. Where are you going?"

"I'm going to see Helen."

Her hair was down. I reached inside the car to run my fingers along a lock of it. Like silk.

"Yeah. A ride would be great. Drop me off at Julien's?"

She jerked her head. "Get in."

The second I folded myself into her passenger seat, I leaned over and took a long, deep inhale. Her head swiveled toward me, confusion drawing her brows together.

"Did you sniff me?"

"You smell good."

She laughed, but it had a nervous tinge to it. "Like outside?"

"You remembered?"

"Just now. That reminded me. You basically said I stunk."

"No. I said you smelled like outside." I picked up a piece of her hair and brought it to my nose. "I meant sunshine and fresh air. Puffy white clouds and blue sky. Fucking delicious."

"Oh." She swallowed hard. "I guess that's nice."

Nice. I wasn't nice. That wasn't what this was. This was so far beyond nice Luciana didn't see it yet. She would. When she was ready, she would.

"It's a fact," I told her.

Luciana was a careful driver, but that was no surprise. She was careful in most ways, which was why the chances she took with skateboarding had been so alarming to me. It also showed me how important it was to her. It had pained me to take it from her, but goddamn, I'd needed her at Savage Academy. More importantly, *she* needed to be at SA.

"Happy birthday, by the way," she chirped.

I was startled out of my thoughts. "Thank you."

"I'm sorry I don't have a gift for you."

"I didn't expect you to."

She sucked in a breath, tapping her fingers on the steering wheel.

"Every birthday since I was fourteen, I've received a bouquet of sunflowers on my doorstep. For a while, I thought they were from an aunt or uncle on my dad's side. And maybe they were, I don't know."

I shifted, facing her profile. I looked at her from this angle a lot. She never noticed, but I had memorized the slope of her nose and the way her chin jutted normally then more pronounced when she was feeling stubborn.

"Ask the question you want to ask, Luciana."

She glanced at me, sucking in a breath when our eyes met. "Were they from you?"

"Yeah. Did you like them?"

"I didn't have a favorite flower before that." She brushed the hair away from her face, tucking it behind her ear. No doubt it would be up in a ponytail soon. "Now it's sunflowers."

"You weren't creeped out by it?"

"No. Helen was pissy the first year, and Theo started questioning me about boys the second year, but now they're just part of my birthday. I'd miss them if they were gone."

This was why I was certain about her. Other girls would have told me I was a stalker asshole, but not Luc. She saw the gesture for what it was: someone who cared enough about her to acknowledge her birthday, even from afar.

"You don't have to worry about that."

Maybe I was a little bit of a fucking stalker. I really had no clue what it was like to feel something for a girl other than what I felt for Luc. I didn't know how to be any other way with her either.

She glanced at me again. "I did get you something, but it's not here yet."

"Yeah? What is it?"

"A surprise, Savage. Don't ruin it."

Breathing out a laugh, I let my head fall back on the rest. "You shouldn't have teased me then. You have to know by now I'm re-lentless."

"I think I'm only beginning to see that, actually." She shoved her hair from her face again. "You know, SA should really do a sweep of the parking lot. There must be nails or broken glass somewhere, considering my tires went flat and now yours. It's an epidemic."

"Yeah? Did you have a puncture in your tire?"

Her teeth dug into her bottom lip. "It's strange, actually. Both times, my tire was fixed when I got back to SA."

"Hmmm. Probably maintenance. We don't pay bank for nothing. The academy is on top of that sort of thing."

She slowly nodded. "That makes sense, although it doesn't really explain why my tires went flat in the first place."

I leaned sideways and forward so I could see her expression and she could see mine. "Do we really want to explain flat tires right now? Because if you do, I will too."

Her mouth tipped. "This is a rhetorical discussion, Savage."

"Yeah." I settled back in my seat, pleased at her little guilty smile. If Luciana ended up being as out of her mind and fiendish as me, I'd be absolutely delighted. "That's what I thought."

A while later, she pulled up in front of Julien and Sera's brand-new house. It was on the tip of my tongue to make some kind of demand that she come in with me, using my birthday as leverage, but I stopped myself. I was letting her choose me. Forcing her would not give me the same satisfaction, nor did I think for a second she would go along with it.

"Thanks for the ride, Ortega."

"Sure." Her fingers grazed my forearm. "Text me when you're ready to head back."

I hopped out of the car and walked away from her before I did anything stupid. Sure, I was disappointed not to have her with me, but that had never been part of the plan. Everything I was getting now was a bonus.

Julien was waiting for me at the door, a crooked grin on his scarred face, his cane clutched in one hand. He'd been hit by an SUV when he was in college, had nearly died from it, and all these years later, he still wore the effects in his limp and scars.

"Happy birthday, Beck."

His arm went around me, pulling me in for a tight hug. Now that I was here, with my brother, most of my disappointment fell away now.

Julien was eight years older than me, the product of our father's dalliance with his family's maid. He'd never taken the Savage name—or, more correctly, our father had never given it—and Gretchen hadn't welcomed him in our home, despite his birth preceding my parents' marriage by several years. That meant he and I hadn't formed a relationship until I was thirteen and had gained some independence from my parents.

The day I'd met Luciana was only the second time I'd seen Julien in several years. I'd pushed my way into his life, though. He hadn't really wanted a brother, but I had, so I'd texted and called until he'd invited me places. Now, I had my own room in his house, which he allowed me to use whenever I wanted.

Sera encouraged it, in fact, but I made sure not to wear out my welcome. I was never not conscious of whether my brother and his wife were still happy to have me around.

"Thank you." I kicked the door shut behind me, grinning when Julien frowned at the use of a foot on his door. "Won't happen again."

He gripped the back of my neck. "Better not. I'll tell Sera."

I sucked in a breath through my teeth. "Anything but that."

He chuckled. "I was going to ask how it felt to be an adult, but you've been an adult since you were ten."

"Now it's official, and I can tell Josh and Gretch to fuck off whenever I want."

His mouth flattened, and he folded his arms over his chest. "Got plans on supporting yourself when your parents stop?"

I shrugged. "You managed."

"Dad paid for my college tuition, Beck. I kept my 'fuck offs' to myself."

I held back a sneer. The idea of willingly being beholden to my dad for a second longer than I had to made me want to leap out of my skin. "And now you work for him, so he's still got you bent over a barrel."

Jules didn't even flinch. "Uncalled for."

"I know." My chest tightened. So much for watching myself. My parents were a touchy subject, and I was already on edge from the weekend. "I'm being an ass because you're right. I've still got to dance the dance like a good little Savage."

He brushed my shoulder. "Once you get rid of that chip and stop looking to have your emotional needs met by our father, you'll realize he's not a villain."

I scoffed. "Sure, Jules."

"I'm not saying he's a superhero either. He's a shit father, we both know that. But as a human, he's pretty neutral. Working for him isn't even painful, and look at my fucking house, Beckett. I get to provide this kind of stability for my wife, for you, for my future kids, because of the job I took working three floors below our dad. You want to be a grown-up, there are things you come to realize. One of them is disliking someone doesn't make them evil. It also means not everything has to be a fight."

At my silence—because what did I even say to my brother laying out facts I couldn't come close to disputing?—he pulled me into another hug. "I love you, kid. I'm happy I get to know you and have you here to celebrate your eighteenth birthday. Honored you chose to spend it with Sera and me."

"Where is my sister-in-law?" I shoved away from him, running my fingers through my hair to give myself a beat to tamp down the rising tidal wave of emotions about to slam into me.

He turned away, giving me the time I needed, and nodded toward the back of the house.

"We're having dinner on the deck. Come on. Let's check out what my girl's been up to."

CHAPTER TWENTY-TWO

Beckett

SERA WAS BUBBLY, FUNNY, annoying, sarcastic, and warm. She was the sunshine to my brother's grump. From the minute we met, she'd liked me. I still had no idea why, but she'd never hidden it. When I came over, she was outwardly delighted. Even when she and Jules had lived in a cramped apartment, there had always been space for me.

For a kid who'd always had to work hard to earn even the smallest dose of affection, she'd made me suspicious. All these years later, my suspicion had died, but I was still waiting for the day she came to her senses and kicked me out of her esteem.

That day wasn't today.

She'd created an archway of balloons over the sliding door leading to the deck. Julien went first, and I followed. Sera was standing beside the table she'd decorated with small vases of flowers and confetti.

She threw her arms out. "Happy birthday, Beckett!"

A chorus of other voices joined her. I went stock-still, sweeping over the people around her. Theo, Helen, and their baby. Rhys Astor looking smug as ever.

My heart picked up, searching over everyone. She wasn't here. How could she not be if Helen was?

Someone tapped on my shoulder, and I spun around, dizzy over the girl leaning her shoulder on the frame of the slider.

"Happy birthday, Savage." Luciana flashed me a smile, conveying how pleased she was for pulling one over on me. "Surprise!"

"What the fuck?" I shoveled my fingers through my hair, practically yanking it out. "You're here."

She stepped out onto the deck. "Yep. Told you I knew when your birthday was for reasons."

Stupefied, I watched her cross the deck to her family, taking the baby out of Helen's arms. Luc rubbed her nose along her niece's downy hair and pressed a kiss to her chubby cheek—a kiss I didn't resent her giving away, for once.

Rhys sauntered over while I was watching her, bumping me with his shoulder.

"I'd like it noted that I'm here too. I also remembered your birthday," he pronounced.

"You always remember my birthday."

"An honor you should not take for granted."

Sera rushed up to us and pressed her hands to my cheeks. "Are you so surprised? I wanted to do something bigger than just the three of us, but I didn't want to overwhelm you. I know how you feel about big parties. Is this okay?"

Wrapping my fingers around her wrists, I tugged her hands away so I could hug her. "It's okay, and yeah, I'm incredibly surprised. The three of us would have been plenty, but this is really nice too."

Words couldn't truly convey how *nice* this was. After Gretchen's extravaganza over the weekend, I hadn't heard another word from her. It didn't surprise me that she hadn't been bothered to do more than send birthday wishes for my father to give me during his perfunctory call this morning, but it did add another nail in the coffin that was my relationship with her.

Though Sera was only related to me by marriage and had only known me a handful of years, she hadn't gone all out to celebrate me because she'd felt obliged. All this was because she wanted to. Which was fucking wild. Hard to believe, yet I did.

She pulled back, keeping her hands on my arms. Her eyes were glistening as she looked me over. "You're such a good boy. Bad at Ping-Pong, but a sweet, good boy."

I chuffed at her sincere compliment. I knew she meant it, but I didn't know how to accept it graciously. "I'm not a dog."

She patted my cheek. "Just say 'thank you, Sera.'"

"Thank you, Sera. What'd you make me for dinner?"

That earned me a harder pat bordering on a slap. "Ribs. You'll eat them and like them. No complaining."

Since Sera's ribs were my favorite, I wouldn't. Then again, she knew that.

Julien passed out drinks to everyone while Helen helped Sera finish up the food. Luciana settled in a cushy, rattan armchair with the baby in her lap. Since I couldn't sit beside her without making a scene, I took a seat where I could watch her. Unaware of my strategic placement, Theo and Jules plopped down right in front of me in chairs they'd pulled from the table. Rhys was beside me on the love seat. I was locked in, no view of my girl.

"How's the season going?" Theo asked, tipping a beer toward me.

"All right. We're undefeated."

"That's awesome, man. Do you enjoy playing?"

I cocked my head. No one really asked me that. All they ever wanted to know was if I was good and where I planned to go to college.

"Uh..." I rubbed the back of my neck.

Theo leaned forward, his elbows on his knees. "Sorry to put you on the spot. I wrestled in high school and college. I won championships but nearly destroyed my body. It was something I did without considering if I even *liked* it. So, when I meet other elite athletes, I always ask that. But you don't have to answer me."

"It's fine." I shook my head, thinking. "I do enjoy it, but it's not my future. If I don't play in college, I'll survive."

Theo leaned back, and Julien narrowed his eyes.

"Have you been scouted?" Theo asked.

"Sure. But I'm not ready to commit anywhere."

"Any thoughts on Savage U?" Julien asked.

I chuckled, my water bottle poised midair. "If I can manage to go to a school that doesn't have my last name attached to it, that would be ideal."

Rhys lifted his chin. "What about you, Luciana? Where will you be applying to college?"

Theo and Jules angled their shoulders to look back at her, giving me a sliver of a peek. Her eyes were wide, the baby's hands patting her face.

"Well, it depends on who wants me to play for them. I'm waiting for offers from UNC and Stanford. They both have incredible field hockey programs, so it will come down to the scholarship."

Theo shook his head. "If she moves to North Carolina, I'm going to have a lot of trouble convincing Helen not to uproot us to follow her."

Julien slapped his arm with the back of his hand. "Why are you acting like *Helen's* the only one who'll have trouble letting her go?"

Theo glanced back at Luc again. "I'm going to be a fuckin' wreck. But I'm proud as hell of my girl. I'll let her go because I know she'll come back."

Jules rolled his eyes. "Big words. Let's see what's happening this time next year."

Luc giggled. "He sends me Stanford stats every week. Don't let him fool you. He's trying to keep me in the state."

Julien raised an eyebrow at me. "You're not moving across the country, are you?"

I lifted a shoulder, and Rhys tried to cover up his snicker. "I'm not ruling it out."

"Savage U isn't so bad," Julien said. "Look how well all of us turned out."

"Are you considering Savage U, Luciana?" Rhys asked.

She got to her feet and walked over to us, the baby snuggled in her arms. "No, sorry, guys. Their field hockey team isn't Division 1."

Rhys probably thought he was digging up answers for me, but I already knew this. I had only applied to schools she was considering, and I was well aware that meant I might end up living in North Carolina. That also possibly meant I wouldn't be playing soccer in college, but I'd easily get over that. As time had proven, the same could not be said for Luciana. Where she went, I went.

However, announcing that when she hadn't yet agreed to be mine wasn't happening. If I let Rhys continue on his merry, maniacal way, who knew what he might've said.

Luck was on my side. Sera and Helen burst back onto the deck with platters of food, and Rhys jumped to his feet, forgetting me to follow them. Luciana started to turn, but I snagged the loop of her jeans.

I stood, my front to her back. "Are you going to stay far, far away from me all night, or will you sit by me?"

She peered over her shoulder at me. "Do you want me to sit beside you?"

"You know I do."

"It's your birthday. You get what you want."

I really fucking doubted she had any inkling of the depths of my want, but spending my birthday with Luciana next to me was more than I could ever ask for, so I'd take it.

For now.

· · · • • · • · · ·

By the middle of dinner, I was feeding a baby.

Luc had asked me to hold her while she grabbed a bottle so Helen could relax. When she brought back the warm bottle, I realized she intended to interrupt her own meal to feed her niece, so I flatly refused to give her back.

That was how I'd ended up with this little creature blinking up at me as she devoured her own dinner.

"Is this the first time you've fed a baby?" Sera had stopped eating to watch me. Her chin was resting on her fists, and I swore she was tearing up.

"It's the first time I've *held* a baby," I admitted.

Luc gasped. "And you let me shove her at you?"

Helen scoffed. "You handed my child over without even asking for his credentials? Some aunt you are." Then she flashed me a grin. "You're a natural, Beckett. She can get cranky about bottles since she usually drinks straight from the tap."

"The tap?" Rhys's brow furrowed.

Helen made a circle in the air around her chest. "This tap. Don't make it weird."

He held up both hands. "I would never. A mother's bond with her baby is sacred and beautiful."

Luciana burst out laughing. "You're so full of shit."

Madelina startled at the sudden sound, her eyes flaring wide. I jiggled her a little and patted her bottom like I'd seen Luc do. She settled back in the crook of my arm, all warm and solid.

I nudged Luciana. "You're scaring the baby. Shhh."

She covered her mouth, her eyes alight with amusement. Leaning closer to me, she peered down at Madelina then flicked her gaze up to meet mine.

"You're cute like this," she murmured. "All nurturing and sweet."

"You thought I'd be mean to a baby?"

Grinning, she reached across me to rub Madelina's hand then mine. "Of course not. I didn't picture you volunteering to feed one, though."

"She's your niece."

Her eyes flared. Maybe she was realizing it really was that simple for me. "Beckett..."

"Don't say my name like that, Ortega," I growled under my breath.

"So," Helen cleared her throat, "I didn't realize you two were such buddies. But look at you over there, whispering like old pals."

She was throwing down a challenge, and I was all ears for how Luciana answered her. Everyone else was too. Conversation dwindled, and all eyes were on us.

Luciana didn't jump away from me. She turned her head to look at her sister while leaning her arm against mine.

"Beckett and I have been running together in the morning. We both get on the track before our teams." She ran her thumb along the seam of her napkin. "You know how it is, you go to school with people but never really get to know them until circumstances throw you together. We run, and we have most of our classes together, so we're getting to know each other."

Helen pressed her cherry-red lips together, and Theo threw his arm around her shoulders while giving me an assessing look.

"It's good you're out there with her in the morning. I don't like her being out there on her own," he said.

"I don't either," I replied, pleased as hell Luciana hadn't denied us by saying something tried like we were "just friends."

Helen's eyes were sharp on me. "Luciana is a good one. She doesn't need trouble."

Sera beamed at me. "Beckett's a good one too. It's perfect they're hanging out together."

Helen lifted her chin at me. "I guess we'll see."

· · · • • · • • · · ·

We were halfway back to SA when I started laughing. Luciana glanced at me.

"What's so funny, birthday boy?"

"Your sister doesn't like me."

"Hmmm."

My laughter cleared, and I studied her pursed lips. "You're not even going to try to deny it?"

She lifted a shoulder. "Helen has her reasons for being suspicious of guys. She started keeping a bat within reach in middle school and still sleeps with one next to her bed. So yeah, with her, men tend to be guilty until proven innocent."

Yeah, my amusement was gone.

"That's why you don't want a boyfriend?"

"Part of it. My mom's part of it too. She had Helen in high school, and I'm not saying her future had been bright before that, but getting caught up in Helen's dad, then a string of other *very bad men*, including my dad, had pretty much ruined her."

She quickly added, "I don't think I'm my mom."

"You're not," I spit out like a swear so she'd hear me.

Sighing, she smoothed a hand over her hair, which was back in a ponytail, like I'd predicted. "I know. But I swore to myself I wouldn't put myself in a position where a guy derailed my future, and Helen's stories of some of the boys she'd known in high school had definitely helped cement my choices."

"I don't know them, but I can tell you without a doubt I'm nothing like those guys."

"You're not." She shifted in her seat. "Hells has had some bad experiences with rich boys."

"She's known me for a long time, Luc. I would like to think she wouldn't lump me in with the idiots from her past."

"She has known you for a long time, but she's never had to consider whether I was interested in you or not."

That gave me pause. I looked at her hard. Her eyes remained on the road, giving nothing away. "Are you?"

She huffed a laugh and slid a smile my way. "I think you know, Savage."

"Do I?"

She finally gave me more than the side of her face, turning toward me for a moment. "Let's wait until we're back at school, okay? This is the kind of conversation I'd like to have face to face."

Fuck.

That did not bode well.

CHAPTER TWENTY-THREE

Luciana

THE ACADEMY CAMPUS WAS mostly quiet and still by the time we pulled into the lot. My stomach was a mess of nerves, but I knew what I wanted to say to Beckett. I'd run my choices around my head again and again until I was certain.

I parked, and we both got out. Then I slipped my hand in his and led him to a bench outside our dorm. It was past curfew, and though we'd been given special permission to be out late, if someone came by, they'd make us go back to our rooms. Luckily, that also meant there weren't any other students around.

"You know it's my birthday."

I laughed softly, pulling his hand into my lap. "I was just at your birthday dinner, so yeah, I do know."

His fingers flexed around mine. "Then why the hell are you torturing me by drawing this out?"

He was clearly out of patience but kept his tone soft and measured.

"I'm not trying to. I wanted to be able to see your face." I licked my dry lips. "You know this is really new to me."

"I know. I'm taking that into consideration when I decide how impatient to feel."

"How impatient *are* you?"

His brow dropped. "It's growing by the second."

He made me grin. I couldn't help it. Beckett was always so intense, and right now, it was multiplied by one hundred. But the fact that this intensity was about me made me nervous and so incredibly flattered I didn't know how to handle myself.

"When you said what you want, that you want everything, I guess...does that mean you want to be my boyfriend?"

"Yes."

I sucked in a breath. "Okay. Well, I've never had a boyfriend."

"I've never been one."

My teeth dug into my bottom lip. "I'm going to need to go achingly slow, Beckett. I don't know if you'll like having me as a girlfriend."

"I will. The pace we go doesn't matter if I know you're mine."

Oh god, the things this boy said. No wonder girls and women sometimes lost their minds over guys. If they said things like Beckett did, I almost couldn't blame them.

"I want to try," I whispered.

His spine straightened. "Yeah? What does that mean?"

"It means..." I brought our joined hands to my chest and pressed his to my heart. "I'm so nervous right now. Do you feel that?"

He reached out with his other hand, cupping the side of my neck. His thumb found my fluttering pulse, caressing the whoosh of blood shooting through my veins, his lips tipping in the corners.

"That's because of me?"

I nodded. "You make me nervous because I like you. I don't pay attention to boys, but I do pay attention to you. I'm scared of this. If this blows up, we still have to live in the same building, sit through all the same classes..."

"It's not going to blow up." He sounded so sure. How could he be?

"You've had more time to think about this."

"That's right, I have. Which is how I know we're going to be good for each other."

I needed him to listen to me before I dove in headfirst. "Do you understand that whatever happens between us won't affect where I go to college? This time next year, I could be on the other side of the country."

"I get that. This thing we're going to have will never be about holding you back. I'd cut off my arms if I ever got tempted."

"Don't do that. I like your arms."

"Christ," he uttered, dropping his forehead to mine. "I think you really do like me."

I released his hand to loop my arms around his neck. "Wasn't that the goal?"

He grunted, rolling his forehead back and forth on mine. "Wanting you is one thing. You wanting me back is another thing entirely." His fingers slid into the side of my hair. "I'll be careful with you, little light."

"I think you will." I let out a soft breath. "Why do you call me that?"

"It slips out." His lips curled slightly. "I looked up the meaning of your name that first day."

"It means light." Though, obviously, he knew that.

"Never knew someone who embodied their name like you do. My little light."

God, this guy. He sounded sort of embarrassed, but I wouldn't let him be. Not over something so unimaginably sweet. How had I never noticed this side of him? How had he hidden it so thoroughly?

"Can I give you a birthday kiss?"

"Is that really a question?"

"Shut up, Savage."

I pressed my lips to his, but that was all he allowed me to control. Beckett took over, tilting my head, coaxing my mouth open with his. His lips were so plush on mine, and when he laved my lips and tongue, I melted into him, a whimper escaping from somewhere deep inside me. He'd coaxed that out too, with his steadfast patience, kissing me like he'd been waiting his entire life to do so.

Not just waiting but planning. Mapping my mouth so when I finally opened my eyes and saw him, he'd know exactly how to kiss me. That was what it felt like, at least.

His hands never left my hair, but I needed to be closer. Drawing my knees under me, I knelt on the bench and scooted farther in his arms. Beckett watched me with hooded eyes and swollen lips.

I nodded toward his lap. "Can I?"

"You can do anything you want to me, Luciana," he rasped thickly.

"I just want to be close," I whispered as I swung my leg over his, sitting astride his thighs. "Is this okay?"

He curled his arms around my waist and pulled me against his chest. My lower body slid forward too, and when his hardness aligned with my core, my breath caught.

"Shit." He tried to ease away from me. "I'm sorry."

"No." I cupped his cheek. "No, it's fine. I don't want to hurt you, but I'm not offended or anything."

His head fell back, and he laughed. "Thank god you're not offended because that is all your fault."

I dug my fingers into his hair, pulling his face back to mine. "Stop laughing at me and kiss me, Savage."

"Anything, Ortega."

His mouth was on mine again, our bodies flush. His fingers splayed wide, the very tips of them dipping low enough to graze my butt. It wasn't a conscious choice to arch my spine, but when I did, my cheeks moved more fully under his palm. He froze for a moment, then started to slide away, but I reached behind me, keeping his hands there.

"I like that," I murmured against his lips. "Do you?"

He answered with a groan, his palms cupping my butt. "Beautiful," he rasped. "Fucking sexy, Luc."

His mouth found my throat, grazing along in a slow, achingly soft path. My breath came out in little pants, and I settled against him even deeper. The feel of him, long and stiff between my thighs, was both wondrous and a major turn-on.

That was because of me. Because he liked kissing me so much. I'd made him feel that way.

I rocked against him, and his groan rumbled down my throat.

"Luc…" His fingers kneaded my butt, and I rocked again, eliciting another ragged sound from him. "Baby, you don't know—"

I slipped my hands inside the collar of his T-shirt, exploring the tight planes of his shoulders and upper back.

"You're so warm," I whispered.

His forehead fell heavy on my collarbone. "I really hate what I'm about to say."

"Then don't say it." I pressed myself down on his thick erection, barely holding back a shudder.

He gripped my hips with a firmness that took my breath away. "Jesus, Luciana. You have to stop, or I'm going to explode. The last thing I want to do is come in my pants on my birthday."

My mouth fell open, and I leaned back so I could see his face. The torture weighing on his brows and tugging at the corners of his mouth was enough that I rose up on my knees and slipped my hands out of his shirt.

"I'm so sorry. I had no idea, but I didn't mean—"

He shook his head, catching my hands at his jaw and keeping them there. "No, god no. It's not your fault you're so hot and feel like a dream come true. You just don't understand the effect you have on me."

My teeth dug into my bottom lip. "I think I'm starting to. I'll be more careful."

"Don't be. Fuck, please don't be."

Dipping forward, I landed a light kiss on the corner of his mouth. "Okay, birthday boy. I think it's time to go inside so you can take care of that thing."

His eyes squeezed shut. "So, you're just going to say whatever you want now?"

I had to grin at his pained expression. "Isn't that what you're going to do?"

With an exasperated sigh, he rose from the bench, placed me on my feet, and started dragging me toward our dorm by my hand.

"Is this fun for you?" he growled.

"Kind of, yes." My fingers threaded through his. "You can't see it, but you turned me on too. It's just lucky I can hide it better than you."

He muttered, "Fuck," and continued charging forward, making me giggle as I scurried to keep up.

"This is what you signed up for," I added. "This is me."

He stopped, yanking me into his chest. His fire and ice eyes burned into me as he peered down at me. Then his hand came up, grazing my hair, my cheek, the line of my neck, my collarbone.

"You are exactly what I want," he murmured, the truth in every word bleeding out.

The warmth pooling between my legs spread over me like a blanket. I wrapped my arms around his waist, my face pressed into his chest. His heart beat a rapid, steady rhythm under my cheek, and his arms circled me with exquisite care.

We stood like that for a long time, holding each other quietly. By the time we finally tore ourselves apart, it wasn't Beckett's birthday anymore but the start of something completely new.

· · · ◆ · ◆ · · · ·

The second my butt hit the cushion in English, Beckett reached over and tugged me, pillow and all, right beside him. So close his thigh was flush with mine.

I put my hand over my leaping heart. "Holy hell. That's one way to wake me up."

"You didn't sit with me at breakfast," he murmured, pushing my hair back from my face.

"I don't think I'm ready to share meals with Rhys and Charles." I shrugged. "And I like my girl time in the mornings."

He lifted his chin. "Charles and Rhys are dead to me. You'll sit with me at dinner."

Rhys cleared his throat. "If my heart were more than a mote of dust blowing around in the hollow cavity of my chest, it would be extremely hurt at this moment. Dead to you?"

I leaned around Beckett to shake my head at Rhys. "He doesn't mean it. He's slightly deprived of oxygen from some of last night's activities."

I whispered this as quietly as I could since I wasn't the type of girl who advertised who she was hooking up with. But Rhys probably knew all about it since he seemed to be the keeper of Beckett's secrets.

Rhys nodded, rubbing his stubbly jaw. "No, yeah, that makes a lot of sense. He was making comments about the weather and how *pretty* the flowers were near the dorm on our walk to class. I wondered if he was suffering from some latent head injury he'd gotten at soccer. It makes more sense his brain was depleted of oxygen from blowing out all those candles."

"It's not an injury *or* from the candles. He says I make him stupid," I told Rhys, which resulted in Beckett shoving me back to my cushion and bodily blocking my access to his friend.

"Don't talk to him," he groused. "You were right, you're not ready for Rhys. You're not going to be friends."

I could *feel* Delilah rolling her eyes. She wasn't opposed to Beckett and me, but she wasn't all in either.

Rhys scoffed. "Shows what you know. Luc and I bonded over poetry. There's nothing stronger than a poetry bond."

Dr. Burns clapped her hands, drawing the class to order. Being the good little student I was, I scribbled notes while she lectured on about class structure in *Pride and Prejudice*. Meanwhile, Beckett was relaxed on his cushion, leaning back on his hands, his legs stretched out in front of him.

When Dr. Burns paused to grab something from her desk, I glanced around the room, snagging on Bianca on the opposite side of the circle. Her sharp, narrow-eyed gaze was aimed at me, and when she caught me looking back, her mouth flattened.

I turned to tell Delilah I didn't think Bianca liked me very much, but she was in a whispered conversation with Ivan, so I left her alone. When I swiveled toward Beckett, I found him glaring at Bianca with death rays.

It was clear Beckett didn't like Bianca, but that didn't keep my
dormant jealousy monster from deciding to wake up and stretch its
arms. My fingers twitched with the irrational desire to yank Beckett's
attention back to me, but if I had to demand his attention, it wasn't
worth anything.

As if he could read my mind, Beckett turned away from her,
finding me. The ice that had frosted over him thawed in an instant.
His knee nudged my leg. I drew a little smiley face with heart eyes on
my notebook. He dropped his shaking head, not doing a great job
of hiding his grin.

Dr. Burns started speaking again, and I did my best to ignore the
warm press of Beckett's leg against mine. It wasn't easy, and I had a
feeling half my notes weren't going to make any sense, but I liked it
anyway.

"Okay. Now to the fun part: your project." Dr. Burns bounced in
her sensible shoes, alight with genuine excitement. "You'll be working in pairs, exploring one of the themes we've discussed in *Pride
and Prejudice*. Let's spend the last five minutes of class choosing who
you'll be working with. I will warn you to choose wisely. This project
will be worth twenty-five percent of your grade."

Beckett tugged on the sleeve of my jacket. "You're mine."

"But—" I turned to Delilah, who was watching Beckett and me
with wide eyes. "Um—"

Ivan regarded the situation with minor interest. "I'll be your partner. Luciana will be his. There. The problem is solved."

"Is that okay, D?" I whispered. "If it's not, I'll tell him no."

She didn't look incredibly happy, flicking her eyes over Ivan. "Do
you care about your grade in this class?"

He inclined his head. "I do. My GPA stays up, my father stays out
of my business."

She nodded. "Fine. We can work together." There was a slight
tremble in her hands as she smoothed out her skirt. Ivan still managed to make my calm and cool friend nervous. "I'm good, Luc. I'll
partner with Ivan."

I swept my gaze over her. "Are you sure? I don't have to work with Beckett. It was him—"

She waved me off. "No, please. I understand. It isn't as though you left me alone. I have a partner too. Everyone's spoken for."

Beckett tugged on me again, and I swiveled back to him, expecting a smart-ass remark from Rhys, but he'd already wandered to the side of the room, where he was speaking very closely to Gavin, one of the smartest kids at SA. Gavin's face was glowing red as he shrank away from Rhys, but Rhys was either oblivious or didn't care because he kept barreling on, moving with Gavin.

"Rhys found a partner?" I whispered.

Beckett chuckled quietly. "He informed Gavin they'll be working together. Gavin accepted his fate."

"Poor Gavin."

"Rhys will pull his weight. He fucks around, but not about school."

"That's good. Are you going to pull your weight or distract me?"

He lifted a brow. "Some of both. I won't let you get a bad grade, though. That's a promise."

"I believe you."

When class was over, Beckett pulled me up from the floor and slipped my backpack onto my shoulders. He then reached for my hand, but I tucked it in my blazer pocket.

The look he gave me stabbed me in the gut. Doubt mingled with hurt pulled down his features, the grin he'd given me long forgotten. Shadows clouded the lightness between us.

"I can't hold your hand?" he murmured.

"You can, but not so...publicly." I barely squeezed the words out. "Can we give it a little time before we're, like, a couple?"

He stared straight ahead, his jaw tight as we joined the flow of students headed to their next classes. "We're not a couple?"

"Beckett—" I brushed my hand over his arm. "You told me you didn't mind going at my pace."

"That's when I thought you were mine." He finally looked down at me. "You told me you were in. You can't keep one foot out. That's not fair to either of us."

"It's been one day. Be patient."

If we walked down the hall, hand in hand, everyone would know. Being Beckett's girlfriend was such a new concept to me it still hadn't settled. Nor did I fully believe it. I was absolutely nowhere near ready for all eyes to be on us and our names on everyone's lips. Especially when I couldn't be sure this would be more than a blip.

It wasn't fair to him or the way I was beginning to feel for him, but this was just so brand new.

"A day for you. For me, it's been years," he argued with an eerie calmness.

I had to let his words slide over me and not soak in. The thought of him wanting me for years was too big for me right now.

I bumped my shoulder with his. "We're together, Beckett. You know there's nobody else. Isn't that enough for today?"

His chest rose as he sucked in a deep breath and slowly relaxed, letting it all back out. "Not really, but I'll accept it." He tugged my ponytail, letting his grip linger. "You're not backing out on me."

Even though he hadn't really formed his statement as a question, I answered him anyway. "No, I'm not backing out on you. I'm in this, but for now, I'm in it with just you—not our entire school's opinion on how odd we are as a couple."

That earned me a scowl. "Why are we an odd couple?"

"I don't think we are, but we're not an obvious match. You're beautiful Beckett Savage. I'm—"

"Fucking gorgeous Luciana Ortega-Whitlock." If possible, his scowl deepened.

"I—" My cheeks were in flames, and my chest was even hotter. Molten. "Thank you."

"You don't have to thank me for telling the truth."

I wanted to kiss his stupidly handsome, disgruntled face, but we were in the middle of a busy hallway, and if I wasn't ready to hold his hand, I definitely wasn't ready to kiss him.

"I'm going to kiss you really hard later."

He stopped walking, closed his eyes, and made a sound that was a mix between a laugh and a groan.

Bringing his hands to his face, he muttered just loud enough for me to hear. "Why? I got the girl and I'm still being tortured. Fucking why?"

Yeah, I'm definitely going to kiss the hell out of him later.

CHAPTER TWENTY-FOUR

Beckett

"FAVORITE MR. DARCY. DON'T think about it, just say it."

Luciana had to have been kidding when she'd told me not to think. That wasn't in my wheelhouse. But in this case, I didn't need to for once.

"I've never seen any of the movies." I braced for her reaction.

She flopped on my bed, dramatic and adorable. Her T-shirt rose, a sliver of the golden skin on her stomach peeking out. My fingers twitched on my knees to graze the line of exposed flesh.

"You're not serious."

"I am."

She scrunched her nose at me. "That's it. We're breaking up."

Something sharp tangled deep in my chest. "Don't joke about that." I recognized that's what it was, but my knee-jerk reaction could not be helped. I never wanted to hear those words coming from her mouth.

Her grin fell at my snap. "Sorry. You know I don't mean it."

She shifted to her hands and knees and crawled to the end of my bed. I was sitting at my desk, where I'd been managing to keep my hands to myself. At least while we were working on our project for English.

It wasn't easy to control myself around her on a normal basis, but it was like bamboo under my fingernails with her on my bed, knowing my sheets would smell like her long after she left.

She reached for my hand. "Come here."

"If I come there, we're going to be done with *Pride and Prejudice*."

Still, she tugged. "Come here, Savage. Don't be stubborn. I want to tell you some things, and you need to be right here for that to happen."

I moved to the bed. If she asked me for anything, I would give it to her. Sitting with my back against the wall, my feet hanging over the side, Luciana swung her leg over mine, straddling my thighs. My dick had been half-hard since she'd walked into my room, but it was at full attention now.

Her warm palms cupped the sides of my neck. "I don't have any experience with boyfriends, but even I know you're really good at being one. I won't joke about breaking up again, but just so you know, there's not even an ounce of me that meant it."

The tangled barbs in my chest loosened. "You like me."

She nodded. "I do."

I reached around her head and slid her ponytail holder out of her silky hair, letting it spill around her shoulders. Dragging my fingers through the subtle waves, I raked my eyes over her earnest expression. Luciana didn't bullshit. She was up front and open, affectionate as hell in private, but still reserved when we were in public.

It frustrated me. She was mine, and that should have been enough, but it wasn't. I kept those feelings locked down, though. I'd promised her patience, so I'd be what she needed.

"I like the hell out of you, little light."

That made her smile. "I know you do. You're one week into this boyfriend gig, and I think you've got the hang of it." She shuffled forward on my lap, aligning her core with mine. She'd changed out of her uniform into a pair of athletic shorts and a tank. The thin material did nothing to muffle her heat, and it fucked with my control big time. "We've done enough work for today, don't you think?"

For a girl with next to no experience, she wasn't shy. She'd been in my room every day for the last week, and each time, she was more daring than the last. Touching, kissing, putting my hands where she wanted them. I realized I needed that from her. I'd spent too long on this island of longing, alone, wanting, and now that she'd washed up on my shore, there was no hiding the depth of my raw need for her.

Luciana hadn't flinched at what she'd seen. She was digging in with me, going deeper each day.

I took her mouth with mine, licking into her. She opened for me, a little moan slipping out. Her fingers threaded in my hair, and mine trailed along the waistband of her shorts.

I spent a long time on that patch of skin, barely dipping below the elastic to areas I hadn't explored, at least not beneath her clothing. We weren't there, and I didn't even let myself venture into what that would be like. To touch the hot, soft places I felt when she pressed herself against me.

It blew my mind I even got to touch her, much less kiss her, until we were both dizzy from lack of oxygen and our lips were red and swollen. I still wanted—no, *needed*, every-fucking-thing she was, but the pieces she'd given me were far more than I'd spent way too much time fantasizing about.

"You can touch me, Beckett," she said between nips of my bottom lip. "Below my clothes. You don't have to stop at those boundaries. I mean, if you want to."

"Of course I want to." I slipped my hand under her tank, splaying flat on the base of her spine. "You're so smooth."

"That's all you want to touch?" She sat up, bracing her hands on my shoulders, her eyes darker than normal, slightly glazed.

My girl.

My fucking girl.

"You know that's not all I want to touch." I slid to the center of her back. "I'm letting you set the pace. We're going slow."

Her bottom lip disappeared between her teeth for a moment, then she leaned back a little farther, gripped the hem of her tank, and yanked it all the way off.

And then my little light was sitting in my lap, completely topless. My mind went blank until she took my hand and pressed it to her breast. Her nipple was like a bead against the center of my palm, the rest of her flesh a perfect handful.

"Baby," I rasped. "You're beautiful."

Her nails lightly scraped my jaw. "You're not even looking at me, Beckett."

I hadn't even realized I'd slammed my eyes shut until she'd said that. My lids lifted. Her forehead crinkled with worry was the first thing I saw.

"You're beautiful," I repeated.

She pressed on the back of my neck. "Look at me everywhere."

I watched her climb off my lap to lie down on my pillow. Her hair fanned out around her shoulders, and she bit down on her lip. Only then did I allow my gaze to sweep down to her breasts. They were as perfect as they felt, mostly because they were hers, but the little raspberry-colored nipples capping the smooth, golden, pert mounds didn't hurt.

"Beautiful," I told her for a third time.

She held out her hand, beckoning me. "You have to come here. Take off your shirt too."

I reached behind my neck and rid myself of my T-shirt, throwing it across my small room. She curled her fingers again, drawing me to her.

I moved over her, my hands bracketing either side of her face as I kept my body apart from hers. Her spine bowed, bringing her chest closer to mine.

"Touch me, Beckett. Put your mouth on me."

My eyes snapped to hers. "I can taste you?"

She nodded. "Please."

This wasn't my definition of slow, but if this was hers, I'd gladly change mine to match it.

Dropping to my side, I leaned over her, lowering my head to her chest. She sucked in a sharp breath when my nose made contact with the silky flesh of her breast. I rounded my hand along the bottom of it, squeezing gently, making my cock throb violently.

It was right then I knew this couldn't last long. Not with the ache in my cock and my barely suppressed need to thrust into something hot and tight. But I'd keep her here, like this, for as long as I could hang on.

I pressed a kiss to her beaded nipple, and when she didn't stop me, I surrounded it with my lips. Acting on pure instinct, my tongue swirled around her, getting a deep taste of the sunshine that poured out of my girl.

She cradled my head to her with one hand, the other exploring the muscles in my back. Each time I pulled her nipple deeper into my mouth, she whimpered and arched closer.

My mind was spinning, dizzy with desire. Circling my arm around her, I gripped her ass and rolled her onto her side. Her leg bent, bringing her knee in alignment with my cock. It was instinct again that had me thrusting against her. Once, twice, a third time, and it dawned on me what I was doing.

Nothing I'd been given permission to do—that was what.

Tearing my mouth off her, I flopped onto my back, heaving for breath. I covered my face, wrangling my slipping control back in place.

Then she touched me. Her fingertips trailed down my abdomen, following the divots of my muscles. She followed them all the way to the waistband of my joggers. My dick was really fucking close to tearing through the waistband to get to her wandering fingers. I clamped down on her wrist, stopping her.

"I want to touch you." She propped her head up on her hand to peer down at me. "Can I touch you, Beckett?"

I shook my head, keeping her clamped down. "If you touch me, I'll lose it."

Her lips tipped up. "Will you come?"

"Yes," I gritted out.

She tried to shake my hold off. "Let me go, Beckett. I want to touch you." Her eyes met mine, a surprising plea softening them. "Please, let me touch you and make you come."

"You're serious?"

She nodded. "I really want to. I don't know if I'll be good at it, but you can tell me what to do."

I slowly released her wrist, not quite believing what was about to happen. "Anything you do will be what I want."

"Okay."

I released my hold on her, and once she had free rein, she slipped her hand into my joggers. Her eyes popped wide when she connected with my cock. First, she only petted it, and even that was nearly enough to make me blow.

"Can I push your pants down so I can see it?" She didn't sound nervous. My girl was brimming with excitement. There was no question this was what she wanted to do.

I helped her out, tugging my pants down to my hips. My cock slapped heavily against my stomach. Luciana didn't let it get lonely, though. Her fingers curled around the middle and slowly slid to the tip.

"Like that?" she whispered.

"Perfect." Tangling my fingers in her hair, I drew her down to me, needing her close for when I inevitably lost my mind. "Keep doing that, little light. You're doing perfectly."

While she pumped my length in her tight, hot fist, I kissed her throat and rubbed my thumb over her nipple. It was sensory overload, the feel of her beside me, holding me, her in my hands and under my mouth. Her sunshine scent invaded my lungs, the sounds of her little pants and whimpers, like she was taking pleasure out of what she was doing to me.

It hadn't been long enough, but there was no way I could hang on, even though I wanted to more than anything. This first time with her should have lasted for hours instead of short minutes, but this was Luciana, and I'd used up all my control over the years I'd waited for her to be ready for me. Now that I had her, there was no stopping this. Not with her half-naked body pressed against mine as she whispered my name in a mindless way that told me she didn't even know she was doing it.

"I'm gonna come." I tried to brush her hand away. No way I could come on her pretty skin. No way she'd want me to. "Let go, baby. I can finish it."

Her hold on me tightened. "I want to. *Please.*"

Unable to deny her a single thing, I relented, rolling onto my back. She followed, her movements matching my quickening, frantic thrusts into her hand. She cooed at me to show her how much I liked it, telling me she wanted to see it. My edges were so frayed her soft, coaxing words ripped me in two.

With that, the last tether of my sanity snapped, and I allowed a tidal wave of ecstasy to sweep me under. My face was buried in Luciana's throat as I came, my stomach flexing and clenching. She pressed tighter into my side, pumping my cock through the last of my jerking spasms. I had to close my hand over hers to get her to stop.

She loosened her fingers but kept her palm over me like a sweet little blanket.

I couldn't believe that had just happened. That Luciana had asked for it to happen. And she wasn't running away in disgust. If anything, she was burrowing into me like she still liked me. Maybe *really* liked me.

"Are you okay?" I asked against her throat.

I felt her nod. "That was really hot. Messy, but so hot." A beat of hesitation, then, "What if—"

"What?" I raised my head to meet her gaze. "Ask me anything you want, Luc."

Her cheeks were rosy, but that could have been from embarrassment or desire. I couldn't get a read on my girl right now, with my brain still cum drunk and hazy.

"What if I touch myself and make myself come?"

"Obviously, I'm in a coma. There is no way you're real." There was no way I could've actually been this lucky. Impossible.

She let go of me and trailed her fingers along her taut stomach. "It's real. Doing that to you really turned me on. I want...I *want*."

This was real. Luciana was real, and this was happening.

My lids lowered as I raked my eyes over her writhing body. Goose bumps pricked her flesh, but she wasn't cold. Not with the heat radiating between us. My girl was turned on, just like she'd said, and there was nothing I wanted to see more than Luciana rubbing her pussy in my bed.

"Do it, baby. Let me see you."

My chest was tight, constricted. I could barely breathe as she slipped her hand into her shorts. Though I couldn't see what she was touching, I knew by the way her mouth fell open she'd reached her destination. My cock, which had barely begun to soften, turned to steel again.

"Are you wet?" I brushed my fingers over her stomach and hip bones.

"I'm soaked." She nuzzled her face against my arm, sighing. "I've never felt like this before. It's you. It's you, it's you, it's you."

Ignoring the sticky mess I'd made on my stomach, I turned to my side so I could get to her. Kissing her smooth skin, sucking her hard nipples, licking a line between her breasts. Mewling, she raised her hips, her hand working inside her shorts.

"Come closer, Beckett," she demanded breathlessly.

"I can't, baby. You don't want to get my cum on you."

Her eyes flared, and her tongue darted out to lick her upper lip. "Come here. I need to feel you on me. I don't care if you make me dirty, I just need you."

That was all she had to say. Lifting her arm over her head, I pressed into her side, my upper body covering hers, my elbows braced on either side of her face. She tipped her head back, her mouth falling open as sharp pants escaped.

"That's it. Look at you, my light. You're so pretty like this. You've never been more beautiful."

I dipped my head down to taste her lips. She moved against me, kissing me, rocking her hips into me. My cock was wedged against her hip, hard again, like I hadn't come at all. Like it'd been decades since I'd released instead of minutes.

"Beckett." Luciana let loose a wild sound from the back of her throat. Her hips were off the bed, her neck arching violently. I thrust against her, over and over, while she cried out her pleasure.

She didn't stop after she came, and neither did I. The friction of her flesh against mine brought me to the tipping point, but the truth was, all she really had to do was look at me to make me lose it.

Her breathing stuttered, and the muscles in her stomach rippled. I closed my mouth over her nipple, taking her the rest of the way, and when she fell, I couldn't stop myself from going with her.

My edges and breath were ragged as my forehead fell on hers. Her panting breaths matched mine, but hers were tinged with a sweetness specific to her. Doubt crept in as seconds passed, then minutes. Luciana went lax in my arms, staying quiet.

I'd gone too far. I'd lost it and violated the immense trust she'd given me. What the hell was my problem? I couldn't even let that be about her without getting my rocks off too? What was wrong with me?

Her eyes opened, locking on mine. "Why do I hear you thinking so loudly? Your brain should be as mushy as mine."

"I'm sorry."

"What?" She pushed on my shoulders, demanding space. I eased away from her even though it was the last thing I wanted to do. "Why are you sorry?"

I tipped my head to my cum, coating her skin and staining the side of her shorts. "You were so beautiful and hot...and I just lost it."

She gripped the side of my neck, frowning. "And you're sorry?" I nodded, and her frown deepened. "I was thinking I might just lie here in your arms all sticky and sleepy after we both got off really hard, but now I feel like I did something wrong by instigating that, and I'm so confused."

"You like being sticky?"

"If it's from messing around with you, yeah, I like it."

She gave me that open, guileless stare while stroking my neck and shoulders, and the twisted, jagged parts of me that were quick to doubt and even faster to blame smoothed out completely. Wrapping her in my arms, I rolled us so she was on my chest, her head tucked under my chin. I was pretty much naked, she was nearly there too, but all I could think about was keeping her.

I was going to keep this girl and never let her go.

That was a fact.

CHAPTER TWENTY-FIVE
Luciana

BECKETT'S ROOM WAS TINY, but over the last two weeks, it had become the hub of our relationship. I found myself drifting to his side of the hall more than my own these days. His room was where the snuggles were. And the orgasms.

The draw was pretty much equal.

Tonight, we were cuddled up on Beckett's bed. He'd set up his laptop for us to watch *Pride and Prejudice*. We were starting with the 2005 version since that was all we had time for tonight, but someday soon, we were going to binge the BBC miniseries.

Except we kept finding ourselves kissing instead of watching.

"This is your fault," he groused once he'd finished devouring my mouth for the third time, not even halfway through the movie. "You're too good at that."

I laughed at his grumpiness. "Too good at kissing?"

"Yes." He took my chin between his fingers. "How many were there before me?"

I squinted at him, having absolutely no interest in answering that. "Are you kidding?"

"No. Yes. I don't know." His narrowed eyes matched mine. "Just tell me, do any go to SA?"

"No." Then I scoffed. "Well, one does."

He stiffened, darkness flaring behind his clear gaze. "Who?"

"Freddie."

He reared back, examining me for the veracity of my statement. "You kissed Freddie Spencer?"

"Yes." I patted his locked jaw. "Freddie has made out with all my friends. It's just a thing."

"Made out? That kid had his tongue in your mouth?" The tendons in Beckett's neck stood out in stark relief.

My lips pressed together. Oh, he was so mad. I wasn't about to give him any more fuel for his anger.

"Does it matter? I only want to kiss you, Beckett."

He grumbled, none of his tension melting. I couldn't believe how disgruntled he was that I'd kissed other guys before him. This wasn't brand-new information, and *no one* had ever kissed me the way Beckett did.

I scooted up on the bed until I was upright, my legs folded. Beckett followed, sitting unhappily against the wall. He shoved his fingers through his messy hair, blowing out a harsh breath.

I took his other hand in mine. "Don't be mad at me."

"I'm not. I'm mad at the guys who've touched you."

"No one's *touched* me. A few terrible, barely memorable kisses aren't anything to get worked up about. I don't even understand why we're having this conversation. I'm not going to ask you to name every girl you've hooked up with."

He jolted, his head jerking back so suddenly he banged it against the wall. "What are you talking about? Was I not clear when I told you I waited for you?"

"You were. I know you saved your first kiss for me. But come on. There are a lot of other things you can do with girls besides kissing. Let's not pretend."

"Who's pretending, Luciana?"

My nose crinkled. I hated how this conversation was going.

"Who you were with before doesn't matter to me. That's what I'm trying to say."

His scowl only deepened. "I told you I waited. There is no *before*."

I shook my head. "You don't have to do that. Just because I'm inexperienced doesn't mean you have to be."

"What kind of man would I be if I felt for you the way I do and still hooked up with other girls?" He clucked his tongue. "I don't know, but that's not the kind of man I am. I have no interest in anyone else. It's always been you."

I wasn't mad before. I got why he wouldn't want to share his past. I hadn't either. But now I was getting pissed. He was looking me in the eye and gaslighting me as if I was going to fall for that.

"Beckett, I heard you and Bianca in the hall when she was talking about giving you—"

"What?" he snapped. "What did you hear?"

"I don't really want to repeat her exact words, but she was saying she gave you a blow job."

His next breath was so frayed and heavy alarm bells started ringing in my head.

"I don't want to talk about it." He clamped his lips together, his eyes going distant and empty. Shut down, just like that.

"Well, I didn't want to talk about my past either, but I didn't lie to your face." Done with this pointless discussion, I unfolded my legs and swung them over the side of the bed. Stuffing my feet in my slides, I snagged my backpack off the floor. I hadn't even opened it, so it was easy to throw it over my shoulder and cross the narrow space to the door. "I'll talk to you tomorrow."

"You're leaving?"

I stopped with my hand on the door and twisted around to look at him. "We're not getting anywhere right now, and I don't want to continue this."

His gaze flipped from vacant to panicked in the blink of an eye, then he was on his feet, wedging himself between me and his door.

"You don't want to continue this?" His fingers sliced into the sides of my hair, and he held my head in his hands. "You're not ending us."

Letting my backpack fall to the floor, I wrapped my fingers around his wrists. "I'm not. I meant this conversation. You're not being forthcoming, and frankly, you're lying to me, so I'm mad. I don't want to be in this room with you anymore. Maybe tomorrow—"

"I was passed out when it happened." Those brittle words shattered as soon as he dropped them.

I sucked in a breath. "What?" I hoped I misunderstood. That I was wrong about what he was saying.

He dropped his hold on me and turned away, bracing his clasped hands on his nape. "Last year, I went to a house party in the hills with Rhys and the guys. I was in a dark headspace, feeling shitty about myself, so I drank a lot. More than I ever have. It was stupid, and my body didn't appreciate it. I passed out in one of the bedrooms, and next thing I knew, Bianca was there, opening my pants. I think I told her no, but I was so fucking out of it, I don't know if anything came out of my mouth. There's no question I did not consent to what she did to me. I couldn't even lift my head off the pillow."

Blood drained from my face, and my heart cracked in two, but I refused to make this about me. As gutted as I was for him, Beckett was the one who'd been harmed. This was about him.

"Beckett—" He flinched when I laid my hand on his back, but I kept it there so he'd know I was listening. I wasn't leaving.

"Rhys walked in and threw her off me. Not before she put her mouth on me. Not before she filmed herself—" His head dropped, and his back heaved with each gasping breath he took.

"Baby," I whispered. "Can I put my arms around you?"

He gave the barest nod, so I circled my arms around his waist and pressed my cheek to his back. When he wanted to face me, he could, but I didn't know if he was ready right now. I'd pushed him too hard already. I wouldn't do it anymore.

"I'm sorry, Beckett. Sorry that happened to you, and so sorry I made you tell me when you didn't want to."

He took my hand and pulled me around to his front. His eyes searched mine, darting back and forth over my face.

"I don't drink anymore," he uttered.

"I don't blame you." I pressed my palms to his chest, covering his thrashing heart. "I want you to know you're safe with me. We never have to do anything you don't want to."

A rush of breath exploded from him, then his forehead was on mine and he had me tucked against him.

"My light," he murmured. "There's nothing I don't want you to do to me. What happened with her has zero bearing on you and me. Now that you know, I want to put it away. That diseased cunt doesn't get to exist here with us."

"If that's what you want."

I breathed him in, feeling him shudder as I tightened my arms around him. I wished there was more I could do. I wished I could take away what she did to him. How it made him feel. Because as much as he said he wanted to put it away, he stood in front of me, calling himself stupid for drinking that much, shouldering the blame for something that wasn't his fault.

"I want her gone," he said lowly. "That's what I want."

"Too bad she came back after her suspension."

His molars gnashed and ground together. "That wasn't supposed to happen."

I reared back, checking his expression.

Grim. Pissed off.

But the vulnerability behind the anger almost brought me to my knees.

"Did you have something to do with that?" I asked, sure to keep any admonishment out of my voice. I certainly didn't feel it.

He lowered his chin, leveling me with a challenging stare. "What's the point of having a mother with a cabinet full of prescription pain meds if I can't use them for my own purposes?" He made a self-deprecating scoff and peered down at me like he was waiting for my judgment.

I raised a brow. "Are you expecting me to tell you that was wrong?"

"I wouldn't be surprised if you did."

Fisting his shirt, I gave him a little jostle. "She deserved it. I'm glad you did it. I hope she was scared out of her mind. But I'm really angry it didn't stick. I don't want that bitch anywhere near you."

He stared at me in silence, heavy breaths filling the space between us. Seconds, then minutes passed, and I never looked away. I wanted him to see I was fully on his side. The door wasn't an option for me.

Finally, he moved, his mouth coming down on mine. He was shockingly careful in the way he kissed me, touching his lips to mine like a gentle breeze over rose petals. I let him take what he needed, sipping from my mouth when I wanted to take big gulps of him.

My heart rattled in my overstuffed chest. My feelings for Beckett had grown quickly. I wasn't sure I'd ever been as close to another person as we were in this moment. This beautiful boy had given me a part of his story he hated, that he was ashamed of. He let me in, and now I was in this land of Beckett, truly seeing who he was.

Yeah, he was a Savage. He was handsome, athletic, popular, rich.

Those were his forward-facing facets. The ones everyone saw. It was the shiny, untouched ones in the back the light rarely touched that made up who he really was.

The loyal friend, sticking with Rhys Astor since childhood.

The doting brother-in-law who was openly affectionate to Mrs. Umbra in the halls.

A boy who saw a girl and made up his mind she would be his. When other kids our age hopped from whim to whim, my Beckett remained steadfast. Though it was crazy and overwhelming to know he truly had waited for me and only me, it was also so heady, all I could do was fall into him without doubting he'd be there to catch me.

"She won't come near you," I promised against his lips. "You're mine."

He smiled against mine. "My ferocious girlfriend. You're gonna protect me?"

"Always."

He rolled his forehead on mine. "That's a big word to me, Luciana."

"I'm feeling big things right now." I tugged him down to my mouth, needing to give him the same gentle kisses he'd given me. My horror and outrage over what Bianca had taken from him had left me ripped open, my raw edges exposed. But each kiss I placed on his lips—lips that were only mine—was a balm.

We held each other through the ugly. And even though Beckett wanted to lock it away, it would always be there, but not between us. Never between us.

CHAPTER TWENTY-SIX

Luciana

I HAD BEEN BECKETT Savage's girlfriend for more than two weeks now, and in that time, he had shown me who he was over and over. I trusted him, and I believed we were solid.

He'd been impatient as hell with my need to keep us low key, but he'd agreed to it. Knowing him like I now did, it went against every one of his natural instincts. He undoubtedly had to fight himself every time he didn't grab my hand or kiss me in the hallway.

To be fair, I'd been fighting too. I *wanted* those things, but I'd been holding on to my fear.

But after Beckett let me inside and showed me his darkness, my fear was lost. And looking back, it had been microscopic in comparison to what we were.

Delilah propped her hip on the bathroom sink beside me. "You're making quite a statement, precious."

"Don't move!" Bella dug her nails into my chin, keeping me in place. "Do you want this paint smeared all over your face?"

We were in a rush, and I wasn't doing the greatest job of holding still due to a combination of excitement and nerves. Beckett's game was starting in a few minutes, and we were holed up in the bathroom near the field, adding last-minute touches to my outfit.

"The statement is the point," I told Delilah.

Evelyn circled her finger near my right cheek. "It's slightly off-center. Is that all right with everyone else?"

I would have grinned at her, but Bella was in drill sergeant mode. She took face paint very seriously. I supposed this *was* serious. Not the paint, per se, but the gesture.

"It's fine with me, Ev." Bella growled at me for moving my face to talk.

"It would bother me." Evelyn peered closer, then at herself in the mirror. "You're lucky things like that don't bother you."

Delilah flicked her hand in her elegant way. "As if you would be caught dead with a boy's jersey number painted on your cheek."

Ev smoothed a hand over her silky hair and smiled. "Not dead or alive. I understand it's your public declaration of affection, but why his number? Shouldn't it be a heart? Perhaps with his name in it?"

The bathroom door swung open before any of us could answer Evelyn's sound logic. Two girls filed in, led by Bianca. Their chattering came to a stop when they noticed the bathroom was already occupied.

"All done," Bella declared, tipping my face side to side to inspect her work. "Y'all, we'd better get out there if we don't wanna miss kickoff."

Bianca parked herself in front of the only unoccupied mirror and went about applying nude lip liner to her full lips. Everything she did nauseated me. I had to swallow several times just so I didn't throw up everywhere.

"Going to the soccer game?" She looked at me in her reflection, arching a brow. "Us too. Although we didn't feel the need to look like a groupie."

No, she looked like a slut in a tiny pleated skirt, a sheer top, and skank heels.

I would *never* call another girl a slut. But Bianca was an exception. She truly deserved far worse. As far as I was concerned, she was an unrepentant rapist, and I would never look at her as anything else.

Her friend, Clarice Chin, who I'd been pretty neutral on until this very moment, got in my face to examine the paint on my cheek.

"Oh my god." She covered her mouth to hide her giggle. "Is that Beckett Savage's number?"

"What?" Bianca slammed down her lip liner on the sink. "You can't be serious."

Clarice circled me, checking out the back of my shirt. "She has his name on her back."

"Wow." Bianca put her hands on her hips. "I don't think I've ever seen anything more pathetic."

"Right?" Clarice moved to stand shoulder to shoulder with Bianca while my girls lined up around me. Even Evelyn stood by me, and she was definitely not one for confrontation. "He's not going to fall in love with you just because you throw yourself at him."

"I honestly thought you were better than this." Bianca lifted her chin in superiority, and that did it.

I couldn't hold it in.

The first laugh came out as a sputter.

And then it was a full-fledged belly laugh, tears springing to my eyes, the ridiculousness of the situation driving me to hysterics.

"That's rich coming from you, B."

Her sharp brow slanted. "What's that supposed to mean?"

My bitter amusement fell away, although the tears stayed. "I think you know, Bianca. I *know*."

I left her ranting in the bathroom, my friends at my sides. They didn't ask me to clarify my meaning, which made me love them even more. Now wasn't the time, and it definitely wasn't my story to tell.

I had a game to get to and a boy to cheer for.

· · · ● · ● · · · ·

Beckett was a graceful player, if that was a thing. He practically danced down the field, swerving around other players while his feet made complicated maneuvers to keep the ball in his possession.

He was already on the field for kickoff by the time we made it to the bleachers, spotting me only a minute or two into the game. I felt the grin he shot me like it was a tangible thing.

I'd been to soccer games before, but I hadn't paid attention to him with the same fervor I was now. It was like I was seeing him through a different lens.

His skill on the field only made me fall harder. The way he pushed his teammates, not just through his words and vigorous pats on the back when a particularly skilled play was made. No, Beckett was the consummate team player. He didn't hoard the glory for himself, always passing the ball when there was an opening.

He played the way I did. Or, at least, how I strove to play.

I didn't see him trash-talking nearly as much as I did, though. But that was a difficult thing to compete with.

When it was halftime, he paused at the bench to grab his water bottle but never stopped charging toward the bleachers. I ran down the steps, my heart in my throat, and we met like we had at his first game: me against the rail, him on the ground below.

He didn't hesitate to jump up and encircle me with a sweaty arm. "You made it."

"I think I love watching you play."

He cocked his head. "What's on your cheek, baby?"

I turned my head to the side to show him. "I'm your cheerleader."

He gritted out, "Fuck," under his breath and yanked me even harder against him. "People will see. They're probably looking at us now."

"I know," I whispered. "Let go of me so I can show you the back."

He didn't let go, gripping my hip to spin me himself. After several long seconds, he wound my ponytail around his fist, and his lips were on my nape.

"You're wearing my name," he murmured.

"So there's no mistake who I belong to."

I spun to face him, taking his face in my hands and pressing a hard, lingering kiss on his mouth. "No mistake."

He squeezed his eyes shut. "Christ, Luciana. I have to go back to my team and my dick is about to explode."

Laughing, I patted him on the shoulder. Man, did I like him so freaking much.

"Do a good job, and I'll help you out with that after the game."

A rough grumble ripped its way up his throat. "Meet me at the locker room."

"I'll be there. Go win the game for me." I pressed another quick kiss to his lips, and he caught me before I could pull away, turning it into something longer and deeper.

"My girl." He looked at me like he wanted to stamp it on me, but it basically was.

"Now everyone will know."

The corner of his mouth hitched. "As they should." He reached around me and gave my butt a swat. "Be good. I gotta go talk to the team."

I watched him run, going mushy over his glutes and calves. Since he ran beside me, I never got to see him from this side, but my boyfriend was gorgeous from every angle.

Once he was back with his team, I returned to my friends, who were wearing plastered-on smiles. Except Ev, who was watching the field, earbuds in her ears, ignoring everything else around her. But that was Ev. She often got lost in her own little world.

I pointed at Bella, Delilah, and Freddie, who had joined us at the start of the game. "What are these faces about?"

Freddie kicked his long legs out, resting them on the bench a row down. "I can't believe you've forsaken me for a Savage. I thought surely you were turning all the boys down because of your hopeless crush on me. But no. I'll just have to count on Delilah for that."

She flicked his ear. "Look elsewhere, Frederick."

Freddie swiveled to Bella. "Doll? You're pining for me, aren't you?"

Bella nodded. "I am. I've already picked out our china pattern. By the way, I won't accept anything under three carats, though four would be optimal."

Freddie scoffed. "Oh, my sweet, darling love muffin, nothing less than five will do for you. I want your finger to shine like a chandelier so everyone knows how much I adore you."

"Okay, okay." I waved my hands around. "Stop planning your wedding and tell me why you guys looked like you smelled something foul when I came back."

"That's because we did," Freddie announced. "Fish cunt is particularly putrid on a sunny day, and Bianca's was assaulting my olfactory senses when she marched herself over here to demand answers about you and Beckett."

I scrunched my nose at his description but swept it aside for the important information. "What did you tell her?"

"The truth," Delilah said.

"Right." Bella nodded. "We told that bitch y'all are crazy for each other and you have Beckett locked down tight. That's your man, and you're his woman."

Freddie snickered. "That bitch wasn't happy. Her face turned tomato red. It was glorious."

Delilah wasn't laughing, though. "It was fun until she began to unload vitriol about both of you. She said Beckett would tire of you quickly and beg for her to take him back, as he always did."

My mouth fell open. "She's delusional."

Freddie, who didn't have a clue about the depths of Bianca's depravity, shrugged it off. "Some people don't know how to accept rejection. Mummy and Daddy never told them 'no.' Actually, that's about fifty percent of the SA population."

"Where is she?" I glanced around the bleachers, not seeing her.

"She left. Poor Clarice got dragged out with her," Bella said.

"Not poor Clarice. She's only as good as the company she keeps." Delilah stole the words right out of my mouth.

"True." Freddie leaned his elbows on his knees, watching the boys take the field again. "Maybe that cunt will get over her unrequited obsession with Savage now."

I bit my lip as Beckett turned toward me from his spot at the center of the field. He lifted his chin and pressed a hand to his chest.

I pressed my hand to the exact same spot on mine.

Bianca was wretched, but she wasn't a factor anymore. She could get herself riled up, spout her delusions, and stomp around all she wanted. I didn't care about any of that.

Today was about Beckett and me. He was mine, and I was his. I couldn't wait to show him how much I meant that when the game was over.

Chapter Twenty-Seven

Beckett

My coach decided today, of all days, was the time to talk about college scouts and do a deep dive into my plans for next year. I was crawling out of my skin by the time I left his office and the locker room had cleared out.

I needed to text Luciana. She probably thought I'd ditched her.

I prowled down the deserted rows of lockers, intent on getting to mine so I could find my phone locked inside.

The row my locker was in wasn't deserted, however. My footsteps came to a stop as I took in the girl waiting for me on the bench.

Clad in a Savage Academy soccer shirt and a pair of cutoffs, my girl was looking like a dream come true. And when she held out her hand to me, I moved to her without a second thought.

"What are you doing in here?"

She lifted a shoulder. "I was waiting outside, then Felix told me you were in with your coach, so I decided to wait here for you."

I stopped in front of her. She tipped her head up at me and smiled, making me feel full all over. My head, my chest, my cock.

"Did the team see you in here?"

She shook her head. "Felix smuggled me in, but a lot of the guys were already gone." Her hands flattened on my stomach and inched down to my hips. There was no disguising the bulge in my shorts, especially not when she was making a frame with her hands on me.

"Baby...let me get changed so we can go back to my room."

Her head shook again. "You won the game for me." A flash of pink. She licked her lips. "Let me reward my boyfriend."

I traced the line of her jaw with my thumb. "How do you want to do that?"

She inched forward on the bench, hooking her fingers into the waistband of my shorts. "Can I suck you, please?"

"I'm—Luciana..."

She opened her legs and tugged me forward to stand between them. Her eyes flicked to mine, then she leaned in and rubbed her face against my hard-on.

"Do you want me to?" she asked softly.

"Do *you* want to?" I countered, because dear fucking god, did I want her to do it. My brain was going to explode from my crazed level of want.

"Yeah, I really do." She kissed the ridge of my cock through my shorts. "You're in charge, Beckett. Tell me what you want me to do."

I sucked in a breath to give myself a second or two to rein myself in. "Take it out."

Her fingers delved lower, tugging my shorts down to my hips, freeing my cock, then she waited.

"Kiss it." Her lips were warm and soft, pressing to the middle of my length. "More, Luciana. Kiss it again."

This kiss was wet and closer to the top.

"Do you like that?" she asked.

"I like anything you do to me, baby."

Her fingers closed around my base. "Can I taste you now?"

"Go ahead. Do what feels right."

She held my gaze as she opened her mouth and my tip passed her pretty lips. Everything was good, mind-blowingly perfect until her lips closed around me. For a split second, I was back to that night, to the dazed panic and helplessness. But she made a sound, a light kitten mew I'd come to know as a sign of her pleasure, and I was brought right back.

This was my girl, giving me pleasure. Pleasure she'd offered and I'd accepted.

No one was here with us. It was Luciana and me. No one else.

"More," I rasped. "Go deeper, baby."

She slid her lips along my length, coating me in her heat. I couldn't take my eyes off her. Her lashes brushed her cheeks, and her lips were pink and puffy around me. Her head was in my hands, but I slipped one onto her ponytail, stroking it then wrapping it around my fist.

Like a fantasy. One I'd had many, many times.

My thumb grazed my number on her cheek, smearing it slightly. I was careful not to ruin it, though. I wanted to keep looking at the way she'd marked herself as mine while she blew me.

"Luciana," I groaned, fighting against closing my eyes. "You're perfect."

She hummed and dug her fingertips into my ass, pulling me closer. I'd never felt anything like this. The wet heat of her mouth was driving me to the edge much faster than I wanted it to. But she kept swirling her tongue around me and flicking it over the ridge below the head, doing what I'd shown her with her hands. It was ten times as powerful with her tongue.

"Can I thrust, Luc? Can you take that?"

She nodded, lifting her eyes to mine for a moment but never taking her mouth off me. More than anything, I wanted to let loose, to lose control, but I never would. Not when this was new for us both. I'd never hurt her. Never let her be hurt.

I edged around the borders of my control, pushing into her mouth while I held her head steady. She moaned and squirmed around on the bench, clenching her thighs together. Her little movements and the sounds she made were a shot of satisfaction straight to my dick. Knowing she was enjoying this made it that much better for me.

"That feels so ridiculously incredible, Luciana. I'm going to come soon. I can't—"

I shook my head, letting my chin fall onto my chest. Her fingers pressed against the base of my spine, urging me on without words. Flexing my hips, I slid in and out of her mouth, making shorter, faster thrusts.

My pulse roared like a storm in my ears, and my knees shook. I couldn't stop watching her swallow me. My girl was so sweet, but right now, she looked anything but. Sexy little light, taking me, licking me, seizing my control from me.

Righting my wrongs and erasing them until there was only this.

Dreams of her mouth on me would replace the nightmares of what came before.

This was hers. All hers.

"Baby, I'm close. I'm gonna come soon." The last thing I wanted was to pull out of her, but I would. "You don't have to swallow, beautiful. Only if you want to."

Her fingers dug into me like she was prepared to battle me if I tried to get away. Those perfect lips sucked me deeper, pulsing around me in a way that made my eyes roll back.

I wanted to keep her in my sight, but my body wasn't my own anymore. My head fell back, and a moan I couldn't contain echoed off the empty room. And then I was pumping deep, twisting her ponytail tighter. She whimpered and clawed, sucking me, licking me, taking everything.

Until the storm erupted and lightning flashed behind my eyelids. A torrent of pleasure claimed me wholly, rippling across my abdomen and spilling out of me. Luciana lapped it up, taking everything with long licks and softening sucks.

I had her in my arms as soon as I could function. Her legs wrapped around my waist, her arms around my neck. I walked with her to the sink area, kissing her neck and jaw and burying my nose in her skin.

I threw a towel down on the counter, then put her on top of it. Cupping her cheeks, I kissed her hard, staying there with my eyes squeezed shut, our mouths connected, inhaling her air.

"I want to go down on you. Let me?"

Raising her butt off the counter, she wiggled her shorts down to her hips, and I pulled them the rest of the way off. Her legs fell open for me. I kneeled between them, grasping her behind the knees and pulling her to the very edge of the counter. She was glistening with need.

I peered up at her. "You have to be quiet, okay? I don't know where Coach is."

She didn't even flinch at the fact that Coach could still be around. That was how turned on she was because Luciana was no exhibitionist.

"I'll try."

I hadn't done this to her. I'd touched her, looked at her, licked her off my fingers, but my mouth hadn't been on her. Well...in my dreams.

I needed it. And from the way her fingers tangled in my hair and gently shoved me into her, she needed it just as badly.

Spreading her with my thumbs, I dipped forward, curling my tongue over her hot, slick flesh. That first taste, straight from the source, burned me alive. She was in my veins, rushing past my heart to invade every corner of my being. Now that I knew, I'd have to have this as often as she'd let me.

There were no slow testing licks. I knew my girl needed a lot more than that, and I had to have it. So, I buried my face in her, soaking up her scent and sweet tang.

"Oh god, Beckett. I love that. Keep doing it."

She drew her knees up, and when I circled the tip of my tongue around her clit, she clamped them around my head. Lapping at her swollen little bud, I pressed her legs down to the counter, stroking the silk of her inner thighs.

"Tell me if I'm doing it right, Luc."

Her fingers curled in my hair. "You're doing it right. Don't stop."

She didn't have to tell me not to stop. That wasn't going to happen. I needed her to come on my tongue like I needed my next breath.

The muscles in her legs trembled and rippled as I lapped at her, letting me know I was doing something right. She was trying to keep quiet, one hand over her mouth to muffle her noises, but there was no disguising the squeaky pants she made when she was close to her peak.

Though I'd have liked to experiment with her body, dig my tongue inside her, tease her until she went wild, I couldn't do that now. Not here. Not our first time. And since I knew Luc responded to pressure on her clit, I flattened my tongue on top of it and pulsed.

She made a low moan I'd never heard her make before. Her hips jerked against my mouth, and she pressed me into her. I gave her what she needed, pressing and licking her clit, until she started vibrating and panting, tugging my hair and almost flying off the counter.

I held her through it, opening my eyes to the beauty of her falling apart because of me.

When it was over, she slumped and slid down so far I had to catch her, or she would have fallen onto the floor. My arms around her, she melted into my chest, clinging to my jersey.

I tugged her ponytail holder out and tucked my face into the waterfall of her hair. And I felt it. The thing I'd kept buried for so long. It was *right there*, at the surface. Too big to keep inside, too soon to share.

I lifted her up and held her tight. She was wrapped around me in the same way, nose buried in my throat, arms and legs surrounding me.

"I need to get you back to my room," I rumbled into her hair.

"I should probably put my shorts back on." She was limp except for her limbs, which were locked in their embrace.

"I'll take care of you. You don't even have to move."

"You're the best boyfriend I've ever had." She yawned and let her cheek rest heavy on my shoulder. "I think I'll keep you."

"You don't have a choice."

"Mmm...good thing I like you a lot and you seem to enjoy going downtown."

I laughed as I attempted to thread her foot into her shorts. She was so fucking floppy, not making it easy on me. I reveled in the struggle, though. I'd done that to her. I'd made my girl limp with my mouth.

"Loved it. Gonna do it again as soon as I get you back to my room."

Like she'd been given a shot of adrenaline, she raised her head, grinning at me. "Best boyfriend ever."

·· • • • • • • · ·

A couple hours later, we were the last stragglers in the dining hall, cramming dinner into our mouths before it closed and they kicked us out.

"I have to tell you something." Luciana crumbled up her napkin, worry pinching her brow.

"Tell me."

"Bianca had a reaction to this." She pointed at her jersey. "An unhinged reaction. She told my friends you'd dump me and come crawling back to her like you always did."

I dropped my fork, my gaze steady on her. "I've never been with her. We were not ever a thing."

Her hand darted out and clamped down on my wrist. "I *know*. I wasn't trying to imply you'd had anything with her. I wanted you to know in case she stirs up trouble."

Flipping my hand over, I threaded our fingers together. "No, I won't let her do that."

"I don't think you can stop her, Beckett. But just so you know, I'm on your side. If she spreads rumors or whatever, I won't listen. They'll slide right off my back."

"No."

Her brows winged. "No? What do you mean?"

"No, I'm not letting her start shit. She's done enough. Fucked me up enough. She doesn't get to be a part of you and me. That's not happening."

She gnawed on her bottom lip, her eyes darting over me with worry.

"Take that look off your face, little light." I swiped a finger along her forehead. "I know what I'm doing."

"*What* are you doing?"

"What I should have done a year ago. Should have gotten rid of her then, but I didn't want to think about it. Wanted to pretend it didn't happen. As long as she stayed away from me…but now there's you. Her staying away isn't enough."

"Are you going to tell me?"

I drew a line all the way down her nose to her lips, pulling the bottom one from between her teeth. "Do you want the details? Or can you trust I'm going to take care of it?"

She slowly shook her head. "If you don't want to talk about it…"

Heaving a sigh, I touched my forehead to hers, grounding myself. "There's a recording. I have it. Soon, her father's going to have it."

Her breath caught. "Beckett—oh god."

"I don't really want to talk about it any more than this, baby. Are you good with that?"

Her warm palm pressed on my cheek. "Yes. Of course. Do what you need to do, and I'll be here with you."

"That's all I need to know."

· · · ● ● ● ● · · · ·

It was done.

The recording was sent, along with a message from me.

If Mr. DeSoto didn't want his daughter's misdeeds leaked far and wide, including to the police, he'd remove her from Savage Academy within the next forty-eight hours.

I'd had this plan since I'd taken the recording from Bianca's phone months ago, ensuring I was the sole possessor of it. But shame and denial had kept me from doing anything else.

Before Luc, I hadn't spoken about what had gone down that night with anyone. Not even to Rhys, who'd witnessed most of it. He'd tried in his own Rhys way, but I wasn't having it.

I wasn't in a place where I wanted to speak about it freely. Hell, maybe I'd never get there. It was enough that Luciana knew. She intrinsically understood what I needed from her and gave it to me.

Like after my game.

A fucking dream.

What she did in the locker room did not erase Bianca's violation, though. Nothing ever would. But my girl showed me how it was supposed to be. She did it with care and more of that deep under-standing.

She made it hot while being safe.

I let go of a knot of barbed wire I'd been carrying in my bloody hands for too long, and with it came a deep swelling of relief. This burden wasn't mine anymore. I didn't have to hold it tight and let it fuck me up.

Luciana did that for me.

My light showed me the way.

CHAPTER TWENTY-EIGHT

Luciana

WE HAD TWO DAYS before the storm came.

Two days to walk down the hall holding hands, confirming with goofy smiles we were indeed a couple.

Beckett's chest was puffy with pride.

And maybe mine was too.

It felt more than good to be publicly claimed by him.

Even better, Bianca hadn't shown for first period either day, so I didn't have to think about her or deal with her shrapnel glares. She'd disappeared with a poof, and I hoped she stayed gone.

Beckett came to my game after school, bringing a few guys from the soccer team with him. They captured my attention when they all started doing a cheer specifically for me, and I laughed out loud when I saw what they were wearing.

During halftime, I met him on the bleachers. "I like your shirt."

He plucked at the white undershirt. "Unlike you, I didn't have time to have one professionally made, unfortunately."

I circled my finger above his head. "Let me see the back."

Grinning, he did a slow turn, showing me what he'd done. It was truly a masterpiece.

He'd taken a white undershirt and scrawled my number on the front with a black Sharpie. On the back, he'd written in big, bold letters, "Ortega-Whitlock's Biggest Fan."

"That's quite a claim," I said when he faced me again. "Helen might dispute it."

"Has she ever made a shirt for you?"

I shook my head. "She's not really crafty."

"Then my claim is unchallenged. It's mine. Besides, did you see my boys? I made those too."

All the soccer guys were wearing my number too. "What's on the back of theirs? The same as yours?"

"Not a chance." He twisted away from me and gave a shout. "Ryan! Show Luc the back of your shirt."

Ryan, a junior I barely knew, stood up and spun around. Scrawled in big, bold letters were the words "Ortega-Whitlock Fan Club."

"Thank you, Ryan!" I yelled.

Beckett snagged me by the nape, dragging me into him. "Don't I get a thank-you?"

"You get a kiss."

"Even better," he murmured before covering my mouth with his.

We were definitely public now. Kissing in front of both our teams, wearing each other's numbers. Declarations had been made on both sides, and it felt right. I would have to tell Helen and Theo, but I'd cross that bridge another day.

Today was for us.

··•·•····

We won the game. Trounced them. I was a good sport about it too, even though a couple tried to start shit about my personal cheer squad.

Now we were in the dining hall at a big table with our friends.

Yeah, Charles and Rhys were there. Felix too. The last two I was getting used to, but Charles still gave me the heebie-jeebies. Especially with the way he was eyeing Ev like a piece of meat.

Delilah noticed too. She was holding her knife like she'd stab him if he even breathed on her sister.

So, all in all, a relaxing dinner.

But the truth was, I was in my little Beckett bubble for the moment. He had his arm around me, my number on his chest, and my name on his back, which made me melty. I wondered if this was how Helen had felt when she and Theo first started out.

They were still *the* couple, even as grown-ups with a baby.

Goals.

Maybe one day I'd have that too. Something I never imagined for myself.

And maybe one day it would be with Beckett.

But that was crazy to even consider. I had too many goals to reach before even thinking about that type of future. I had to build my own life first. One that was just mine and no one could take from me, no matter how much my world shook.

I pushed those thoughts away and leaned into him as I chewed on a dinner roll. Staying in the right now was more than enough.

Freddie pointed to Beckett's T-shirt. "I'm trying and failing to picture you making these. Walk me through it."

Beckett's fingers curled around my upper arm. "I happened to have a pack of undershirts, a few Sharpies, and a girl I wanted to impress. Simple as that."

"Oh god," I whispered, my heart flipping in dizzying circles.

"Wow." Bella flopped back in her seat. "Do they make y'all on Amazon? And can I personalize you? I'd like one with curly hair and a few tattoos."

Grinning at her, I grabbed Beckett's jaw and squeezed. "Are you saying this boy isn't perfect?"

"Perfect for *you*. I want my man to be edgier. Like, when I first see him, I won't be sure if he's going to hit on me or rob me at gunpoint."

Felix shook his head. "Please tell me you're not influencing Isla."

Bella laughed, her cheeks flushing. "Oh, come on, Santos. With how overbearing you are, your sister is ripe for sneakin' off with a bad boy."

He shot her a death glare. "You're banned from talking to her."

Bella gave him a thumbs-up. "Definitely not going to happen, buddy."

Rhys crossed his arms over his chest. "I'd like to hear more about this cheer you came up with. It's dreadful that I missed it. Feel free to re-create it here and now."

"It was very complex," Delilah drawled. "They spelled her last name."

Rhys leveled Delilah with his attention. "Interesting. Which one did they go with? Or was it both?" She opened her mouth to answer, but Rhys waved her off. "What little bit of interest I had died off by the time I asked the question. I don't care anymore."

I threw my napkin in his direction. "They spelled Ortega. I expect you to be at my next home game, cheering with the boys."

He tapped his chin. "Hmmm. Thank you for the offer, but no. I have an appointment for an asshole bleaching that day that can't be missed. Mathilde loses her temper when I cancel. You really don't want an angry aesthetician coming near your asshole." He flicked his fingers. "Actually, who am I to kink shame? *I* don't want an angry woman near *my* asshole, but if that's your thing..."

A laugh sputtered out of me. "Who are you even talking to?"

He flung both arms out. "The ether."

"I know far too much about your asshole," Beckett muttered.

I glanced between my friends, who were wide-eyed and speechless. Then again, Rhys's friends were too.

The awkward silence was interrupted by a shrill scream ringing in pure fury. My head swiveled to the source.

Disheveled and red-faced, Bianca DeSoto beelined for our table. Beckett was up on his feet before she made it, heading her off at the pass. I hopped up to stand beside him, but Rhys reached him before I did, shoving himself half in front of Beckett.

"What did you do?" Bianca screamed, bringing the last conversations around us to a halt. "My dad has people packing up my room. He's making me leave, and I know this is your fault. What did you do?"

"Nothing you didn't deserve," Beckett told her lowly. "You did this to yourself."

Clarice was hovering a few feet behind Bianca, present but not actively backing her up like normal. Bianca was swinging by the noose of her own making, all by herself.

"I didn't do anything." She stomped her bare foot. She'd forgotten her shoes, which only added to her unhinged look. "I can't leave. My life—no. I can't leave. Fix it."

"No." Beckett's jaw rippled. "You crossed one too many lines."

Her fingers dug at her scalp, all her dark hair wild and messy. "I'm sorry, okay? I was drunk and—"

"No." He folded his arms over his chest. His demeanor was eerily calm. I would have believed it if I didn't know him so well. "I would have let you exist in my presence if you'd left her alone. But you chose not to."

"Who?" Her crazed eyes darted around. When she found me, she took a step forward. Rhys put his arm out, completely blocking her. Bianca sucked in a sharp breath and jabbed a finger at me. "Her? You're doing this for her? You're ruining my life, Beckett!"

He peered down at her, deadpan, with no emotion in his expression or words. "You ruined your own life the second you looked at her. I don't know why you came here looking for sympathy. You won't find it here. I don't care about you. You're nothing to me. But you talked shit to my girl, and I have no patience for that. So, you're gone."

"But I—" She pressed her hands into the sides of her head. "You can't—"

A man in a slick suit strode toward Bianca with fire in his eyes. As he drew near, he barked something low in Spanish.

The Spanish I knew was rudimentary, but I picked up that this was her father and he was out of patience for his daughter.

He gripped Bianca's bicep and yanked her backward. "Leave this place now," he hissed in Spanish. "Go to the car."

"Papa—"

"No." He brooked no argument, and she didn't even try.

She scuttled backward, giving Beckett one last pleading look, then she turned and ran. I thought I should feel sorry for her, since her father clearly cowed her, but I just couldn't find it in me to care.

Mr. DeSoto addressed Beckett in a thick Spanish accent. "You will have no more trouble from Bianca. I expect this will remain between us, as gentlemen."

Beckett's nostrils flared. "You're not in the position to extract promises from me."

Mr. DeSoto reared back slightly but nodded. "No. I don't suppose I am. Then I will go. The flight back to Spain will be long."

He took his leave, and the dining room fell silent. Beckett turned to me, holding out his hand. I wove my fingers through his, needing him to know I was here and wasn't leaving.

He pulled me into his side and started for the door, bringing me with him, but stopped and turned back to the deathly silent room. Clarice was standing in the same spot, and Beckett looked her square in the eye.

"I hope you understand now. I will go to *war* over this girl. You hurt her, I will ruin you." He swiveled his head, taking a sweep of the room. But he didn't have to. All eyes were on him. On us. "That goes for everyone. You don't want to battle me. When it comes to my girl, I am a berserker. I will tear your world apart, and I don't care what happens to me in the process. No one comes near her or you'll have a fight on your hands—and I will win."

We walked out of the dining hall together, hand in hand. Beckett kept his gaze straight ahead, his jaw clenched, for the trek to our dorm and the elevator ride to our floor.

When we were locked in his room, only then did he exhale.

I pushed him onto his bed and climbed on top of him so we lay chest to chest, heart to heart.

His arms banded around me, his nose buried in my hair. We held each other, and each minute that passed, a strong sense of calm settled over me. From the steady thrumming of Beckett's heart, it settled over him too.

The storm had passed, and we were still here. Still standing and whole.

"She's gone," I whispered.

"Yeah."

"Are you okay?"

"Got you in my arms." He heaved a sigh. "I'm okay. You?"

I propped myself on his chest, needing to look at him. And then I needed to touch him, curving my fingers along his jaw.

"You protected me when I should have been protecting you."

His hands shot out to take my head in his grasp. "You—" He closed his eyes for a beat and exhaled. When he opened them, they were clear and sure. "I love you, Luciana. I love you so fucking much."

My fingers went to his mouth, needing to feel the words he'd just said. But they weren't there anymore. They'd landed in my heart, pumping through my veins. They traveled down to my toes and up to my brain until all my insides knew them and felt the truth.

"I love you too, Beckett."

He lifted his head. "You do?"

I nodded. "I only just realized it, but yeah, I do. I love you."

Without warning, he jackknifed, taking me with him, so I was in his lap, facing him. My head was in his hands, and his eyes were boring into mine, a little feral.

"Say it again, Luciana."

"I love you, Beckett."

The breath he released brushed across my smile. "I thought it would take a lot longer than this. I thought I'd love you on my own while I waited for you to get there."

I touched his lips again, wondering how I had never seen how soft his heart was. I'd missed it for so long, but now that I knew, it was glaringly obvious to me.

"I think you waited for me long enough. I'm here."

"I would've waited forever."

My lids lowered, heavy with the magnitude of his words. "And you're surprised I love you?" I pressed into him, flattening my chest to his. But it wasn't close enough.

I needed more.

We'd both waited long enough.

Chapter Twenty-Nine

Luciana

SOMETIMES, A STORM PRECEDED the kind of beauty that seemed unreal. Through the clouds and gray came a rainbow. It was fleeting and special, an intangible experience that made the wind and rain worth every second.

Beckett and I were holding each other, kissing and touching, shedding our clothes bit by bit. We'd never been fully naked with each other, and we were at the point where we'd normally stop.

"I want to keep going," I told him.

"Are you sure?"

I nodded. "I've never been more sure." I raised my leg, draping it over his hip, bringing our pelvises together. He was hard and warm between my thighs, our underwear the only thing separating us. "Are you ready?"

He huffed, his fingers dipping under the band of my underwear. "I want you. I've always wanted you."

"I want you too."

His chest shuddered, then his mouth was on mine again while he slipped my underwear down my thighs. I kicked them the rest of the way off, then worked his down his hips, needing us both to be bare so I could feel him everywhere.

Beckett gently rolled me onto my back, hovering over me. I trailed my eyes along the length of his tautly muscled torso to his thick erection jutting from his hips. My fingers followed the line my eyes had traveled to wrap around him. I gave him two pumps before he jerked out of my hold.

"I need to go slow," he uttered softly. "This is important to me, Luciana."

"To me too."

He showed me how important I was to him, kissing me gently on my mouth, then working his way down my body. He caressed the lines of my waist and hips while his lips closed around my beaded nipples. Beckett had taken his time to learn me. His patience and devotion to my pleasure lassoed me to him. I wanted his hands on me always. I trusted him with my body. He was the first to see it, to touch it, to taste me, and he'd made it so I was never self-conscious.

He was so beautiful, all sinewy muscles and hard planes. Plush lips and fathomless eyes. When he reached my core, my thighs over his shoulders, my ass cupped in his palms, his eyes met mine and locked.

We were connected that way at the first swipe of his tongue along my slit. He vibrated at the same time I trembled. I reached for him, threaded my fingers through his hair, and sighed his name.

Then he buried his face in my core and feasted, lapping at me from one end to the other, taking his time at my entrance, teasing me there, circling his tongue around it. It was strange and new, but I liked it. God, did I like it. My hips rocked against his mouth, and he pulled me closer, delving inside with the tip of his tongue.

"Please," I cried, asking for something, but I didn't know what.

He hummed and pushed his tongue farther into me. The heat of his breath on my pussy combined with the feeling of him entering me, even just a little bit, had my eyes rolling back in my head.

But he didn't linger there long. His tongue slid to my clit, giving it the attention it craved. While he swirled around it, he brought one hand forward, then his finger took over where his tongue had left off, pressing into me. He slipped inside me and pulled out, repeating a slow, steady pattern.

My hold on his hair tightened, pulling him closer, rubbing myself against his mouth, taking his finger deeper. He hummed again, and

I whimpered from how good that felt. My mouth stayed open to allow panting breaths to escape.

Beckett pulled his finger all the way out, and I almost cried in frustration, but then he was back, pushing two fingers inside. He went slow, an inch at a time, and I was so full. It almost scared me, but he didn't allow me to fall into fear. Not with his tongue and lips on my clit, pressing and sucking.

"I'm close," I rasped, but he had to know. I was rocking and jerking my hips, heaving for breath like I'd run a marathon. "Please, *please*."

A surge of heat flooded my belly, spreading over me until I was liquid heat melting into Beckett's hold. I moaned his name, coming all over his mouth. He never let me go, riding the wave with me to the very end.

I tugged at his hair, needing to see him, to press my lips to his.

He climbed up my body, kissing me up the center until our mouths joined. His lips were impossibly soft now, and so hot, I somehow melted even more. Bending my knees, I raised them to his hips. His cock wedged between us, grazing my throbbing clit.

"I need you," I murmured.

He pulled back, peering down at me. "Are you still sure?"

I nodded. "I love you."

A rush of breath heaved from his lungs. "I love you too, Luc."

He reached inside the table next to his bed, ripping open a box of condoms. His hands shook slightly as he opened a blue packet and took out the condom.

"Do you know how to do it?" I asked.

His eyes lifted to mine, the corner of his mouth hooking. "I've never tried it, but I'm thinking it's foolproof."

I smiled back at him, a sense of pure happiness striking at my heart. I really loved him, and I was so glad my first time was going to be with him.

Proving himself right, Beckett rolled the condom on easily, then he was over me again. My pulse stuttered, and a swarm of butterflies attacked my belly, but when our eyes connected, my nerves fell away.

This was right.

Nothing had ever been more right than us. Now.

He touched my face as he pressed into me. My lips parted, exhaling at the surprise of the burning stretch between my thighs.

"Don't stop." If he knew it was hurting me, he would, and I didn't want him to. Never, ever.

"You sure?" He sounded strained, his shoulders vibrating. I brought my hands up to his shaking muscles, stroking him as I nodded.

Releasing a sigh, he slipped all the way into me, our pelvises flush together. Then he dropped down on me, shoving his face in my throat. I wrapped my limbs around him, touching my lips to his jaw and the tendon along the side of his neck.

"Can I move?" he asked.

"Please."

And then he did, starting a slow rolling pace, barely retreating before pushing back in. It took time, but my body loosened, got used to having him inside me, and the pain receded.

Beckett pushed up on his arms to stare down at me. I trailed my fingers along his torso, peering down to where we were joined.

"Look at us," I whispered.

He lowered his head, and together, we watched his cock disappear inside me.

"Fuck," he grumbled. "That's—"

"I know."

His eyes found mine again. "I want to say a lot of things, but I'm losing it here, Luc."

"It's okay. Lose it. Tell me after."

He shook his head and bit down on his bottom lip. "You feel too good. Never thought it would be like this. Never want to stop."

I turned my head to kiss his shaking arm. "I love having you inside me. It's perfect."

"Shit." He was throbbing, swelling against my tight walls. "Too good, Luc."

His movements sped up, but he wasn't rough, even as he became more frantic. I stayed with him, matching his pace. I couldn't take my eyes off him. I'd never seen him this way, his control strained to the breaking point but his eyes soft on me, his love for me spilling out of every pore.

He gripped the back of one of my legs, raising it higher, so it was almost pressed to my chest. His cock carved out an impossibly deep place inside me, and once he was there, his movement stuttered.

A hoarse groan rumbled from his chest. He stared at me with awe as he pushed into me one final time, planting himself there, in the place he'd created for himself. I would never be the same after this. Beckett had personally shaped me for him. He'd changed me, molded me, not just where we were joined, but my heart.

"You're mine," I whispered.

"I'm yours," he agreed, pressing his forehead to mine like he always did.

A minute or two passed before he rolled us to our sides and eased out of me. I didn't look. If there was blood, I didn't want to see, and thankfully Beckett didn't say.

Once he'd gotten rid of the condom, he gathered me against him. For a while, there was only our quiet breathing. Then he spoke.

"I've never belonged anywhere until I belonged to you."

I pulled away from his chest to look at his face. "What do you mean? You belong. You have family...your brother—"

"I know. But belonging is a feeling. I've never had it. Not until you." He pushed a lock of hair away from my face. "Is that too big?"

"It's a lot," I admitted.

"It's true, though. I've always had to work hard at being loved. I pushed myself on Julien. He didn't want a brother."

"He loves you."

"Now he does. I hounded him into it, though. I'm still on my best behavior so he doesn't get sick of me. And he could. I'm never not conscious of it."

"I don't think that's true. You're very lovable."

He took my chin between two fingers and scanned my face. "To you. Because I belong to you. Don't I?"

I nodded. "I told you you're mine. I love you."

"I love you too, baby." He trailed his fingertips along my spine to cup my ass in his palm. "Did I hurt you?"

"Only a little, and only because it was the first time. You were careful with me."

His brow furrowed. "I hate that I hurt you at all."

"I know you do. But next time you won't." I wiggled closer, stealing his body heat. "Did you like it?"

"Fuck yes," he rasped. "You couldn't tell? I lost my mind in you."

I cracked a grin. "I could tell. I just wanted you to say it."

He spread his fingers on my cheek. "I have never felt closer to anyone than when I was inside you. I want to live in you. Never let you out of my bed so I can fuck you over and over, only stopping to eat your sweet pussy. I loved every second of that—except for the ending. I never wanted it to be over." He tapped my cheek. "Is that what you want to hear?"

My smile widened. "That pretty much covered it." I propped myself up on my elbow. "When can we do it again?"

He finally laughed. "Whenever you're ready, baby. I'll never say no to you."

CHAPTER THIRTY

Beckett

IT WAS SIGNING DAY for Luciana.

I was standing in the back of the library, watching the ceremony her coach had set up.

Over the last month, Luciana had received offers from UNC, Stanford, and a handful of other D1 schools. She'd warred with herself over which to choose.

True to her word, she never asked me where I wanted her to go. I would have told her it didn't matter to me, anyway. I'd find a way to follow her. But I didn't want to sway her in any way. This was her decision.

After long talks with her coach and current players at her top picks, she'd made her choice.

In the end, she chose Stanford.

Her sister and brother-in-law were standing behind her as she signed her letter of intent. They didn't hide how pleased they were Luc was staying in state, but I'd like to think they would have been celebrating if she'd chosen North Carolina too.

Bella smacked a kiss on Luciana's cheek and plopped a Stanford hat on her head. My girl looked good in Cardinal red.

Her team, her family, and her coaches all took turns hugging her. Getting a full ride to play college field hockey wasn't easy. Going to one of the best schools in the country was even more incredible.

I was proud as hell. This was what I wanted for her.

But something possessive twisted in my stomach. She wasn't only mine. Intellectually, I knew and accepted that, but seeing her surrounded by the people who loved her made me want to snatch her up and keep her for myself.

I had to pull myself together.

After almost two months of being her boyfriend, I'd thought I would have leveled out somewhat, but nah, I was incapable of chill when it came to Luciana.

The ceremony came to an end, and after being hugged and kissed by a hundred people, Luciana finally made her way to me.

"What are you doing back here?" She leaned into me, flashing me a giddy grin.

I curled my arms around her middle. "Watching the star. I'm proud of you."

"Thank you." She tapped a finger on the base of my throat. "You should have been up there with me."

Helen and Theo approached, their daughter attached to his chest. She'd doubled in size since I last saw her on my birthday. At least, it appeared she had. I didn't really know how quickly babies grew.

Luciana moved next to me, and I kept my hold on her waist.

"Hey, Beckett." Theo patted my arm. "Nice to see you."

Helen eyed me skeptically, as she always did now that she was aware Luc and I were together. I'd gotten used to it.

"Beckett." She arched a brow. "We're taking our girlie to dinner. Are you coming?"

Not expecting the invite, I glanced at Luc, and she nodded eagerly. I guessed I was going to dinner. "Yeah. I'd like that. Thank you."

·· • • • • • • • ··

Three long hours later, Luciana and I were finally back on campus, riding the elevator up to our floor.

"She still hates me, you know."

Luc laughed. "She doesn't, I promise. Hells is just a hard-ass." She wove her fingers with mine. "You taking Madelina outside when she started crying probably made massive inroads."

I scoffed. "At least *she* likes me."

She encircled my arm with hers as we stepped out of the elevator, turning to my side of the hall where we spent most of our time. "*I* like you."

"Thank Christ for that." I turned my head to press a kiss to her hair. "Stanford girl."

Her head fell back as she laughed. "What? I still can't believe it. Scrappy, crusty-Dickies-wearing *me* is going to Stanford. I'm *playing* for them."

I nuzzled into her hair, grinning at her happiness. "They're paying for you to play for them, baby. That's all you. Crusty Dickies and all."

As soon as I kicked my door shut, Luc jumped on me, wrapping her legs around my waist. I had her pressed against the bathroom door, my mouth over hers, her hands digging in my hair.

"I love you," she moaned.

"Love you so fucking much."

She tore at my shirt until I threw it off, and hers followed. I pushed the cups of her bra down, taking her breasts in my hands. Her nipples were beaded, begging to be teased and sucked. But my mouth was too busy on hers. Kissing Luciana was still my favorite thing to do. If we didn't have other obligations, I would've spent my days doing it.

"Fuck me, Beckett." She nipped at my lip, then sucked it between hers.

My cock was hard, throbbing behind my zipper. Aching for her. Hearing her say that, demanding what she needed, only made it worse.

Or better.

It was impossible to say, only I knew I got to be inside my girl and she loved it. We had spent nearly as much time having sex as we had kissing over the last month. We hadn't tried everything, but we'd tried a lot. Luc liked to be on top. I liked anything where I could see her face and watch her tits bounce.

When it came to her, though, I wasn't picky. As long as I got to have her.

My girl wasn't shy, not with me. We explored what we liked and got to know each other's bodies inside and out. It was hot and always, *always* loving, even when we got messy. I couldn't imagine *ever* wanting to do this with anyone else. She'd ruined me for life, but I was more than happy to be ruined by her.

I thrust my erection between her spread thighs, making her suck in a breath. And then she started pushing back, arching her back off the door so she could press down on me. She rocked and rocked until the cloth of her shorts was wedged between her pussy lips and I could feel her through my shorts. And dear god, did she feel good, even like this, through too many layers of clothing.

But we both needed more. I had to put Luc down to tug off her shorts and mine. Then she was back in my arms, her legs around me. I sat on my bed, my back against the headboard, her in my lap. She rocked her wet pussy against me, sliding her clit over the head of my cock.

My head fell back against the headboard with a thud. Laughing, she cupped the back of my head to protect me.

"Careful. I like this head," she admonished breathlessly.

"You're too good to me." My tongue delved into her hot mouth, kissing the hell out of her. "Taking care of me, baby. So sweet."

"Of course I take care of you."

I reached between her spread thighs and rolled my index finger over her swollen clit. "I'm gonna take care of you too. Need you to come for me. My Stanford girl."

Her giggle was cut off by a gasp as I slid a finger into her and ground the heel of my hand against her clit. She rode my hand while clinging to my neck. Her nose was touching mine, and I inhaled each of her panting breaths.

"Beckett..."

"You don't even know how beautiful you look right now, baby. Never seen anything like it. Your cheeks are so rosy, and your lips look like a place I want to spend the rest of my days."

Her lashes fluttered as her eyes opened to find mine. "How do I feel?"

I groaned. "Oh god, like heaven must. You're so hot and tight. I want to get my dick inside you so bad, but I need you to come on my hand. I want to feel you squeezing me. Will you come for me?"

Lip caught in her teeth, she nodded. "Soon. Keep doing that and I'll come for you."

I curled my fingers inside her, rubbing this spot we'd discovered that drove her through the roof. Her limbs started to shake, and her cute little chin quivered. She lost control when I rubbed that spot. Combined with pressure on her clit, and she was helpless.

I watched as she let herself fall apart in my arms, sighing and moaning with abandon. Her eyes slammed shut, and her head lolled on her shoulders, all that silky hair spilling down her back like a waterfall. Leaning forward, I touched my lips to her exposed throat, her cries vibrating against my lips.

"Beckett," she moaned.

"Got you, Luciana. Fall, baby."

Her eyes opened and locked with mine as she released softening whimpers. We stared at each other, intense yet light. The corners of her mouth lifted, and mine were pulled right along with hers.

"So good," she sighed.

"So beautiful," I told her.

I rolled on a condom when her climax started to wane, and she shifted to her knees.

"Come here." I took her hips in my hands, and she inched forward, rising over my erection. Slowly, torturously, she lowered herself onto me, not stopping until her soft ass met my thighs. She tightened around me, forcing a deep groan out of me.

"I want it hard." Her pussy clenched again. "Are you ready?"

I stared at her for a beat to make sure she was real. "Fuck yes, baby. Ride me."

"Yes." She rolled her hips once. "God yes."

Luciana used her muscular thighs and lifted herself to my tip and plunged downward, taking me deep. She held on to the headboard for leverage, riding me hard. I helped her move, gripping her narrow waist and thrusting up into her when she slammed down.

We found our rhythm, fucking each other with fervor. I sucked her little nipples, and she nipped at my earlobe and licked my throat. And we kissed and kissed and kissed. Sweet and savage. Every kind of kiss.

Her pretty, perky breasts bounced in my face, and her ass slapped my upper thighs. I still hadn't gotten used to the fact that I got to have sex with her. My beautiful girl. I tried hard to last as long as I could. To make it good for her. But there were times when she went wild on me, and I knew she was testing my control. Trying to push me over as fast as she could.

It was impossible to resist her, but I worked at it, because I never wanted this to end.

"Need you coming on my dick, little light. Need it bad." I shoved two fingers between us, pressing on her clit. She cried out, her fingers digging into my nape.

"Beckett, keep doing that. Feels so good."

"I won't stop if you won't."

"Never."

She worked herself up and down my length, and at the bottom, circled her hips in a new way that almost made me lose it. I rubbed her clit at the same speed, taking her to the edge with me.

Perspiration beaded on my forehead as I held on to control by the skin of my teeth. She was so wet, I could feel her slickness through the barrier of the condom. For a split second, I let myself imagine taking her without a condom one day, feeling that cum all over my cock, her making me shiny with her arousal. But I couldn't spend too much time thinking that or I'd come before her.

And that wasn't gonna happen.

Gripping her hair in my fist, I tipped her throat back to bury my face there. With my other hand, I cupped her hip, then I started to pound into her from below. Luc wrapped her arms around my shoulders, grinding down on me hard. A couple weeks ago, she'd learned when she did this, her clit rubbed against my pelvis and she could get herself off that way.

We were panting and writhing, clinging to one another, so close, so fucking close. She murmured my name, and I told her I loved her. I said it a lot, on repeat, while I fucked her roughly.

Her inner walls started clamping down on me at the same time her back arched and her head tipped to the ceiling. I had no choice but to follow her over this time, coming hard while planted as deep inside her as I could reach.

It took a while to come down. I held her in my lap, stroking long, slow lines down her back until I had to take care of the condom. Then I placed her gently on the bed and went into the bathroom for a minute.

When I came back out, Luc was wearing one of my shirts and sitting on the side of my bed, her head in her hands. I shoved my shorts on and kneeled in front of her.

She lifted her head, and I was stunned to see tears welling in her eyes.

"Baby." I smoothed her hair away from her face, horror filling me. "Did I hurt you?"

"No," she squeaked urgently, her hands coming to my face. "No, no, no. You didn't hurt me."

I swiped at a tear with my thumb. Her assurance didn't make me feel any better. Not when she should have been all languid and relaxed and was anything but. "Then what's this about?"

"I'm—" She pressed her lips together and tried to turn away, but I kept her facing me. "I know I said I wasn't going to let you and me affect where I go to college, and I'm not. But it hit me just now. I'm going to have to leave you, and it's going to kill me, Beckett."

"Nope." I shook my head, relieved this was something I could fix. "You don't have to leave me."

Her brow furrowed. "But—"

"Do you want me to tell you something that will reveal the level of my madness but also might reassure you?"

"Yes please," she whispered without any hesitation.

I'd been hoping to conceal how intricately I'd planned what would happen between Luciana and me, especially since my plans had been completely blown up in the best way. While Luciana knew I was crazy about her and had been for a long time, I didn't think she was aware of how *crazy* I was about her.

"Little light, I've known which colleges have the best field hockey team. I've known who was looking at you. When it was time to send in applications, I sent mine to those schools. I got my early admission to Stanford a couple weeks ago. There's no full ride like my girl, but that doesn't matter. We'll both be wearing Cardinal red in the fall."

"What?" she breathed. "Beckett—*what?*"

Worry struck me hard. I couldn't get a read on her reaction. "You don't have to miss me, Luc. I'm going to be with you."

"What?" She bounced once on the mattress. "Are you kidding?"

"No, I don't kid."

Her eyes narrowed. "But...what about soccer?"

I shrugged. "I'll be a walk-on. Coach Watts has been talking to the Stanford coach for me, but if I don't make the team, I'll play intramural. It's not important to me. Being where you are is."

"I—" Her mouth fell open, but only a creaking sound came out.

"What? I can't tell what you're thinking, Luc. Talk to me."

"I can't believe you." She shoved at my chest. "I can't believe you didn't tell me. You should have told me."

And then the tears, which had temporarily stopped, came flooding. She heaved a heavy sob and fell against me, and all I could do was wrap my arms around her, holding her while she cried on my shoulder.

I'd never seen her cry, and it was killing me. There was a tight fist in my chest. I wanted to take this sadness away from her, but dear god, I had no idea what to do or what was going on in her mind.

"Luc, please talk to me."

She lifted her head. "I'm—" She gave her head a shake and sniffled. "I didn't realize how worried I've been about what was going to happen with us until now. And I'm so freaking relieved I don't have to worry anymore. I love you, and I think—no, I'm pretty damn sure I won't stop."

"Christ, baby. I thought you were crying over my crazy."

"No." She wiped her wet cheeks with the back of her hand and gave me a wobbly smile. "Well, a little, but only because your crazy is giving me you, and you are what I want."

My eyes fell closed, and I let out a heavy breath. "Then I guess you're lucky, because I'm not going anywhere."

"Except to Stanford. With me." Her lips touched the corner of my mouth. "My college boy."

I opened my eyes to grin at her. "Now I just have to make sure you keep liking me, because I am planning on following you off the ends of the earth."

She cupped her mouth like she was telling me a secret. "The earth is round, Beckett. There's no end."

My grin widened. "*Now* you're starting to understand."

Now that I had her, there was never going to be an end to us.

CHAPTER THIRTY-ONE
Beckett

AFTER A BRIEF AND excruciating visit with my parents, where I informed them I'd be attending Stanford in the fall, *not* Savage U, I headed out early to pick up Luciana.

She'd gone to visit Helen and Theo first but should've been with her mom by now. I still had time to kill and would've hung out with Jules and Sera, but they were in Oregon visiting their friends for the weekend, so I was at loose ends.

I decided to park and wander through the paths of Chance Park, ending up at the skate ramps. Of course, Luciana wasn't there, but there were plenty of other skaters around.

I found a bench in the sun and kicked back on it. Sliding out my phone, I sent Luc a message.

Me: *How's your visit going, baby?*

Luc: *It's going. Mom's asleep, so I'm cleaning her place up a bit. How are your parents?*

I knew what that meant. Her mom was passed out and her trailer was filled with trash. It killed me that Luc had spent any time living in that environment. It was even worse that she kept going back.

That wasn't her.

She didn't belong in a place like that.

Me: *Gretchen sobbed over me moving 5.5 hours away. I told her not much would change since I already don't see her on a regular basis.*

Luc: *How'd that go over?*

Me: *Poorly. It turned into me reassuring her she isn't a failure as a mother.*

Luc: *And your dad? How was he?*

Me: *No sobbing.*

Luc: *Haha, is that the best part of his reaction?*

Me: *No, Josh is on board with Stanford. He gets to brag about it to his friends and colleagues, so I didn't get any pushback. He's pissed about my soccer situation being up in the air, but he'll get over it.*

Luc: *I'm sure they're both proud of you in their own way.*

Me: *Now you're being funny. Can I come get you yet? I miss you.*

Luc: *Give me an hour. I want to get my mom up and dressed, make sure she eats.*

Me: *All right, baby. Be careful. I'll see you soon.*

Luc: *Love you, Beckett.*

Me: *I love you, little light.*

I tucked my phone away, feeling better for having touched base with her. Another hour away from her was doable.

Normally, I wasn't so pathetically codependent, but spending time with my parents always threw me off-kilter. I knew one minute with Luciana in my arms would right me again. That was all I needed.

I watched the skaters to take my mind off the shitty parts of my life. Luc would be back out there soon. I'd wrap her up in padding, but she missed this too much to keep her from it, and I looked forward to watching her. The first and last time I'd seen her skate, I'd been too pissed off and horrified to really appreciate her skill.

Things were different now. Yeah, I'd be worried about her falling. That would never go away. But she wasn't going to be careless, not with her future within her reach.

A couple dudes with boards under their arms walked by me. One stopped and turned back.

"I know you."

Squinting, I peered up at the guy who spoke, instantly recognizing him. Johnny, the Savage River High player with a big mouth who'd put his hands on my girl.

I rose to my feet, my arms loose at my sides. "I know you too, Johnny."

His friend circled back to stand at his side. He seemed familiar, but I didn't think he was on the soccer team. I had no beef with him other than him keeping poor company with this douche canoe.

"Last time I saw you, you were with little Luciana Ortega." He held his skateboard in front of him, almost like a shield. "How did that work out for you?"

"Just fine." I shook out my hands. This kid wasn't getting anything from me. "You make it out of there without speaking to the cops?"

"Cops?" Johnny's friend glanced between us. "Oh, wait. You're talking about the bonfire? That shit was out of hand."

"Yep." Johnny raised his chin toward me. "I was having a friendly conversation with Luciana that night, and this cat came barreling in like some off-brand superhero."

My jaw clenched. I managed to hold my tongue. I had no need to correct his version of events. We both knew what he was saying was complete bullshit.

The other kid snapped his fingers. "Oh shit, do you know her friend? The thick one with the bomb accent? I went looking for her, but I had to head out before I found her."

Delilah. Had to be Delilah.

"I know her."

"Cool, cool. Tell her Cris was asking about her if you see her. I'm at this park every weekend. She can find—"

Johnny backhanded his chest. "Don't be desperate, man. That rich cunt isn't gonna dumpster dive with you. They all think they're too good for us. Being around them has rubbed off on Luciana too." His nostrils flared as he raked his eyes over me. "You fuckin' her?"

I glared at him, unwilling to entertain his questions.

The other guy made a choking sound in the back of his throat. "That's uncalled for, J. Those girls were chill as hell that night. Maybe Luc isn't into *you*, but that doesn't mean she's a cunt."

Johnny didn't even seem to register that his friend had said anything. "You're fuckin' her, aren't you? You *rescued* her at the bonfire, and she played damsel for you."

"Keep her name out of your mouth, *Johnny*."

Yeah, all right. I couldn't keep my mouth shut any longer. I'd been pretty patient up until this point, but he wouldn't stop talking.

"You know, girls like Luciana aren't meant for guys like you. You'll fuck her, but you won't respect her. You'll never understand her." Johnny gestured over to the skate park. "My boy Adrian has a mad crush on her. He gets her, knows where she comes from. You might get your dick wet, but you'll never *get* her."

"You won't either." I leaned toward him, violence filling my veins. I wouldn't touch him, but that didn't mean I wasn't fantasizing about taking his skateboard out of his hands and bashing his skull in. "Keep dreaming about something you'll never have. Hope it keeps you warm at night. Luciana is never going to be yours. She's not going to be Adrian's. She's gone, and you'll never touch her."

He scoffed. "Okay, rich boy *Beckett Savage*. When you're done slumming, Luciana will find her way back where she belongs."

"Never happening." My fingers curled and uncurled at my sides. "If you see her, you keep walking. She has no interest in you, and she belongs exactly where she is."

Johnny threw his head back, releasing a mad cackle. I took that as my cue to exit, which I should have done five minutes ago. As I stalked away, Johnny called after me.

"Keep telling yourself that. I hope those lies keep you warm at night, Savage."

Luciana was done with this town. Ready or not, I was going to get her. The thought of her spending another minute anywhere near Johnny and the likes of him set me on edge. I needed her back at SA, behind the gates, where I could keep her safe and away from the bullshit of her old life.

CHAPTER THIRTY-TWO

Luciana

I HAD TO PUT my mother in the shower, and it wasn't the first time I'd done it. At least when she emerged, she was more clearheaded than she'd been when I'd first woken her.

"Lovey," she rasped, an unlit cigarette between her lips. "You cleaned."

I was at the stove I'd scoured, making her a grilled cheese. "I did. You can't let your place go like that, Mom. It's not healthy for you to have trash everywhere."

I didn't say anything about the needles and pills I'd left untouched on the coffee table or the empty bottles I'd carted out to the dumpster. Mom didn't mention any of that stuff either, although her gaze lingered on her cluttered coffee table.

She waved me off. "I forget, lovey. The days get away from me, and you know how I get. Sometimes I'm just too sick to get off the couch."

High. Hungover. Jonesing.

"Still, can you at least try?" I flipped her grilled cheese onto a paper plate and brought it to the small dinette set I'd scrubbed earlier.

My mom took a seat across from me and started picking at her sandwich without a word of thanks.

"I'll try." Her face scrunched. "When you don't visit me, I just get so sad..."

It had been a few weeks since I'd last stopped in. Helen had her groceries delivered like always, but I hadn't made the time to come by in person. Admittedly, that was because I'd been swept up in Beckett, but I'd also just been busy. Studying, practice, games, friends, and a boyfriend took up all my time. And quite frankly, when I had a spare second, I really didn't want to spend it scouring my mom's disgusting trailer while dodging dirty needles.

"Well, when I go to college, it's going to be much harder for me to stop in, so you're going to have to fend for yourself."

I wanted her to ask me about college so I could share the news. And then I wanted her to be awash with pride at my achievement the way Helen and Theo had been. I longed for that from her with a deep, unabating ache.

When she didn't give me that, I wasn't surprised, but my heart still cracked a little.

"As long as Helen keeps sending me a little bit of food every week, I'll get by. I don't have to live in a palace, unlike some people."

"Mom." I placed my hand over hers, and her glassy eyes darted to mine. "I have really good news."

"Oh yeah? What is it?"

"I'm going to Stanford in the fall. They offered me a full ride to play field hockey for them." I held my breath and crossed my fingers she wouldn't let me down. This was her second chance to come through.

She pulled her hand away and used it to rub the picked skin along her jaw. "Hmmm. That's a good school. Even I know that."

My lips formed a tentative smile. "It is. You're right."

"Good job, lovey. That scholarship come with cash? Spending money? If it does, maybe you can pass some of it to me. After all, I'm the one who signed those permission slips when you wanted to start playing field hockey. One could say this is all due to me."

My smile fell as my lips parted in shock. I honestly couldn't believe she remembered signing permission slips when she was clearly whacked out of her addled mind.

"No, there's no cash," I whispered.

"Oh." She shrugged. "You should demand they throw some in there. You know what I always say, lovey: never take the first offer. Rich school like Stanford has to have deep pockets."

I shook my head. "I'm not—no, that's just not a thing, Mom." I blinked back disappointed tears. "Aren't you proud of me?"

Before she could answer, there was a loud knock on her front door. Mom pushed herself up from the table with surprising speed, beelining to answer it. She flung it open and stuck her head outside.

"Oh, hello, handsome. How can I help you today?" She propped herself in the doorway, arching her back to push out her skeletal chest.

"I'm here for Luciana."

Oh crap. There was no mistaking Beckett's deep, resonant tone. I didn't miss the fury behind his clipped words either. Was I late?

"You've come to the right place." Mom stepped back from the door. "Come on in, honey."

Hoping to cut him off, I raced to the door, but Beckett was already inside, scanning the small, run-down space.

"Beckett, I thought I was meeting you at Chance Park." I moved directly in front of him, but there was no missing the moment he spotted the detritus of my mom's addiction on the coffee table. "Can you wait outside? I'll just be a minute—"

His eyes jerked to mine. "It's time to go now, Luciana."

I felt my mother behind me. "Is this your boyfriend?"

I glanced at her over my shoulder. "Yes. This is Beckett. He's driving me back to school—"

"You don't have to leave so soon. Let him come inside and sit down."

Beckett sucked in a lungful of the stale air no amount of disinfectant spray could've disguised.

"Let's go," he ordered lowly, his gaze blazing into mine.

"Now wait a minute." My mother clamped her fingers on the back of my arm. "You don't come to my home, not even introduce yourself, and make demands of my daughter. That's not how things are done."

He turned his attention to her. "From my untrained eye, there is heroin residue on the burnt spoon on that table, along with pills I'd guess are not prescribed to you, and god only knows what other illegal, dangerous substances. Luciana doesn't belong anywhere near that shit, and I have no inclination to introduce myself to the woman who would force her to be in its proximity. So, no, I will not be introducing myself to you, and I *will* be taking my girlfriend out of here."

"Mom," I whispered. "I'm going to go now. I'll see you soon."

Her fingers dug into me. "You don't have to leave with him."

I shrugged off her feeble hold. "I want to." Then I leaned in and hugged her, getting absolutely nothing in return. "Remember what we talked about."

Nodding absently, she wandered into her bedroom without another word. I was staring after her when Beckett took my hand in his and pulled me out of the trailer, only slowing to allow me to close the door.

I stumbled after him as he stormed over the cracked pathways of the trailer park. His broad shoulders were tense, and the muscles in his jaw rippled. I didn't know what I'd done wrong, but I did know he was angry at me.

Beckett shut me in his car and circled to the other side, sliding in and slamming his door. The locks engaged, and he sped out of the parking lot in thick silence.

I let the air remain quiet between us even though I had a strong urge to defend myself. But why? I didn't even know why Beckett was so furious.

We were halfway back to SA when he spun the wheel, kicking up dust and gravel as he pulled into a scenic overlook. There was room for maybe two or three cars, but we were the only ones there.

"You're never going back there," he announced with finality.

"What?" I reared back, hitting the passenger door. "To my mom's?"

"Yeah. That's done. You won't set foot in that piece-of-shit trailer again. Fuck that whole town. You're done with it."

A spark of fury lit low in my belly. "You don't get to decide that."

He looked at me sharply. "The hell I don't. Try to go back there and see what happens. You think Helen will let you when I tell her what I saw?"

Oh, that did it. I didn't play that "snitches get stitches" game, but in this case, I'd make an exception. Beckett was going to have a serious case of stitches if he thought he could tattle on me to my sister.

"Drive me back to SA. I don't want to be in this car with you for any more time than I have to."

"I'm not taking you back there until you agree with me."

"Fine. I'll walk." I threw myself out of the car, knowing full well my threats were empty. I just needed away from him.

Beckett didn't give me that, though. He was out of the car and on me in a blink. He crowded me against the back door, his hands bracketing my head, trapping me there.

"There were drugs all over her living room, Luciana. You expect me to let you go back there?"

"You can't *let* me do anything. That's my mother's house. I'm going to visit her whenever I want to."

I'd been disturbed by the contents of her coffee table too. She normally hid it from me when she knew I was coming. But it wouldn't stop me from going to see her. It wasn't like I hadn't known she pumped poison into her veins on a regular basis.

"But why?" He shoved his fingers into the side of his hair. "You don't have to. You got out. In a few months, you'll be on the other end of the state. I get that that's your past, but that's all it is."

"That's my *mother*. She's an addict, but she's still my mom. My only parent. How can you even think to presume to tell me I can't see her? Did you think I'd just merrily skip along and agree? Because, no. That's not happening."

"Why did you work so hard for Stanford if you're not leaving all that behind? I don't get you. That trailer isn't you, Luciana. You're so much better than that."

"Maybe, but the person inside the trailer is who I came from. She's messed up, but she's my mom. I won't give her up. Going to Stanford doesn't mean I'm leaving my family behind. How could you expect that?"

"You have Helen and Theo. They're your family."

"Helen isn't my mother. Helen and Theo have their own kid, their own home." I slapped his chest. "You told me you never felt like you belonged until you belonged to me. Well, how do you think I feel, Beckett? I'm a guest everywhere I go. I'm at SA at the behest of some rich benefactors. Before that, I was living with Theo and Helen, but I'm not theirs. My mom might live in a piece-of-shit trailer, but at least I know when I'm there, I'm not intruding or on borrowed time. She will always want me, even if she wants things from me too. I will *not* give up my mother."

He heaved a heavy breath, his eyes darting wildly between mine. "You've never said any of this to me."

"You've never tried to forbid me from seeing my mother." I hit his chest again. "Why do you think you and I feel such a strong pull toward each other? We're the same, Beckett. Neither of us has belonged. Your parents make you feel like crap about yourself, but do you think I would ever try to stop you from seeing them? I wouldn't because I get it. I know under the crap, they do love you, and you love them."

He shook his head and turned away from me. "You're better than all that."

"How did you come to that conclusion? I'm *lucky* because I can play field hockey. How does that make me better? Those are my origins. Nothing can change that, not you denying it or forbidding me from going back. If you don't like where I'm from, where I'll always be from, then you need to tell me that now so we can end this. I won't ever be able to make you happy, and I know I won't be happy being squeezed into a mold of someone I'm not."

"You're purposely misunderstanding me so you can be angry." He took two steps away from me then spun back. "I don't give a shit where you're from. That isn't what this is about. This is like you skateboarding, putting yourself in another dangerous situation—one you do not have to be in anymore—and I'm forced to act. I will not stand here and watch you get hurt."

"She would never hurt me," I hissed.

"Wouldn't she?" He took two big steps, erasing the space he'd created. His palm cupped my cheek, forcing my face to tip up to his. "Allowing you to step even a single foot inside that place says otherwise. I don't want you going back there, Luciana. If you want to see your mom, take her to lunch. You can't put yourself in that situation. I won't let you."

I was too mad to listen to him, even though he'd adjusted his tone to be calm and rational. If anything, it made me lean into my anger.

I shoved at his chest for the third time. "Give me room, Beckett."

"No. I understand why you're pissed at me. I didn't react well when I walked into that trailer." His thumb caressed the line of my jaw as he murmured softly to me. "I had a run-in at the park with that asshole Johnny and was already on edge. Seeing the condition of that trailer, your mom...it tipped me over to a place I don't want to be when I'm with you. I'm sorry for raising my voice. I'm not mad at you. I'm furious at things I can't control, and if you want the bare fucking truth, I'm terrified something bad's going to happen to you during one of your visits there."

I tried to scowl at him, but it came out weak. "Why do you have to be so good at apologizing?"

"It's because I mean it. I reacted in a way I shouldn't have and I'm sorry for that."

"Okay. I forgive you for yelling." I sighed. "But that doesn't take away the fact that you expect me to go to Stanford and never look back. Maybe you don't know me as well as you think you do if you believe I'd do that."

"I don't want you going to that trailer again."

"And I don't want you telling me I can't see my mother. I *especially* don't like you threatening to tell my sister."

He stared at me long and hard through narrowed eyes. "I don't want to control you. I want to keep you safe."

"But it has to be your idea of safety or nothing? That's controlling, and I won't put up with it."

"You're not breaking up with me over this, Luciana."

I rose to my tiptoes so I could look him square in the eye. "Then you need to figure out how to compromise because what you're doing right now is a deal breaker for me."

He grunted. "Don't talk like that."

"Figure it out, Beckett." This came out as more of a plea. Now that some of my anger was wearing off and I could see straight, I needed him to make this better so I could let him wrap his arms around me.

His hand slipped back to my nape, squeezing me, and his eyes stayed locked on mine.

"Don't go alone," he uttered.

"To my mom's?"

"Yes. I'll go with you. Or take Theo or Hells if you don't want me there. Don't go there by yourself. Even better, meet her at the T. Have lunch with her and let her take care of her trailer on her own."

"That's your compromise?"

He released a heavy breath across my lips. "You can't live with me telling you not to go there, and I can't live with you going there on your own. So, yeah, that's my compromise. Can you meet me here? It's as middle ground as I can get."

I nodded slowly, forcing my stubbornness away. If Beckett could bend for the sake of *us*, I absolutely could too.

"I'll meet you."

CHAPTER THIRTY-THREE

Luciana

I SHOVED OFF THE car and tucked myself into his chest, closing my arms around his waist. As soon as he registered what I had said, he lifted me off the ground and buried his face in my throat. My legs locked around him, and I dug my fingers into his thick hair. Tears pricked at the backs of my eyes. Being at odds with Beckett was my least favorite thing.

He spun and opened the back door of his car, climbing in with me in his lap. The door slammed, and we stared at one another. I was panting, my emotions too big for my heart.

"Don't talk about deal breakers. We don't break," he snapped.

"Fine. Don't talk in absolutes," I retorted.

"Fine."

His nostrils flared, and his hands traveled to the small of my back. In one swift motion, he gripped my ass and placed me on his swelling cock.

"I love you," he growled at me.

"I love you too," I snarled back.

Not even a beat passed before we collided, kissing and clawing at each other. I rucked his T-shirt up, and he yanked it over his head, followed by my sports tank. Then our chests were flush, but it wasn't enough. My nails sank into the rippling muscles along his spine, attempting to bring him closer.

It was daylight. We were barely concealed from the highway. Anyone could have pulled off and seen us, but I didn't care. Those concerns were barely whispers in the back of my mind.

Throwing myself off Beckett's lap, I managed to pull my shorts off. I had every intention of crawling back into place, but he had other ideas. He flipped me onto my stomach, pinning me against the seat. His hot mouth connected with my nape, kissing and sucking. I arched into him, wedging his dick between my cheeks.

"Beck...come on."

"I'm coming, baby."

I turned my head to watch him roll a condom down his thick dick. Then he slid his arm between my stomach and the seat, lifting my hips in the air. First, his fingers prodded my entrance, no doubt finding me slick with desire.

"Need you," I slurred, drunk on him.

The head of his cock slipped between my lips and barely inside me. His thumbs stroked along the valley of my ass, the rest of his fingers curling around my hips. The next moment, he slammed into me and gave me no time to rest. Not that I wanted it.

I just wanted him.

Brutally. Completely. Untamed.

My love.

My Beckett.

He fucked me hard but not fast. Each thrust was filled with purpose. I used my hands on the door to press back, allowing me to take him even deeper.

"I love you," he gritted out.

"I love you."

"You're mine, Luciana."

"I'm yours."

Slam. He never stopped moving into me, but one hand wound around to my front and between my thighs, cupping my pussy.

"I'm going to take care of you." His fingers found my clit, the slow circles in direct contrast to his rabid thrusts. The contrast was what drove me wild. I could barely get my mouth to cooperate to form words.

One word was all he got from me.

"Okay."

That seemed to be all he needed.

He became unleashed then. Pumping hard, our bodies slamming into each other. He knocked the breath out of me, and I found I didn't really need air anyway. Beckett made me feel alive and wanted. No, *needed*. Necessary to him.

Since our first time, my body had learned his. He'd carved a path inside me that was only his. We'd experimented with positions and with our mouths and hands. We hadn't tried it all, but we'd tried a lot.

What we were doing now was brand new. This feeling of frantic need. The force with which Beckett pounded into me; the vigor with which I called him to me. My mind and body spiraled from the utter loss of control. I'd been reduced to a writhing, desperate being who couldn't go on without quenching this dizzying thirst for more, more, *more* of Beckett.

His passion reassured me.

Each thrust of his thick cock against my slick inner walls was a confession of his love for me and only me.

He held me tight because he wasn't letting me go.

We could fight and disagree, but we were still us. We still had each other.

My logical mind knew that, but fear was irrational. When Beckett put his foot down on top of my boundaries, it felt like the first step to our ending.

Without warning, Beckett pulled out of me. I whimpered, bereft and empty. But then he spread me apart, and his mouth was on my slit, his tongue lashing at my clit. Groaning, I pressed back onto his face, desperate for more of what he was giving me.

"That feels so good, Beck. Oh god, don't stop," I begged.

He didn't stop even for a second. His tongue swiped the length of me, then his lips wrapped around my clit, suctioning gently but fervently. My nails scrabbled on the door, and my head reared back to let out a scream.

Yeah, a scream.

It was guttural, wild, and out of my control.

Beckett flipped me to my back, held my legs as far apart as he could in the confines of his car, and rammed into me. He fucked me hard, his eyes locked with mine, except when they drifted down to watch my breasts jiggle from his thrusts.

My climax had waned, but the friction of his pelvis grinding into my sensitive clit drove me back to the pinnacle again.

"Beckett," I moaned. "I love you."

"Love you," he grunted. "So good, baby."

His brow dropped, and his teeth trapped his bottom lip between them as his thrusts became concentrated. Shorter, faster, more vigorous.

He pushed into me once, and his mouth fell open. Another time, his lids lowered. A third time, his entire face went lax with euphoria.

He came quietly, his moans stuck in the well of his chest. His eyes remained on mine until they dropped closed and his head fell back.

I curled my fingers around his wrists, rubbing his fluttering pulse with my thumbs until he released a heavy exhale and pulled out of me.

Falling back on the seat, he got rid of the condom and gathered me onto his lap.

"We need to get dressed," I murmured.

"Yeah." He nuzzled my hair, making no move to actually follow through.

"Anyone could pull in and see my boobs."

He made a disgruntled sound. "No."

I laughed. "You can say no, but that doesn't make it untrue."

His head lolled on the seat as he stared at me. "Are you okay?"

"Mmhmm." I trailed my fingers along the curve of his bottom lip. "Are you?"

"I am now." He pressed a firm kiss to my temple. "Let's get you dressed and back home."

· · · · ●· ● · · · ·

Beckett didn't let go of me until we were behind his room's closed door. And even then, he only let me use his bathroom before swooping me back into his arms.

We both needed it.

The out-of-control sex in the back of his car had been us reclaiming each other, but this was the tender aftermath.

We lay face-to-face on Beckett's bed, our hands intertwined between us.

"I let that douche Johnny get in my head," he admitted.

"What'd he say that was so bad? He doesn't even know me, so I can't fathom—"

"He said I'd never get you."

"But you have me."

The corners of his mouth tipped slightly. "I know, baby. But he meant I'd never understand you because we come from such different backgrounds."

"Ah. Well, he's not wrong."

Beckett jolted. "You think so?"

"We did grow up differently. There's no getting around that, but that doesn't mean you won't ever understand me. There are parts of me that are mirror images to parts of you."

He released a breath. "I don't want you to be the same as me. I like the other parts of you that are nothing like mine. I fucking adore your light."

"I adore your shadows." I pressed on the furrow in his brow with my fingertip. "We've been living in a happy bubble. Today was bound to happen."

"What do you mean?"

"As much as I want to will the rest of the world away, I can't. You and I are different, and I like that about us, but that means we're going to clash sometimes. And, Beckett, we have to be able to clash without it being a knock-down, drag-out fight."

He nodded sharply. "I messed up."

"I did too. I got mad at you instead of stepping back to see the big picture. I shouldn't have threatened to break up."

"Made me crazy that you could even think it."

"I'm sorry. I'll try hard not to go there again."

"I would appreciate that." He touched his lips to mine. "My little light has a temper off the field too."

"You're lucky I didn't throw elbows."

"My ribs thank you for your restraint."

I giggled softly. "You know Johnny isn't my friend and never was, right?"

His lids lowered, and he nodded once. "I know. I let him get under my skin because he pushed on my one weak spot."

"Me?"

"Mmhmm. I spent so long wanting you, most of the time I still can't believe you're mine. Being the one who chases is a vulnerable position to be in."

"You're not chasing me anymore, Beckett. I'm here."

He hummed and didn't argue, but I didn't think he was completely settled. There was an edge to the way he buried his nose in my hair, a slight desperation to his arms tightening around me. I tried to hug him back with equal force, to help him understand that he *did* have me and no outside forces would scare me away.

He'd have to be the one to do that.

CHAPTER THIRTY-FOUR

Luciana

BECKETT: *SEND ME A picture.*

I handed my phone to Delilah. "Can you take a picture of me?"

She arched a brow. "Of course. Is this for Beckett?"

"Yep. I think he wants to know what I'm wearing to the party."

The phone was poised, but she didn't take the picture. "He knows you're dressed for the pool, doesn't he?"

"He knows. And he'll see me in person in a couple hours." I lifted a shoulder. "He also knows I'm not going to change my clothes, no matter what his opinion of my outfit is. Take the picture please."

Two really peaceful weeks had flown by since our argument. Last weekend, I'd had brunch with my mother at the T. Beckett had shown up at the end and actually apologized to her, completely unprompted by me.

My mother was a mess of a human, but I couldn't help the satisfaction that had brimmed inside me when she'd very clearly approved of Beckett.

This afternoon, Delilah and I were headed to Giselle's apartment complex pool for her birthday party slash cookout. Beckett was playing in a tournament an hour away, but he'd be joining us as soon as he got back.

He hadn't been happy I was going.

"I won't be there."

"You'll come late. Delilah will be with me, and I love Giselle. I don't spend enough time with her anymore, so I can't miss this. It's her eighteenth birthday, Beckett."

He pulled me onto his lap, scowling at me as he gently stroked my hair. "Who else will be there?"

"I asked, and Johnny wasn't invited. I know that's what you're worried about."

He grunted. "Among other things."

"I think you'll like Giselle. She's sort of like Bella."

"Do I like Bella?"

I smooshed his face with my hand. "Shut up. You love all my friends."

That had ended the discussion, but just like after our argument, I felt Beckett's edges rising. As much as I would have liked to soothe his worries away, I couldn't. I wasn't going to give up my friends or my past just because certain things made him uneasy, so I held on to the hope that time would be the solution. The longer we were together, the more assured Beckett would be that we were real and I wasn't going to leave him.

Delilah took my picture in the parking lot of Giselle's apartment complex, and I sent it to him, along with a selfie of D and me.

Beckett: *Fuck. I'm leaving the game. Coming now.*

Me: *No you're not. You promised to win for me. Anyway, it's just a bikini top.*

Beckett: *I didn't even know you owned a bikini. Now some assholes are seeing you in it before I do. Not happy.*

Me: *Don't pout. You're the only one who's ever seen what's under it.*

Beckett: *Christ, baby. Now I'm hard and I'm surrounded by my teammates. Go have fun. I'll be there as fast as I can. Be safe. Love you.*

Delilah tugged on my wrist, tired of waiting for me to end my text conversation. I tapped out a quick *I love you*, then stuffed my phone in the pocket of my cutoffs.

The funny thing about Beckett's jealous texts was I *didn't* own a bikini. I'd borrowed the top from Evelyn, not bothering with the bottoms since I didn't know how to swim and had no plans of putting more than my feet in the pool.

Delilah agreed with my plan. Instead of a bathing suit, she was wearing a cute little sundress that showed off her boobs and nipped at her waist before flowing over her round hips and ass.

Giselle has no such qualms. She met us at the gate of her pool in a teeny-tiny bikini that barely contained her petite goods.

"Oh my god, you look so hot! Happy birthday!" I threw myself into her open arms, squeezing her tight.

"You look awesome too, girlie." She released me, then hugged Delilah. They'd only met a handful of times, but Giselle greeted her with the same enthusiasm as she did me because she was awesome like that.

"Happy birthday," Delilah said.

"Thanks, D." Giselle gave her a long once-over. "I don't know how I feel about you looking hotter than me at my own party." Then she bounced on her toes and snapped, "Actually, I do know. I've got the hottest bitches at my party, so that must make me a hot bitch too. Come on."

Giselle's pool was in the center of the complex, with apartments surrounding it on three sides. The buildings were older, but they had nice balconies overlooking the pool, and the landscape was well maintained. I'd spent a decent amount of time here before I lived with Helen. The walls were thin, but it was safe, and for the most part, the neighbors looked out for one another.

I was eager for Beckett to get here, not just because I always wanted to be with him but because I wanted him to see this. To spend time with Giselle. To know my prior life wasn't just made up of a rusted trailer and guys like Johnny.

· · · · ● · ● · · · ·

An hour later, I was relaxed and having fun. Giselle's parents had cooked a truckload of food, so I'd been sampling some of everything while talking to a few girls from SRH and lounging next to the pool.

I was stuffing a tamale into my mouth when three guys walked through the gate. Adrian, Cris, and freaking Johnny. The bite I'd just taken turned to sawdust.

Absolutely wonderful.

Delilah bumped my leg with her foot. "Isn't that the guy who was bothering you at the bonfire?"

"Mmhmm. Beckett hates him."

Adrian spotted us first, visibly lighting up. I waved back at him, but I didn't want to encourage him to come over since Johnny would undoubtedly follow. I hopped up and took Delilah with me to find Giselle on the other side of the pool.

She was groaning when I walked up. "I didn't invite him, Luci. I told Ade not to bring him, actually."

"I know you didn't. Don't worry about it. As long as he stays away from me, we're fine."

She stared at the three guys with her hands on her hips. "I'm gonna go talk to them and make sure Johnny knows what's up. He can't be here to cause trouble." She pointed to the patio on the bottom floor of the apartment building next to the pool. "A cop lives there. He's like the neighborhood watch. We can't even talk too loudly when we pass his place or he gets bent out of shape. No idea why he moved into an apartment next to the pool, but that's not my problem."

She charged over to Johnny, her hands flying as soon as she reached him. I tugged my phone out of my pocket, dreading Beckett's response to the new situation.

Me: *Hey, I know you're probably on the field right now, but I wanted to let you know Johnny showed up uninvited. I'm staying away from him, and as long as he does the same, I'm going to stick around. See you when you get here. Love you. xoxo*

When I looked up from my phone, Giselle was still letting Johnny have it, but Adrian and Cris were headed our way.

"That's the boy who was flirting with me, isn't it?" Delilah whispered.

"Yep. And he's looking at you like he's a kid and you're the candy store."

She snorted a laugh. "That is revolting."

"But not untrue."

Adrian and Cris joined us, pulling up chairs beside ours. Cris raked his eyes over Delilah and grinned.

"Not-A-Chance, we meet again." Cris then lifted his chin at me. "Luciana. Nice of you to bring your friend to me."

"No, dude. We only came because we were told you wouldn't be here," I replied.

Cris chuckled and patted Adrian on the shoulder. "Nah, we know that's not true. Your beef is with Johnny, who followed us here. We couldn't shake him."

Adrian nodded. "He's not lying. We tried to tell him not to come, but he heard 'party' and 'girls,' and there was no way he wasn't going to show up."

I rolled my eyes. "Giselle's not too pleased. Couldn't you guys have circled the block a few times to confuse him?"

They both laughed like I was making a joke, but, man, life would have been a lot easier if they'd actually done that.

My phone vibrated while Cris and Adrian joked with each other. Dread twisted in my stomach as I read the screen.

Beckett: *I'm on my way.*

That was all it said, but he might as well have said a thousand words. He wasn't happy. Possibly displeased with me for staying or even coming in the first place. He was going to be in a pissy mood when he showed and would want me to leave with him.

With a sigh, I set my phone down on the table. If this party was going to be cut short, I'd try to enjoy myself until Beckett got here.

"Are you ever going to tell me your real name?" Cris asked Delilah.

She arched a brow. "For your diary entries?"

"Yeah. Writing 'the most beautiful girl I've ever seen' is a little long and it's making my hand hurt."

Adrian threw his head back and laughed. "Oh, boohoo. Your poor widdle hand."

Cris held up his right hand. "Hey, I need this guy since my dream girl won't give me the time of day."

I winced. "Oh god, no one needs to know that."

Cris sent me a pointed look. "What are you thinking about? Did you think I was talking about masturbation? Because wow, Ortega, I was referring to how often I have to wipe my tears, ya perv."

I rolled my eyes, but Delilah seemed amused by this fool.

"It's Delilah," she told him.

He pressed a hand over his heart, his eyes widening. "Gorgeous. Suits you perfectly."

Her cheeks went pink. Was she actually charmed by him? It sure seemed that way.

"Get your asses over here and sing to me!"

I swiveled around at Giselle's holler. She was standing beside a two-tiered cake, waving a lighter.

Adrian smiled at me. "I think that means we have to go sing to the birthday girl."

"That lighter feels a little threatening, so yeah, we better," I quipped.

The four of us headed over to the crowd, dutifully filing in around Giselle and singing to her at the top of our lungs. Her cop neighbor stuck his head out his sliding door and gave us the stink eye, but that only served to make us laugh.

Thankfully, Johnny stayed far away from me while we ate cake with Giselle and the rest of the group. Delilah and Cris were actively flirting while Adrian and I talked a little about skating and our college plans with a couple other girls.

My worry over what would happen when Beckett showed up was on a low simmer. Maybe it was my optimism, or maybe it was the cake, but I was having such a nice, laid-back time I really hoped he'd get here, feel the vibe, and join in.

CHAPTER THIRTY-FIVE

Beckett

"SLOW DOWN. I HAVE plans to die young, but not yet. Give me ten years, then you can career me off a cliff," Rhys drawled dryly.

"Check my phone again."

"Nope. Not while you're driving. I already told you how unforgiving Mathilde is. Death isn't an excuse for missing an appointment."

Furious, I slammed my hand down on my steering wheel. "Fuck you. I'm not in the mood for your jokes. If you won't check my phone, then give it to me."

He'd confiscated my phone when the first text arrived and my vision went black. I'd already been on edge, knowing Johnny was at that party with Luciana. When I received a selfie of him from her phone, I lost it. My mind, my sight, my ability to steer the car properly. If Rhys hadn't taken the wheel, I probably would have driven us off the road for real.

He continued to send messages and pictures with her phone. Pictures of my girl talking to that skater punk I kept seeing her with. Zoomed-in snaps of her tits and stomach. Her laughing. That guy touching her shoulder.

Rhys stopped looking after the fourth or fifth text and fucking refused to let me see. There was nothing I could do except haul ass to get there.

I trusted Luciana.

I did not trust anyone else.

"Have you even thought of what you're going to do when you get there?" Rhys asked in an infuriatingly calm manner. "You know Luciana better than I do, but I'm assuming she won't appreciate you storming the castle with your guns blazing."

"I'm focused on getting there."

"I'm all for chaos, Beck, but I don't think you'll like the results if that's what you bring this time. We're ten minutes out. Seven if we don't hit any more traffic lights. Take the fucking time to get your head on straight. This guy is antagonizing you to get a reaction. Think about it."

I heard him. I knew he was right.

I simply did not care.

· · · ● ● · ● ● · · ·

We got there in six.

Music hit my ears first, then laughter. I didn't pause to try to decipher if it was Luciana's laugh. I needed to see her with my own eyes. Then I'd pause.

With Rhys at my back, I entered the pool area, swiveling my head back and forth. I spotted Luciana on the far end with the skater. Delilah, another guy, and a few other girls were with them, but when she gave the punk one of her smiles, betrayal stabbed at my gut.

It was irrational. She wasn't doing anything wrong. But I was too angry to see rationality.

I started for her, but I was cut off by a smirking clown.

"Savage. Fancy meeting you here." Johnny crossed his arms, blocking my path. "Who invited you?"

"I'm not interested in you. Move." I tried to swerve around him, but he jumped in front of me.

"Nah, my boy is finally getting his shot at the girl he likes. I'm not about to allow you to get between them."

"Not happening. Move, or I'll move you."

"Beckett." Rhys laid a hand on my shoulder, and I shrugged him off.

This motherfucker needed to be dealt with. He'd come for me one too many times.

Johnny narrowed his eyes. "You think you're something special? All you have is a quick foot on the field. That's *it*. Must be why you're so insecure, can't even let your girl come to a pool party without needing to supervise." He glanced over his shoulder. "Although, maybe you were right. Luc and Ade have been really fucking cozy since we arrived."

He took another glance at them, and I used that opportunity to shove his stupid ass out of my way. He stumbled back, but only a step.

"Now, that wasn't very nice." He'd dropped the jovial act, his face reddening and awash with fury. "Say you're sorry and I won't react like I really fucking want to."

"You have to move on, Johnny. No one gives a shit about your opinions." I bumped my shoulder into his. "I'm going to get my girl."

He took me by surprise, fisting my shirtsleeve and hauling me back. Rhys caught me, keeping me from going down.

"Don't think she's your girl anymore," Johnny gritted at me, yanking at my shirt so hard the fabric started to rip. "Never really was."

"Hey, no fighting at my party."

A short girl tried to push her way between us, but I was too far gone to listen. She started yelling at Johnny, but the roaring in my ears made it impossible to make out what she was saying.

Whatever had been holding us both back snapped at the same time. We collided in a ball of flying fists and untethered aggression.

This kid needed to know when to shut up. He had to learn he didn't come between me and Luciana. No one did. If I had to teach him the lesson in blood, at least he'd learn it.

His fist landed on my jaw, knocking my head back, but it didn't slow me. He danced back, and I chased him, not giving him a second to take a breath to recover. This wouldn't be over until he was on the ground, fucking begging for the end.

Johnny picked up a lawn chair and heaved it at me. I dodged it easily, and it landed in the pool, water spraying onto the concrete.

Someone grasped the back of my shirt, but I was a freight train, barreling down tracks I wouldn't have gotten off if I could have. Johnny was my destination. Tunnel vision narrowed until he was all I saw.

My fist connected with his stomach, his jaw. He yelled vitriol in my face, spit flinging off his lips, but I had shut down the part of my mind that could hear anything but the blaring alarm rattling in my skull.

Johnny flew at me, punches landing on my chest, stomach, the side of my head, and I returned with twice the power. Head. Nose. Jaw. Kidney. I wasn't a fighter, but he'd turned me into one.

Another splash from the pool. Water sprayed my lower legs. There were screams around me, more splashing. My shirt got yanked until it was halfway ripped off me.

Then Johnny was gone. Three guys had him, pulling him away from me. I would have gone after him. Jesus, did I want to. I was nowhere near done.

But I wasn't on my feet anymore.

Without warning, someone took me down from behind. A knee forced me prone on the concrete, and pressure on the back of my neck kept me from lifting my head. Was it one guy? Had to be more. I couldn't buck them off.

Then Rhys was crouched beside me, snapping his fingers in my face. "Stop, Beck. Stop. Luciana...she's hurt."

I went still, his words sinking in. "Luciana?"

He moved to the side, and my world crumbled when I found her. She lay on the concrete too, but on her back, soaking wet. Delilah was kneeling beside her, her head to Luc's chest.

"What?" I had a hard time believing what I was seeing. Luciana was too still and soaked to the bone. Why was she wet? Why wasn't she moving? She had to move. Wake up. Make a sound.

Luciana jerked, her feet kicking in front of her, and my heart started beating again. Delilah and Adrian rolled her to her side.

I watched, unblinking, not breathing. Luciana jerked again, then water flooded out of her mouth as she coughed and gagged.

"Luciana!" I needed her to know I was here. I couldn't get to her, but I was here. "Baby, you're going to be okay. You're okay."

Delilah pushed Luc's hair off her face as coughs racked her body. Adrian patted her back, both speaking gentle, quiet words to her.

I couldn't see her face. Did she hear me? Know I was there? A wave of panic shot through me when I considered she might be afraid. Holy fuck, I needed to get to her. I had to hold her, chase her fear away.

Bucking hard against the weight on my back, I spit and cursed, clawed at the ground to find purchase. If I couldn't stand, I'd crawl with this heavy motherfucker as a passenger. I couldn't just lie here when my girl might be scared. It was my job to chase it away.

But it was no use. The weight wasn't budging, no matter how hard I fought.

"You can't arrest him," Rhys yelled over my frustrated grunts. "He was defending himself."

His words registered a second before my arms were jerked behind me and tight cuffs were banded around my wrists, keeping them together.

The weight finally lifted off my back, but not to give me freedom. I was dragged to my feet. I took one lurching step toward Luciana before being hauled in the opposite direction.

"Luciana!" If I couldn't get to her, I'd give her my voice, hoping it would give her some kind of comfort.

I twisted my head, rationality finally coming back to me little by little. I needed to reason with the man trying to take me from her. The cop who had me in handcuffs. "That's my girlfriend. I need to make sure she's okay. Let me check on her, then I'll come with you. I won't fight."

He was uninterested in anything I had to say. My pleas fell on deaf ears. He continued pushing me toward the gate, reciting my rights with each step away from the only person I wanted more than my next breath.

My last glimpse of Luciana was of her being cradled in Delilah's arms, beads of what I hoped was pool water trickling down her cheeks.

More likely, though, they were tears.

Chapter Thirty-Six

Beckett

No one would tell me anything. Not even if she was okay.

I sat in a windowless room for what had to be hours. But again, no one would tell me anything and I didn't have a phone, so I had no idea how much time had truly passed.

I hadn't been booked. At least, I didn't think I had. No one had taken my fingerprints or my picture. What that meant, I didn't know.

Common theme.

All I had to keep me busy was my thoughts.

Luciana's face occupied most of them.

Other than that, there were questions. How did she end up in the pool? Had she been knocked unconscious? Was that why she looked like she had drowned?

It was driving me crazy, not knowing how she was doing or where she was. Had she been taken to the hospital?

Was she angry at me? She had every right to be.

I'd messed up. I knew that. Getting arrested was a slap in the face. A wake-up call. I'd barged into that party with a thirst for blood and hadn't slowed down to assess the situation, allowing that idiot Johnny to goad me into a fight I never should have been in.

I should have gone straight to Luciana.

I should have listened to Rhys.

Even through all my disordered thoughts, one thing became clear: I was the reason Luciana had ended up in the pool. I was the reason she was hurt. That was all on me, my ego, the arrogance of being sure I knew what was best for her—that *I* was best for her.

Look where that had gotten her.

Had gotten me.

The door opened, and the officer who'd put me in this room held out his arm. "Your ride's here, Savage."

I got up from my chair, eyeing him warily. "I'm leaving? No one fingerprinted me."

His scowl deepened beneath his thick, black mustache. "That's because there were no charges pressed against you. We can change that if you want."

"No." I walked toward the door, my gut churning over what waited for me on the other side. "I hope I never see you again."

He chuffed. "On that, we agree. Get your spoiled ass out of my station. Next time, keep your hands to yourself."

Julien was waiting for me in the reception area. He shot me an even deeper scowl than the police officer. It slid right over me, though. I didn't give a shit about myself at the moment.

"How is she?" I rushed out.

He sighed, leaning heavily on his cane. "I talked to Helen. She said Luc was tired and grumpy but doing fine. Hells is going to take her home in the morning."

"Is that safe? Shouldn't she stay in the hospital?"

He squeezed my shoulder. "They ran tests, now they're observing her. She's going to be fine. Helen is a nurse. She can take care of her sister." He jerked his head toward the door. "Let's go."

She's tired. She's grumpy. But she's going to be fine.

She had Hells now. Hells wouldn't let her be afraid. She'd wrap Luc up and keep the demons at bay. Hells would do what I should have done. Be the strong one. The one who stood between Luc and danger—*not* shove her toward it. As much as it killed me not to be with her, being with Helen was the best choice. The safest one, that was for sure.

In the car, I checked the time. It was late. Past midnight.

"Thanks for picking me up."

He grunted. "Not something I foresaw having to do for you."

"Me either."

"I'm taking you home. We're going to talk about this in the morning. I'm too tired to have a productive conversation with you tonight."

"All right." I let my head fall back on my seat. Something told me none of this would be any less bleak in the morning.

······

I woke up and dressed in some of the clothes I kept stashed at Jules's house. When I ventured out to the kitchen, he was eating breakfast alone.

"Sera sleeping?" I asked.

"Mmhmm. She's not much of a morning person." He shoveled a spoonful of cereal into his mouth.

I made my own bowl and sat across from him, eating in silence, barely noticing what I was chewing and swallowing.

Julien got up and rinsed his bowl. I followed suit a minute later, then took my seat at the table.

"Do you want to talk about what happened?" he asked.

I shrugged. "Not really. I know I screwed up. I let my anger get the better of me."

He nodded. "I want you to look at me. My face. My cane. Think about how I got these scars. I am the result of someone letting their anger get the better of them. You need to stop and think before you act, Beckett. You don't get to fly into a rage just because you feel like it. There are consequences to every action."

The driver who hit Jules with his SUV hadn't done it by accident. He'd been aiming for Julien's friend, Amir, as retribution for a beef they had. But Jules, being the kind of man he was, stepped into the path, saving Amir and nearly dying in the process.

The driver lost his life, and my brother would never be the same, all because of some stupid vendetta.

"I get what you're saying." My head fell forward, heavy with shame. "I don't like how I acted. I don't want to be someone who lets his anger rule him."

He patted my hand. "Then don't. Next time you're in a volatile situation, you can look back on this experience and remember how this felt. Then you walk away. That's what you have to do."

I nodded. "You're right."

Jules leaned back and chuckled. "That was a lot easier than I expected. Where's the signature Beckett attitude?"

I shrugged. "Got trampled when I saw my girlfriend nearly drown, followed by me being led away in handcuffs."

"That'll do it." He lifted his gaze to mine. "Speaking of, I'll text Hells to see if Luc is ready for a visit."

"No." I gripped the edge of the table. "She needs to rest."

He cocked his head. "What? I thought for sure you'd be shoving me out the door to get to her. You're telling me you *don't* want to see her?"

"I don't." I pressed the heel of my hand into my eye, grinding it down hard. "I have to end it with her. We're not good together."

Saying those words made me feel physically ill, but not more than when I pictured Luciana as she lay unmoving on the concrete. I'd done nothing but think about that since I found out she was going to be all right. I had to do this. There was no other choice.

"That's your guilt talking. Don't make a decision you'll regret, Beck. You love that girl."

"I do. But I thought I knew how to take care of her and look where that got me. She could have *died* because of me."

Punch to the solar plexus. My lungs refused to fully inflate.

"You fucked up. Does that mean you're going to blow up your whole world?"

"I'd rather my world blow up than hers."

There would be no me if she did not exist.

His brow dropped. "And if you're her whole world?"

I shook my head. This part was easy. "I'm not. I've loved her for a long, long time, but this is new for her. It won't be hard for her to move on from me."

He stared at me like I was an alien who'd been dropped into his kitchen. "You have the weekend to sort yourself out. You need to really think about what you're doing before you make a move. Right now, you're letting your fear speak for you. I get that. Believe me, I do. But listening to your fear isn't going to get you anywhere you want to be."

A bang against the front door interrupted our conversation, and I was relieved. I didn't have anything else to say. My mind was made up.

I had to let her go.

Julien started for the door, and I got up, following him when more pounding commenced. Sera emerged at the top of the stairs, her hair wild, her eyes sleepy.

"What's going on?" Her shoulders jumped as the door rattled.

I pointed at her. "Go back upstairs. Stay up there until we come get you."

She frowned at me but didn't argue. Spinning around, she marched back down the hall to her bedroom in time for Jules to open the door.

I should have known he'd come.

Our dad stood on the front porch, his fist poised to start pounding again.

"Dad," Julien greeted flatly. "You should have called."

He jabbed his finger at my brother. "I could say the same to you." Then he found me standing behind Jules. "And you. Did you honestly think I wouldn't find out?"

Jules sighed and stepped aside, making room for our dad to come in. As he stepped into the entry, Jules pressed a hand to his chest.

"I'm allowing you to come into my house because I don't want you making a scene on my front porch. But my wife is upstairs sleeping, so I will not hesitate to ask you to leave if you disturb her peace. Remember that."

Dad grunted, but he didn't argue. He strode into the house with less arrogance than he normally had, deferring to Julien to take the lead. My relationship with my brother was separate from my dad, so I didn't see the two of them together often. It took me by surprise that Dad actually listened to Julien.

We ended up back in the kitchen.

Jules poured Dad a cup of coffee then joined us at the table.

"You were arrested," Dad stated.

"I was."

"You called your brother."

I nodded. It was true. I hadn't even considered calling my father.

A vein in his forehead twitched. "Did you think I wouldn't find out? My last name is on almost every building in this town. If my son is arrested, that news will get to me."

"I knew you'd find out, but I didn't want to deal with what you had to say." If I was going to blow my world up, I might as well start at the core.

Julien clamped down on my shoulder, halting my words. "There were no charges brought. Beckett knows he screwed up. We've been talking about it this morning. He understands it can't happen again."

Our father threw up his hands. "You've talked, therefore I can't? That's bullshit. This is my son."

Julien gestured for him to go ahead. "If you have something constructive to add, feel free. I'm only telling you the ground Beckett and I have already covered."

Dad's attention whipped from Julien to me. He wasn't happy. That vein was popping.

"I talked to my contact at the station. He informed me you were fighting over your girlfriend at some apartment complex in Savage River. I looked up this girlfriend of yours. Her criminal father is dead, her junkie mother lives in the Palisades."

Yeah, he was going to need to stop talking about Luciana right about now.

"I'm aware," I intoned.

He flattened his palms on the table. "That's over. You will no longer have anything to do with her."

He was right. Luciana and I were over, but he had nothing to do with that decision.

"What will happen if I don't listen to you?" I challenged.

His laugh was dry and bitter. "Scholarships can be pulled at any moment. I can force your separation if I need to."

I pushed back from the table and shot to my feet, my chair tipping over behind me. "You aren't going to threaten her. You aren't going to go anywhere near her."

"Sit down. You're hardly in a position to make demands." He glared at me, unimpressed and implacable. "Anyway, I'll have no cause to threaten or go near her if you end the relationship."

"You don't know anything about this girl," Julien said. "Do you realize she's the younger sister of one of my best friends? That I've known her since she was in middle school? No, you don't care about any of that. It suits your narrative to cast her as the troublemaker dragging Beckett down rather than taking a closer look at your son to find out why he's so angry that he ended up getting arrested."

My father clamped his mouth shut and slowly turned back to me. "Do you have anything to say?"

I shook my head. I had things to say but nothing to him.

He inhaled slowly, then released a long exhale through his nose. "Then you'll end it with her."

Julien rose from his chair to stand beside me. "That's enough, Josh. Luciana is a really good girl. Beckett screwed up, she didn't. If you even think about leaving here and making trouble for her or trying to split them up in any way, I will remove myself from your life completely."

Dad chuckled. "That's not much of a believable threat since you work for me."

Julien lifted his chin. "I'll leave Savage Industries. Not only that, but you won't be welcome in our home anymore. That means when we bring our new baby home in the spring, you will not have a relationship with them or us."

I turned to him. "Sera's pregnant?"

He nodded, one corner of his mouth lifting. "We found out a few weeks ago. We weren't going to tell anyone yet, but now seemed like the right time."

My dad stood, his arms crossed over his chest. "You—" He stared at Julien, then me, some of his arrogance crumpling. "When your child is older, I think you'll understand where I'm coming from, Julien."

He shook his head. "No, I won't. My child won't be a reflection of me. They'll be their own person. If you want to be around to see that happen, you'll back off Beckett and Luciana. If I even hear a whisper of a threat toward her again, you will be cut off so fast and completely I won't remember your name."

There wasn't much for my dad to say after that. He blustered for a minute or two, extracted a promise from me to visit my mother soon, then left.

Jules and I watched him drive away. "How'd you know that would work with him?"

My brother faced me and clamped his hand down on my shoulder. "Because, despite being an asshole with an ego the size of California, family is important to Josh. You probably think it's important just for appearances, and that might be part of it, but it's not the full story. He adores Sera, or I wouldn't allow him to be near her, and I think he'll love our child."

"And he loves you."

Jules shrugged, dropping his hand. "He does, in his own limited way, just like he loves you. He's not ever going to be the dad you deserve, but he does care. And that show he just put on? That was classic Savage blustering due to fear. I don't think he'd actually go after Luciana."

"You can't be sure of that." And I'd never give Josh that much credit. "It's moot anyway. Luciana and I don't have a future."

The words were like fire ants crawling over my tongue. Even after they were gone, the sting and burn remained. They didn't taste right or sound true, but it was how it had to be. I'd nearly gotten her killed.

Julien gave me a slow once-over. "Whether that's true or not, at least Josh won't be breathing down your neck, so you can make the decision on your own."

"It's made."

He exhaled. "You need to talk to her. And not by text. You need to look her in the face, see she's alive and well, and have a real conversation."

Footsteps on the stairs made us both swivel in that direction. Sera peeked down, all dressed, her hair less wild.

"Is it safe to come down now?"

Jules met her at the bottom of the steps, taking her hand. "Josh threw a tantrum."

She rolled her eyes. "And you spilled the baby beans." She grinned at me. "Uncle Beckett has a nice ring to it, huh? I'm going to need you to come home every break to bond with your niece or nephew."

I laughed, even though I didn't really feel it. I'd be happy about this news when I wasn't so fucking miserable about my own shit.

"You're going to need me to change diapers, right?"

Sera came straight for me, pulling me into a tight hug. "Sure, that, but we *always* want you around, kid. I hope you know that."

I didn't really feel that either, but it was nice as hell to hear.

"He thinks he's breaking up with Luciana," Julien said, amusement tingeing the news.

Sera pulled back and pressed the back of her hand to my forehead. "Are you sick? Did you hit your head during the fight?"

I shook her off. "No, and it doesn't need to be a big discussion. When you almost kill your girlfriend, it's time to walk away. I'm not good for Luciana."

Sera glanced back at Jules. He laughed. "His record's stuck. He keeps saying the same ridiculous things. But he won't go talk to Luc."

She blew out a heavy breath. "Okay, well only a jackass wouldn't contact his girlfriend after what happened. Even if you do end up breaking up, you're not going to do that to her, Beckett." She slapped my chest. "Don't be a dick. If you let her go by ghosting her, she's going to be mad. And you know what girls and women do when they're mad at their exes? They revenge date. I think Luc and Rhys would make an adorable couple."

"Shut up, Sera. That's not funny."

"Hey." Jules put himself between his wife and me. "Don't tell her to shut up. I don't care how upset you are, you're not going to talk to my wife that way."

"I know." My eyes fell closed, and I tried to exorcize the thought of Luc and Rhys being together from my mind. "I'm sorry, Sera."

She peeked out from under Julien's arm and offered a soft smile. "You're forgiven. I'm sorry I pressed on a sore spot. But I do want you to think about what walking away from her means. She *will* date other guys. Not Rhys, because she's sane, but for sure other guys, and you won't be able to say anything."

She wielded the truth like a machete in the jungle, slicing through everything in the way of making me hear her. All I could do was nod. She was right.

But how could I keep Luciana when I had proven, in Technicolor, I wasn't any good for her?

CHAPTER THIRTY-SEVEN

Luciana

So, I DROWNED.

It had been as embarrassing as it'd been terrifying. One second, I'd been running toward the fight. The next, I was hit by a chair Johnny threw and went flying into the deep end of the pool.

The last thing I clearly remembered was thinking I should have taken Delilah up on her offer for swim lessons a lot sooner. Then it was all a blur.

Delilah had filled in the blanks for me.

Adrian was the one to notice me at the bottom of the pool. He dove in and brought me up. I'd been unconscious, but my heart had been beating.

The embarrassment part kicked in when I vomited pool water all over Adrian and Delilah. I shouldn't have been dwelling on it since, you know, I could have died, but I kept replaying the moment Adrian leaped away from me over and over.

I suspected it was my mind's way of protecting me from the rest of the horror that had gone down.

"Hey, girlie." Helen plopped down on the bed next to where I was stretched out on my back. She'd checked me out of the hospital as soon as they would release me and had bundled me up in my bedroom at her house. "How are you feeling?"

"I'm fine. I don't know why I can't go back to school."

She leaned toward me, frowning. "You need to rest."

"I can rest at school."

"He's not there, Luc. You know that."

My breath caught in my throat. "I know. But maybe he'll be back soon."

My phone had been in my pocket when I went into the pool, which meant I no longer had a working phone. Helen had been in contact with Julien and Sera over the last two days, so I knew Beckett was out of jail, and he had been told I was with Helen, but we hadn't spoken directly.

This wasn't like him.

Not at all.

I was hurt by his absence.

And frankly stunned by his silence.

The sooner I got back to SA and saw Beckett, the better. I just had to figure out how to make my jailer set me free.

Helen stroked my hair, her eyes raking over me. "Can't you just humor me a little? I need some Luc time before I send you back."

"You don't have to worry about me."

"It's my job."

I blew out a heavy breath. "I'm eighteen now, and you have your family to take care of. I'm good. Scratch me off your worry list."

Her fingers went still in my hair, and she pulled away, frowning down at me. "Back up a second. You *are* my family. You're never going to be off my list, no matter how old you are. Why would you say that?"

"No, I know you love me. But you have Madelina and Theo. You don't have to pause your life just because I'm a dummy who can't swim."

Helen went silent. I chanced a look at her, and she turned away, her fingers opening and closing in her lap.

"Helen?"

She slowly turned back to me, and my breath caught at the wetness in her dark eyes that mirrored mine.

"Do you know that when your dad moved away with you when you were two, I cried for three days straight? I couldn't sleep because

I was so worried about who was going to change your diapers. Your dad didn't know which book you liked to be read to you at bedtime. He didn't know the song I'd made up to soothe you back to sleep if you woke up crying. I physically ached for a solid year after you were gone. And when I got you back all those years later, I did crazy, unimaginable things to make sure you were permanently mine."

"Hells—"

She shook her head. "You're more than my sister, Luciana. The way I love you is different from how I love Madelina, but it is no less big or important. You are my girl, and there is no me without you. You will never, ever be a burden to me. Do you get that?"

"I'm—" A tear slipped down my cheek. "A lot of people have given me up. I never wanted to put you in a position where you had to."

My parents both gave me away. If you couldn't count on your parents to want to keep you, how could you trust anyone else would?

"You really don't get it." Helen swiped my tears away. "You are the light of my life and, for a long time, my reason for becoming better. I'm pissed you don't know that. How can you not know that? Theo and I talk about how much we miss you pretty much every day and conspire ways to get you back here. You'll never put me in a position to give you up, and I *won't*. You're not my daughter, but you *are* my girl, and you have been since birth."

I hated seeing my badass sister with tears welling in her eyes, especially knowing I'd put them there. I held my arms out to her, needing her to hug me just as badly as I needed to comfort her.

"I'm sorry for not getting it," I whispered. "The thing is, I'm starting to realize I'm a little bit broken."

She nodded into my hair and squeezed me tighter. "I know something about being broken, girlie. Sometimes we have to push harder to get through all the scar tissue."

I sighed and pressed my face into her shoulder. After a few minutes, I was brave enough to ask her the question that had been weighing on my mind. "Do you know why Beckett isn't here?"

She pulled back, her gaze filled with sympathy, which made my stomach twist. "Julien just said he needs time. He asked about you, of course, but I'm getting the feeling he's dealing with a lot of guilt."

"This isn't like him."

"I hope not." She huffed. "I'm not impressed with Beckett Savage right now. I know you love him, kid, but ghosting you like this isn't cool. Let's hope he pulls his head out of his ass before I have to be the one to do it."

I pressed a hand against my aching stomach. "Let's hope so."

······

By the time Helen let me go back to Savage Academy, I was crawling out of my skin. It was Tuesday evening, and I hadn't heard a word from Beckett since Saturday afternoon. According to my friends, he'd come back to SA the night before.

Anxiety rode me hard as I turned down his side of the hall. I had to take a deep breath before I could knock on his door. I had never been this nervous to see him. Beckett had always gone to great lengths to make sure I was comfortable with him.

Something was wrong.

And I was certain I wasn't going to like what was waiting for me in his room.

I knocked anyway. I couldn't wait any longer for answers.

The door swung open moments later, a solemn Beckett filling the doorway.

"Luciana."

He made no move to allow me into his room, and my heart sank like a stone.

"What are you doing?" I whispered.

His head cocked. "I was studying. I guess you're back. That's good."

"What are you *doing*?" I asked slightly louder.

He finally stepped back. "Let's talk in my room."

Like I was taking a walk to my doom, my steps were leaden. Beckett moved as far from me as possible so there was no chance of me touching him.

He closed the door, and we stared at each other from opposite sides of his tiny room.

After long, tense moments, he spoke. "Are you feeling okay?"

I shook my head.

The corners of his mouth dipped as he raked his gaze over me. "Is it too soon for you to be back?"

I stared at this stranger I loved more than anything. "Do you care?"

He blinked at me. "Yes. I care."

"You're not very good at showing it."

His shoulders fell, and he looked away from me. "Things got messed up, Luc. Everything was so intense. Too intense."

"*Too* intense?"

He turned back but didn't quite meet my eyes. "Yeah. I had a lot of time to think, and I realized I couldn't do this. You're great, amazing, but I'm not in the right headspace to be as serious as we are. I can't be a good boyfriend to you, which I think is evident from how things went this weekend."

As his complete absence had continued, my darkest thoughts had gone there. To Beckett ending us. I'd told myself I had to be wrong. The boy who'd watched over me for years would never walk away from me without a fight.

Yet here we were.

I clearly knew nothing about this person.

"So, that's it? You're done with me without even having a conversation?" I pressed my lips together to stop them from trembling, but there was nothing I could do to prevent the tears from welling in my eyes.

"There's nothing to talk about. I can't be your boyfriend."

He wasn't sorry. There was no apology. He'd reverted to the Beckett Savage I once thought he was. Cold and uncaring. Had I missed that this was always who he was? Had I just convinced myself he was more?

"You made a lot of promises to me, Beckett." I was proud of myself for my voice not cracking.

He lowered his chin, still focusing on a spot beyond my shoulder. "I shouldn't have. There was nothing behind them. They were empty."

"Just like you," I whispered. "You should try out for the spring play. You're a really great actor."

Tears fell in silent streams down my cheeks. My arms were too weak to bother wiping them away. It wasn't as if Beckett was looking at me anyway. At least he allowed me to bear the shame of loving a boy who didn't love me back all alone.

I rushed to the door, gripping the knob hard in my fist. With my back to him, I let my hurt take over. "I hope it goes without saying that I want you to stay the hell away from me."

I didn't slam his door or stomp off.

My dignity and pride wouldn't allow it.

I held my head high as I calmly shut his door and walked back to my side of the hall.

It wasn't until I was inside my suite, surrounded by the friends I never doubted would always have my back, that I allowed the first sob to break through. And once it did, I fell apart, wholly and completely.

CHAPTER THIRTY-EIGHT

Luciana

IT TOOK ME FORTY-EIGHT hours to come to the conclusion that Beckett Savage was a liar.

My suspicions began during English the day after he dumped me.

We were finishing our *Pride and Prejudice* project, preparing to present it, and Dr. Burns gave us the period to work on it. Beckett and I had no choice but to work together. During the entire hour, he never once looked at me.

At least, not while I was looking at him.

But when I glanced down at my notes, I caught him sneaking peeks. The first time, he visibly winced at the sight of me. I didn't blame him for that. I was a mess. Red-nosed, glassy-eyed, falling apart at the seams.

For someone who didn't want to be with me, he seemed to care about the state I was in an awful lot.

Throughout the day, I caught him watching me again and again. I also caught Rhys shaking his head at Beckett like he strongly disapproved of what his friend was doing.

Those occurrences alone wouldn't have brought me to my conclusion that Beckett was a liar, though. He had held far too firmly in his stance that we were over for me to jump there on my own.

That came later, but my suspicions rose higher during a conversation with Coach Thompkins Thursday afternoon.

My locker was cleaned out. Nothing of me was left behind.

I picked up my bag filled with shin guards, jerseys, protective gear, and cleats and stopped at Coach Thompkins's office.

"I'm all done."

She looked up from her computer and shot me a grin. "It's the end of an era. It won't be the same without you next year."

I hitched my bag higher on my shoulder. "I'll miss this place." Before I knew they were coming, tears dripped down my face.

Coach got up and circled around her desk, drawing me into a hug. "Don't you dare make me cry, Ortega."

I laughed. "Sorry. I've had a weird few days. It's all hitting me at once."

"I'll bet. Going under had to be scary as hell."

People kept saying that, but those few minutes were a blank for me. I'd be happy to go the rest of my life never remembering what it had felt like to drown.

"I barely remember it, to be honest. I think it was scarier for the people who saw it happen."

Like Delilah...and Beckett.

Delilah had hugged me for a solid half hour when she came to visit me at home. And Beckett...well, he'd gone the other way, shoving me out of his life as fast as he could.

Because...he was scared?

Was that it?

Coach and I talked for another minute or two, then she hugged me again.

"You had an outstanding season," she told me. "I wish I could thank the anonymous donor who funded your room and board. Having you here twenty-four seven was key."

My brow dropped. "Wait. It was one donor? I thought my scholarship had been expanded...?"

She shook her head. "No, actually, it wasn't. You have a big fan. The donation was to be strictly allocated for your room and board."

I was staggered. "Does that happen often?"

"I've never heard of it. But let's not look a gift horse in the mouth." She winked. "Someone really wanted you here."

· · • • • • • • · ·

The bomb Coach dropped had rattled in my head the rest of the day.

Someone really wanted you here.

Someone really wanted you here.

There was only one person who could have wanted me here so badly he would have found a way to make it happen, underhanded or not.

Then he dumped me.

Because our relationship was too intense.

The captain of Team Intense had claimed *our* relationship, which was as easy as breathing, was too intense.

Now that I wasn't standing in front of him, having my heart utterly shattered, I was able to mull over his words.

He hadn't said much.

He'd made sure not to touch me. He'd barely looked at me.

"I can't be your boyfriend."

He'd been kind as he broke my heart, making sure to tell me how amazing I was. Beckett wasn't the type to be kind to spare someone's feelings—especially when he was finished with them.

It was in the dining hall at dinner that the truth really sank in.

I couldn't eat, not with the boulder lodged in my stomach. My friends were around me, chatting with each other in between throwing worried glances at me. I wanted to join in with them, to think of something other than the absence of my person, but it was like I was behind a thick glass wall. Seeing them but completely separate.

Beckett strolled by with Felix and Charles. He didn't look my way, but Felix did. The expression of sympathy Felix shot me flipped me inside out. He knew. They all did. And they felt sorry for me.

I didn't want their pity. I wanted my heart.

And Beckett was my heart.

Ivan shifted beside me, leaning in close to be heard over the din of conversation. "You are sad."

I tore my eyes off Beckett to turn toward Ivan, bringing our faces close together. He eyed me curiously and without pity. Freaking *finally*.

"It's been a rough week. I'm sure you've heard."

"I did hear, and I was surprised Savage is the type of guy to let his girl go." Ivan picked up a lock of my hair. "He's looking this way, you know."

I tipped my chin up but didn't dare check to see if Ivan was right. "Is he?"

Ivan nodded, tucking my hair behind my ear. "He's frozen. I do not think he appreciates me being so close to you."

"He doesn't care."

He grunted. "His friend is now clamping down on his shoulder, preventing him from getting out of his seat, I think. If he were to get up, where do you think he would go?"

"Ivan..." I choked out a soft sob. "Don't give me hope where there is none. I can't take it."

"I'm only observing a situation that does not make sense to me." He gently placed his wide hand on my shoulder. "Come. I will hug you."

I let him pull me toward him, really needing a hug. Ivan palmed the back of my head, pushing it down on his shoulder, then dipped down so his mouth was beside my ear.

"Look at him, Luciana," he whispered. "He's near detonation."

My eyes snapped open, landing on Beckett across the room. He was locked on Ivan and me. The tendons on either side of his neck were thick ropes, and his face was so red it was nearly purple. Rhys was talking to him on one side, and Felix had ahold of his shoulder on the other.

"He's jealous," I murmured.

"I suspect he is being eaten alive with jealousy." Ivan threaded his fingers in the back of my hair, pulling me from his shoulder to peer down at me. "When he comes back to you, don't make it easy. A man who can walk away from his girl, even temporarily, should be made to suffer so he never considers doing it again."

"You think it's temporary?"

He nodded once. "I think Savage will try to kill me when he next has the chance." Then he smirked as if amused by the idea.

Ivan released me and went back to his dinner. I still couldn't eat, but I no longer felt like hiding the fact that I was staring at Beckett. As soon as our eyes connected, he ripped his away, studying his plate.

That was when I knew for sure.

Beckett Savage was a liar.

The flimsy reasons he'd given me for breaking up weren't real. He didn't mean them. And he wasn't even close to letting me go.

I hadn't fought him when he'd ended us because I'd been so shell-shocked and broken. I saw things clearly now. He'd made that decision out of fear, and that wasn't acceptable.

Determination spurring me on, I rose from the table and took my full tray to the trash. Then I spun around and marched straight up to Beckett's table. All his friends stared at me with wide eyes, but he was my sole focus.

"I do not accept," I announced calmly.

He cocked his head. "What?"

"We're not broken up. I don't accept it. That doesn't mean I'm not very angry at you for abandoning me. I am, and I expect you to grovel for a while to make up for it."

Rhys started cackling, but Beckett didn't take his eyes off me. "Luciana, it doesn't matter if you accept or not—"

I held up my hand. "I get it. You got scared. Maybe you blame yourself for what happened to me. You set me free so I'd be safe, or however you explained it to yourself. Except I don't want to be set free. If you're my cage, then I'm closing the door, locking it, and throwing away the key. I'm yours, and you're mine. That's nonnegotiable."

His mouth fell open and closed, but I kept barreling on before he tried to deny me again. I only had so much bravery left, and Beckett's refusal still hurt like acid on my skin.

"I won't accept anything less than you down on your knees, Beckett."

I lifted my chin, swiveled on my toe, and marched out of the dining hall.

The night air hit my face, my eyes burned with tears, and my empty stomach revolted, but I kept going. If I stopped, even for a second, I would falter.

False bravado only took me so far.

CHAPTER THIRTY-NINE

Beckett

LUCIANA WAS STANDING OUTSIDE the dorm when I walked out. Unlike the past few days, she was smiling. Her eyes weren't so bloodshot, and the shadows beneath them weren't quite as deep as they'd been.

Still, seeing her was a knife to the heart. I had to stuff my hands in my pockets to keep myself from reaching for her, my fingers closing around the hair tie I'd been carrying every day since I was thirteen. The girl was part of my system. She was everywhere, and I didn't know how to even begin the process of extracting her.

Not that I wanted to. I never would. So, I'd have to learn to live with a gaping wound in my chest.

I put my head down, aiming to walk past her, but she fell into step beside me.

"Ready to grovel?" she asked cheerfully.

"Come on, Luc. Don't do this."

"I take that as a no. That's okay. Last night, I was thinking about how long you wanted me and made plans to be with me before I finally saw you for who you really are. You were patient. Now, it's my turn to be patient with you. Again, that doesn't mean I'm not pissed off. I am. I'm very, very mad and hurt beyond measure, but I know you'll make it right."

I glanced at her, frowning. What was she doing?

"There's no making it right. I told you I couldn't do this. That remains true."

She brushed my words off. "I remember everything you said, and I don't accept it." She nodded toward the dining hall. "Are you getting breakfast?"

"Uh. Yeah."

"I'll go with you, but I won't be eating. I haven't really eaten in days because your abandoning me has made me physically ill. It's strange. I feel empty, but I also feel like there's a boulder lodged in my stomach. That makes eating difficult, but I'm hoping you'll come to your senses soon and buy me lots of food as part of your groveling process."

I stopped walking to stare at her. Luciana blinked up at me, a picture of innocence as if what she just said wasn't completely insane.

"You have to eat. You'll make yourself sick."

She pressed both hands to her stomach. "I think it's too late for that. I guess it's good that field hockey is over since I don't really have any energy right now."

I wasn't certain whether I wanted to throttle her or pick her up and carry her to the infirmary.

I chose a third option.

"You're eating. Come on."

She scurried along with me into the dining hall and over to the bakery. Luciana loved chocolate chip muffins, even though she rarely allowed herself to eat them. I ordered two then picked up a yogurt, fruit, milk, and apple juice.

My tray was loaded when I put it on an empty table. "Sit."

She took a seat, and I placed the food in front of her. She divided everything, pushing half the food over to me. When I didn't take a seat, she looked up at me.

"The only way I'll take a bite is if you sit down and eat with me," she said.

I figured as much, so I folded myself into the chair beside hers. My arm brushed hers, and though two layers of clothing separated us, I still felt her heat, which was why I'd been avoiding exactly this.

The urge to wrap my arms around her was almost overpowering.

Luc pinched off a microscopic piece of muffin and slowly chewed it. I twisted in my chair to watch her eat. Her lips were pursed in a sour expression, and her face had lost most of its color. She really was making herself sick.

More to the point, what I'd done to her was making her sick.

She sucked in a breath. "Delilah's going to start giving me swim lessons."

I went still, blood draining from my face. If she noticed, she didn't slow down for me to figure out how to handle my rising sense of panic.

"She and Ev basically grew up in the water. You know Ev's a great swimmer since she's on the team, but Delilah is too." She showed me her shaking hand. "I'm nervous. I would have been no matter what, but after what happened last weekend, I'm pretty terrified."

"So don't do it," I ground out, attempting to rein in the violence surging through my veins. Imagining Luciana in another pool made me want to break things.

"It would be easier not to. But I can't just not do things because they scare me. What kind of life would that be? Besides, once I know how to swim, I'll basically be invincible."

I grunted, still stuck on the fact she was willingly going back in a pool after she almost died.

"It's too soon."

She pinched off another piece of muffin but didn't eat it. "I don't think so. The longer I wait, the worse it'll get. Fear doesn't get to rule me."

Then she pushed back from the table with her muffin in one hand, the apple juice in the other. "I'm going to get going now. I'll see you in class."

"Eat," I called after her.

She spun around, waving her muffin and juice before disappearing outside, leaving me wondering what had just happened. What kind of spell had she just woven over me?

· · · • •• • •• · ·

I had no explanation for my presence in the stands lining the sides of SA's Olympic-size indoor pool. Luciana had waved at me when she spotted me as if she'd expected me to be right where I was.

She and Delilah were in the pool now. My focus never strayed from Luciana. I hadn't even taken a breath since she'd dipped her toe in the water ten minutes ago.

Delilah had her on her back, floating on the surface of the pool. Luc's eyes were closed, her face relaxed, but my heart was about to hammer right out of my chest.

They were in four feet of water.

Luc could touch the bottom with her feet if she stood.

She wouldn't drown if Delilah let go of her.

Not that she would. Delilah hadn't taken her eyes off Luc even for a second.

I still didn't trust her with Luciana's safety. With her life. So, I stayed, watching, making sure everything was all right. Even as blackness closed in on the edges of my vision.

Without warning, Luciana's peaceful floating turned to panicked splashing. I sprung to my feet and darted down the steps toward the pool in sheer panic. Before I reached the bottom, Delilah had already helped Luciana climb out, and she was sitting on the edge, gasping for breath. Delilah was beside her, her arms around her, speaking quietly in her ear.

I stood behind them, helpless. I'd given up my right to comfort her, but Christ, it was all I wanted to do. But I could only watch from a distance as Delilah calmed her. Luc's breathing slowed, and she nodded at whatever Delilah was murmuring.

Luciana sucked in a deep breath. "Okay. I'm ready. Let's get back in."

Delilah ran a hand down the length of her back. "Are you sure, precious?"

Luc nodded. "If I quit now, I'll never get back in. That was just a temporary freak-out." She slowly lowered herself into the water, keeping a death grip on the side, and grinned up at Delilah, her eyes flicking to me for a moment. "See? Not so scary."

Still holding on to the side, she submerged herself fully for long, dragging seconds before bursting back up again. Delilah dropped into the pool and pulled Luc into a tight hug.

Then...they got back to it. Floating. Treading water. Putting her face in the water. Luciana did it all, never giving in to her fear.

I always knew she was better than me, and this was just another piece of evidence to add to the pile. My knees were so fucking weak from my lack of control over just about everything. I paced the edge of the pool, going out of my mind.

Luciana and Delilah carried on like I wasn't there, which was good since I was being an absolute lunatic and couldn't stop myself. I'd used up all my calm, cool, and collected in the years I'd waited on Luciana. My chill had gone to pasture.

After a thousand years, the two of them climbed out together and headed for their towels. I stopped pacing to watch Luciana dry off.

Maybe if I hadn't been watching her as closely as I was, I would have missed her tells.

The hitch in her breath.

Her vibrating hands.

The subtle downward tug of her mouth.

My brave girl wasn't doing okay. I saw it the moment she broke.

The towel slipped from her fingers, and her body bent in half.

Whether it was my place or not, I went to her, dropping to my knees in front of her. Her sobs were quiet but violent, racking her body.

"Luciana." I gripped her hip and cupped the side of her face. "You're okay. You're safe. Nothing's going to happen to you."

Delilah was behind her, rubbing her back, telling her the same things, but Luc was leaning into me, her cheek against my hand, her body listing in my hold. I curled my arm around her back, giving her more support, and pressed my face against her quivering belly. Her fingers dug into my hair, violent sob after violent sob sending quakes down her spine.

"Baby, you're safe. I promise nothing's going to happen to you. You were so brave to get back in that pool. I've never seen anyone more brave."

"I remembered—I remembered going under."

My face was wet from her swimsuit, but not just that. I couldn't say when the last time I cried was, but Luciana's sobs cracked me in two, and there was no stopping the tears from leaking down my face.

"You never have to do that again, Luciana. No one will ever make you go in a pool. I promise you that."

She took a shuddering breath, then dropped her hands to my shoulders. I looked up at her through glassy eyes, finding her staring back at me with a pained expression.

"You don't get it," she rasped. "Fear doesn't get to rule me."

She swiped her thumb along my cheek. This time, it was me leaning into her hand.

"You're so fucking brave." My eyes flicked to hers. "I don't know how to be like that."

Her thumb kept up its gentle sweep. "I don't feel so brave right now."

"You are. You really, truly are."

Before I was ready, Delilah pulled Luciana away from me, taking her into the locker room for a hot shower. She needed it. Her quakes had turned into trembles, and goose bumps dotted every inch of her exposed skin, but now that she was out of my arms, I didn't know how to get myself up and move.

Fear doesn't get to rule me.

I'd let it rule me. I'd thrown my whole world away because I was too fucking afraid to latch on to it with both hands.

Even if I could claw my way back to Luciana, I wasn't sure I was worthy. Not when I'd done exactly what she accused me of—abandoning her when she'd needed me most.

That was fear talking again. Convincing me not to even try.

Fuck being afraid.

Fuck backing down.

If I wasn't the best choice for Luciana, I needed to work harder, not quit when I was falling behind.

Down on my knees beside an empty pool, I couldn't fathom how I'd forced those parting words past my lips. Now that I'd gotten my hands on her, felt her hands on me, there was no going back.

Luciana was mine.

She was always going to be mine.

Now, I had to prove it to her.

CHAPTER FORTY

Luciana

I DIDN'T HAVE TO chase Beckett down. He was waiting for me outside of the locker room. I was bundled up in a thick hoodie and sweats, the shivers finally passing.

I was too tired to do much more than nod at him.

"I'll walk you back to the dorm," he stated.

Delilah and I exchanged a glance. She was worried Beckett was going to continue to hurt me, and to be honest, so was I, but she also understood we needed to have a true conversation.

"I'm going to the library." She leaned in and gave me a hard squeeze. "I'll see you back at the suite, precious."

"Thank you, Delilah. I couldn't do this without you."

She winked. "You'll never have to."

I watched her walk off in the other direction before turning to Beckett. His eyes were already on me.

"She's a good friend to you."

I agreed. "The best of the best."

"I don't think I could have gotten in the pool today like you did."

A dry laugh burst out of me. "I won't argue with you. I think we both know who the brave one is in this relationship. That's okay, though. When you get stupid out of fear, I'll set you straight."

"Luciana..."

I was too tired to keep up this cheerful act. Swimming, choking, swimming, sobbing, then silently crying some more in the shower had taken it all out of me.

"I'm actually a little hungry. Let's have dinner."

He heaved a sigh, his shoulders rolling forward. "All right."

SA's campus was massive, so the walk to the dining hall wasn't a short one. Somewhere along the way, Beckett's pinkie brushed mine. The first time might've been an accident. The second time felt purposeful. The third time culminated into his whole hand engulfing mine.

He was watching me instead of the path in front of him. I looked up at him, remembering the tears he hadn't hidden from me when he'd fallen on his knees in front of me.

"You really hurt me," I whispered. "But I want to be able to forgive you. Can you try to make it easy for me?"

His neck bobbed as he swallowed hard. Then he lowered his chin, his gaze blazing into me. "Your work is done. It's my turn, baby. Just relax, and I'll make it better."

The knot in my chest unfurled a tiny bit, and I leaned against his arm. "I'm going to trust that you mean that."

"I do. You'll see."

The dining hall was packed, but Beckett steered me into a quiet corner, away from our friends. He left me there and returned a few minutes later carrying two trays laden with every food item the dining hall made, placing them both in front of me.

"I...don't think I can eat all this."

He nudged the trays. "Eat what you can. If you want me to, I'll feed you."

I turned sharply toward him. Judging from the way he was scowling at all the food, he wasn't kidding.

I plucked soup from the tray and a hunk of bread. "This looks good. You eat too, or I won't be able to."

For the first time in almost a week, I consumed a full meal. My stomach still didn't feel quite right, but I wasn't seconds away from throwing up either. Beckett watched me the whole time, even as he ate his own dinner.

As soon as I put down my spoon, he spoke. "I'm sorry, Luciana. You are right about everything."

"I know."

He brought his hand up to cup my nape. "I convinced myself you were better off without me. It's my fault you ended up in the pool. I let this kid I don't even care about goad me into a fight I never should have been in. That's all on me. No matter how guilty I was feeling, I should have been by your side as soon as I was able to."

"You were in the clink. Did they scare you straight?"

He huffed a dry laugh. "Seeing you lying still on the concrete did that."

I flinched. I really hated thinking of myself like that. The fact that Beckett had seen me that way and still left really jabbed at me hard.

"Did you think I wouldn't want to see you?"

His brow pinched. "I don't know. I thought you *shouldn't* want to see me, and I didn't deserve to see you."

I'd figured all this out on my own, but being right didn't make me feel vindicated. Anger was the predominant emotion at the moment.

"You hurt me. That you could stay away from me after everything absolutely kills me. I know you paid for me to live here this year. I know that was you. You did all that and then you just gave me up when I needed you the most."

His fingers flexed on my nape, and he brought his forehead down to mine, breathing in my pain. "I'm sorry, Luciana. In my warped, terrified mind, I thought I was doing the right thing. But I realized pretty fucking fast I was doing the cowardly thing. I have no excuse other than panic. I love you, and that will never be untrue. I told you forever, and even if you never look at me again, I'll keep on loving you."

He was digging under my skin with gentle claws. If I allowed it, he'd be all the way under again. But he'd introduced mistrust between us, so all I could think of was Beckett walking away again and ripping me apart.

"Prove it," I murmured.

"I'm going to."

Beckett took me back to my suite, holding my hand. We rarely spent time here, but when he turned to leave, I invited him in. I wasn't ready to see him retreat yet, worrying I'd wake up tomorrow to find he'd changed his mind again.

"Hang out for a little?" I asked.

"You don't even have to ask."

I turned on the BBC *Pride and Prejudice* miniseries and stretched out beside Beckett on my bed to watch. The lights were low, and fatigue tugged at me. He opened his arm, inviting me closer. His chest looked like a perfect pillow.

"This doesn't mean I forgive you," I told him as I settled my cheek in the spot I'd claimed as my own.

He wrapped his arm around me, pulling me tight to his side. "I know, little light. We'll get there."

··········

I didn't wake up until morning, and I was alone. My laptop was closed and put back on my desk, and my phone was charging. Beckett must have done that before he'd left.

I checked my phone first, my heart lightening when I found a text from him.

Beckett: *You were knocked out last night. I wasn't sure if you'd want me to stay so I went back to my room. One of the hardest things I've ever done. Text me if you wake up before morning and want me back. If you don't wake up, I'll see you for breakfast. I love you.*

This was the first morning in a week I didn't have any trouble getting out of bed. I showered and dressed, my stomach finally sending signals to my brain that I was hungry.

It was early and the weekend, so my suitemates hadn't emerged yet. Beckett was probably still asleep too. But I couldn't stay inside my room any longer.

I stepped out of my suite and carefully closed the door behind me. Before I could take another step, I jumped, releasing a little squeak.

Beckett was sitting on the ground, clutching a bouquet of sunflowers, tracking me with tired eyes.

I crouched beside him to bring us to eye level. "What are you
doing down there?"

"Waiting for you. I didn't know when you'd wake up." He shifted
to his knees, one hand hovering beside my face. I tipped my head into
it so he was cupping my cheek. The breath he released was ragged,
filled with both relief and pain. "Good morning. I'm sorry. I love
you so fucking much."

He tugged me into his arms, and I allowed it because I'd needed a
hug from him since forever had been invented.

"Did you get me flowers?" I murmured into his shoulder.

"Yeah. Had to drive around to find them."

I squeezed my eyes shut to stop myself from crying. I'd done
enough of that already, and Beckett buying me flowers shouldn't
have affected me so profoundly. But he was the only one who ever
had. Back when he had loved me on his own up to now when we
loved each other but couldn't quite get it right.

"Thank you. They're my favorite."

"One day, I'll take you to a field of sunflowers and buy all of them
for you."

"You don't have to buy them if you promise to have a picnic with
me in that sunflower field."

He pulled back enough for me to see his frown. Oh, my grumpy
Beckett.

"Name the day," he uttered. "I'll always be there."

"Keep your promises and maybe I'll believe you."

·· • • • • • • ··

Beckett stayed with me all day. He didn't ask for my forgiveness, and
I didn't offer it. I needed him, but I was much too raw to fully let
him back in. It was unlike him not to demand, but he allowed me to
set the pace.

He was waiting outside my door Sunday morning too. This time, he brought me chocolates. Piles of them to make up for my week of not eating.

We ate chocolate and muffins for breakfast on a blanket in the courtyard. The same spot I'd discussed E.E. Cummings with Rhys. Beckett showed me a sunflower farm on his phone he promised to take me to when they were in bloom. Then we lay in the sun with full bellies, our pinkies touching, sneaking peeks at one another.

He turned to his side, so I turned to mine. He curled his arm around my back, tugging me against him.

"I love you," he said.

I gave him a smile. I wasn't ready to say that again yet either.

He smiled back and dipped down to press his lips to my forehead. "That's an 'I fucked up' kiss."

He pressed his lips to the corner of my mouth. "An 'I'm not going anywhere' kiss."

His lips touched the tip of my nose. "That one was an 'I'll never love anyone but you' kiss."

His mouth landed right next to mine. "That was a friendship kiss. I'm going to be your best friend, always."

I kissed my fingertips then pressed them to his lips. "That's an 'I'm not ready to do more than this, but I'm getting there because of you' kiss."

His breath traced across my lips. "There's no rush. We're together, and we'll find our solid ground again."

•••••••••••

On Tuesday, I stared at Beckett as he studied on the floor beside where I was sitting on my bed. A frothy kind of anger bubbled in my stomach.

"Eventually, you were going to have another girlfriend."

His head jerked up. "What?"

"If I had accepted you breaking up with me, one day, you would have moved on and found someone else. You can deny it all you want, but it would have happened." I pressed a hand to my stormy belly. "All these sweet kisses you invented for me would have belonged to someone else."

He set his book aside and rose to his knees, bringing him to my eye level. I tried to turn away, but he grasped my chin, keeping my face pointed at his.

"It would have taken me a while longer, but I know myself, Luciana. I wouldn't have been able to stay away from you forever." He stroked my bottom lip and chin, peering at me with pleading, soft eyes. "It's easy for me to say that now, and it has to be almost impossible for you to believe. I'm sorry for that. I'll never stop being sorry I did this to us. But I've learned patience when it comes to you, so I'll be here until you're able to believe I won't let fear rule me again."

I closed my eyes to him, the hurt outweighing his words of reassurance. "I don't know how to get past this, Beckett. You became another person to give me up, and I hate that you're on that list."

"I hate it too," he whispered. "I love you, Luciana. To the ends of the earth."

Nodding, I fell forward, and he caught me, pulling me down into his lap. Swamped in doubt, I let Beckett hold me until I no longer felt like I was drowning.

· · · · ● · ● · · ·

In between the soft moments and the pricklier ones with Beckett, Delilah and I continued my swim lessons. Beckett never missed one. He spent them pacing the side of the pool and watching me like a hawk.

After that first lesson, I wasn't so afraid of the water. Each time, my fear dimmed, and my confidence grew. Conquering the thing that nearly killed me was a pretty big boost.

Not that I was a fish or anything, but I could dog paddle and put my face in the water without feeling like I was going to die.

Beckett walked Delilah and me to the dining hall and had dinner with my table full of friends. They were even more wary of him than I was. But I guessed watching me fall apart because of him hadn't exactly endeared them to him. He had mountains to climb to win them over.

As he spoke affably to Freddie and Bella, some of my doubt started to fade. If I was being honest, each day he stuck like glue to my side, a little more faded. Even though I refused to kiss him or return his "I love yous," he never wavered in his devotion.

That night, after he left me in my room, Theo called to check in.

"How's my girl?"

"I'm doing pretty well. I had another swim lesson with Delilah." I leaned back against my headboard, the day hitting me hard.

"Yeah? You have to come home soon and show me your new skills in our pool."

"Maybe. I might need Delilah with me. I'm not sure I can get in a pool without her."

"Bring her." He cleared his throat. "How's it going with Beckett?"

I sighed. "He's being great. Better than ever, to be honest."

"But...?"

"I don't know how to move past this. I want to forgive him, but I keep getting mad all over again when I think about what he did."

He went quiet for a moment. "You know I broke up with Helen, right?"

"I remember."

"I did the same shit Beckett did. Probably worse. I wasn't nice about the way I ended things. But I realized pretty quickly I'd made a massive mistake."

"Of course you did. It's Hells. Who would break up with her?"

He chuckled. "A fucking idiot, that's who."

I grinned even as tears pricked my eyes. Man, did I love Theo.

"How did she forgive you? That's what I'm struggling with."

"I took concrete steps to change so I would be worthy of her. But our story isn't the same as yours, Luc. Hells and you aren't the same. I will say that even though she let me back in, it took a long time for her to fully trust me. And I was okay with that. We had to be together, loving each other, for her to see I was in it for the long haul. If she'd kept me at arm's length, we never would have gotten to the place we needed to be."

"She took a big risk."

"Right. She did because I had already screwed up monumentally. She had to choose to risk being hurt again. *I* knew I was all in with her, but she couldn't read what was scrawled all over my heart. It was her risk to take, and she did it."

"And she's never been sorry that she did," I whispered.

"I like to think I've never given her a reason to be sorry."

"Thank you, Theo. I think...this helped."

I may have been brave by getting back in the pool, but I *had* been letting fear rule me when it came to Beckett. As much as I wanted to dive deep with him, I'd been staying in the shallow end, where I could escape if it became too much.

My risk was low this way, but so was my reward. My heart ached every time Beckett and I were together, but not *really* together. He'd done everything right, yet I continued to wait for some type of sign that told me everything would be okay.

I didn't think everything would be okay until I was fully back in Beckett's arms. To get there, I had to take a risk.

"Always. Whatever you decide, Hells and I have your back."

"I know." I finally did.

As soon as we hung up, I shoved my feet in my flip-flops and flew down the hall to Beckett's door. He opened after one knock, pulling me into his room.

"What's up?" His gaze swept over my face. "Have you been crying?"

I shook my head. "Almost, but I held it in." Then I pushed him to his bed. He sat down on the side of it, and I took my spot astride his legs.

He frowned in confusion. "Not that I don't love that you're here, in this position, but you need to tell me what's going on, baby."

"I'm working hard to forgive you."

His lids lowered, and he released a shuddering breath. "I know you are."

"But I don't want to hold you at arm's length while I do." My palms flattened on his cheeks. "I love you, Beckett. I want to be with you even though sometimes I might get mad at you and you might have to help me out with that."

His fingers dove into the sides of my hair, and his gaze was steady on mine. "I love you too, Luciana, and I will do whatever it takes. You can get mad at me. You can question me. You can ask me to make you promises. I'm not going to go anywhere. I'm yours in every way."

"Okay."

I pressed my lips to his for the first time in what felt like forever. The rightness of being here, opening myself up to Beckett this way, struck me hard and fast. This was where I was supposed to be.

"I love you," I murmured against his lips.

He inhaled my scent and rubbed his lips back and forth against mine. "I love you too. Never going to stop."

My eyes fluttered open. "I saved one thing for you, Beckett."

"Give it to me," he demanded.

I grinned, laughing lightly. My bossy Beckett.

"My heart. It's yours. Be gentle with it."

He went still except for his hand, which he spread on my chest. "I'll wrap it in velvet and carry it with me always." Then he took my hand and spread it on his. "I saved mine for you too. I won't ask you to be gentle with it because I already know you will be."

I pressed a kiss to his lips. "To the ends of the earth."

He cupped my face, and his eyes met mine. They were clear and true. There was no deception or doubt anywhere in the way Beckett stared back at me. He was here, and he wasn't going anywhere.

"To the ends of the earth, Luciana."

It was a risk to think it, and even more so to say it, but with risk came reward, and being completely, fully in love with Beckett Savage was the biggest reward of all.

So, I took the risk and dove in headfirst.

"I believe you."

EPILOGUE
Beckett

Five Years Later

WHEN I PROMISED TO follow Luciana to the ends of the earth, I meant it.

My promise turned out to be literal.

We graduated from Stanford a year ago, and Luciana became a member of the national women's field hockey team. I used my communications and marketing degree, as well as my family connections, to land a job working for Team USA.

It was a pretty solid job. The pay was shit, and Luc's wasn't any better, but I had a trust fund I wasn't the least bit ashamed to dip into since it meant I got to give my wife the kind of life she deserved.

My wife. Still getting used to that.

We got married straight out of college after a two-year engagement. I would have married her the minute we graduated from Savage Academy, but Luciana was far too practical for that. Besides, she never said it, but I knew, in my gut, she'd still been working through me abandoning her.

There were moments when I caught her watching me with wariness. They were fleeting and not often, but I never once blamed her for having lingering doubts.

Both of us came with baggage. They weren't quite matching, but it meant we were able to understand each other in a way not many people could.

My love for Luciana had never once wavered.

Not during the crazy college parties we attended separately and together. Mostly together because nothing was as fun as it was with her.

Never once during group projects with other girls. They existed, but not in the way she did. Other people were background noise. She was under the spotlight. The only one I ever saw clearly.

During my away games and hers, we stayed connected.

I never wondered what being with someone else would have been like. It never crossed my mind. Loving Luciana was part of my physiology. It was something I couldn't change—not that I ever wanted to.

Loving her had taken me to places I had never expected to go. Chile, Ireland, China. Today, I was in London, standing with the coaching staff of the USA women's field hockey team, while my wife and her teammates were awarded the Olympic gold medal.

Somewhere in the stands were Helen, Theo, Madelina, and their son Mateo. With them were Sera, Jules, and their kids Jakob and Amara. My parents were here too. Victoria hadn't been able to pull her shit together enough to make an international flight, but I hoped she was watching her daughter having her shining moment on TV.

·· • • • • • • • ··

After interviews, autographs, and a dinner out with our families, I finally had Luciana to myself. Her languid body rested against mine in the oversized bathtub in our hotel suite.

I dragged my fingers up and down her taut, smooth belly. "How do you feel?"

"Perfect." She reached back to hook her hand behind my neck. "How about you?"

"I don't think I've ever been better."

She twisted her head around to look at me. "Aren't you tired of following me around?"

I raised a brow. "Are *you* tired of me following you?"

"No, never," she rushed out. "Sometimes I worry you're giving up what you could be doing in order for me to fulfill my goals."

"Do I lie to you, Luciana?"

"You don't."

"When I tell you I'm exactly where I want to be, I mean that. I don't want to be apart from you."

"I don't either."

"Good." I planted a kiss on the top of her head. "Beyond my need to be near you, you know I like my job." I wasn't playing anymore, but I got to be a part of a team, which was something I'd discovered was more important to me than the competition aspect. Still, I got off on watching my wife win. "I have more than I could ask for."

She spun around in the tub and shuffled forward, straddling my thighs. I reached underwater, cupping her ass to bring her closer. When my cock was wedged between her lips, I settled back, content in this position for now.

She bit down on her bottom lip, her eyes sweeping over me. "I want kids with you, but I'd like to compete in one more Olympics first."

My cock jolted at the idea of getting her pregnant. "We have time."

Her worried expression melted into a grin. "I felt that. What were you just thinking of?"

"You, round with my baby." I slid my palm down her flat stomach. "We should practice so when it's time, I'll know what to do."

Her forehead dropped to mine. "I love you, Beckett Savage."

"To the ends of the earth, Luciana Savage."

Epilogue Two

Luciana

Five Years Later

My back ached.

My feet were swollen, and my hands were sore from carpal tunnel.

The only things that fit me were Beckett's sweatpants and T-shirts.

I always pictured myself like Helen had been during pregnancy: all belly. That was not the case. I was a bloated monster. Belly, ass, thighs, face—all of me had blown up like a balloon.

I waddled into the kitchen where my husband was cooking me breakfast number two. It wasn't that I ate a lot. The enormous baby currently lodged in my abdomen made it impossible to eat large meals. Or even average-sized meals. A few bites, and I was full for an hour or two, then I became ravenous again.

I pressed myself against Beckett's back. "I can't get close enough to you," I whined.

He reached for me and pulled me to his side. "Is this better?"

"A little."

He chucked my chin with his knuckle. "You're pitiful, aren't you?"

I poked my lip out. "Yes. And it's all your fault."

He laughed, turning off the stove so he could give me his full attention. "I know, and I'm sorry you don't feel good, but you're sexy as fuck, and I love you for carrying our little girl so well."

My eyes welled up. "Shut up, or I'll cry. I've already cried once today. That's my limit." I pushed up on my toes to kiss him. "I love you too, you know."

"I do."

He steered me to our kitchen table and put a plate with a feta and spinach omelet in front of me. Then he sat beside me with a mug of coffee between his hands.

I dug in, sighing as the first taste passed my lips. Beckett could cook not just omelets but most things. He'd taught himself, and since he was much better in the kitchen than I was, he made most of our meals. I was something of a clean freak, so I washed up when he was done. After being married for six years, we had a system.

Of course, it was all about to be upended when Baby Savage made her appearance in the next week or two. But I was looking forward to a little chaos.

I was *really* looking forward to seeing Beckett as a dad.

· · · ● · ● · · · ·

One month later...

I woke up in a panic.

The house was too quiet, and I was way too well rested. I'd only lain down for a minute but checked the clock. It had been more like two hours.

Throwing off the covers, I padded out of the bedroom and ventured toward the quiet voices coming from the vicinity of the living room.

There, I found a lovely sight. Beckett was sitting beside Julien, who had our three-week-old daughter, Serena, cradled in his arms.

We'd named Serena for a beach town in Chile called La Serena, where we'd taken a respite after one of my field hockey competitions a few years ago. While we were there, we'd spent a lot of time talking

about the shape of our lives to come. Beckett mentioned he liked
the name of the town for a future daughter, and it had stuck with us
both.

"Hi, guys."

They both turned to me. Beckett hopped to his feet and crossed
the room to pull me into his arms. He placed a gentle kiss on my lips.

"Good nap?"

I nodded. "You let me sleep too long, though. My boobs are going
to burst."

He laughed and peeked at them through the loose neck of my
shirt. "Yeah, they're getting close."

I swatted at him. "Shush."

"I think your daughter's ready to help you out with your problem.
She's been trying to find my milk for the last ten minutes," Julien
called.

Beckett led me into the living room, his hand resting on the small
of my back. Jules stood from the couch, passing a squirming Serena
to me before giving my forehead a peck.

"I'm going to head home and give you privacy." He squeezed my
shoulder. "Sera will be over tomorrow with lunch and dinner."

"She really doesn't have to," I reminded him.

He cocked his head. "I'm not going to be the one to tell her to stop
making you food. You'll have to do that."

I laughed. "I mean if she insists..."

He shot me a crooked grin. "Yeah, she definitely does. And it gives
her an excuse to get her hands on Serena. I hope you don't mind. I
don't have an excuse for stopping in. I just wanted to hang out with
the baby."

My chest tightened. "I don't mind at all."

It was true. Once we'd let them, our families rallied around us.
They'd supported us as a couple from the beginning, but since we'd
become parents, they were all over us.

Respectfully, of course.

They never stayed long unless we asked them to, which we did
sometimes.

Having a newborn was tough, man. Thank goodness I had Hells and Sera to give me guidance since my own mother was still very much lost and I wouldn't be letting her near my daughter.

Theo and Jules were pretty much amazing too. Beckett had only grown closer to them over the years.

Serena latched on to me like a starving little bird, and I settled back against the couch cushions, stroking her dark hair and relaxing. Beckett sat beside me, alternating between watching her and me.

"Gorgeous," he murmured.

I gave him a loopy grin. Nursing Serena always made me feel a little high. Since she was born, I felt like I'd fallen in love with Beckett all over again. He was the dad of dreams and the husband of fantasies.

Beckett had supported my athletic career through two Olympics. And when I decided to retire from the team, he urged me to make certain I was definitely ready.

It had been time. As much as I enjoyed competing, I wanted a family with my husband—the man who'd never stopped loving me since we met when we were thirteen years old. That love had grown and matured. I had never been so secure in my life as when I was with Beckett. Adding Serena to our family had only made it bloom a thousand times over.

"I love you."

He stroked my hair away from my face, then touched his lips to my temple. "Love you too, baby."

"Do you need a nap?"

He sighed and placed a hand on Serena's back. "Nah. I nodded off for a while when Jules was here."

"Because you knew he was watching over her?"

His grin was sheepish. "You know me too well."

That was a fact. We were an inextricable part of one another's lives, and on top of being married, Beckett had fulfilled his promise of being my best friend. We had friendships outside of each other and spent time apart doing our own thing, but when we reunited, it was always with a sigh of relief. He was my home base, and I was his.

"I do. You're obsessed with your girls."

He studied me and then Serena, a look of contentment that was fresh and new suffusing his features. It had come along three weeks ago and had yet to wane.

His crystal-clear eyes met mine. Heavy-lidded, with dark smudges beneath, they were just as beautiful as ever.

My husband smiled at me. "That's never gonna change, little light."

I touched the place on his chest where he carried my heart wrapped in velvet.

"I know."

· · · · ●· ● · · ·

Read Helen and Theo's story in Soft Like Thunder https://my-book.to/SoftLikeThunder

Read Sera and Julien's story in Real Like Daydreams https://my-book.to/RealLikeDaydreams

Playlist

"Chance with you" mehro
  "Burn" David Kushner
  "Dark Red" Steve Lacy
  "Save Yourself" Save Ok Rock
  "Hideous" mehro
  "Another Love" Tom Odell
  "The Loneliest" Maneskin
  "Drop the Game" Flume, Chet Faker
  "Cringe" Matt Maeson
  "Cleopatra" The Lumineers
  "I Wanna Be Yours" The Arctic Monkeys
  "It's Called: Freefall" Rainbow Kitten Surprise
  "Would That I" Hozier
  "Please, Please, Please Let Me Get What I Want" The Smiths
  "First Day of My Life" Bright Eyes
  "Bruises" Chairlift
  "Loving Is Easy" Rex Orange County
  "Glue Myself Shut" Noah Kahan
  "Where's My Love" SYML
  "Mine" Sleep Token
  https://open.spotify.com/playlist/6tSYNE6eKGfuzk9kv8NE6F
?si=6ffdd30f20c94f1d

STAY IN TOUCH

JOIN MY READER GROUP! It's the easiest way to get in touch with me, and learn all my book news first!
https://www.facebook.com/groups/JuliaWolfReaders

Acknowledgments

When I wrote Start a Fire, I thought it would be a standalone.

Ha! 2020 Julia was so cute, right?

I couldn't have imagined I'd be writing my third Savage series. But you guys love this world as much as me. Don't tell anyone, but I already have an idea for a fourth series. I joked that eventually I'll be writing Savage Nursing Home.

That being said, I have to thank my readers for loving these books! They make me happy to write, and I adore how connected you are to this town, which keeps expanding with every book.

Big shout out to my main writing buddy, Alley Ciz. I wrote a sports book without any games. Aren't you proud of me? I wouldn't be able to write *any* sports without your guidance.

Thank you to Jenny for beta reading. I love your commentary and the insightful points you always bring up.

Thanks to Kate Farlow for always rocking my covers and being patient with me.

Thanks to Daniel Jaems for the absolutely stunning cover picture. I love it so much.

I couldn't publish books without Monica and Rosa making my words make sense. Don't ever quit me.

Last but not least, thank you to my author group chat friends. You make me laugh and keep me sane. Best coworkers ever!

ABOUT JULIA

Julia Wolf is a bestselling contemporary romance author. She writes bad boys with big hearts and strong, independent heroines. Julia enjoys reading romance just as much as she loves writing it. Whether reading or writing, she likes the emotions to run high and the heat to be scorching.

Julia lives in Maryland with her three crazy, beautiful kids and her patient husband who she's slowly converting to a romance reader, one book at a time.

Visit my website:

http://www.juliawolfwrites.com

Printed in Great Britain
by Amazon

25452780R00190